MATTHEW J. HEFTI

A HARD AND HEAVY THING

TYRUS
BOOKS

Published by
TYRUS BOOKS
an imprint of F+W Media, Inc.
10151 Carver Road, Suite 200
Blue Ash, OH 45242. U.S.A.
www.tyrusbooks.com

Hardcover ISBN 10: 1-4405-9187-3
Hardcover ISBN 13: 978-1-4405-9187-7
Paperback ISBN 10: 1-4405-9188-1
Paperback ISBN 13: 978-1-4405-9188-4
eISBN 10: 1-4405-9189-X
eISBN 13: 978-1-4405-9189-1

Printed in the United States of America.

10 9 8 7 6 5 4 3 2 1

Library of Congress Cataloging-in-Publication Data
Hefti, Matthew J.
A hard and heavy thing / Matthew J. Hefti.
pages cm
ISBN 978-1-4405-9187-7 (hc) -- ISBN 1-4405-9187-3 (hc) -- ISBN 978-1-4405-
9188-4 (pb) -- ISBN 1-4405-9188-1 (pb) -- ISBN 978-1-4405-9189-1 (ebook) -- ISBN
1-4405-9190-X (ebook)
I. Title.
PS3608.E3385H38 2016
813'.6--dc23
2015025805

Cover design by Elisabeth Lariviere.
Cover image © iStockphoto.com/sx70.

This book is available at quantity discounts for bulk purchases.
For information, please call 1-800-289-0963.

For Monica,
my own life's love story.

And for Madeline, Lillian, and Zoe,
the amazing ladies that make everything worth everything.

ADUMBRATION:

It's Not a Suicide Note; It's a Love Song

God made clay; the clay made men; the men made war. They fingered the triggers on their rifles as they labored under the rucksacks. They were mules, trudging along the path. Silhouettes and eyes hovered in the windows of the huts while the soldiers fought the muck. The tread on their boots gripped the wet clay, turning their feet to anvils. Their thighs burned as they heaved the weight. No one spoke a word, and the downpour drowned the sound of their panting.

Levi walked point. Water fell from his helmet and streamed in front of his eyes, so he did not see the battle erupt. He did not hear the shots because of the storm. He did not hear the explosions because of the thunder. Levi focused on the road ahead, and the road did not stop; so Levi kept walking.

While the men behind him killed, Levi walked. When the men cried for their mothers, Levi took off his helmet. When the lieutenant barked orders, Levi had gone miles past the men.

He was tired from all the fighting and leaving and returning. All the fighting, leaving, and returning. The fighting, leaving and returning, and fighting.

He was tired, so he dropped his pack and ammunition. When the blood mixed with the water, and when the dying men lay on the path wondering how it had all happened, Levi didn't look back. When the men cried out to God to stop the fighting, Levi put down his rifle and walked out into the world.

The world he had left was not ready for his return; or rather, he was not ready to return to the world he had left. After years of the slow agonizing burn of his own guilt, which stood in stark contrast to the sudden and violent flames that caused it, he sat on a rock near the edge of the mighty Mississippi, longing to ease himself into the river's dark currents.

He could not make sense of all that had happened, but he had to explain it somehow. He owed his friend that much. So he left the river for home, where he wrote and remembered. He wrote in such a way as to ignore his ego, a task that still remained difficult despite his narrative tricks.

[I did exactly what you told me to do, Nick. Didn't you tell me to just write the stupid book already? And that even doing the worst thing on the planet had to count for something? Well I can't think of anything worse than what I'm about to do, which is why I think you deserve an explanation. And maybe after you read it you'll realize why I don't have the hope that you have. The truth is this: We begin and end alone.]

When Levi was done explaining everything, he would do it. He would ease himself into those cool waters and embrace the end on his own terms.

It took an entire life to get to this point, but what was a life? A life was a red hole in a forehead. A life was a man suspended against a backdrop of smoke and flames, one bootless foot covered with a green sock. A life was the maddening immutability of the past, the monomania of the present, and the frightening black hole of the future. Out of ten thousand days, he only carried a handful. Single moments exploded in detail and vibrancy in his memory, yet entire years had disappeared.

So starting. Starting was difficult.

A life was a story, and a story was nothing more than a promise that something bad would happen. It was a promise that people would desire and want and ache and burn, but it was not a promise that they would find what they sought.

And what did any of them want?

All Levi ever wanted was to be a writer.

But that's not exactly right. Levi wanted other things. He wanted kicks. He wanted greatness and immensity. He wanted to be one of Kerouac's people, the fabulous yellow roman candle people. The mad ones. Levi was desirous of everything at the same time. He wanted big parties, loud music, risks, gunfire, and explosions, and vastness, and immortality, and romance, and—

He wanted what Nick had. He wanted Eris.

And what did Eris want? Like her mythical namesake, all she ever wanted was to create mayhem and sow discord.

But that's not true either. She simply wanted someone to pay attention to her. She wanted someone to listen.

And she wanted Nick.

And what did Nick want? He simply wanted to do good. To be good. He was mad to be saved. That was good enough for him.

It wasn't good enough for Levi. He wanted more and his desires burned through him like the flames from a roadside bomb. But that's not true either. It wasn't fast, violent, or exciting. He wanted more and his desires burned through him like acid. Burned through them all. He didn't know when he began wanting to destroy Nick. He didn't know how he ended up with his fingers around his neck, staring at the bulging eyes of his best friend in a murderous rage. [And how can I begin to tell our story when I'm so perplexed about my own motivation?]

The start of their story, this story, could have been way back when they were children wrestling on the sticky floor in Oma's Pub, when Nick learned he would be an orphan. The start could have been that first time Nick saved Levi without cause—the time in middle school when their principal caught them smoking in the ditch behind the chain-link fence of the playground. The time Nick told Oma he stole the cigarettes from her purse, not Levi. As she snapped the leather belt Opa left behind when he died, Nick pleaded with her to believe him when he said Levi was blameless. That was the first time Levi said nothing to stop Nick from getting hurt.

It could have started freshman year when Eris's older cousin, Jesse, answered the ad Levi posted at The Deaf Ear record store as he and Nick went looking for a drummer to round out their fledgling punk band, A Failed Entertainment. Or, it could have started when they opened their first practice in Jesse's basement and Eris appeared at the bottom of the stairs with one hand on her hip. She glared across the room at Jesse sitting behind the drum kit. She held up a middle finger for two and a half minutes as they ran through their first song. When they finished, she walked upstairs without a word.

It could have been the night Nick and Levi got drunk, threw bottles at invisible foes from the roof of their apartment, cut themselves so they bled for America, and pledged to join up because it was just past September 11th, 2001, and they took that hell personally even though they were a thousand miles from those towers.

It could have started when Nick woke up in the burning rubble of a Humvee on Main Supply Route Tampa in central Iraq, the weight of another man's severed arm on his chest; it could have started right at that tense moment when Levi's face appeared in his field of vision with all the sad, unspoken truths about how they got there ignored to make Levi look like some hero. But that was more of a climax, wasn't it? Only twelve minutes of their lives at the top of the mountain.

[And if that was the climax of our lives, I'm telling you now, it came too soon. I cannot handle this long slow denouement that my life has become. This slow burn that makes me want to drive drunk, get high, jump off bridges, get in fights, and do whatever I can to make things feel real again.]

The story didn't start—and this was obvious—until some time before a cloudless midnight in early spring many years later. It didn't start on the bank of a stream that flowed into the La Crosse River, where both of their faces dripped blood on the green grass that had already begun to accumulate dewdrops in the rapidly chilling air, where each of their knuckles screamed to take out on each other what they couldn't take out on their enemies [whom we rarely knew], or their leaders [who sent us there], or the ghosts that still haunted them months and even years after they had left.

That is to say, it didn't start tonight.

They hadn't always been broken. They used to be tight like the skin of burn scars. But by that time, it was far too late for them to recognize what had pulled them apart, what had grown into a cancer so large and so irreversible there was nothing left to do but risk death in order to extract it—to get it out in the open air where it could be examined, studied, dissected, and then kept for posterity: something ugly and sad in formaldehyde.

Levi James Hartwig
6 April 2010

BOOK ONE

WE JOINED IN A FIT OF YOUTH

1.1 DEAR NICK, LET'S BE HONEST; WE WERE BROKEN BEFORE THE WAR EVEN STARTED

September 8th, 2001

They were only able to find Eris dying in the bathtub because she was making woofing and growling noises like a very large dog. By then it was late night or early morning, and Nick and Levi believed they were alone. They were rolling hard on designer drugs, and it was not their first time. It was, however, the last time.

It was always the last time.

Levi lay on the floor of their apartment and complained about how bored he was until he realized that his complaining was picking up speed. With that realization came other realizations. He noticed the wiggling of his toes. He noticed the way he sucked his cheeks between his clenched teeth. He recognized that the hollow drumming sound that now filled him came from the rapid tapping of his hands against his sternum. With that, he realized he wasn't bored anymore.

Nick—still amped from their band's show that night—noodled on his unplugged electric guitar, already completely entranced by how he was able to watch the notes bounce off the useless pickups with each strum, after which they floated in a glorious arch over to Levi's ear.

Levi's ears still rang with tinnitus. He turned onto his stomach and buried his face in the brown carpet, which smelled of the earth. "Shut up. Will you please shut up, please?"

"Me shut up?" Nick said. "I didn't even want to do this tonight, and now that we're doing it, you're telling me to shut up?" He banged on the guitar. "I can't just do this stuff like you can, with no guilt or pangs of conscience." He held out his hand. It trembled.

Levi got up and went to the closet in the hallway.

Nick called after him. "But you always get your way, right? And like always, even though I resist at first, I give in to the temptation and the sense of anticipation that sits deep in my bowels like a bowling ball."

"Shut up." Levi grabbed his ex-girlfriend's pink earmuffs from the floor of the closet.

"Ooooh," Nick moaned. "For the good that I would: I do not, but the evil which I would not, I do."

[You really did talk like that when you got conflicted about things. Sometimes you still do.]

Levi snapped the pink earmuffs over his ears.

The telephone rang. Nick played on. The phone rang again, and the LCD on the caller ID window displayed KEVIN & CHARLOTTE HARTWIG, Levi's parents. The guitar grew louder; the thin treble of the unplugged strings battled against the high-pitched ringing. Levi screamed, "Will the noise never end?"

Even with the earmuffs, Levi heard his mother's voice when the answering machine kicked on. "Levi?" she said. "If you're there, honey, can you pick up?"

Nick stopped playing and leaned forward on the couch.

Levi lifted the earmuffs from his ears and let them snap back around his neck.

"Levi, sorry it's so late, but, I thought you should know." She sniffed. She waited.

He waited.

"It hath pleased Almighty God—" She cleared her throat.

"Who?" Levi asked the answering machine.

Because Levi and Nick had spent their lives surrounded by this kind of phraseology, they knew what was coming. Because they had endured hard wooden church pews for fifty-two Sundays a year for eighteen years—to say nothing of extra services for Advent, Lent, or Holy days—they knew that nothing good served as the referent of That Which Hath Pleased Almighty God. Because they had spent twelve years in parochial school, they recognized the preludes to bad news. Because every moment of their youthful lives had been punctuated by liturgy, they knew that they were about to learn that someone had kicked the bucket. "Who?" Levi asked again.

"It hath pleased Almighty God—" She sniffed. "To summon out of this vale of tears the soul of your grandfather, Randall Hartwig." She took one loud breath and rapidly exhaled the rest into the telephone's receiver. "Your father and I are trying to figure out the funeral. Call us as soon as you get this."

Levi closed his eyes. Finally. He had his silence.

Nick set the guitar down. "Man. I'm so—"

"Ssssh." Levi placed an index finger in front of his lips.

"I'm sorry."

"Ssssh." He kept his eyes closed and he held his breath.

With the house finally silent, Levi heard the noises coming from the bathroom. It sounded more animal than human. He cocked his head.

Nick eased himself to his feet. Levi marched down the hallway without hesitation. Always one to cross busy streets without looking, he found himself glad for the diversion.

"Dude, wait," Nick said before following in a crouch. "Aren't you going to call your mom back?"

Levi followed the noise, knocking through the bathroom door with his shoulder. Once inside, he flung back the shower curtain to find Eris.

The last time Levi had seen her that night was shortly before A Failed Entertainment took the stage for their final show of the summer. He stood on the fire escape of The Warehouse smoking a cigarette. Eris had looked like she was in a hurry the way she was

trucking through the alley two floors down. Levi dropped a lit cigarette in front of her to get her attention, but it accidentally landed
on her head. The orange sparks bounced off her black hair, and she
jumped and swatted at the air as if she had stepped into a spider web.
She looked up and yelled at him. Threatened to kick his ass. Her big
green eyes matched her flannel shirt. As the sun dropped behind
the old brick buildings downtown, her skin looked like it had been
tanned brown like a farmer's, not orange like a co-ed's. "Where you
going?" he had yelled. She shook her head and walked on down the
alley. He didn't see her at the show.

Now in the bathtub, her fierce eyes were closed and her skin was
pale. They realized she was the one making the dog noises. Her flannel
shirt soaked up long tendrils of thick drool. Her knees were tucked
into her chest, the pale patellae popping out of the holes in her jeans.

Nick pushed past and turned the shower on. He spun the knob
to cold and flung the curtain closed. "This is bad. This is bad. I didn't
even know she was still here."

"Still here? What do you mean still?" Levi opened the curtain
again.

"You were at the store. The cigarettes. She was drunk. I told her
our plans. She left in a huff." He opened the curtain just a bit to look
in. "Oh God, what do we do?"

"Do?" Levi said, looking oddly triumphant, like his plans for the
night had finally materialized. Like he had been hoping for some
disaster like this to happen so he didn't have to be bored anymore.
Like even a dying girl in his bathtub was better than calling his
mother to confirm that his grandfather actually was dead, and that
what he had heard on the answering machine wasn't a mere auditory
hallucination. "We save her, of course."

[This was denial.]

"We gotta call 911."

Levi opened the curtain again and turned off the water. "Nuh
uh. No way. We gotta save her ourselves."

16

He climbed into the tub behind her and placed his feet as wide apart as the tub would allow. He squatted down, hugged her around the chest, and stood. Her head dropped forward, her neck twisting as it dropped to her chest.

She slapped at his hands; the right one cupped one of her small breasts. "That's no way to touch a lady," she said, the thick drool falling from her lip, down her chin, and onto Levi's wrist.

"Here. Gimme a hand," Levi said.

Nick was the larger of the two, the solid first baseman in high school, the strong power forward in summer rec leagues, but now he stood motionless, his mouth hanging slightly open. He lifted a hand and brushed it over his light sandy hair, which was just long enough to be soft and fuzzy. He rubbed his hand over his hair again. His dilated eyes took up half of his round boyish face, which was now slack. His hand went over his hair a third time.

"Nick," Levi said, exasperated. "Take her."

Nick moved like a man underwater, but he hugged her and pulled her from the tub. He lowered her to the floor, where the water from her clothes pooled around her limp body.

Levi put both his hands on his chest and felt his damp T-shirt. "We need to get her to a hospital."

"We need to call 911."

"And what do we tell them?"

"I can't drive."

"We tell them you can't drive?"

"You can't drive." Nick reached down and touched the pool of water on the floor as if testing its viscosity. He rubbed the wet flannel of Eris's shirt between his thumb and forefinger as if he doubted that it was tangible. He straightened up. "We are definitely not driving."

That's how they ended up dragging her through the heart of La Crosse, her toes skimming along the cracked asphalt of back alleys lined with six-bedroom Victorian frat houses and low-income apartment complexes. They rushed past dimly lit parking lots as they tried to stay out of sight, until finally they had no choice but to drag her along the sidewalk next to busy South Avenue as they neared Gundersen Lutheran Hospital.

[Most people don't realize how things can get serious so quickly. One second you're face down on your carpet listening to bad guitar-playing, and the next second there's a dying girl in your bathtub. One second you're playing with your best friend and his GI Joes under the pool table, and the next second Oma is pulling you off the barroom floor trying to explain that the crash was really bad and you have to leave right now, right this second, and then all you can do is stand next to your newly orphaned best friend as two caskets get lowered into the ground. Or, you're cruising along in your super-cool-guy Humvee thinking about chicks or cheese curds, and your best friend's truck disappears into a Hollywood ball of smoke and flame. The next thing you know, you're covered in blood and you're tossing around the severed limbs of your friends.

These things can happen to anyone.

But of course, you already know that.]

They dragged Eris under a canopy of trees on the sidewalk, and the illumination from the stars and the streetlights disappeared. Cars whooshed past. For a brief moment of darkness, their mess felt invisible to the world.

"Levi," Nick said. "We cannot keep taking drugs."

Levi had nothing to say to that. He had nothing good to say about their small town hemmed in on all sides by bluffs, rivers, and coulees. He was dissatisfied with their small shows, their uneventful lives, and his boring conservative family. He felt the drugs were the only excitement in his life so he said, "It's the only excitement in my life."

After a few more cracks in the sidewalk, they were back under the streetlights. A maroon Park Avenue slowed; the silver-haired driver stared at them stumbling beneath the streetlights, and then he moved on.

Levi used his free hand to grab her shoulder and shake her. "Hey, wake up." With the hand that was on her back, he grabbed a handful of wet flannel and bra strap. He pulled and snapped the strap. "Help us out here."

Eris was a small girl, but the work was taxing for both of them. Levi could see the blond fuzz of Nick's upper lip collecting sweat. With Eris sandwiched between them—her arms slung over their shoulders—they trudged the final block to the auto-opening doors of the hospital. Drops of sweat pooled on Levi's forehead, slowly growing until they swelled to critical mass and had no other avenue but to travel down, plopping from his eyebrow to his lip, where he grabbed the drops with his tongue to feel their salty wetness.

Eris, on the other hand, had stopped sweating, or she had never been sweating to begin with. Maybe her clothes and hair were only wet from the shower. Levi didn't know. He put a hand to her cool, dry face. He urged Nick on and pleaded for him to walk faster; act cool; don't act weird.

They set her in an empty wheelchair, which they found by the elevator. Levi checked her pulse with his fingers on her neck. He stuck his forefinger in his mouth to wet it and he held it under her nose.

"Oh God, is she still alive?" Nick said.

Levi pushed the wheelchair. "Of course she's still alive."

Eris opened her eyes, rolled her bobbing head around, and closed her eyes again. Her chin dropped onto her chest.

"Chip off the old block, huh?" Levi said. Her dad was long gone and her mother spent a considerable amount of time at the Hazelden Rehabilitation Center in Saint Paul, Minnesota.

They followed the hallway to reception, where a large fleshy lady sat back in an oversized office chair, her feet on an upside-down wastebasket. Levi stopped the wheelchair so Eris faced away from the desk. He turned and stood between the woman and the wheelchair, and he put both hands on the desk to show that if he was anything at all, he was serious. "This lady needs to see a doctor."

The woman dropped her feet off the basket and stood. She moved to her left, leaned over the desk, and looked at Eris's soaking wet clothes, the black hair plastered against her face, and her unresponsive limbs dangling by the wheels of the chair. The woman said, "Ma'am?" All this was to say nothing of the not-so-slight smell of vomit emanating from Eris's clothes, a smell that Levi was just now noticing in the sterility of the hospital. "Did you drag her out of the river or something?" the woman asked.

"Mmm," Levi said, nodding his head. "Yes. Exactly. Fished her right out of the water. This ox right here probably saved her life." He pointed at Nick, who looked up from the floor, mouth open, eyes wider and blacker than before.

"Oh my," she said. She lowered herself back to the edge of her chair and rolled slightly from the desk. "This is Labor and Delivery. She needs to go to the Emergency Room."

"This is Labor and—?" Levi looked around. There were no doctors bustling. No one sat waiting in the wide chairs. Down the hall, two nurses casually whispered and sipped from oversized mugs. Levi smacked his forehead with a palm. He pointed in the direction of the hallway from which they came. "So then the emergency room is—?"

She pointed in the opposite direction.

"Of course." Levi flashed a smile and grabbed the handles on the wheelchair.

The woman picked up the telephone on her desk. "I can call someone to come get her. Let me call someone."

Nick spoke up. "No, no. That's fine. No need. It will be faster if we do it. We can do it. You can put down the phone." He spoke rapidly, and he chewed on his tongue after he stopped. His jaw worked, and he looked from Eris to the receptionist, from the receptionist to Eris.

"Is he okay?" she asked.

Levi shrugged and started moving. "You'll have to pardon him; he's had a bit too much to drink." In that town, a town where the bars outnumbered houses, such an explanation wouldn't raise an eyebrow.

She raised an eyebrow. "He has?" She started punching in numbers. "And what's with you? What's with the earmuffs?"

"Huh?" Levi said. "Oh these?" He stopped, pulled the earmuffs from his neck and held them out to look at them. "Tinnitus," he said. He put the earmuffs over his ears and yelled out, "Experimental treatment." He once again grabbed the wheelchair and started down the hall. "Walk faster," he told Nick. "I think she's calling the cops, man."

Nick gripped Levi's forearm. "Hey, what are you planning here?"

"What do you mean what are we planning? We're dropping her at the emergency room."

"And then what? Leave her there?"

"She's underage. We're underage."

Nick lowered his voice to a whisper. "Yeah. This is bad." He nodded as if realizing all of this for the first time. "Plus we're on drugs."

Sometimes Levi wondered if Nick was really a cop.

"But we can't just leave her here."

Levi turned a corner and stopped. "This is a hospital, Nick. I think we need to step back and appreciate that we've got a lot going on here." He lowered his own voice to a whisper to match Nick's. "We were faced with a situation; we made a decision, acted with some poise, and saved the day, right? I mean, really, we're doing the best we can here. I'm going to drop her off at the emergency room where the professionals can handle it, and then you and I skedaddle."

Nick shook his head no.

"There's no sense lingering here." Levi looked around and started walking again.

"But—"

"But nothing. There's no sense in waiting for the cops. We had nothing to do with this."

Nick stopped again and grabbed Levi's T-shirt.

"Look, buddy. Do you trust me?"

Nick nodded mutely. His teeth chattered together.

"I'm as freaked as you are. Really. I am. But let's be rational. We're in a hospital. Let the professionals handle this. We'll push her to the emergency room, and then you'll follow me out the door. We'll act natural, and we'll just walk down the block. Then we'll call for a ride home so we can avoid any further discord as we ride this thing out." He patted one of Nick's cheeks and dropped his hand onto his shoulder. "You tracking?"

"We can't just dump her off."

"Can we pump her stomach? Can we give her the medical care she needs? If she gets taken to jail, can we bail her out if we too are in jail?"

Nick shook his head. "I'm staying."

"Suit yourself." Levi dropped his hand and pushed Eris down the hall. They took a few more turns. Nick reached out to touch the wall as they walked, his finger tracking the horizontal line where the teal paint met the purple. His finger jumped each time they passed a doorway. They followed signs and ended up at a crossroads.

A set of doors in front of them led outside. A set of doors to their left led to the emergency room reception desk. Levi pointed outside. "Wait for me out there."

"I'm not just going to—"

"Nick. Trust me. Just wait for me outside. Find a pay phone. Call someone for a ride. Just go outside."

Nick hesitated.

Eris opened her eyes again. Levi put his hands on her shoulders and bent down to look at her face. "Hey, hey. You doing all right?"

She pushed his face away and staggered up out of the wheel-chair. "Outta my face," she said. She took a step and stumbled into the wall in front of her before turning to face him.

"What the—" Levi could not believe what he was seeing.

She made like she was going to slap him across the face, but she was slow and her fingers just grazed his cheeks. It felt like flirting. "You just gonna leave me, asshole?"

"What did you take? Did you take anything? Are you just drunk? Are you faking?" Levi turned and paced back and forth in the hallway before stopping in front of her again. "Have you been faking this entire time?"

Nick's eyes went wide. "Oh thank God, thank God, thank God. Thank. God."

"He's got nothing to do with this." Eris smiled and winked at him. A drunk, wide, sarcastic smile. She swayed on her feet like a tired boxer.

"Are you—" Nick stopped. Scratched his head. "Are you okay then?"

"Of course she's okay," Levi said. "This whole thing here is just her sick idea of a good time. Some sort of cry for help. Isn't it, Eris?"

Eris swaggered up to Nick, leaned against him, looked up into his innocent and confused face, and said, "You saved me."

[I would have done anything to have heard those words myself. You didn't even notice.]

Through the double glass doors of the emergency room, Levi could see two women talking in the hallway. They glanced up at him. He stormed outside and left Nick and Eris, each in the arms of the other. Once he made it to the fresh air, he put a palm against the stone enclosure that held the trashcan. Anxiety and adrenaline washed over him when he left Eris there, fine, but not fine. The ordeal left him lightheaded and weak and furious. He took a deep breath and exhaled through quivering lips.

Nick helped Eris out the double glass doors of the hospital. She giggled. He walked her over to a bench near an ashtray.

The entire time Levi had known her, Eris's crass confidence, tie-dyed Phish shirts, and frayed jeans had all marked her as a girl apart. She was fun. She was dangerous. She was beautiful. She did not fit into the Abercrombie/American Eagle/GAP hierarchy like the private school girls Levi knew. He couldn't help but steal glances at her constantly, to the point where it wasn't stealing glances; it was leering. Yet, he found he couldn't even talk to her. Nick, on the other hand, had developed a theretofore alien aplomb in her presence, and he had no problem talking to her. In fact, here she was now, hanging all over him.

Levi started across the parking lot.

He heard Nick running after him. "Where are you going?"

Levi kept walking away, across the parking lot, and away from whatever cruel joke was going on.

"Dude, relax. She's been worse."

Nick caught up to him. They walked side by side for a while. The night air felt cooler. It felt better now that the girl was gone and they weren't dragging dead weight between them.

At Perkins, Levi used the phone at the cashier's counter while Nick waited outside.

When Levi returned, Nick said, "Wish you wouldn't have done that. We could have walked back."

Levi sat on the bench in front of the restaurant.

"We should go get Eris."

Levi lit a cigarette and stared at the drifting smoke. He waved it in front of his face and watched the trails behind the cherry-comets streaming through the maples beyond the parking lot.

Nick paced.

They were quiet a moment. Then Nick stopped and said, "So when are you going to call your mom back? You know, about your grandpa?"

Levi looked up at the sky, which was black, cloudless, and full of stars. All the memories of the man came flooding back to him.

The slimy blood from the inside of a rainbow trout. The heavy panting of a young boy trying to keep up. Copper pennies underneath starched white pillowcases and the tonguing of empty sockets where baby teeth once grew. Holding a hand covered in rough scabs and burn scars from long days welding boilers. *Gunsmoke*, John Wayne, and *Bonanza*.

He stood up. "I don't know." He stepped on his cigarette butt. "Can you believe the way my mother broke the news? I mean, it's my grandpa, not some random person. It hath pleased Almighty God? Really?"

"I don't know." Nick stepped on his own cigarette butt. "I mean look at all this." He spread his arms out to demonstrate the expanse of the night sky. "None of it is an accident. I mean, like, he was sick anyway, right? And was probably going to die anyway."

"Just stop," Levi said. "I know where you're going, and don't. Just stop."

"But just listen for a second. If he didn't die when he did, then your mom wouldn't have called when she did, and if she didn't call when she did, we may never have heard Eris making noises in the bathtub." He looked at the ground and started moving again. He waved his hands and spoke more rapidly, as if he were having a revelation. As if his visions were divine and not neurological misfires manifested from chemical reactions to the acid-molly cocktail he had dropped earlier in the night. "If we never heard Eris making noises in the bathtub, we'd still be dinking around in the living room. Who knows when we would have found her? I mean, probably not until we took a shower. If we didn't find her when we did, we couldn't have brought her to the hospital, and who knows what would have happened? She could have choked on her own vomit, died in her sleep, or who knows what. I mean—" He stopped and rubbed his big meaty hand over his fuzzy hair again. "I mean isn't it possible that God took your grandpa at just the right time? For your own good?" Nick stopped pacing and looked at his friend. A hopeful smile played at the corners of his mouth. He lifted his light eyebrows in query above his big, dark, tripping-black, deep-space eyeballs.

Nick had been so focused on his revelation that he couldn't have seen Levi's demeanor grow dim. He couldn't have seen Levi clench his fists. And when he looked up hopefully, he couldn't have had time to register the right jab coming at his face.

Levi's fist connected with Nick's nose as soon as he looked up from the ground. He felt Nick's nose crack under his knuckles.

[This was anger.]

His much-larger friend fell to the ground without even drawing his hands to his face or dropping them to the ground to brace his fall. Nick looked up from the ground with his forehead folded in confusion. Blood streamed from his nose, over his mouth, and down his chin.

Nick put his hand up to his chin, touched the blood, and apologized.

"I'm sorry, Levi," he said as he looked at the blood on his fingers. Nick wiped his palm across his mouth and chin. He wiped his bloody hand across his jeans.

Levi wanted to scream down at Nick that he was naïve, he didn't understand, didn't know how Levi felt. But he couldn't say any of those things because they weren't true. If anyone knew the pain of losing someone, it was Nick. Instead of making things worse, which is all he really wanted to do, he walked away.

He walked aimlessly for several blocks before he returned to the hospital. The fluorescent lights in the hallways burned his eyes. He found the chapel and walked into the dimly lit room. He contemplated walking to the front to say a prayer at the altar. He had seen people do that in movies. He sat down in the back pew.

[This was bargaining.]

From the vaulted ceilings high above the red carpet and wooden pews hung fixtures with amber globes that dimmed the light shining through them. He thought of taking a candle from the altar. He could touch the small flame to the ornate paraments until flames engulfed the entire place for all its false hopes and unanswered prayers.

The night before his grandpa left for Arizona, where the weather was supposed to help keep him alive, they drank beer together and pissed in the backyard of the house his grandparents had just sold. Grandpa said, as he always said, "Don't tell your grandmother." That night, the generation gap narrowed. It seemed like a small crack in an old sidewalk; spiders could touch both sides. But now, with a head full of acid, Levi clearly saw that his current mess of a night reflected the aggregate of his life. A Technicolor map of mazes with no ends. Realizing this, he saddened. The generation gap now seemed huge, like the great Grand Canyon. Nothing could touch both sides.

He folded his hands and bowed his head and tapped his toes until the restlessness grabbed him around the throat and squeezed and forced him to get up and move.

Levi dropped his pink earmuffs into a trashcan outside the door of the hospital. He breathed in the fresh air of late summer, and he felt the cool breeze from the river on his face. He began walking back to the house that held his upstairs flat.

He stopped only briefly to decline a ride from a truck driver looking to spread the Gospel. The man scared Levi as he pulled up, engine roaring. He hung out the window, leering. His wrinkled face, pushy demeanor, and evil smirk were all incongruous with the collared shirt and tie he wore inside the cab. "Need a ride?" he called down before spitting a line of tobacco through the gap where his front teeth should have been.

When Levi shook his head no, the man called out, "Been saved?"

"Not interested."

"You should be."

"Move along old man," Levi said as the man's trailer-less big rig crawled along beside him, out of place on the nearly deserted residential road.

"Suit yourself," the man said before closing his window and driving ahead.

Levi squinted against the sun that was just beginning to rise. He walked through town under streetlights. Each one seemed to turn off at the moment he passed. He walked through the bar districts, playgrounds, and parking lots. When he reached home, he kept walking. He didn't want to go inside and explain to Nick—who wouldn't understand—where he went and why he went there.

1.2 MY OWN EGO AND
THE MAJESTIC PLURAL

Hours later when he arrived home thirsty, lightheaded, and weak, he found his mother had left a message on the answering machine pleading with him to make the twenty-minute drive back to Bangor to be with the family. And if he wouldn't come home, would he at least please call her so she knew that he knew about Grandpa?

Levi lay on the couch without his shoes. Too tired to do anything, but too strung out to sleep, he allowed colors and images of the night to pulse and dance and flicker on his eyelids.

He heard the fridge open. When he looked up, he saw Eris through the pass-through window. She lifted her eyebrows in surprise as Levi caught her drinking directly from a jug of apple juice. She returned the bottle and wiped her mouth with her arm. She stood in the doorway of the living room and flipped her black hair. Her face was scrubbed clean of makeup, but she still looked like she was blushing. She wore a small pair of purple boxer shorts, which revealed taught calves and curved hamstrings, nearly all the way up to the rondure of her bottom. The white cotton tank top she wore was cut low enough to reveal the tan line that separated the summer-kissed skin of her chest from her alabaster breasts. She was not wearing a bra.

"What are you doing here?" Levi asked.

She yawned and stretched, oblivious to the fact that Levi had seen girls in magazines selling sex with the same poses while wearing more clothes. He turned on the couch to hide his arousal. He heard her bare feet stick to the linoleum with each step as she walked away. He rolled onto his back.

Sometime later, she returned holding a pair of strappy cork wedges. She now wore a black dress that clung to her hips. He looked at the ceiling to avoid staring. She looked better to him in the dress than she had just moments before.

She sat on the edge of the couch, her back pressing against his side. She put her shoes on the floor and slipped her feet in. "You need to come to church with us," she said.

"You're going to church?" Levi asked.

Some people are church people, and some people are not church people. Eris was not a church person.

Nick, on the other hand, he could understand. Or at least, tolerate. Nick was born a church person. His Uncle Thomas was a preacher and, if Lutherans had nuns, his Oma would have been one. Those old saints were the only family Nick had left, and he had to cling to something.

[If this were one of the creative writing workshops I took in school, no one would buy this. Everyone would probably say acid + ecstasy + dying girl = okay, but acid + ecstasy + dying girl turns out just fine + they wake up early to go to church = implausible, but obviously they don't know you like I do. And I don't need to explain to you that teenagers + incongruity does not = implausibility.]

Levi got off the couch and went to the kitchen. He grabbed the jug of juice from the fridge and made a show of wiping off its mouth before drinking from it himself. He was about to tell Eris off, tell her to not bother asking again. He wasn't going. Not now. Not ever again. And she should know better. But when he turned the corner, he saw Nick shuffling out of his bedroom.

Levi met him down the hall and whispered, "Did she stay here with you last night? And she's going to church with you? What's going on?"

Nick took the jug from Levi and drank. He wiped his mouth with the back of his hand. "I'll tell you later."

Levi raised an eyebrow.

"I will," Nick said.

"Okay," Levi said, skeptical.

[We told each other everything. I know you like you know yourself.]

"Want us to wait for you?" Nick asked.

Levi looked down at the floor because he couldn't bear to look at Nick's disfigured face. His nose was crooked and swollen, obviously broken. The trauma had bruised the skin under his eyes a deep purple. Despite his wounds, Levi sensed no checked aggression. On the contrary, Nick's eyes were full of a naked, earnest hope.

Levi stalled on the rejection speech he had planned. "No. I gotta figure out what's going on with my grandpa," was all he could muster as he disappeared down the hall to his room.

• • •

Hours later, Nick opened Levi's bedroom door and turned on the light. "There are three messages on the machine from your parents."

Levi nodded against his pillow.

Nick threw open the curtains. The lancinating light of the noon sun streamed onto Levi's closed eyes and turned the dark orange of his eyelids to a bright white. He put his head down and his hand up to shield his eyes.

"Levi, you have to call your parents. Just let them know you're alive, will ya?"

"I just need a minute." Levi got up and closed his door. He pulled out the lone drawer of his pressboard desk, reached into the back corner, and removed a 35mm film canister of weed. He packed a small bowl for himself and sat on the window ledge. He looked down into the empty alley as he smoked. He was static for long periods of time with his hands in his lap, the bowl cupped in one and a lighter cupped in the other. He passed an hour or two, crippled by the anxiety and sadness that followed his comedown. The absence of pedestrians and traffic on an otherwise bustling street and the silence of the neighborhood made his chest swell with a sense of impending doom. Shards of broken glass on the asphalt made him want to cry. Despite the early hour, when there was nothing left in the bowl but blackened ashes, he took off his clothes and went to bed.

[This was depression.

Also, contrary to popular belief, this is where the process ends. In my experience, acceptance is a myth.]

The weed helped some, but he slept fitfully and didn't leave his room until the next morning. When he rose, he felt far better than he had the day before. He ate a bowl of cereal, showered, shaved, and tried to make himself look presentable. His eyes were no longer dilated, and apart from a little melancholy, he felt relatively normal.

He had no desire to encounter the suspicious, calculating glare of his father the litigator and the litany of questions that went along with it. He was also in no mood for his mother's fawning and expressions of worry. Nevertheless, he had put it off long enough. He skipped class and drove east on I-90 toward home. Levi's dad balanced a stuffed suitcase on the edge of his Buick's trunk. Levi parked over all the old oil spots that still remained from the beater he drove in high school.

"Mom inside?" he said.

"Yeah." His dad shoved the suitcase the rest of the way into the trunk and slammed it. "If you wanna talk to her, you better hurry. We're about to leave."

"To where?"

"Whaddya mean where? Arizona."

"Arizona? We're having the funeral there? We're not bringing him back here?"

His dad turned and walked toward the house in a rush. "Who's we? Like the royal we? We're we; i.e., your mother and I are we. If you want a funeral here, someone has to physically get him and bring him back." He stopped at the steps and turned around. "You obviously got the messages. Was it too much to call back? You live twenty minutes away, for God's sake. It shouldn't be this hard to get a hold of you."

"Dad, I'm—"

His dad turned and went into the house and called for Levi's mother.

Levi reached up and touched his dad's shoulder. "Dad, I'm sorry." His dad turned and looked down into his eyes and frowned. "I was just having a hard—forget it. I should have been here sooner. He was your dad after all." Levi looked down at his shoes. "How are you holding up? Are you okay?"

His dad unclenched his jaw and his face relaxed. He let out a deep loud sigh and hugged Levi. He squeezed and patted his son's back. "I'm fine, Son. I'll be fine."

This was his father, and these were the pendular swings between fearsome judgment and bold, shameless compassion.

When Levi pulled away, his father took to the professional tone in which he felt most comfortable. "Your mother and I will go to Phoenix and help your aunt clean out his room. We'll help her make the arrangements, and we'll bring Aunt Trudy when we come back with the body on Thursday. It's not set in stone, but the funeral will most likely be Saturday. At Immanuel."

"Uncle Thomas officiating?"

"Yes, Pastor Anhalt officiating." His dad turned to get in the car.

Levi's mother came fumbling with the keys and an oversized handbag as she tried to hold the storm door open with one foot. She dropped the keys, and as she bent to pick them up, the bag slipped off her shoulder. Levi picked up the keys for her.

"Oh, hi honey." She put her hand on one of his cheeks, stood on her tiptoes, and kissed his other. She was flushed and out of breath.

"Oh, honey. I'm so glad I got to see you before we left. I was worried. Are you okay?"

"What about you guys?"

"Oh you know your father. Crisis mode."

Levi looked down the walkway at his dad standing by the driver's side door. His father's smooth, tanned forehead held a slight sheen of sweat. He pulled a comb from his back pocket and fixed his thick black hair, which he wore with a side part. He put the comb away and rubbed the side of his face as if feeling the closeness of his shave. He tapped his fingers on the top of his car. He unbuttoned his two-button black suit coat so that it hung open. He loosened his tie and climbed into the driver's seat. He rolled down the passenger's window and leaned across the seat, looking impatiently at their prolonged hug.

When they broke, Levi walked his mom to the car and opened her door for her. When she was in, he leaned down and looked into her window. "I'll be around. Available all week, I guess. And so, let me know if I can do anything on this end."

His father nodded and started rolling up the window.

"Seriously," Levi said. "If you need anything here, just call?"

His dad tossed up a dismissive wave as the window closed against the seal. His mother blew a kiss.

"I'll answer the phone this time," Levi shouted as the car backed out the driveway.

1.3 HOLLYWOOD CAN'T MAKE EXPLOSIONS LIKE THIS

On Tuesday morning, Levi looked down at his watch as he strolled into the periodicals department office at 7:51 A.M. Central Standard Time and tried to put on his most carefree smile. He fully expected a disapproving frown and a shake of the head from his already exasperated middle-aged work study supervisor, Doris. He expected a suppressed giggle from plain Jane Poorman, his periodicals coworker, who even as a senior was still plenty happy filing copies of everything from *The American Journal of Physiology—Endocrinology and Metabolism* to *Revista de Música Latinoamericana* every semester for $5.15 an hour.

"Just in time," he beamed, knowing full well he was nearly half an hour late. Neither of them, however, paid him any mind. Both of them sat in the far corner of the room huddled over the old transistor radio that Doris used to listen to NPR every morning.

Levi pulled the industrial steel cart from its home in the corner to a more accessible spot next to his beech-veneer desk. The cart carried three teetering piles of periodical journals and magazines. In his three-hour shift, Levi needed to check each one into the online library catalog, place a white sticker on the top right corner denoting the volume and issue, and apply a Tattle-Tape strip to the interior of each publication. Then he needed to shelve all of them. He had no time to dawdle on any normal day, and having already lost a sixth of his shift, he would have to hustle to get it all done in time.

He could barely hear the radio in the back of the room. He focused on his ancient monitor with the dark background and monochromatic amber printing.

"Hey," Doris called up to him. "Listen to this."

"What are they saying?" Levi said without turning around as he typed *The Annals of the American Academy of Political and Social Science* at a pace of approximately ninety-three words per minute.

"A plane flew into the World Trade Center in New York City."

"Wow. Terrible," Levi said as he set aside the first journal and started typing *Der Spiegel*. He flipped through that one because sometimes the foreign magazines had pictures of women with their tops off. Not a year, he thought. Not a year goes by that some Cessna driven by some amateur doesn't smash into some building.

"They say," said Doris, "that it's some kind of terrorist attack."

"How do they know it wasn't some kind of accident?" He placed *Der Spiegel* on top of *The Annals of the American Academy of Political and Social Science* and picked up *The Journal of English and Germanic Philology*.

Jane shushed them both and then said, "Quiet, I'm trying to hear this."

Levi finally broke from his rote cataloging and turned around. Jane leaned far over on her chair as if she were warming the bench in a close basketball game. Doris sat upright with her back straight. Every few seconds she reached up and put both palms on her head and ran her fingers through her shoulder-length gray hair.

"Could you turn it up?" Levi asked. The volume level didn't change. He continued his work.

When he had finished shelving his first stack, Doris and Jane hadn't moved. "So what was it?" Levi asked. "Like a puddle-jumper or something?"

Doris's eyes grew large and she shook her head. "No," she nearly whispered. And lowly and slowly, as if she were telling a ghost story to her children in front of a campfire she said, "A passenger plane."

She continued to shake her head in the slow, deliberate way in which she had begun.

"A passenger plane?" Levi said. "Like a jet?"

"Ssssh," Jane said.

Levi raced through the next dozen journals. His work was sloppy and the Tattle-Tapes were slanted and clearly visible on the pages, but he didn't have time to open the bindings wide enough to hide them. As he stood at the end of a center aisle placing *Infinite Dimensional Analysis, Quantum Probability and Related Topics* on a bottom shelf where he was sure it would never be touched again, he saw Doris pass by holding a rabbit-ears antenna. Jane followed with a boxy 19-inch color television set.

Levi went back to the empty office and flopped back into his desk chair. The pile of journals didn't seem to be getting any smaller. He picked up the receiver to make a quick phone call while Doris was out of the office, but he couldn't decide whether to call his aunt's house in Phoenix to see if his parents were in or Nick to hazard an apology.

[I still don't know if I ever apologized for punching you in the face that night. Compared to everything else I've done to hurt you, breaking your nose doesn't seem like that big of a deal, but for what it's worth, I'm sorry for that too.]

Doris held onto the doorjamb and swung her torso into the room. She was flushed and out of breath. Levi jumped and dropped the receiver onto its cradle.

"C'mon," Doris said.

"Why, what's up?"

"Just follow me."

She made a beeline straight toward the main doors of the library, but veered at the last second and went up the burgundy-carpeted stairs to the second floor. Doris led him down a hallway, all the way through the graduate-student carrels, and she turned the handle on the last door. It was a small room, cramped like an elevator. Jane found a clear picture on the television by holding the antenna and standing to the side of the set.

At 8:01 A.M. Central Standard Time, the picture of dense black smoke billowing, boiling, pouring, overflowing from the top floors of the North Tower of the World Trade Center came into focus on live television.

The television program was *Good Morning America*. The digital clock on the bottom right-hand corner of the screen said 9:01 and the temperature read 68 degrees. To Levi, it looked no different there than in Wisconsin. The sky was sunny and clear and he could almost feel the crispness of the autumn air. The exception was the dark smoke obscuring the screen.

Doris pointed and stuttered. "We were right there. Gary and I. Right there. There's an observation tower there. Tourists everywhere. Restaurants. The place is like a city by itself." Diane Sawyer confirmed what she said and Doris nodded, as if to say, "See, I told you."

"We remind you again," Diane said. "There was a terrorist bomb that did go off at the World Trade Center years ago."

"Why is she saying that?" Jane said.

"What do you mean?" Levi said.

Jane switched the hand she used to hold the antenna. "They said it was a plane. Are they just trying to scare people?"

Charles Gibson said, "Absolutely no indication that this could have been related to that."

[The extent to which the media not only entered, but practically controlled the dialog would become all too clear to us as the day went on—hell, as the entire decade went on.]

Charles and Diane went by telephone to a man who described rescue efforts. It all seemed so mundane to Levi at the time. So journalistic. So newsy.

Until—

Levi, Doris, and Jane all saw the second plane—and it was a huge plane—enter the screen. Charles, Diane, and even the man on the telephone were entirely incognizant about what was going to happen.

Hollywood can't make explosions like this, was Levi's first thought.

The man on the telephone with Charles and Diane shouted, "Oh my God," and it wasn't so much like blasphemy; it was an echt and ingenuous prayer.

"Where did these planes come from?" Levi said. "Where were they going? I think—" Levi thought his brother was flying home from DC that morning. Or maybe it was the next morning. He couldn't think. "I think that maybe—" He couldn't bring himself to say it aloud for fear that he would make it so.

The mother in Doris took over and the open-mouthed shaking of the head vanished. All slack left her face. Even her tired eyes grew taut and she looked ready to spring into action.

"Both of you," she said, "can stay here and watch if you'd like. Or you can go home. Or you can do whatever you need to do, call whomever you need to call." She reached back and grabbed the door-knob, stopping to address the practical items. "Of course, whatever you decide to do, don't forget to clock out. I, for one, will be using sick hours because this makes me sick." She sucked in her breath as if something dawned on her. "Oh, I need to call my daughter. Her husband is in the army."

Levi backed slowly toward the door, looking back and forth between Jane and the emptiness where Doris had stood. "Jane, what about—"

Jane lifted a hand and waved him off without taking her eyes off the screen.

Levi ran down the stairs two at a time. He pushed through the double doors into the lobby. When he reached the exterior doors, it dawned on him that he didn't punch out. "Screw it," he said aloud as he continued down the sidewalk at a jog on his way home. He had to turn on the news to see where those flights came from. He had to figure this thing out. He had to get home to check the e-mail itinerary his brother had sent him. He had to—

1.4 [. . .]

You know what? Forget it. How can I write about this when all I did was sit on the couch and get high? I had five tense minutes as I ran home and waited for the modem on the computer to hiss, pop, groan, and screech as it tried to connect to the Internet. If I'm going to be honest, all dramatic tension dissipated when I looked at my brother's itinerary in my e-mail and saw that he wasn't due to fly until the next day.

How can I write about all this when I wasn't in any danger? When no one I knew was in any danger? When I was just an eighteen-year-old kid who was far far away? When I spent the day in the safety of my living room? What right do I have? And what purpose would it serve?

After all, you saw what I saw.

Or did you? I don't know that I'm as intuitive as most people. I think you're better at grasping the gravity of things.

You probably placed yourself in their shoes. You did this because you have empathy. You probably imagined yourself at a desk in a cubicle full of people. Maybe a New York Yankees souvenir pennant hanging on the wall and a picture of your gray cat, Nuggets, tacked up above your computer. Type. Input data. Click. Verify. Repeat. Take a sip of coffee. You look over your shoulder to see if your coworker is watching. Do an AOL search for "readings in the village this weekend." Minimize that screen and bring back the data entry program. Glance over at a window to see a passenger plane coming right at you.

Did it all happen in slow motion? Did the pilot have fear in his eyes or was it resignation? Did you, from your desk by the window, see the maniacal grin and the hatred in his eyes? Did you duck for cover by instinct or did you instead drop your coffee mug in slow motion and stare at the plane head-on? Did the mug shatter into pieces on the floor in similar slow motion while the plane made contact, sweeping you away into ashes on the way through?

It's possible, even probable, that you took a moment to imagine what it felt like to be those men holding those box cutters against the rough whiskers of another man's neck. Knowing you—you who have learned to live with such common sinners as us—you probably tried to feel what they felt, to learn what drove them to it. You would grasp at any illumination like a man falling down a cliff reaches for grass. You'd take hold of any reason to forgive, wouldn't you?

You saw more than I did. You had to have seen more. It affected you differently because you're good. You can see that people—other people—are hurting, and you can feel for them. You love. Which is more than I can say for myself most days.

You knew before we ever went anywhere and did anything that there was a whole world out there. We lived somewhere; but other people lived somewhere else; and other people lived in entirely different countries—which may as well have been different worlds to me—but to you, people were people; and everyone else was just living, like we were living; and now, for reasons completely unknown to me, people were literally dying on live television right before our very eyes. Yet, you knew things about the world without having been told, because you understand the nature of things.

I didn't feel like I should have felt for all those people who were dead and dying. My own grandpa had just died. Instead of imagining these people a thousand miles from our home in Wisconsin, I imagined Grandpa in some freezer with a toe tag. I imagined the mortician sitting over some small TV on his desk, caring more for the dead people on the news than for the dead people in his array of freezers with the roll-out trays. I could tell early on that it affected you more. I could tell as soon as we had huddled on the couch in the living room, even before we had watched the second tower fall. Eris sat between us. She and I passed the little bong, green-and-blue hand-blown glass (remember that?). While the two of us took big pulls and sunk into the cushy flower-patterned couch you got from your grandmother, you were glued—like, hard, two-part epoxy glued—to the little black box in front of us. Eris tried to pass you the bong a few times, but you pushed it away. You leaned forward on the couch and you turned up the television.

Meanwhile, I looked over at Eris to admire her magical and mysterious teenage pulchritude. The way her lips plumped up when she slowly blew the smoke out. She made eye contact and smiled when she passed the bong back over. We were young, we were listless, we were stoned, and we were blissfully dumb.

When they went to Jamie McIntyre at the Pentagon to announce that it, too, had been hit, you moved your hands to your head like you do. You knew before we did that everything had changed. That we were no longer children in a safe world. You opened your mouth and I thought maybe you would finally say something, but then you closed it again when they cut to Aaron Brown at the New York site—at the site we have all come to know as Ground Zero. They didn't cut quickly enough for us to see it happen, but the reporter described the chaos, explosion, smoke, and falling debris with painstaking impromptu detail. "But just look at that," he said. And in the pregnant silence that hung in the room, we did look. We looked at the smoke that rose up to the sky, high above the North Tower, which we could see, and then down through what had to have been miles of city blocks below. Aaron could not tell us what was behind the North Tower, because there was no longer anything at all. After he had gathered himself, Aaron told us, "That is about as frightening a scene as you will ever see."

You still said nothing.

I, for one, thought about the rhetorical nature of that statement. I thought, *Isn't it kind of assumptive for this guy to assert to an audience of millions that some grainy pictures on TV will be the most frightening thing they ever see?*

Perhaps if I'm being honest with myself, if I'm making any effort toward realistic self-assessment, I would admit that these are the only conversations in which I feel comfortable: Yes, the ones in my head, but not just that. The arguments. The back-and-forth over semantics. The little digs, the baseless opining about anything, the straw men, the false feeling of superiority that comes with the territory, the emotional stuntedness that keeps me from directly addressing any issue in any sort of real and meaningful way. Growing up, I trained well for these diversionary conversations. Perhaps it's genetic: the need to press, deflect, then litigate.

Don't get me wrong, I was horrified, but the attacks horrified me in an existential and detached way. The event seemed important, but it was not an importance I could grasp, though I tried. It didn't touch me in the same way as, say, Bobby Withrow killing that guy over at the Conoco in Holmen by hitting him over the head with a forty-ounce bottle of Mickey's. Remember? We took that trip to the prison for our American Government class and I saw him there. The guard escorted us through a hallway lined with thick security windows, which overlooked a common area filled with octagonal steel picnic tables bolted to the epoxied concrete floor. Several groups of inmates crowded around televisions suspended near the upper corners of the large room, but Bobby sat alone at one of the tables in the center of the room. He was playing solitaire, moving the cards from one pile to the next, straightening each pile as he went. When he shuffled, he looked up at us. All of us high schoolers, just like him. I swear he made eye contact with me.

The chilling thing was that Bobby held the eye contact, and he wouldn't look away. The guard had warned us not to lock eyes with any of them because they were like animals and it was a dominance thing with them, but you know, I didn't see any hatred, malice, or ill will in his eyes; he only had this kind of loneliness and forlorn sadness. I can still remember every detail of that moment. That was the year my parents threatened to kick me out; I had gotten that minor-in-possession charge, and it was after my second time totaling the Caprice. I remember thinking, "Damn, dude. That could be me."

But this? This was a grainy 19-inch television screen. This was the wreckage, the smoke, the flames—this was the apocalypse that wouldn't look real in a movie.

You made a guttural sound in your throat.

Eris put her hand on your back, and I began fuming that she was apparently our new houseguest. I resented you for finding another best friend, albeit one with breasts and benefits. Or so I imagined. And the absolute worst part about it was that she seemed to know it. She made eye contact with those savage green eyes, and she smiled. She knew everything she was doing, and she mocked me.

But that's not true either. How could she not love you? You who have always been so good. Do you remember what you wanted to do? You wanted to drop out of school to drive to New York and help. You spent two weeks' worth of pay on bottled water and first aid kits, and you packed up the Prizm to go. Nothing anyone said could convince you that quitting work, dropping out of school, and leaving town was a bad idea. Finally, your Uncle Thomas had to guilt-trip you into staying by telling you Oma needed you, which was a lie. That woman never needed help from anyone. And because Uncle Thomas is a Protestant minister, he made sure to remind you that you can't be saved by your works.

You agreed. What was it that you said? What was it that you fired back at him, nodding and snarling in a barely contained paroxysm of frustration? "Good works can't save you, but they might save someone else."

The truth is, we should have let you go.

No. We should have gone with you. All of us. Every last one of us should have gone and handed out water, food, and clothes. We all should have dug through the rubble to save the bloody, bruised, and broken souls trapped underneath the weight of it all. We all should have cleansed the hurting, rubbed ointment on their wounds, and wrapped them in the whitest of bandages. We all should have walked away from our paychecks for those who needed it. We all should have done what you would have done. We all should have given up what we had to go help in the search for the lost.

We should have done that instead of what we did later, which was drive to the recruiter's office to become part of the problem.

You grabbed my arm and turned up the volume on the television.

The top of the second tower fell.

Aaron Brown once again spoke to us from New York. "Good Lord," he said. The top of the tallest tower on the world's greatest skyline kept falling and falling and falling until nothing remained but smoke and ash. "There are no words."]

1.5 I THINK ABOUT GOD A LOT

Levi woke to a dark room, his mouth dry and sticky. His legs lay across Eris's lap. The television's blue lights flickered, still replaying The Attacks, but it was muted. Eris slept sitting up, her head back, her mouth open. She snored softly.

Nick sat in the recliner. He leaned forward and looked at them both. "Do you think you could wake her?" he said. "I've been listening to that for hours." It was not acrimony he displayed with his tone, with his posture, and with his gaze, but it was also not adoration.

The telephone rang once, then stopped. Nick got up from the chair, picked up the cordless, and looked at the caller-ID window. "It was Oma." He tried calling back, but no one answered.

The three of them moped out in single file to go check on her. They took the slick black Altima paid for by Eris's father. Nick and Eris spoke in low voices up front. Levi stared out the window at the river as they drove toward the freeway from downtown.

When they pulled off I-90 in West Salem, still five miles from Bangor, Eris turned to answer the question he didn't ask. "I have to drop my mom's keys off at home real quick. It'll only take a minute."

A tan Lexus sat in the driveway of the new split-level bungalow Eris shared with her mom. Eris pulled in behind it. "That son of a bitch." She took a set of keys from her console and slammed the lid down before storming up to the house, leaving her door open and the ignition dinging.

Levi thought of following her in, but Nick stayed put, so Levi stayed put. He wanted the least amount of drama. Eris had left the front door of the house wide open. He could hear yelling.

When Nick didn't seem to register that the car was dinging at them, Levi got out to smoke a cigarette. He only got a few good drags before he heard the house door slam. He turned and saw Eris storming toward their car, but she turned and went back to her house again. She opened the front door and leaned in. "You're just helping him cheat on his wife," she screamed. She slammed the door, and then she opened it and slammed it again.

Levi flicked his cigarette out into the road and got in. Nick had turned sideways in his seat and was looking at Eris with respectful concern. "The guy with the ear?" he asked.

Eris said nothing. She held the heels of her hands to her eyes and she cried. After a time, she slammed both her fists against the steering wheel and gulped, as if trying to swallow her own tears. She took a deep breath, and wiped the tears from under her eyes with an index finger. In silence, she backed out of the driveway.

[And once again, my failure to get close to her was my own fault. I said nothing. I held my breath, scared to death of saying the wrong thing, when instead I should have just said something.

This is always how things went. She had tried to make inroads with me, but I had failed to see what she needed. She had shared innumerable poems with me and asked me to look them over, to give her feedback. Literature was our one unique connection. I had read them all, sad confessionals chock full of abstract language and shadowy angst, each verse utterly devoid of any concrete images, but each line crying out for company, each word screaming out her loneliness and frustration.

Utterly intimidated and ultimately apathetic, I had no framework with which to respond. What did I know of her life? What did I know of a parade of ergodic men marching through the halls of her home doing unspeakable things with her mother under the influence of God knows what? What did I know of the leers of her cousin's friends, the comments and gropes and calls of the couch-dwellers and freeloaders who paid her so much attention? What did

I know of a life in which my family wouldn't notice if I came home or not, if my bed remained empty and no phone calls were made? The answer is nothing.

Her life apart from us was foreign to me, and thus, her poems were foreign to me. They made me uncomfortable. They made her seem too vulnerable, and I didn't like to see her as vulnerable. I liked the girl she projected—the street-smart punk, the general artist, the mysterious and aloof poet—but I could not grasp the girl she was with all her history and stark reality. And her poems were as unknowable as she was. I was terrified of saying the wrong thing, so I simply said nothing. I said they were great and asked for more. But I never responded. Not really. I never talked to her. I never asked the basic questions that showed I cared, because I was too afraid to sound callous. First, do no harm. Nothing ventured and nothing gained.

And this is why you won. You turned the unknowable into the knowable. By talking. By asking. By listening. Ultimately, by caring. You saw her as more than the angsty girl next door; you saw her for what she was: a complicated, feeling, living, breathing, thinking, independent young woman who just needed a friend. It's why you knew about the specific guy with the ear, whoever that was, and it's why I didn't.]

When Eris turned on the radio after a few minutes, Nick reached out and put his hand on her leg and gave her thigh a gentle squeeze.

"No," she said. "The guy with the neck."

They spoke in code riddled with subtext. Levi didn't understand and he didn't dare ask, though he wanted to be the one touching her. He wanted to be the one she leaned against to say, "You saved me."

[Don't think I didn't/don't recognize that it wasn't exactly fair or selfless—to put it mildly—to begrudge her the comfort that she needed in her state of emotional distress, preferring that she go without comfort rather than get it from my best friend. I only bring all this up to let you know how conflicted I was/am/maybe always will be in your presence, that is, your combined presence.]

After a few moments with Nick's hand on her leg she said, "You and me both, buddy. We got something in common."

"What's that?" Nick asked.

She patted Nick's hand and then let it linger there. "You're not the only orphan, Annie."

• • •

Uncle Thomas turned in his stool when the door jingled to signal their entrance. He waved with one hand and snuffed out a smoke in an ashtray with the other.

"Well, now that you've got some company, I'm going to head home and get back to work." He leaned down and gave Oma a chaste kiss on her cheek. He passed Nick and clapped a hand on his shoulder.

As Nick hugged his grandmother and sat next to her, Uncle Thomas stopped in front of Levi and shook his hand firmly. "Long time no see, my boy."

"Yeah. It's been a while," Levi mumbled.

"Been going to church with your folks back home then? Here in Bangor? Haven't seen you in La Crosse with Nick."

[And I have to admit, this type of thing was not an insignificant factor in my latching on so quickly to your idea to sign up and skip town. Small towns = glass houses, and glass houses + everyone is religious = everyone guilt-tripping you all the time about everything.]

Levi looked up and made eye contact. "No," he said. "Just a busy summer, I guess."

Uncle Thomas maintained a firm grip, even as Levi tried to move along. He pulled him closer and in a low voice he said, "I heard about your grandpa. Real sorry to hear that. He was a good man. I served him for many years." His breath reeked of coffee and stale tobacco. "If you need anything, anything at all, you let me know, okay? Even if you just need to talk, drop by anytime, okay?"

Levi pulled his hand away.

"Tell your folks I said hi, will ya?"

"Sure thing."

"Okay, then Levi. Okay." He left and the bells on the door rang behind him.

There were no customers. Oma watched the evening news. They all sat in a row next to her.

When she broke the silence, she sounded sad and tired. "You kids have class today?" She kept her eyes on the screen mounted on the wall.

"I don't know," Nick said.

She turned and put her hand on Nick's cheek, just below where the pale skin below his eyes turned a sickening shade of blue. "What's the other guy look like?"

Oma moved her mouth without opening it, as if she were talking to herself, the way she did sometimes when she got anxious.

After only a few minutes, Nick's grandmother broke the silence again. "Oh, get out of here," she said. "Let this old woman watch her country fall apart in peace."

Nick put his hand on her forearm. "I can stay."

She patted his hand and shook her head. "Scram."

"Let us take you out to dinner," Eris said.

She shook her head. "People need a place to go sometimes, and I need to be here for them. This is where I need to be."

Eris got up and gave her a silent hug. Nick kissed her cheek, and they left. Levi looked over his shoulder at the old woman sitting alone at the bar, staring at the television, twirling her wedding band around her skeletal finger.

• • •

Eris dropped them off, but didn't come in.

On the television the president sat at his desk in the Oval Office, his hands folded, his lips pursed and twitchy.

After he had finished speaking, Levi turned toward his room. "I should probably call my parents." He dialed his Aunt Trudy's from his desk. No one answered. He tried reading, but he found himself repeating sentences. He tossed his book aside and went for a walk through the deserted streets of a world that made no sense.

He found himself passing in front of the church, and he crossed the street to the parsonage where Uncle Thomas lived. He walked up the two steps to the door that entered directly into the study, and he stood there a moment picking juniper berries from the bushes by the door. He knocked once and heard Uncle Thomas's raspy bellow to come in.

The desk inside was broad enough to dominate the room, but it was not a pretentious desk; the immensity of the scratched steel frame, monochromatic legs, and chipped laminate top only served the functional purpose of holding enough books to allow for uninterrupted study, transcription, and translation. The old pastor sat in front of the typewriter with his black tie loosened and the top button of his starched white shirt undone. He crossed his arms over his chest. A burning cigarette sat in the amber glass ashtray next to the typewriter, sending smoke up to the heavens. A Bible sat open on the other side of the typewriter.

Uncle Thomas didn't look up from the paper in the typewriter. "Nicodemus? The one who comes under the cover of night's darkness."

"Am I interrupting anything?" Levi asked.

Uncle Thomas brought one hand up and rubbed his chin. "Just an old man and his lucubrations," he said.

The two plush chairs for the visitors who frequently came for counseling—the meek, contrite, and brokenhearted—were more comfortable and lavish than the preacher's own squeaky, fake-leather office chair. Levi took a seat and waited. Uncle Thomas continued staring at his page. He typed a sentence or two in a fury of clicking and then leaned back again.

Levi looked around at the thousands of books. Three of the four walls were themselves bookshelves. The books they held were not arranged alphabetically, but rather, dogmatically. They weren't separated by language, but by doctrine. The books in Greek mingled with the Latin and they brushed spines with the Hebrew. The ancient Aramaic pressed hard against the German, and the English books were there for when the man needed a break. There were, of course, Bibles in all of these languages, and although Levi had learned long ago that the man at the desk knew every word, their spines were broken and worn.

Uncle Thomas once again began typing, but he broke their comfortable silence. "What's on your mind, my boy?"

Levi hesitated. He had been weighed down by his conscience for months, unwilling to believe, yet unwilling to leave. He had come to confess. He had come to bare his unbelieving soul, to explain that he wouldn't be returning to the church. He had come to beg absolution for his apostasy and ask the old man's advice, and if it was denied, to sadly depart anyway. Now, however, he faltered. "I dunno. What's on anyone's mind? It's like I woke up this morning and the world was one way, and then out of nowhere, the world is another way. This is like," he paused, lit his own smoke, and tried to find the word. "Unprecedented."

"Ecclesiastes one, verse nine: 'What has been will be again, what has been done will be done again; there is nothing new under the sun.'"

"So maybe 'unprecedented' was too strong a word."

"Indeed," Uncle Thomas said, still focused on his page.

"So what then? America's under attack, but just another old day under the sun?"

Uncle Thomas rubbed his chin again and still didn't bother to look up at Levi. "Matthew twenty-four, verse six."

"Which says?" Levi said, already reaching forward to grab the Bible from next to the typewriter.

Uncle Thomas beat him to it. "'You will hear of wars and rumors of wars, but see to it that you are not alarmed. Such things must happen, but the end is still to come.'"

"Convenient. What do you tell the people trapped under the rubble or the family members?"

Uncle Thomas clacked away on the typewriter.

Levi dropped the Bible onto the desk with a thud. "Well?"

"Luke thirteen, verses four and five, 'Or those eighteen who died when the tower in Siloam fell on them—do you think they were more guilty than all the others living in Jerusalem? I tell you, no! But unless you repent, you too will all perish.'"

"So that's it, huh?"

"Maybe this will get people of this apostatical age to think about God. Has it gotten you to think about God?"

Levi took his chance to say what he had come to say. "I think about God a lot."

"Good. And what do you think?"

"I think god-awful. I think when things get really awful, people put god in front of it all, and that makes everything worse. God-awful." It had not come out how Levi had wanted. He closed his eyes and took a deep breath, trying to figure out how to disassociate himself from things he didn't believe without separating himself from those who still believed them.

Uncle Thomas ripped the page out of the typewriter, crumpled it, and threw it into the trashcan under his desk.

Uncle Thomas finally turned and gave Levi his attention, but he changed the subject altogether. "How are your folks doing? Your dad in particular. He holding up okay?"

"They're fine," Levi said.

"You doing okay? I know you and your grandfather were close."

"I'll be fine."

The old man frowned and shook his head. "Blessed are those who mourn."

Levi threw up his hands in exaggerated exasperation. "Don't you have anything to offer for yourself? Or does it all come out of that book?"

Uncle Thomas turned away again and inserted a new page in the typewriter. He manually turned the platen knob until he had it where he wanted it. "Oh, what do I know? 'The one thing needful' isn't exactly a reference to my own personal musings."This is how the man always spoke, how he lived. Everything he said pointed back to the Gospel, and Levi couldn't figure out how to get a real conversation going.

"Sure. Go on back to your typing." Levi sat there tapping his feet. "I didn't come here for a sermon, you know."

"Well you haven't been around on Sundays, so I have to give them to you when I can."

Levi grabbed his pack of smokes from the edge of the desk and shoved them in his pocket. He leaned forward to go. "Forget it. I shouldn't have wasted my time."

Uncle Thomas turned toward him again. He leaned back and laced his long fingers behind his head. He looked down his nose at Levi for a moment. He didn't bang his fists on the desk or lift his trembling hands up toward the heavens as he thundered his message in the way that Levi had seen him do so many times from the pulpit. He spoke gently, conversationally, as a man talks to his friend.

"I've known you since you were a small boy, Levi. Watched you grow with my nephew since you were knee high to a grasshopper. I've seen you hit your Little League balls and I've seen you scrape your knees. But you're no longer a child." He reached up and took his glasses off. He chewed on the stem for a moment before twirling them between his thumb and forefinger. "To be honest, I don't know exactly why you came here. But I do know one thing." He set the glasses on the desk and leaned forward. His mouth turned down and he stared at Levi with pale blue eyes that seemed to somehow cut through him. "You sure as hell didn't come here to shoot the shit about the evening news."

[That was my opening, I suppose. I had been lingering around, waiting for him to ask me point blank why I had come, and I should have known that's as close as he'd ever get. In a way, I guess, I had lost my nerve. Or maybe there was some kind of mustard seed remaining deep inside my unrepentant soul. It's more likely that I simply realized that you can't break up with your pastor like you can with your girlfriend. You can't just waltz into his office and say, "I'm done with you and your kind, but let's all stay friends." They'll never let you go.

You'll never let me go, will you? Giving me the space and freedom I want isn't your idea of love, is it? You'd rather cut me deep on earth to spare me pain in hell, whereas I think hell is right here.

I'm recalcitrant, and you're indomitable. We're all impervious to change.]

Levi stood up and pushed his chair back with his legs. "I don't know why I came here. Maybe to confirm what I already knew."

"And what, my boy, did you already know?"

"That I can't just pretend." He waved his hand around. "That this hell is the product of some benevolent deity. Turn on the news. Not just tonight, but on any given night." Uncle Thomas stared at him and the silence grew uncomfortable. Levi looked down at his shoes and muttered, "God is dead."

"You can't pretend? And quoting philosophers now? You've got it all figured out? Big smart grown-up, full of logic and reason?"

"Oh forget it."

"Oh, did I offend you?"

Levi moved to the back of the chair and pushed it in, but made no move to leave.

"Fair enough and perfectly natural, I suppose," said Uncle Thomas with a shrug. "Young men are often filled with doubt, with restlessness and aimless wanderings. No direction really." He leaned back in his chair again, and gripped the armrests with each hand. "But you come in here tonight, I try to help you find that direction somehow, and what do you do? You hear something you don't want to hear, and you stick your fingers in your ears and say la la la la. I didn't expect that from you."

Levi walked to the door. "And I didn't expect to hear the rote recitations of a brainwashed old preacher."

He walked back through town, through dark alleys, and then he went out of his way to walk along the river. He pulled leaves and twigs from the trees as he walked, picked them apart between his fingers, and dropped them on the ground.

[I spent so much time that year walking alone, trying to figure it out, trying to articulate in my own mind why I was so full of ennui and discontent, but I couldn't. I still can't. Maybe restless is just how it feels to be young.]

When Levi finally returned home, Nick sat smoking a cigarette on the landing at the top of the stairs with his back against the wall. The bruising under Nick's eyes had turned a sickly yellow at the edges. When Levi reached the top of the stairs, he sat next to his friend.

They smoked together in silence for a while. The weight of that strange day hung between them.

"Hey Nick?" Levi said.

"Uh huh." He exhaled and stared ahead at the cigarette held up in his lap.

"Remember that first time you did Ex with me? The day when your Opa died?"

"Don't remind me."

"You disappeared and I found you two hours later in your bedroom rocking back and forth. The notebook was open where you wrote over and over, 'I'm going to hell. I'm going to hell. I'm going to hell.'"

Nick didn't say anything. He just nodded slightly and took another drag from his cigarette.

"I'm sorry I made you do that," Levi said.

Nick turned toward Levi and cocked his head and squinted an eye. "I know."

Levi stood and stepped over Nick's legs to get to the door.

"And Nick?"

Nick looked up.

"You're not going to hell."

Nick looked back down the stairs. "I know."

1.6 IN A WAY, IT WAS WRITING THAT GOT ME INTO THIS MESS IN THE FIRST PLACE

The university canceled classes on Wednesday. Nick went off to work a double at Oma's Pub while Levi sat on his couch watching the talking heads on the news. He smoked cigarettes, and every few minutes he'd spark his bowl and take a deep pull. At some point during mid-morning, his dad called.

Levi picked up the cordless from the floor in front of the couch.

Not one for pleasantries, his dad got down to business. "I think it probably goes without saying, but just so you don't complain later that no one told you, we won't be having the funeral there on Thursday. All the flights have been canceled."

"Got it, Dad." Levi kicked his feet up onto the couch and rested on his elbow. "So when do you think you'll be back?"

"How in the world should I know?"

"I dunno," Levi mumbled. "I didn't know if maybe the airlines told you when you could fly again or anything."

"Nope. It's a mess."

"So like, what's up with Grandpa's body then?" Levi pictured the body of his grandfather sitting in the back of some truck on the flight line of the Phoenix airport. He pictured the skin drawing tight against the cheekbones, and he imagined the makeup on the face of the embalmed corpse drying out and cracking as it waited. He could see the gray skin underneath the cracked makeup practically sweating in the heat of the truck's boxy cargo bed. He pictured blue embalming fluid leaking from his dead grandpa's eye sockets as his waxy face melted.

Levi heard his father sigh with impatience. "What do you mean what's up with it?"

"I mean like, how long can it wait? You know." Levi flipped through the channels and stopped on some hip hop music videos.

"No, Levi. I don't know. How long can it wait? Wait for what? He's dead."

Levi sat up. "How long before it rots, Dad? How long before the body rots? I mean, geez. Don't act like you don't know what I'm saying. It can't just sit there forever, right? It's already been like what, four days? Five?"

"I have no idea. I'm sure it will be fine. Aunt Trudy's been talking to the funeral home. She has a guy."

"She has a guy? Like a funeral guy?"

"I don't know. Yeah. A funeral guy. Some friend of hers. I'm sure he'll know more. Hey, I gotta go. Call me tonight and see if I have an update."

"How about you call me? I can't afford long distance."

"Maybe work more than five hours a week stacking magazines and you could afford long distance."

"In the meantime, you call me."

An hour later, his sister called. She lived in one of the big new houses on the south side with her husband and was working on starting a catering company. She had good credit.

"Hear from Dad?" Levi was sure she already knew the answer to her own question. He was also sure she had just gotten off the phone, but her conversation with their dad would have been far more detailed and protracted.

"Yup."

"Can you believe all this?" she said.

"Believe what? Like The Attacks or that Grandpa's body is rotting in Phoenix?"

"What? Grandpa's body is rotting?"

"Forget it."

She moved on and spent considerable time lamenting that they hardly saw each other even though they lived in the same town. She asked him a lot of questions about what was going on in his life, if he needed a job, and he gave a lot of monosyllabic answers rather than ask her the obvious, which would have been, "Why are you just now for the first time taking an interest in what's going on in my life?" He flipped through the channels some more.

Finally, she drew out her words in resignation. "Guess I'll letchya go."

"K, bye."

"Love you," she said.

He hung up the phone and went back to watching television.

• • •

This is how things went. By Thursday, pragmatism beat out reflection in most of Levi's classes as many of his professors got back down to business. The Logic professor's aide taught syllogisms; History of the Civilized World through 1850 hosted a guest speaker with a giant mustache and a propensity for dropping f-bombs, who gave a lecture on misogyny in American politics; and Professor Brendan, a big-breasted post-grad adjunct with thick-framed glasses that drove Levi wild, gave a PowerPoint called "*Godot,* or No? Minimalism in Modern Casting." None of the professors dared start a discourse about The Attacks, with the exception of Dr. Buddy Jackson, the Creative Writing transplant from Purdue prone to tie-dyed Kafka T-shirts tucked into his khakis. He had Einstein hair that matched his bright white tennis shoes.

He burst into the room in a flurry. [This is a cliché he would have hated, but it literally was like a flurry with much movement and papers seeming to fly around him at all times like snowflakes. He also would have hated the shifting points of view, these constant regressions into the colloquial first-person, and that's what he would have called them: regressions. I'm almost certain he would say I was unsure of my own authorial voice, that I was uncertain of my own narrative authority. And did I really need to intrude into the story using brackets like hugs? And did I need a hug because I lacked confidence? To which I now reply: If I sound unsure of myself, it's because I am.] He shouted that he was tossing the syllabus because in light of recent events, it was no longer needed.

Dr. Jackson pointed at some mousy girl in the back. "Do you remember when Kennedy was shot?"

She shook her head. He asked the same of all the eighteen-year-old kids in the room and everyone shook their heads no. Finally, he came to Louise, a nontraditional student who looked old enough to be Levi's mother. "How about you?"

She pulled a streak of her gray shoulder-length hair from her mouth. "A little. I was in kindergarten. I just remember they took everyone to the cafeteria and we all watched the television. It was a big deal." She put the hair back in her mouth.

Dr. Jackson clapped and hopped up into the air. "Exactly. Everyone was crowded around the television. Everyone can say where they were. Everyone can remember the images—you know, Jackie climbing over the back of the convertible to pick up pieces of her dear husband's brain." He paused. A respectful silence. "Do you at least remember those images from the day? I know you're a young lady, but do you remember the footage on the news of the president being shot?"

Louise lifted her eyebrows in rapt attention and nodded.

"Oh, so can I," said Dr. Jackson. "I can remember it so vividly. The breaking news. The color video clips—blue sky, Jackie in her pink Chanel suit. The gruesome home video of the president's head just—" he put his hands together and pulled them apart, fingers splayed.

He shook his head and looked around the room. "Except you all remember it the same way I do. It's fake. Artificial. I didn't even have a color television screen. They didn't show footage of the president being shot that day. And the Zapruder film with the clearest depiction of the assassination wasn't shown to the public until twelve years after it happened, when Geraldo Rivera showed it to the world on *Goodnight America*." He bent his knees and looked around with his eyebrows up, waiting for reactions.

Levi looked around. Some people stuck their tongues in the corners of their mouths and furrowed their brows, pressing their ballpoint pens into their composition books as they doodled. Some people chewed on their pens and looked out the window. Some chewed their gum with the bored look of cows on pasture.

[This is our generation: Here we are; now entertain us.]

Dr. Jackson stood up, disappointed. "I'm lamenting here, people. No one can even tell the difference anymore between what they remember from that day and what they remember from a decade later. Isn't that a tragedy? And now, with the constant news and the World Wide Web and all of that, it won't take a dozen years to corrupt the collective consciousness, I'll tell you that for free."

No one said a thing.

"Hemingway famously said it is valuable to a trained writer to crash in an airplane that burns. He also said there's no rule about how soon one should write about it. Apropos for this week, no? So use your imagination. Imagine yourself in one of those airplanes or one of those towers. Or the Pentagon. Or a field in Pennsylvania. You have ten minutes to write as many carefully chosen words as you can on The Attacks. And make it personal. Ten minutes. Ready and—" he looked down at his watched and waited for seconds to tick off. "Go."

[We had not been trained as writers and we had not crashed in burning planes, but Dr. Jackson paced through the aisles assuring us that we would definitely want to keep what we were writing. This would be our shield against the false memories created by the shifting landscape of media. This would ensure that we created our own consciousness instead of falling victim to the collective consciousness, thereby enabling us as writers to help *create* the collective consciousness rather than be manipulated by it. And five, ten, or twelve years from now—when other people finally got comfortable writing about this stuff—novelists would be writing about nothing more than news clips and iconic photographs, e.g., poignant images of men walking out of the ashes and ruffled men in suits jumping to their deaths, instead of anything they actually experienced. Or even worse, they'd all be writing about how they *should* have felt or what they were *supposed* to be feeling rather than what they actually did feel. But what we were doing, he assured us again, was our inoculation against all that. What we were doing—he stamped his foot again—was creating something that could last generations.

No one told him he told lies.

No one spoke up and said that what he proposed was inappropriate and opportunistic. Revolting and immoral. No one told him we were too far away while real people were too close. No one told him it's a sin to create drama where there is none. It's a sin to steal the stories of those who have earned them.

No one told him these weren't our stories to tell.]

Levi attempted the exercise, but he had already been corrupted. He had not one original thought. As he closed his eyes and tried to think of something personal to express about what had happened, an image from some Internet news site kept obtruding. It showed the parallel lines of a building's windows running from the top left to the bottom right of the image. The visible part of the building in the lower half of the picture was clean and light gray, but a jagged and diagonal swath of flame split the image in two, leaving the upper half of the photo a black, charred, and smoky ruin. Yet, it was not the orange flames cutting across the building or the smoke that obscured the bit of sky visible in the top right of the image that drew Levi's attention. It was the shape of a falling man, clothes rumpled by the wind, spread against the sky, suspended in the lower left of the image and backdropped by those perfect lines that ran parallel to gravity. The only image that spoke to him personally was the photograph of someone in such deep despair that jumping remained the only option.

[Now, so many years later, that picture still haunts me, but now the man has one bootless foot covered in a green sock. His pants are unbloused, and he stays like that, weightless in front of the smoke and flames, never falling further than that single moment in time.]

• • •

As Levi walked back to his apartment after class, he played the lecture over in his head. He thought of rebuttals, mouthing the words he would have said in response if he would have thought of them at the time, or if he had any courage. He walked past the cracked apartment parking lots, overflowing dumpsters, and back porches in various states of disrepair. The longer he walked, the more his anger dissipated like fog from his breathing. Why should he care anyway? The guy had a few chapbooks and a PhD. What had he ever done? It was a joke.

All of school had been something of a joke thus far, at least in terms of the challenge it presented, or rather, failed to present. Levi spent a lot of time writing, sure, but even thinking about that made him laugh when he was honest with himself. More than writing, he smoked weed and doodled in notebooks. He had probably written more random haiku than anyone in history, but so what? That didn't exactly give him any moral authority. His righteous indignation had turned him into a phony, and he hated phonies.

After all, what in the world did Levi have to write about? He had no stories of his own, but he could fill books with the things he hadn't done. Huge sets of *World Book Encyclopedias* full of stuff he hadn't done. He hadn't traveled the country on a wild and reckless road trip. He had never been to a bullfight, never been to the running of the bulls, never acted like a bull in a china shop, never even been to a china shop. He had never gone deep-sea fishing, had never battled anything bigger than a Mississippi catfish, had never taken a boat or a raft all the way down the Mississippi. He had never gone mountain climbing, skiing, or big-game hunting, had never even gone deer hunting. He hadn't, he decided, really done much of anything. He hadn't even had the chutzpa to ask out Eris, the girl he'd been crushing on since he figured out what girls were. He'd never done a thing. Everything he had ever done that was in any way worth writing about could fit in a single red milk carton crate full of black-and-white composition books. If he stuck with his academic plans, he'd end up nothing more than a Dr. Buddy Jackson, purveyor of fine arts and bullshit.

Later, as he lay on his back devouring a book of Denis Johnson short stories, the phone rang. It was his dad again.

"Big change of plans, Son. We're going to have a funeral service here."

Levi sat up and dropped his book on the floor. "There? I saw on the Internet that they're letting people fly again today."

"Yeah, well, even so, it's not that simple. The backlog is three days long. But the real problem is your aunt. She's refusing to fly. She also won't drive that far because of the blood clots. So, change of plans. Pastor Anhalt referred us to a pastor down here. We'll do a small service so Aunt Trudy can participate, and then we'll come home."

"Grandpa's already got a burial plot here next to Grandma." Levi began pacing. This was worse than the body melting in a truck on the tarmac.

"Would you just let me finish? With all the flight delays we can't get a solid answer on air transport. We could have the funeral home here drive him to Wisconsin, but that's cost-prohibitive and not exactly practical under the circumstances."

"Cost-prohibitive? Geez, Dad. Should I write that down for when I plan your funeral? God forbid you die in a different city than Mom."

There was a long silence. Finally, his dad cleared his throat and continued in his professional, restrained, I-deal-with-scum-like-you-for-a-living voice. It was the voice that meant he was bothered. "After the service here tomorrow, we're having him cremated. We'll hand-carry his remains."

"You're cremating him?" This is not how Levi pictured things.

His dad finally raised his voice. "Would you cut me a break here, Son? Dust to dust or ashes to ashes, what difference does it make?"

"I don't know. It all just seems—" Levi wanted to yell at his father, wanted to hang up on him, wanted to tell him this wasn't how it was supposed to be, but he didn't know what to say that wouldn't sound petulant or foolish.

"We're doing the best we can, okay? Think we're happy with all of this?"

The silence between them hummed.

"You know how you can help, Son? There's a box of photos in the attic at the house. One of those big tubs. Has a gray base and blue lid. Call your sister to help you, and pick some photos of your grandfather that cover the years. Make sure there are some of him and Grandma too. We'll set them up at the reception."

Levi imagined the pictures on a folding table, everyone talking in hushed tones, heads slightly tilted to the side when they talked—the tilt of the head being the universal body language of sympathy, and before he knew it, he was there.

1.7 WE SURE HAVE BEEN TO A LOT OF FUNERALS TOGETHER

Levi's parents returned with a cherry-wood urn that resembled a miniature coffin. Before the internment, they had a small memorial at Immanuel with just family and friends. Levi arrived early, and before the service, he hovered by the door of the sacristy where Uncle Thomas sat hunched over his desk. He knocked.

Uncle Thomas looked up and smiled at him. "Hi, hi," he said softly, his voice raspy and soothing. "How're you holding up?" He got up and came around the desk.

"I just came to say sorry for last week. Or, two weeks ago. The way I acted in your office that night," Levi stammered. "It doesn't mean that I don't think—well, but, the thing is, regardless of what I think, I was rude and—"

Uncle Thomas grabbed Levi's right hand, and put another hand on his shoulder. "No, no. Don't worry about it. I've heard worse."

Levi had read in his horoscope once that guilt was his Achilles' heel, and too often, that was true. Despite his best attempts to break out of his shell and exhibit just a modicum of intellectual honesty, to explain that he didn't have all the answers, his parents didn't have all the answers, Nick didn't have all the answers, Uncle Thomas didn't have all the answers, the church didn't have all the answers, and he sure couldn't hear God giving him any answers, Levi still felt guilty for leaving Uncle Thomas's office the way he had the night of The Attacks. He had dreaded this moment, but felt it necessary to apologize, to show some deference to the older man who had always been there for Nick, for him, a kind of surrogate father figure for both of them. The pastor's gratuitous kindness made him want to apologize all the more. "No, but really I had no right. You didn't say anything spiteful and I should have been more—"

Uncle Thomas squeezed his shoulder. "All is forgiven, my boy. We can talk another time if you need to, but don't worry about it today. Okay?" Levi nodded but left frustrated because he couldn't explain himself. As he ushered Levi out, Uncle Thomas said, "You make sure you take care of your parents today, okay?"

After the service, as they waited for everyone to arrive at the cemetery, Levi's mind drifted through memories of his grandfather. They rose and fell, swelled and diminished like the small waves behind the wake of his grandpa's fishing boat. He pictured him spitting over the side of the boat as they rocked by a bridge, a big bulge of tobacco in his cheek. He'd always wink and say the same thing, "Don't tell your grandmother." When Levi grew older and stopped in to visit between school and drama practices, his grandfather would sniff the cigarette smoke on him, and Levi would wink and say, "Don't tell my mother." His grandpa would smack him on the side of the head, but he would never tell. Levi felt the urge to cry, but he chewed on his lip to keep himself from breaking.

His dad stood straight with his chin held high. The wind whipped his overcoat, and the brim of his fedora fluttered, but his eyes didn't water. Levi looked across the open grave at his brother Paul, who stood at ease and chatted in a low voice with a rarely seen great-uncle named Gilbert.

Nick stood like a stoic, nodding at Levi as if to say, "Hang in there, buddy. You can do it."

And yet—

It was not late autumn, but most of leaves had already fallen. The maples stretched out black and skeletal against the ashen sky, which drizzled a frigid rain that soaked the cemetery turf but refused to freeze. The bluffs towered over them as colossal shadows in the mist, reminding them of the earth's longevity and their own mortality. No day had ever *been* more perfectly funereal; no day had ever *been* more perfect for crying.

Uncle Thomas spoke a few more brief words at the grave, reminding them all of the Resurrection to come while the small contingent rocked and shivered. The men blew into their hands and the women pulled their hands into their sleeves. With great reverence, they each placed a single flower on the table next to the urn, which waited for its descent into the earth.

When the crowd left for the parking lot, everyone headed over to Immanuel's grade school gymnasium to eat sandwiches and drink the bottled water Nick had meant for New York. Levi's father remained by the table with the ashes and photos. Levi hung back like a voyeur. His father reached out his hand and touched the wooden box. He took a deep breath and his slumped shoulders betrayed great sadness. He pulled his fingers along the visible grain of the heavily lacquered and impossibly smooth wood, as if to determine its finite nature. He patted it and slowly turned. Levi expected to finally see tears, but his dad's eyes weren't even moist. He looked surprised to see Levi hovering there and he turned his mouth up slowly in a reassuring half-smile. He put his arm around Levi and walked him to the parking lot, their feet squishing in the wet grass over all those dead bodies.

1.8 WE JOINED IN A FIT OF YOUTH

That was it. Levi's parents went back to work. Paul went back to DC. Elizabeth went back to juggling her fledgling catering business and her new responsibilities as a mother. Levi and Nick went back to school. Life went on with one less person in it.

With each day at school, Levi grew more claustrophobic. His restlessness only grew. But in early October, something changed. Levi and Nick sat in their living room and watched America strike back. The war entered their small apartment in the same way The Attacks had: live and in color. There was tension when the news report started, but unlike the shock and nausea brought on by the spectacle of September 11th, the night of October 7th sparked a strange satisfaction, gestating an abstract, but visceral blood lust.

The satisfaction grew into a sense of wonder and then jubilee at certain victory as the video kept streaming in. Dim and shaky footage filled the screen for several seconds before light from Tomahawk cruise missiles illuminated formidable battleships and aircraft carriers. Warplanes fired their afterburners and flew off of massive floating cities owned by the United States Navy. Mountain ridges filmed with night-vision settings exploded into a wash of emerald light before dimming again as the differing shades of green smoked and smoldered. Red, white, and blue meteors streaked across the sky in massive displays of American firepower.

Levi poured shots of Captain Morgan rum, and the two of them toasted the victims of 9/11. They toasted the brave pilots dropping their bombs. They looked up Afghanistan on the Internet to find out where it was and what it was like, and then they toasted the Special Forces troops sneaking through caves and mountain complexes.

They toasted any other GI Joe who was over there to roll up those terrorist fools.

The more they watched, the more they drank, the more excited they got by the war in their living room. "Sleeping giant," Nick yelled, grabbing the bottle of Captain Morgan from Levi so he could drink straight from the bottle.

"No one messes with the good old U-S-of-A," shouted Levi. "No one."

One of the three girls who lived downstairs pounded a broomstick on her ceiling. Nick stomped on the floor. "Didn't you hear, ladies?" He yelled at the floor. "Someone messed with the wrong country."

"Shut up," they heard a shrill voice yell back.

Nick swirled the last swallow of rum in the bottom of the bottle. He poured it down his throat and looked at Levi with wide eyes. "Dude," he said. "Follow me."

"Idea?"

"Idea."

Nick rushed out the door, down to the outside of the house, and around the corner to the porch that led to the downstairs apartment. He plowed through the flimsy screen door and kicked the cat's food dish, spilling kibbles all over the floor.

Levi stopped short behind him and held his breath. Nick held a finger to his lips and then pointed at two boxes of Rolling Rock at the back of the porch.

After a moment of standing there in silence, when it became clear that no one was investigating the clatter, Nick made a show of tiptoeing over to the beer. He handed a box to Levi and picked one up himself. He nodded in the direction of the screen door.

Levi led the way up the stairs. When he set his box of beer on the counter, Nick said, "Nuh uh. Follow me."

Nick went to his room and climbed out the window that went to the flat patch of roof over the porch where they had stolen the beer.

He stepped to the ledge and cracked a bottle open, throwing the cap into the alley. With one hand he pulled out a hard pack of cigarettes.

They stood in silence at the edge, smoking and drinking.

Levi turned around and looked up at the few stars and his breath.

"Man. Just think," Nick said.

"Think what?"

Nick gestured up at the ridge, a wide sweeping motion with the hand that held the bottle. "If we climbed high enough, we could probably see it going down."

"See what going down?"

"The bombs bursting in air, dude. Raining down some justice tonight."

"True."

"Yeah," Nick said. "Yeah. Yeah." He said it slowly, in a whisper. He had that crazed look again. The same one he had when he packed up his car to go to New York in the wake of The Attacks. The same one he had when he got drunk and walked around downtown passing out twenties to every bum who asked.

He blurted it out. "Let's join the army."

Levi snorted and spit out his beer. "What?"

"Let's join the army."

Levi stared off down the alley.

[Sudden? Yes. But this is the way I remember it. It was that sudden. And I don't know if that was the moment the idea came to you or if that's the moment you finished turning it over in your mind. Knowing you, you had the idea days, or even weeks earlier, and you thought about it, and you stayed awake at night praying about it. But unlike some of your other ideas, this one didn't make me laugh; it made me sit down so my feet could dangle with nothing solid beneath them. I sat there on the ledge sadly, stung that I had nothing better to do than drink on the sticky tar roof of some old Victorian full of co-eds.

You couldn't have struck at a more vulnerable moment. An image flashed in my mind. It was just a glimpse, but it enthralled me just the same. For a moment, I saw myself screaming, face covered in gunpowder and dirt, flashes of artillery behind me, a steel safari helmet jauntily askew, riding pants and tall boots, wool tunic with the mandarin collar unbuttoned, rifle with fixed bayonet in hand, charging forward with my war face on.

Then another. You and I leaning against some drab army truck smoking cigarettes together. Cocky smiles and big belt buckles. Somehow, the washed-out tans of the uniforms put us on equal footing. In this image, I wasn't some small skinny kid with hair falling into my eyes and a shyness I couldn't shake. Our denuded military scalps looked the same, and in this image, I had bulked up from our training and I now look self-assured. The big boots made me grow six inches—at least—and I could finally look you in the eye without feeling bad about myself, about how I always dragged you down. I could, for once, let you drag me up.

And wasn't it in my blood? I thought of that picture of my grandpa as a young man in uniform. His smile was huge. His eyes sparkled. His pompadour made him look like a movie star. It was hard to imagine a guy who looked that happy guarding surrendered Nazis. But why shouldn't he look happy? By the time he was our age, he had done more than we could imagine. He had traveled, he had helped save the world from tyranny, and he had helped liberate millions.

Then, of course, my own dad fought in Vietnam. He probably told you more than he told me. He never said a word about it to me until after I got back, and by then I didn't want to hear it, but I had seen that one sepia-toned picture in my mom's underwear drawer when I was a kid. Rather than the thick Vitalis side-part I knew, the man in the picture had long hair swept to the side. Instead of the close shave, soft jawline, starched collar, and fat Windsor tie knot of my father, the man in the picture wore a mustache that cascaded over his upper lip and flowed around the edges of his mouth. His green shirt was open in the front, revealing a hairless chest and stomach. The man in the picture had the kind of sharp abs, malnourished ribs, hollow cheeks, and well-defined jaw muscles that underwear models envy. He was standing, but leaning slightly, reaching for the rifle against the row of sandbags behind him. A smile played at his lips and the photo froze him like that forever: *You caught me without my rifle. Busted.* The smile made it look like he was actually having fun.

Then it struck me: I had never lived a day in my life. Thinking about my grandpa and then that picture of my dad, I realized that for all my talk and complaining about how boring our lives were and how we never did anything exciting and how my parents just didn't understand, I was the one who didn't understand. I was the one who had never taken a risk. I was the one who played it safe and stayed near home for college. I was the one who was all talk and dreams and no action.

And I thought, hell, why shouldn't I take a risk? I was no younger or less worldly than Grandpa or Dad when they set out to conquer the world.

But also, I thought, taking a deep breath to calm my own growing giddiness, this isn't just some fanciful idea, some daydream. We could really be a part of it all. The army was a real thing. Real people made up the army. Maybe real people weren't actually slaying dragons with swords like in the commercials, but actual sailors were firing those missiles off aircraft carriers. Flesh-and-blood soldiers were jumping out of airplanes with guns. Perhaps a future Nobel Prize-winning author was sitting behind the controls of a medical helicopter at that very moment, scribbling in a notebook as he waited for the call to fly. And that guy, the guy in the helicopter with the notepad, was actually earning his story, unlike the Dr. Buddy Jacksons of the world. Men with histories and childhoods and mistakes and successes and hometowns and varying levels of education were huddled in tanks and trucks and planes, and they were all taking action. They were taking the fight to evil people.

And just like the army was a real thing made up of real people, the recruiter's office was a real place. It was an office down on State Road on the south side, in the middle of a trashy strip mall. It was made of bricks and mortar and drywall and whatever other materials trashy strip malls are made of, and it was a tangible place where we could drive. If push came to shove, it wasn't so far away that we couldn't walk.

And perhaps my response came quicker than you expected. Perhaps it was the exact opposite answer of what you were expecting. Maybe you were looking for me to save you from yourself, to talk you out of it. After all, you had so much more to give up. I was going nowhere while you had your entire life mapped out for you. All you had to do was finish your degree and the family business would be yours.

Perhaps it was the wrong answer, and perhaps I should have told you that you were crazy. Perhaps it took you by surprise, but I thought about it some. A whole lifetime of thought went into those few seconds back then, back when we had a whole lifetime left to live.]

"Okay."

Nick stopped pacing. "You'd actually do it?"

Levi waved his bottle at him, a gesture of effrontery. "What the hell does that mean?"

Nick took a breath and tried to speak judiciously. "It means sometimes you talk. Sometimes you spout opinions and grand ideas and nothing ever happens. It means I'm asking if you'd really do it, and not just talk about it."

"Hell yeah, I'd do it. It's about time we actually did something."

"That's the whole point," Nick said, sitting down next to him. "To do something. Seriously, it's a good idea. I think they pay for education, so we can still finish that. But the great thing is, instead of just going to school and not doing anything, we'll actually be making something of ourselves. We'll be contributing. We'll be doing something important, something bigger than ourselves. We'll be standing up for people who can't stand up for themselves. We'll be doing something good.

"When those planes flew into those towers and killed all those innocent people—all those people just going about their lives who never put a uniform on, never held a gun, never went out looking for a fight—the world changed. The world changed overnight. Now it needs guys like us—no, men like us—to stand up and do what needs to be done. Now our country needs men like us to shelter her in this new and terrible age. It needs people willing to do more than stick flags out by their windows and call it good. And if we don't go, who will?"

Levi nodded, enjoying the way Nick could get his sermons rolling. He brought his cigarette to his lips. He blew the smoke out. "Okay, sure."

"Seriously. This is like, our generation's defining moment. This is the time for action. Not for witnessing the action on some little TV."

Levi laughed and swilled his beer. "I already said okay." He got up, walked across the roof and exchanged his empty bottle for a fresh one.

Nick looked at Levi, narrowed his eyes, took a sip of his own drink.

"Levi, it's more than just an alternative to doing nothing. There's meaning in it. There's *nobility*. You'd really join the army? Put it all on the line?"

"You trying to convince me or yourself?"

Nick smashed his bottle of Rolling Rock against the cedar siding, grabbed Levi's skinny right wrist, and sliced the green glass across his outstretched palm until it dripped deep red onto the roof, his heavy-handed way of letting Levi know that covenants meant nothing without the shedding of blood.

Levi, caught mid-swallow, pulled his bottle of beer from his lips and looked down at his bleeding palm. Nick held out the shard of glass in his left hand and stretched out his own right palm.

Levi shrugged again, as if, "Why not?" was the only thing he knew how to say. He took the glass in his bleeding hand. He tilted his head back and poured the rest of his beer down his throat. He heaved the bottle into the air while releasing a jubilant bellow—a "Whoooooooo" that filled the town, surrounded them, and bounced between the Mississippi River and the bluffs that hemmed them in. He held Nick's hand and put his face close to concentrate on what he was about to draw there. When he heard the crash of the bottle on the street, he carved a line to match his own, appraised it with pride, looked at Nick, and shook his hand.

Silence followed. They looked in each other's eyes, searching for weaknesses, wavering confidence, a way out, a hedged bet.

"Well, all right then," said Nick.

"Apparently."

"Hit the recruiter tomorrow then?"

"Yup."

• • •

And so, they signed away their lives in a fit of youth. Long before they bled for each other, before they bled because of each other, they bled with each other for an America that, to them, on that day, was worth every drop. Standing on the soft tar of the flat roof of their off-campus house on a brisk autumn night, mere weeks after starting college, they figured out their whole lives. They joined in a fit of idealism and naïveté. They joined in a fit of patriotism and zeal. They joined in a bout of underage drinking and hands covered in blood, in a fit of juvenescent exuberance with no intentions of ever looking back.

1.9 LOUSY SERVICE

Levi winced against the pain as he grabbed the nozzle to turn the shower on, wondering if Nick would say anything about their blood oath. Maybe he would act as though nothing had happened. As if it were just another one of many drunk and stupid nights, no different from when they held cigarettes on each other's forearms trying to win a bet, and no different from when they wound up wrestling for an hour on the concrete patio by the Schwartz's pool, each of them earning an oozing road rash, which left them in daily pain for over half the summer.

This morning, in the aftermath of it all, Levi didn't know if Nick had been serious or just drunk enough to get caught up in romantic notions. With the television off and his buzz long gone, he had a hard time feeling any excitement for the idea. The most he could muster as he stood in the shower, lightheaded and slightly nauseous, was a half-hearted desire that he could leave all his temptations behind, sober up, and make his own way in the world.

Awake and clean, but not refreshed, Nick and Levi drove to Oma's Pub, the bar and grill on Main Street in Bangor, their hometown. Oma was just opening, so Nick and Levi pulled all the chairs from the tables while she walked around flipping the switches and pulling the chains to illuminate the assorted Miller Genuine Draft, Pabst Blue Ribbon, Leinenkugel's, and Green Bay Packer lights and signs.

They sat at the bar. They sipped on sampler-sized glasses of Schlitz, hoping the hair of the dog would cure what ailed them.

Nick still hadn't mentioned the previous night, but he kept turning his hand over and looking at it. Nick's gash looked far worse than his own, which was barely discernible from the lines in his palm, but it hurt like hell all the same. Levi grit his teeth and wondered why he had cut his friend so deeply.

While waiting for their late morning breakfast of deluxe bacon burgers and fries on the house, Nick looked up and broke the silence. "Well, Oma, you can finally retire for real. No more school for me; no more tuition for you." Now that they were sober and in the presence of a witness, Levi felt a sudden tightness in his chest. As if Nick saying it aloud somehow closed any doors that might allow either of them to back out.

From the grill, Oma turned to look over her shoulder and raised one eyebrow. "Is that so?"

"Yup." Nick looked down and picked at the scab on his hand, which he held under the bar out of sight. He looked back up at her. "You know what you should do? Sell this joint, buy a boathouse on the Mississippi, spend all morning drinking coffee and catching sunnies off the dock. Spend the afternoons playing euchre with your friends. That sounds like the life, right?"

"You think so?" she said as she deftly flipped a burger in the air.

Nick's breezy tone betrayed the seriousness of the conversation. Levi knew it couldn't have been easy for Nick to throw away his birthright so rakishly. Nick had been groomed to take over the bar since he was young. That's not to say that he wanted it—in fact, it was the last thing he wanted—but everything his grandparents had built, everything they had done had been for him.

Levi gulped the last swallow of his beer. He nudged Nick and put his hands up to question what he was doing. Nick shrugged, as if to say, "What?"

Oma turned and crossed her arms. She stuck one foot out and frowned. "Why don't you tell me what's really up."

"Nothing's really up."

"Won't take long for you to figure out that playing guitar for beer doesn't pay the rent," Oma said, leaning forward. She rested her forearms on the bar. "Big market for death metal these days?"

"Punk rock," said Nick quietly, swirling his tepid beer.

She slapped his forehead with her metal spatula, and her eyes did not twinkle with playfulness when Nick looked up in surprise. Levi was glad it wasn't him. "Tell me what's really going on," she said.

"Nothing's going on." He rubbed his head, smearing the grease left over from where he was stung. He pulled his napkin from under his beer to rub it off. "What'd you hit me for?"

"I'm going to ask one more time. What's going on? Why are you coming in here on a school day, obviously not in school, telling me you're quitting school." She hit him again.

"Knock it off," he cried, stepping back off his stool. "I'm not just dropping out. We're joining the army." Nick looked over at Levi for concurrence, but all Levi could do was fold his hands and look down.

"Why in the world would you do a fool thing like that?"

Levi could feel Nick still staring at him, but he kept his gaze on his feet.

"Levi wants to rid the world of tyranny and needs someone to look after him."

Levi looked up at him for the first time. His head reared back as if he had just been accused of a crime. "It's not just me."

Nick shrugged. "We just kind of feel like we should actually do something. You know?" He eased back onto his stool, keeping his eye on the spatula as he did so. "Help me out here, Levi." He furrowed his brow and looked hopefully at Levi.

[In that look you gave me, I knew you needed me. Your heart was pure as were your intentions, but in the face of your grandma's admonitions, I know the words were failing you. We needed all the emotions and spirit and tangible reasons and plans of the night before gathered in a pile so you could once again set it on fire and convince Oma of the righteousness of the thing.

But the only thing I burned for was a glass of water. Maybe a nap. Once again, I wasn't there when you needed me.]

After seeing that Levi had nothing to offer, Oma turned her attention back to Nick. She stood with one hand on her hip. The other hand held the spatula, which she slapped against her thigh. "I'm old, Nick."

Although it went unstated, the implication was clear. She couldn't hold on to the place forever. Nick could be giving up more than just school.

Nick stammered at first but managed to mumble off a semi-coherent speech about how this new war—this response to The Attacks—was the defining struggle of their time, and it was time for their generation—the young and bright men of the world—to step up and do their part. As he went on, he seemed to gain steam. Oma actually tilted her head to the side, like she was taking him seriously.

She turned around again and flipped two buns onto the grill. "Well," she said, still looking away. "You're both idiots. The war will be over by the time you get out of boot camp. You'll end up shoveling shit in Louisiana for three years. Or you'll polish tanks or count bullets or some other such nonsense." She stood silent for a while. She brought a hand up to her face. "I suppose your Opa would be proud." Even after she pulled the buns from the grill and adorned them with onions and ketchup and mustard, she remained facing away. "So would your parents."

Levi looked over at Nick, but he didn't look back. He stared down at the bar, conflict just beginning to take its toll on his rounded, boyish face.

"Anyway," Nick said. It was barely a whisper.

"Anyway," said Oma, sliding the burgers from the spatula to the buns. "And what do your parents think of this, Levi?"

"You're the first person we've told," said Levi.

"Isn't that just special?" She slid their plates in front of them.

Nick began to speak, but his voice cracked. He cleared his throat and shook his head. Resigned, he held up his empty glass. "How about a refill?"

Oma put her palm under his chin and squeezed both of his cheeks with one hand. "Forget it. When you're done here, get your butt to class."

She made trips back and forth to the back room to get ice, lemons, and boxes of beer. Levi chewed and stuffed steak fries into his mouth, but he felt sick. He stared at the poster ahead of him and read Vince Lombardi's "What It Takes to Be #1" for the millionth time. A flickering neon sign that said "Lousy Service" flickered just above that. After finishing half his sandwich to be polite, Levi pushed his plate away and inspected his chewed fingernails.

Nick stuffed the last of his fries in his mouth and asked, "Ready to do this?" but on account of the fries, it sounded like, "Weddy ta do vif?"

Levi nodded. They stood. They placed both hands flat on the bar like seasoned old barflies.

Oma walked out, wiping her hands on a towel. "Okay boys. Make sure you come say goodbye before you take the train to boot camp."

Levi put his hands in his pockets and looked at his feet. "Oma," he said. "If you could not tell my parents about the whole army thing just yet—"

She lit a cigarette and cackled. "I'm a barkeep, honey. People pay me to listen, not to talk."

1.10 COURT-MARTIALED WITHIN A YEAR? (I SHOWED THEM, EH?)

They drove back to La Crosse with the windows of the Geo Prizm down. They pounded on the dash and steering wheel while they sang along with a mixed CD filled with NOFX, Pennywise, and Lagwagon songs. When they reached the campus, Nick passed Vine Street and kept going through town all the way to the south side. Levi stopped singing and sat back in his seat as he realized they were really going to do it. They were going to stand in line at the recruiter's to sign their lives away.

The scene that greeted them inside the recruiter's office was not what Levi expected. He wasn't sure what it was supposed to look like, but in his mind he pictured sturdy steel desks, a tall blond soldier with a flattop or crew cut. He'd be sitting tall and erect behind the desk, dapper in his full-dress uniform, medals across his chest. He would give them gruff congratulations on being some of the few courageous boys left in the world. He'd give them a brief speech about how what they were about to do was not easy, no. But it was rewarding. And they would grow to be men. Walking through that door was the first brave step. And then he'd ask them one time, just to be sure they weren't pansies, if they really wanted to do this. With full confidence, his voice already stronger and deeper, Levi could reply, "Where do I sign?" and the soldier would nod and pass the sign-up sheet across the desk, unsurprised, as if he knew all along these two fine young boys were made for his United States Army, and asking if they were sure was simply a matter of formalities and regulations.

Instead of what he imagined, what greeted him were cheap office furniture, the smell of moldy carpet, and an obvious air of apathy. One portly sergeant sat hunched over a computer monitor, which faced away from the doorway, while another robust-looking sergeant stood behind him. They were both laughing at whatever was on the screen, and when the door opened and the bell jangled, they didn't bother to look up.

Nick and Levi stood there in awkward silence until the two men finished whispering. Then, flashing his most patronizing smile, the sergeant who had been standing said, "How can we help you men?"

"We want to join the army," said Nick, stepping in front of Levi.

"Of course." The sergeant put his hand on the shoulder of his colleague. "This here is Staff Sergeant Duffy. He'll be more than happy to help answer any questions you have." He patted the shoulder he had been grabbing, and he walked away to sit behind a computer in the back corner of the room.

Sergeant Duffy forced a smile, obviously put out, and in a southern drawl said, "Take a seat fellas."

They sat in the oversized chairs in front of the desk. The vinyl upholstery squeaked as they sat, and both boys gripped the wooden armrests. There was no ceremony, no patriotic speeches, and no hard-sell. There were only clipboards, pens, questions, and a strange sense of wonder at how simple it was. The speed of execution was shocking.

Within thirty minutes they had each filled out paperwork, scheduled a pre-test for their urinalysis, and arranged a subsequent trip to the Military Entrance Processing Station in Minneapolis over Christmas break.

Before Levi even knew what happened, he stood to leave. He forced a smile, and shook the recruiter's warm, squishy hand.

Despite the strange inertia that carried them along, Levi held the news of their enlistment close to his chest. Not until they had visited the recruiters several times, filled out more forms, and taken the Armed Services Vocational Aptitude Battery; not until Sergeant Duffy watched them holding their privates over a little plastic cup to pee clean, both Nick and Levi kidney-shy and ashamed; not until they had ridden a Greyhound bus to Fort Snelling in Minneapolis to duck-walk in their underwear, to pee in another cup, to swear they had only smoked pot twice and they didn't even like it, to have their ears, throats, and anuses prodded by a creaking elderly doctor; not until they had signed their contracts and chosen 11B Infantryman as their Military Occupational Specialty; not until they had repeated the oath of enlistment in front of an air force major, who threatened to arrest them for desertion if they reneged and didn't report for boot camp when the school year was over; not until he had told all his neighbors, friends, and drug dealers; not until he felt that it was a done deal and there was no turning back; and not until he felt confident that he could answer all his father's pragmatic questions while alleviating his mother's concerns did Levi finally feel comfortable telling his parents he had joined the United States Army.

He anticipated an argument with his father because he'd be leaving college. He anticipated a scene from his mother, who had already lost her oldest son to a law firm in DC and her daughter to a husband and the all-consuming nature of entrepreneurship. Levi chose a Sunday morning two days before Christmas to break the news. His sister Elizabeth, her husband Chris, their baby, and his older brother Paul were all at home for the holiday.

He nearly broke the news while they all sat around drinking coffee before church, but then he envisioned his mother stoically walking to the front pew of the church with smeared mascara and eyes puffy from crying, too proud to skip church and too proud to be late just because makeup was cascading down her face. He pictured his father clenching his jaw as he gallantly and protectively ushered his wife into the pew. Meanwhile, Elizabeth's baby would probably be shrieking from all the fighting and yelling, and his sister would keep sighing, rolling her eyes and flipping her silky blond hair, looking at him like it was all his fault. Chris would stuff his hands in his pockets, wondering how he ended up in the middle of such a mess. He'd repeatedly look at Levi and shrug like, "What can ya do?" and Paul would pat Levi on the back as he hung his head and shuffled into the sanctuary, wanting to die.

Instead of risking the brawl that the privacy of the Hartwig kitchen would enable, and instead of risking the scene he was sure would follow, he opted to wait until after church. He told them all over heaping plates of mashed potatoes, pot roast, and macaroni and cheese at an Old Country Buffet in Onalaska. Levi sat directly across from his father.

Levi began by clearing his throat. He banged his knife against his glass, hoping to signal everyone to quiet down, but because his glass wasn't a glass at all and was instead a plastic amber tumbler made to look like glass, it made a dull ticking noise. It did not make the dramatic tinging for which he had hoped.

No one noticed except Paul, who looked at him smacking his plastic cup of pop. Paul said, "What are you doing, Bro? Get Tourette's while I was gone?" He stuffed a carrot in his mouth and chewed, holding one eyebrow up like all the Hartwigs loved to do when they thought someone was acting like a moron.

Levi cleared his throat again.

"Need a glass of water?" his dad said.

"I have an announcement to make." Levi's voice quivered with nerves. "A pretty big one."

Liz kept talking to their mom, but their dad wiped his mouth with a napkin, set it on the table, and folded his hands. "Oh?"

Levi nodded.

Paul nudged Chris. "Levi has an announcement. I think baby brother is about to come out of the closet."

Liz reached across the table and smacked him with her napkin.

"Well, Son. What is it?" said his dad.

Everyone at the table had finally stopped eating to stare at Levi. *I should have just sent them all an e-mail on my way out,* Levi thought. "Um. Nick and I. We joined the army." He glanced at everyone except his father to gauge their reactions. "We leave in May. After the school year? They've worked it out so we'll be in the same unit. At least to start with?" He cleared his throat again and took a sip of Dr Pepper.

When he finally looked at his dad, he was surprised to see him almost smiling. "Sure you want to do this? Thought it through?"

Levi couldn't find his voice right away. He nodded and hid behind his cup.

"It's not just some rush job or impulse decision based on emotion, pride, fervor, and all that?"

"Yeah. We've actually, uh, been working with the recruiter for like, forever. Like, almost two months now."

Levi's dad leaned back and folded his arms. His cuffs popped from under his suit coat and the shoulder seams stretched. He looked over Levi's head as if deciding how to react. Finally, he allowed himself a full smile. "That's great, Son. I think that will be good for you." He brought his eyes back down to Levi's face. "Yeah," he said. "I think that will be good."

This was not what Levi expected. He looked over at his mom. She was crying, as he had expected, but not in the same manner. "Oh honey," she said. "I'm so proud of you."

Levi blushed, pleased with himself. Yet, he also felt confused and perturbed at their immediate acceptance of the news that he had joined the army smack dab in the middle of a war. Sure, Liz and Chris peppered him with questions between trips to the buffet to get their bread pudding and ice cream—Infantry? What will you do there? When do you leave? Are you scared? Will you go to Afghanistan right away?—but no one tried to keep him around. His dad had never looked more pleased. Levi tried to answer their questions with energy and excitement, but it gnawed at him that no one tried to talk him out of it.

Later that night at the Hartwig house, after the bottles of home-made wine from Liz's catering company had been drunk, after the board games had been put away, and long after Levi had surrendered his keys to his dad, the married people went upstairs to bed. Paul stayed at the dining room table, his top shirt button undone and his tie loosened. He sat in front of his laptop answering e-mails and doing whatever work it was that young lawyers did when they were on vacation.

Levi sat at the end of the table and sipped on Glenlivet 18, the smooth scotch being the only liquor he could find in the house. He tried to keep his movements slow and small. Each time he set down his glass, he eased it onto a cork coaster, trying to refrain from making any noise that would disturb his brother, who was the definition of concentration, a fact that astounded Levi considering Paul had drunk as much as anyone that night.

The more he drank in silence, the more he grew annoyed that Paul hadn't moved, hadn't gotten up to go to the bathroom, hadn't stretched, hadn't even stopped typing. He started to make little noises to grab his attention. First, he coughed, as if something had gone down the wrong tube. When that didn't work, he poured tiny sips into his glass and drank them like shots, slamming the tumbler onto the table after each one. He retrieved a bag of cheese curds and flopped into his seat, making sure to bump the table on his way down. Paul continued working, unfazed. Levi belched and threw a cheese curd into the air and tried to catch it in his mouth on the way down. He caught about one out of every three. He leaned over the table to catch one on the way down. It moved the table several inches and his elbow knocked the bottle of scotch on its side.

It was empty enough by now that only a few drops fell out, but the disturbance finally made Paul look up from his computer. He glanced at the tipped bottle as if to ensure that its contents wouldn't flow in his direction and ruin his computer. When he was satisfied he was safe, he looked up at Levi, raised his why-are-you-a-moron eyebrow, and returned to his work.

Levi crossed his arms in a petulant huff. He stewed. The only sound in the house was the steady hum of the forced-air heater and the clicking of Paul's keyboard. The silence was too much for Levi, and he grew dizzy with his drunkenness.

"Why didn't you say anything at lunch when I told you I joined the army?"

Paul didn't look up from his work. "What did you want me to say?"

"I don't know." Levi stood up. "Maybe that I shouldn't do it. Maybe talk me out of it?"

"Okay. How about this? You're an idiot for wanting to join the army."

"Dad and Grandpa were both in the army. Are they idiots?"

"They were drafted, moron. They hated it. They're both practically pacifists now. Well, Dad is anyway. Grandpa's dead."

"Thanks for the reminder, dick." Levi sat back down.

Paul shrugged. "Okay, let me try again? You're a total shrimp. Your life's dream is to smoke weed and write books all day in your underwear. You play in a punk band and do exactly the opposite of whatever anyone in authority tells you to do. The first thing they'll want to do is buzz your head and shave off that stupid soul patch, but you won't let anyone touch your hair or those ridiculous sideburns. And you're going to join the army and all of a sudden be GI Joe? You'll be court-martialed within the year."

"You're such a dick."

"It's your life," Paul said. "What do I know about it?"

Levi picked up the tipped bottle and sucked down the last few drops. "Yeah," he said. "It is my life. And you don't even care if I lose it in Afghanistan?"

Paul laughed and pushed his computer forward. "You haven't even left yet and I'm supposed to be worried about you dying?"

"Well, we're in a war, aren't we? And I'm your little brother, aren't I?"

Paul spoke slowly, as if he were explaining something to a small child. "Let me take those points one at a time, starting with the latter." He held out a thumb. "One. Yes, you're my little brother. I care for you deeply. But I can't pretend to know what's best for you when I see you maybe once a year. The last time I really knew you? As in knew you, knew you? As in when we lived together? You were nine years old." Paul added an index finger to his outstretched thumb. "And fighting a war? Do you want to know how many United States military personnel have died in Afghanistan from hostile fire since we invaded?"

"Probably a lot," Levi said.

"Take a guess at how many."

"I dunno. Nineteen."

"Zero," Paul said. "Zero military deaths from hostile fire. You're more likely to die of dehydration in boot camp or a training accident on the grenade range than you are to die by hostile fire in Afghanistan right now. So no, I'm not going to try to talk you out of your grand adventure."

Levi dropped his head to the table, and then remembering something, he popped back up. "That can't be right. What about that helicopter?"

"Crashed. Not shot down. Accidents happen. Could have happened anywhere."

"Wow," Levi said slowly. "Well, that's great though. Means we're kicking their butts."

[But, to be honest, which is what this letter is all about, this revelation saddened me, angered me even, because it seemed to diminish what we were doing. It made it feel like our war wasn't big enough or bad enough to mean anything.]

"Yup," Paul said. "And I'm sure it will be over by the time you even finish training, so if you think you're going off to be some big war hero, you better think again." Paul pulled his computer back toward him.

"Well, what about everyone else? Mom and Dad didn't try talking me out of it. If Dad's so anti-army, why didn't he talk me out of it? They don't care if I finish school? They don't care if they lose me?"

Paul shook his head. "You don't get it, do you?"

"Get what?" Levi spat back.

"Brother, they feel like they lost you a long time ago." Paul closed his laptop, slid it into his leather messenger's bag, and stood up. "Maybe they feel like the army will shape you up and they'll finally get you back." He walked around the table and patted his nonplussed brother on the shoulder. "If you want to join the army, join the army. If you don't, don't. But if you are going to do anything, do it for you and not as a cry for help. Just grow up is all. Just grow up."

1.11 STICK YOUR FINGERS IN YOUR EARS AND SAY LA LA LA LA

January turned into February with no discernible change, and Levi thought the end of the school year would never come. He thought the long Wisconsin winter would last forever and the sun would glare off the snow for the rest of his life. The ice would never melt, leaving the fishing shanties forever on the lakes and the salt forever on the roads. But spring did come and the ice did melt and the boats emerged from their docks once again to cruise the three rivers in search of their bass, crappie, and sunfish. Before he knew what had happened, Levi found himself setting the little blue exam book from his last final on a stack of little blue exam books before walking out the door of the lecture hall, elated.

Levi had already boxed up his journals, and both he and Nick had boxed up all their other sentimental items like high school yearbooks and old DIY concert posters. They took them to the Hartwig basement for indefinite storage. They had not, however, packed their guitars. Both Levi and Nick decided that their going-away party would be one final show at The Warehouse the night before they left for Fort Benning, Georgia. The owner of the club gave A Failed Entertainment the honor of headlining. Instead of drinking before the show started, instead of sneaking pot into the backstage hangout room while the other bands played, Nick walked around talking to all his friends and the few local fans they had come to know over the past few years. Levi sat alone with an ashtray and a pack of cigarettes in the room behind the sound booth. He didn't hear the door open and close.

"You have an ashtray right there on the table. Why don't you use it?"

Eris stood in front of him in a pair of Docs, tight jeans, and a ripped-up form-fitting NIL8 T-shirt. Her makeup was thick, her eyeliner dark. He had rarely seen her since he and Nick had told her over coffee that they were leaving. She had done everything possible to avoid them. Levi had noticed, and he had missed her. And now, here in front of him, she looked broody and gorgeous. She sat in a folding chair in front of him.

"So you wanna tell me why?" she said.

"Why what?"

"Why what do you think? Because of The Attacks last fall? Because you're bored? Because why? Why, Levi. Because why."

"Well, yeah. But not only." He stuffed his cigarette out in the ashtray.

"Well, what else?" She leaned forward in her chair, her elbows on her knees. If it weren't for the coffee table between them, Levi was sure they'd be touching.

"It's complicated and probably sounds dumb, and so." She looked at him in a way that made him feel naked. "Because I want to do something exciting. Be exciting," he said.

"And why Nick?"

"I don't know." Levi stood up. "I have to get out to watch the next band."

"Sit down."

He obeyed.

"Why Nick?"

"I don't know." He threw his hands up and let them drop in his lap again. "He wants to do good. Be good?"

It must have been something in his voice or in his look, but she took a deep breath, licked her lips, and sat back in the chair. She crossed her legs. Before she spoke, Levi had thought she might tell him he was the most exciting person she'd ever known, and that he was good too. Even if it wasn't true, maybe she'd say it to get them to stay. Instead, she said, "If you want to be good, don't go halfway around the world to kill people."

[That stung. It had never been about that for me. It had been about leaving a life that was boring and going nowhere. Sure, I had vaguely contemplated the possibility of being killed, and that's where the excitement and allure was—in the danger—but until then, the thought of killing other people had never even crossed my mind. Not once.]

Levi said nothing to dispel her notions of why he was leaving; he didn't spill his guts to her like he did years later in retrospect, after his mind had been destroyed. Instead, he leaned forward over the table and earnestly reverted to parroting Nick's fervent speeches. Levi thought phrases like, "The Defining Struggle of Our Generation," and "The Only Time for Action Is Now," and "We Weren't Created for the Sidelines," sounded thin and cheap coming out of his mouth—[I don't have your heart. The naked sincerity. The earnestness in you that I admire so much. I couldn't strip the irony from it no matter how hard I tried. Still can't, but I'm working on it.]—yet he spouted them anyway. He was too afraid or too in denial to get at the heart of the matter.

When he had finally finished, he sat back in a mix of exhaustion and exasperation.

Eris stood. "When did you become such a follower?"

"Like you've got all the answers?"

"And what if I do?"

"Do you have a single reason why we should stay?"

"What if one was standing in front of your stupid face?"

"A reason for whom? A reason for Nick?"

She held a middle finger up in front of his face, stood still for a moment, and walked away. She slammed the door. Levi picked up the ashtray and hurled it against the wall where it shattered in silence against the feedback, open chords, and clanging cymbals of the opener's finale.

He sat there in angry silence until he heard the next band begin. A mass of teenagers swelled against the stage. Levi waded out into the group until he was surrounded, and the group started moving, and swaying, and bobbing in beat to the lazy introduction of the first song of the set. He allowed himself to be swallowed by the crowd until they were all one body with a thousand feet shuffling on a splintered wood floor, all of them wearing thin sheens of sweat. Cigarette smoke drifted at the pace of the thin noodling of the lead guitarist, which soon gave way to a heavy riffing. The music consumed all of them as the early bobbing turned into a raucous rocking of the entire upper half of the collective body until one touched soul started thrashing about through the crowd. Each pointy, frightening tip of the spikes on his wristband glinted in the lights of the stage in the small and dingy club. He pumped his fist along with the beat of the double bass drum, a pounding which by itself had the power to make their collective heart want to burst out of their collective chest in celebration of the freedom that they were experiencing in the music that preached independent thought in pursuit of an honest and more upright world. Or the agony in it all, which Levi could feel when the music stopped just for a millisecond, during which time each heart stopped with it.

The sparkle of light that had been dancing on the spiked wrist stopped. The smoke that had been drifting toward the ceiling from endless cigarettes stopped. The hand that triumphantly held a gray nylon guitar pick in the air stopped. Levi's thoughts stopped. In the silence, he locked eyes with Eris, who stood alone in the corner. Only the hum of the amplifier tubes remained, nearly indistinguishable from the hum of silence, until the weight of all that hope and desire and youth and angst and sweat lust fire idealism freedom longing potential independence difference confidence became so much to bear that the music came crashing down once again so they could all move, unsure of how to live, or be still.

[When my turn came to stand on the stage, emote until my throat was raw, and jump from my half-stack like a madman; when our turn came to keep perfect rhythm during improvisational key changes simply by making eye contact with each other and with Jesse behind the drums; when our turn came to sweat under the lights, to announce our penultimate song, to flow seamlessly into our finale; when my turn came to fall trustingly into the crowd, it was finally a time in which I could forget myself.

That's only one kind of release that I miss.]

Long after the lights had come up, after the crowd had dispersed, after they had finished carting their amps and drums down forty-nine stairs to Jesse's van waiting on Pearl Street, they shook hands with the owner of the club and said goodbye to an era. They gave Jesse casual, choreographed handshakes, and he was off. For Jesse, the end of the band couldn't have come too soon; he was newly twenty-one, and now he had other opportunities for mayhem. His mind hadn't been in the music for weeks.

Nick and Levi sat at the top of the tall staircase leading down to the street from the first level of the club, and they smoked one last cigarette in silence, not wanting the night to end. Finally, they walked down and out together.

Eris sat on the sidewalk, her back against the building. When they opened the door and walked out onto the street, she stood up and brushed the dirt from the back of her jeans. "Took you forever," she said.

"Hey, hey," Nick practically shouted. "You waited."

"Just cuz you're leaving doesn't mean I have to."

Levi shrugged. "Fair enough." He looked over at Nick, who was beaming.

Eris folded her arms over her chest and kicked at a rock on the sidewalk. "Is there a big after-party you have to go to? Some big goodbye bash?"

"Nah," Nick said. "We figured it'd be depressing."

"Well," she said, looking up and making eye contact with both of them. "Wanna maybe at least have a small goodbye bash with me?"

Nick put his arm around her. "Depends. Will you give us a ride?" They walked off toward the alley. Levi followed, steps behind.

Three hours, nearly a handle of rum, and four liters of pop later, Nick lay passed out on the living room floor, a sweatshirt for a pillow. Levi and Eris looked down at him and giggled.

"One second," Eris said. "He was out in, like, literally one second."

"No kidding, right?" Levi said. "One second he wants to go steal a keg from downtown, the next: boom. Down for the count."

"Let's go soke," Eris said, leaning into Levi.

"Soke?"

"Let's go soke a smigarette."

"Okay." He put his arm around her. "We can go soke a smigarette."

"Shut up," she said. She hit him in the chest with an open hand and let it linger there. "Know what I mean," she said. Or commanded. Levi wasn't sure which.

Levi let go and led her outside where they smoked one cigarette in silence. They sat near the top of the stairs, Levi on the landing and Eris three steps below. When Levi snuffed out his cigarette on the bottom of his shoe and made like he was going back inside, she said, "Just one more. There's nothing better than smoking when you've been drinking."

Levi lit the cigarette dangling from her lips. She looked at the cherry of it as she smoked. She blew her smoke on it with each turn. Levi watched her lips purse, and he watched the cherry glow brighter with each of her breaths before it faded again.

Wanting to break the silence, he said, "Thanks for throwing us this party. I, for one, think it turned out pretty great."

She brought a hand up and wiped her eye.

"Are you crying?"

She shook her head and sniffed.

"Hey, hey," Levi said. "Why are you crying?" He paused but she did not answer. "I wasn't being ironic or sarcastic or anything."

She turned her head away.

"Look, Eris, I'm sorry about—" he looked down at his hands. "Look, tonight, this right here. Being with you before we leave. This was perfect."

She wiped her eyes and said, "Stop talking already."

Then quietly, "Is this because Nick's asleep already?"

She turned and looked up at him with something like disgust on her face. Her tears had moistened her eyes and had made them shimmer in a way that caught the light from the naked bulb hanging in the landing. "Why would it be?"

"Aren't you two . . . you know."

"No, I don't."

"Aren't you two, or weren't you two like, sleeping together?"

"Ha," she turned away from him again. "You really are dense. You live with the guy and don't know that he hasn't slept with anyone? Let alone me?" She took a deep breath in through her nose. "He doesn't want damaged goods." She put her elbows on her knees. "I can't believe how stupid you are sometimes."

Wounded and confused, Levi sat in silence. Should he leave her to be by herself? Should he console her? Should he apologize? And if he did apologize, for what would he be apologizing? Finally, he scooted down two steps and put his feet on each side of her so he sat behind her. He put his hands on her shoulders. He did it with caution, not knowing how she'd react. "You're not damaged," he whispered. To his surprise, she leaned back into him. He held his breath.

She turned slightly to the side and rested her head on Levi's thigh. "You have no idea," she mumbled.

"I don't care." He took a finger and brushed black hair over her ear so he could see her cheek and the contour of her chin. He bent down to kiss her head, in a manner that he could pass off as paternal or brotherly if she balked. He barely noticed how uncomfortable it was to lean down so far. When she did not turn and slap him, when she did not rear back to elbow him, he breathed. He leaned over further to kiss her cheek, and as he grew close, she turned and arched her neck so her lips met his. They kissed. She reached a hand up and touched his face. She turned completely around so she was on her knees on the stairs. She put both of her hands on his cheeks, and she kissed him. And she kissed him. And she kissed him.

At first he was blinded by the brilliant flashes of light behind his closed eyes, and the blindness was water, and all his thoughts drowned. Then every thought in the world went through Levi's head. Memories of high school, of how he had longed for this moment and for a million like it. He pictured himself sulking as a third wheel as Nick and Eris developed such a close friendship. Now, as he kissed her, Levi laughed at being jealous about it all, knowing that what he had wanted—and was now getting—was something Nick had never had or even wanted. He thought of Nick on the floor upstairs alone.

[Everything I thought back then was foolish, and shallow, and sad.]

Levi thought of how he no longer had a bed, only a few pillows and blankets on the floor of his room. He thought how she must be getting uncomfortable on her knees for so long. He thought how in just a few hours he'd be getting on a Greyhound bus to Minneapolis. He'd get on an airplane for the first time and hold his breath as the plane accelerated and left the earth in the same way that he had held his breath before he kissed her. Then he thought of how he should be thinking of the kissing instead of buses and plane rides. *Think of this kissing, he thought. You'll want to remember this kissing forever.*

She pulled away, and he opened his eyes. She stared at him with wide eyes, surprised. She shook her head, almost imperceptibly. She stood. "It's getting cold," she said. "We should get inside."

He followed her in, wondering where she'd lead him. She walked to his bedroom, and he held his breath again. She stood in the middle of the empty room and crossed her arms over her chest. "I'm cold." She shivered.

Levi picked up a rumpled blanket and shook it out over the floor. He did the same with a folded quilt. She got on the floor and climbed under the blankets, and Levi followed suit. He leaned in to kiss her again and he embraced her, but she held her elbows in close to her abdomen. She balled her hands into fists under her chin, keeping her forearms as barriers between them. She shivered. After the blankets trapped their body heat, after Levi had let his hands wander on her back, her legs, and other places, she rolled onto her back and took off her shirt. Levi hurried to take off his own. They explored each other's bodies, but they did not make love.

When the aching became too much, Levi stopped moving. Eris rolled on her side and faced him. He searched her face, but she closed her eyes. In that moment, he felt his entire life rested in the hands of that girl, and he was helpless. He thought he saw a small smile play at her lips. He took his finger and moved hair behind her ear again. He watched her for a while. "Eris," he whispered. "Just tell me to stay."

BOOK TWO

WE CARRY THE WORLD

2.1 THIS IS WHERE I HIT MY STRIDE

15 May 2005

Levi had been awake for nearly an hour, continuing his journey through the stack of paperbacks his mom had mailed him. The Humvees pulled up to the staging area outside their appropriated home, the old hardened ammo bunker that had been left relatively undamaged after the Americans invaded Iraq. After the gravel stopped grinding and crackling beneath the tires, the roar of the engines and the opening and closing of truck doors remained. Soon, the vehicle engines ceased. The generators continued their perpetual hum, and the scattered voices of the returning soldiers grew closer.

He stretched and slid his bare feet into his flip-flop sandals. Not bothering to put on a shirt, he pushed aside the woobie poncho liner that served as a door to his bunk. He wandered into the common area. The members of third and fourth squads stormed into the bunker as he reached the door. Someone flooded the bay with light, and Levi squinted and crossed his arms over his chest, chilled by the cold morning draft.

He stepped back so his toes didn't get squashed by their tromping. Three water bottles were strung up to the door with parachute cord to keep the door closed, and since no one bothered to hold the plywood door open for the next man, the water bottles pulled the door shut with a slam after every second or third soldier. Then the next man would fling the door open and the process would repeat, prompting the members of first and second squads to yell profanities from their beds.

Midway through the stream of men piling through the door, helmets and body armor in hand, a private dropped the Meal, Ready-to-Eat that he had been carrying between his teeth. Levi bent down to pick it up for him. "How'd it go?" Levi asked.

As he lifted an arm so Levi could tuck the MRE into his armpit, the young kid smiled. "Outstanding. We rustle up more bad guys by 9 A.M. than first and second squads round up all day."

"Is that right?"

His broad mustachioed team leader, Staff Sergeant Shane Havens, walked in behind the grunt and kicked him to get moving. "Hell no," Havens said. "Most boring ten hours of my life."

During their first few months in country, the contact had been frequent and the improvised explosive device strikes had been plentiful, but the past few months of winter had been dead. The activity seemed to die almost instantly in late fall, and as the days with no action ticked by and as the string of boring patrols grew longer, every mission felt like an odd letdown. It felt like they had somehow won the war without doing anything. The deeper into winter they got, the more inevitable it seemed that each patrol was a perfunctory exercise in pretending their presence was needed. The winter rains seemed to keep everyone down, troops and insurgents alike. Levi was glad the slow winter was now over. From his perspective, the entire platoon had escaped a dangerous few months in which they had traded their motivation for complacency, and complacency killed more than the enemy.

Rumors of the spring fighting season had so far been all talk, but the anecdotes from visitors on the logistical convoys had been enough to get them back into squaring each other away. The PowerPoints the LT showed them once a week with storyboards and SIGACTS from nearby villages had been enough to remind them of the hell of the previous summer when they had still been green and gung ho. Now that they were on the back third of their tour, they all seemed to have snapped out of their malaise, and now they were just waiting for the inevitable day when their own AO would explode again.

Levi stumbled out into the dark, and not wanting to walk the fifty meters to the bathroom Cadillac, he looked around to make sure no one remained outside before he walked around the corner of the massive concrete bunker to take a leak in the rocks. He looked up, trying to determine if it would be a dry day. In the cloudless desert sky, every star shone brighter than if he were on the bluff back home. As he looked straight up, he tried to force himself to think a pastoral thought about the stars and moon being the same no matter where you are. He tried to think of something poetic or significant, but the sting of diesel exhaust in his nose and the roar of the generators ruined the nostalgia and sentimentality of it all. He shivered and tucked himself back into his PT shorts before returning to the bunker to get dressed and supervise his truck's checkout before patrol.

The bunker had turned into a bustle of men in various states of dress. Most of the returning members of third and fourth walked around in nothing but unbuttoned DCU pants and flip-flops, towels thrown over their shoulders. The remaining bleary-eyed soldiers milled about with bottled waters and shaving bags. Nick sat on an ammo box outside his cubicle with one boot on. He held one sock and stared at the ground.

"Ever gonna put that sock on?" asked Levi.

Nick didn't move. "Eventually. But it's hard work. And it's early."

Levi banged on the plywood next to Nick's bunk. "Hooper," he yelled. "Let's get this party started. An invocation please."

From behind the blanket covering the entryway he heard a loud belch. An empty can of Mountain Dew covered in Arabic scrawl came flying over the plywood. "Hooah, Sar'nt," came the cry from Specialist Tom Hooper. Tom, along with nearly everyone else in the company, ignored syllables and said sergeant in the slow, southern way. The army way. Though Levi had been in the unit for the better part of a year, he still thought it sounded incongruous mixed in with the northern accents and swallowed vowels of the National Guard members from his home state.

Tom flung aside the woobie across his door and stepped naked into the middle of the bay. His arms were tanned dark and the hair had been bleached by the sun, but his hulking torso was pasty white and covered with curly red hairs. He held a bullhorn to his lips. "Friends, Archers, countrymen," he yelled. "Lend me your ears. I come to bury Ali Baba, not to praise him."

"Preach, brother," came a yell from down the hall.

Tom turned and continued his monologue toward the voice. "The evil that men do lives after them; the good is oft interred with their bones. So let it be with Ali Baba." Tom looked around. "Who's with me?" he yelled.

He was met with indifference. The men of Archer platoon had heard Tom recycle the same mangled Shakespeare soliloquies ad nauseam. The novelty had worn off for most of them. Levi, however, still loved it.

"Thank you," Levi said. "I have chills."

Tom nodded and ducked back into his cubicle. The plywood walls buzzed as he turned on the stereo he had bought from the PX on Anaconda their first week in country. Rowdy honky-tonk filled the bay. More yelling ensued, but the groggy obscenities at the rude awakening were shortly followed by grunts and whoops, guys playing grab-ass and pumping themselves up for the coming mission.

Levi started to walk back into his own sleeping area, partitioned with more plywood and sheets, when he heard his name shouted from deeper down in the bay.

Sergeant Havens waved him over. He leaned against the two-by-four frame that led into the LT's room. When Levi reached him, Sergeant Havens clapped his hand onto Levi's shoulder. "Ready to get called up to the bigs today?"

Levi peered into the LT's room. Second Lieutenant Michaels sat on a folding camp stool tying his boots. "Sure," Levi said. "What's up?"

The LT stood up and turned to face a Humvee's rearview mirror, which he had hung on his wall after it had blown off his truck in an IED strike last year. He brushed his long sandy hair, which never would have flown among the active duty officers Levi knew before he went Guard. "Your platoon sergeant, Staff Sergeant Roper, is at the battalion aid station. I guess he spent the whole night with rice and curried lamb coming out both ends."

"I got it covered, sir. No problem." He tried to sound cool, but these were the moments he lived for. He was doing something important. He finally had a role, a place in the world, and he had gained a small modicum of responsibility with his new stripe. And now, his leadership entrusted him with more.

Sergeant Havens spoke up. "Sir, I can just go out with you again. It won't be a problem."

The LT shook his head and felt his hair with the palms of his hands. "Nuh uh," he said. "You can't lead third and fourth on missions all night, come back, and head out for another twelver. That's crazy talk."

Sergeant Havens ignored him. "Sir, it's not that big a deal. Under the circumstances, it's our best option."

The lieutenant put down his brush, tucked in his shirt, and cinched his belt. "We all know you could go out again. Lord knows that no man has ever needed as little sleep as you." He punched the staff sergeant in the shoulder as if he had just left his frat at UW-Whitewater a week ago. "Hotshot here can be my number two today. Can't ya, Hartwig?"

"Yes, sir. As long as you don't call me hotshot anymore." He said it with a smile, hoping to get his point across without sounding butt-hurt.

Sergeant Havens turned on him. "He's the leader of this platoon, which means he gets to call you whatever the hell he wants. Do you understand that, Sergeant Hartwig?"

"Roger that, Sergeant."

"It wasn't that long ago that you were a specialist," Havens said in his low, patient voice. "Pretty sure we can make that happen again if we need to."

"Ease up, Havens," said Lieutenant Michaels. "Levi's my right-hand man today, the one to keep this greasy butterbar in line." He flashed a grin at his own self-deprecation. "And hotshot?" He walked out his door and put his arm around Levi. "Just take it as a compliment. Including Havens here, you're the only NCO in the platoon with any active duty time. Which means—" He paused and elbowed Sergeant Havens in the ribs. "You have more experience than this tubby beer drinker right here, what with his one weekend a month and two weeks a year." He elbowed Havens again. "Ain't that right, Shane?"

Sergeant Havens popped to attention and snapped off a mocking backwards salute. "Sir, yes, sir," he said. He relaxed and chuckled at himself.

Levi took it as a point of pride that he had been regular army before joining the Guard, and this irreverent behavior was still new to him, but he finally felt he had found his home. Contrary to what the other 99 percent supposed, the entire army wasn't made up of dummies, rednecks, and gang bangers. It was made up of solid guys with colossal work ethics. It was made up of pragmatic souls, each with a strong sense of civic duty and a willingness to do something rather than talk about it. Most of the kids in the company had joined the Guard to pay for college and had educations themselves or would otherwise finish them soon enough. The Guard officers recognized that and often lacked the unearned moral superiority Levi had run up against too often in the active duty ranks. He wouldn't trade his new unit for anything.

The LT walked down the hall a few feet and grew serious. "All joking aside, Hartwig. You are the number two today, whether you like it or not. It shouldn't change much, but be a second set of eyes and ears for me. I'll ask for advice if I need it, but otherwise, take care of your truck and your guys like you always do. If we split up on contact to hold a cordon or for any other reason, you take second and I'll take first squad. We'll have Corporal Gassner fill the TC seat for Roper. It's not optimal." He shrugged. "But with these around-the-clock ops, we don't have any more NCOs to spare."

"What about the empty seat?" Levi asked.

"We'll bring along Jellybean. Battalion has nothing planned for him today. We're not planning on stopping to chat with anyone, but if we have the open seat, it can't hurt to bring someone who knows the language."

Lieutenant Michaels slapped Levi on his bare back and started walking away. "And one last thing you need to know," Michaels said as he turned around. "If I die, you're in charge. And that would mean everyone is screwed."

"Easy, sir. Just don't die." He turned and went to get dressed and kitted up.

• • •

An hour later, Levi stood next to his Humvee while a small circle of troops gathered in a huddle to pray before their mission. The few that there were—Nick, Tom Hooper, Specialist Pete White, who was Levi's driver, and a few others—all took a knee in the gravel and started muttering together. Levi, meanwhile, paid attention to the things that could save him. He did one last check of his gear, one more inspection of his weapons, one more COMCHECK with the TOC.

When the faithful had finished, Lieutenant Michaels, call sign Archer One-Six, gave the same briefings he'd given for the past 243 days since they had left the States. The same actions on contact. The same directions to blow through IEDs. The same questions to the privates about the rules of engagement, known as the ROE. The only thing different before this patrol was that when they went through the mission's chain of command, Levi was second to the lieutenant.

The speech was littered with letters, each set equaling words and phrases: TOC = tactical operations center; FOB = forward operating base; LSA = logistical supply area; PX = post exchange; QRF = quick response force; TC = truck commander; PMCS = preventative maintenance checks and service; victor = vehicle; HMMWV = High Mobility Multipurpose Wheeled Vehicle = Humvee; MSR = main supply route; PL = platoon leader; AO = area of operations; AIF = anti-Iraqi forces; ECM = electronic countermeasures; SIGACTS = significant actions; BOHICA = Bend over. Here it comes again.

Instead of joining the circle of troops around the lieutenant, Levi lit a cigarette and let it dangle from his lips as he lifted his flak vest high enough to get to his fly. He pulled out his business and took a leak against the Humvee tire, squinting to keep the cigarette smoke from his eyes. He watched his stream wash the fine desert caliche from the rubber. Nick tossed bits of gravel at him from the staging area.

"Pay attention to the briefing, numbnuts," Levi said through the corner of his mouth. Nick laughed quietly, trying to avoid the ire of the lieutenant, and he tossed more rocks, trying to lodge them between Levi's back and body armor. One of them stuck and fell right to the middle of Levi's back.

Levi prepared to set Specialist Nick Anhalt straight in a very grandiose and theatrical way so he could get a laugh and so he could show all the privates that—best and oldest friend or not—no one could dick with Sergeant Levi Hartwig, platoon sergeant, acting.

Before he had a chance to showcase his machismo, Archer One-Six shouted, "Mount up."

Levi flicked his cigarette at Nick's face. "Hey, thanks a lot, Annie. Now I've got this rock sticking in my back for the next six hours." He started putting on his Kevlar helmet. "Here. Help me get it out."

"Stop being a pussy."

"For real, dude. Hold my rifle for a second. I'm not going on this whole mission with this rock back here." Levi jumped up and down but nothing happened. "It's stuck in there. Right between my shoulder blades." Levi's voice carried an edge. The sun had just come up, and the temperature had already soared to 90 degrees. His boxer shorts had already grown damp from the sweat.

"I'll get it, I'll get it," Nick said. He knelt and reached his arm up Levi's back from the base of his flak vest. He rooted around the tight space, his arm sliding around against Levi's sweaty back.

Tom Hooper called down from the turret, "What the hell are you two cupcakes doing? Playing without me?"

The LT stood by the shotgun door of the third Humvee as he buttoned his chinstrap. "You two can snuggle later. Mount up."

Nick stood. "Got it. Here ya go."

Nick dropped the pebble into Levi's hand. As Nick walked away, Levi dropped it down the back of his friend's body armor. Nick wiggled and tried to get it out while he walked. Before he climbed into his own Humvee, he called over his shoulder, "Really, Levi? You really are a one-way prick. You know that?"

"That's Sergeant Hartwig to you," Levi called, only half in jest. He stood by the right side of his own truck, the second one in line. "Love you, Annie. Eyes up out there." He grinned at him, amused with himself for getting the upper hand. Nick was still hopping around by his driver's side door when Levi buttoned up his own victor and started briefing his men.

For months after, Levi often stared sleeplessly at the billowing canvas vents above his cot thinking, *So much depends upon a piece of gravel, dusted in desert sand.* For years after, he stared sleeplessly at his popcorn-textured ceiling, marveling that it was little details on which the whole world turned. For the rest of his life, he would obsess about the stupid, galling, rebarbative, pestilent, abrasive, carking rock.

2.2 DON'T ACCUSE ME OF PUTTING WORDS IN YOUR MOUTH; I'M JUST TRYING TO LEARN EMPATHY

OR

FEEL FREE TO KEEP CONSIDERING ME AN UNRELIABLE NARRATOR

Nick squirmed behind the steering wheel of the lead Humvee, unable to take his mind off the rock that had been digging at him for the past sixty minutes. He tried leaning forward to relieve some of the pressure on his shoulder blade, but that proved futile because the added girth of the body armor made it impossible to move behind the steering wheel, and it wasn't like he was a small man to begin with. The piercing of the rock and the sting of sunburn on his back made him imagine the road opening up and swallowing him to put an end to it all. The narrow dirt roads lined on each side by deep canals filled with sewage water—perfect for corralling convoys into kill zones—were likely to open up in a flash of fire and steel anyway. He figured it might as well happen when he was already miserable.

To make matters worse, his acting truck commander was now Corporal Brody Gassner, who was a stickler for the rules. He cut his sideburns straight off, right above his pasty white ears, and he wouldn't let anyone in the truck smoke. All the privates called him

Gasser behind his back, and the noncommissioned officers had no qualms about saying it to his face.

"I'm dying here, Gassner. Let me smoke." Nick took his eyes off the road and looked over at his TC to see if he might give in.

"No chance, Annie."

Nick's mood darkened even more. "Don't call me Annie."

Gassner looked out his window over the butt stock of his down-turned rifle, his right foot resting on the row of sandbags that covered the floor of the Humvee.

Nick kept himself from cursing at his squad leader and he tried to control his mounting rage. "Stop being such a gas, Gassner." It sounded juvenile, even to his own ears, but the guy was unreasonable.

The comment only caused Gassner to hole himself up in his professionalism even more. He donned his mask of combat readiness and slipped on the rules like a pair of comfortable house shoes. "Look alive, Specialist Anhalt. Eyes front."

Nick tried all the tricks he could think of to keep his mind off the rock against his sunburned back. He sang at the top of his lungs. He started with "Don't Stop Believin'" by Journey, but the register was too high and he broke into a coughing fit before anyone joined him. He sang mad parodies of patriotic country songs, but no one paid him any attention. His squad mates stared out into the tall grasses that lined the canals, perking up only when they passed inhabited qalat compounds. No one in the vehicle was in a mood. Or, they were all in a mood.

Nick started hitting Tom Hooper's leg, which rested behind his right shoulder. Tom stood tall and ominous in the turret of the Humvee, not apt to think twice about putting a .50 caliber projectile through the torso of a brown man digging on the side of the road after curfew. Nick kept turning in his seat and hitting Tom's leg. Nick shouted, "We'll put a boot in their ass, right Tom? We'll put a boot in their ass?" Eventually, Tom—in whose mind Toby Keith was only slightly less culturally significant than William Shakespeare—took great offense to Nick's scorn of hard-working and righteously angry Americans. He kicked Nick in the head from the gunner's sling that sat in the middle of the Humvee. This shut Nick up for a while and he went back to stewing in his own sweat and frustration.

The routes in their AO were all named after snakes: Cobra, Boa, Asp, Rattler, Trouser, Alabama Black. They rumbled along the dusty canal roads for hours, unsure of their mission. They rarely stopped, and they didn't make friends when they did.

The longer they bounced along, cramped and sweating, the more Nick boiled. He slammed his fists against the steering wheel. "You know what we're doing here? Nothing. We're just driving around waiting to die. Just driving around waiting for someone to key a radio so some artillery round can take my legs."

Gassner didn't stop scanning. "Shut up, Annie."

"I gotta piss."

Gassner handed him a wide-mouth Gatorade bottle.

"I guess if you want to get technical," Nick said. "We're driving around waiting to validate our presence. Commanders have this hard-on about relevancy. We have to be relevant. The only way to be relevant is to be in contact, to either take casualties or dish them out, just so we can make this look like an actual war, which we all know it's not."

"Leave that shit at home," Gassner said. "Save it for your political science class at whatever fancy college you go to."

"Yeah, shut your mouth, Annie," Tom shouted down at him. "You're killing my morale."

"No use," Nick said. "I'm a dropout. But seeing as we can't set our own IEDs, and since we don't take much direct fire because these people are all cowards, we're pretty much driving around waiting to get blown up in these rickety, flat-bottomed boats." He kicked the door of the Humvee with the rusty steel plates, which were stolen and then thrown on by curbstone welders, eighteen-year-old privates and specialists who didn't want to die from something as silly and unglamorous as a stray bullet fired by some running-scared kid whose idea of jihad was spraying and praying from cover. "Just driving around waiting to die. Just so some general can say we're relevant. And for what? To fight an insurgency? We're not fighting an insurgency; we're creating one."

"Yo," said Jalaladin, their translator in the backseat. "This is a movement, dudes. A movement to contact because we are some bad dudes. This is a show of force to demonstrate that Archer don't take no crap from nobody."

Nick turned in his seat. "What do you know, Jellybean? They won't even let you hold a gun."

"I'll take yours when you get shot at and start crying like a little girl, Annie."

"And also," Nick said, going back to his rant. "This is exactly what I'm talking about." He squeezed the steering wheel. "Show of force? Cruising around in makeshift armored trucks, covered in body armor, sweating our balls off? Being too terrified to stop to take a piss is what they call a show of force?"

Gassner turned and actually looked at him for once. "Shut your mouth, Specialist."

"We look like scared little kids. At best, we look like dickheads. More than anything, with all this gear on? To these people, we look like alien weirdos from another planet."

"I'm not going to say it again. Zip it." Gassner fiddled with the radio and then said, "You know what your problem is? You listen to Hartwig too much. All his philosophizing. You're starting to sound just like him."

Nick closed his mouth and looked straight ahead. It wasn't true. He didn't sound like Levi. Not anymore anyway. Whereas Levi started out philosophical, intelligent, political, and angry—sometimes contradicting himself but always entertaining—he didn't stay that way. He didn't sound like anything anymore except a sergeant in the United States Army. Levi had drunk the

Kool-Aid. Slurped it down like a sacrament. If you want a guy to lose his mind and forget who he is, pat him on the back and give him another stripe.

The silence of Nick's teammates ate at him, and he got to the point where he couldn't help talking. "Case in point," Nick said. "About looking like jerks? So last week, Ali Baba happens to be walking around in his man dress, herding his sheep. One of these underfed lambs gets a little frisky, runs in front of my truck, and you think it's some master plan to get us to stop so they can ambush us. I try stopping and you yell at me to keep going, so what do I do? I follow orders like a good little soldier and I run over Ali Baba's sheep. Now even though he wasn't an insurgent before, he is now, all because we're driving around for no stupid reason, scared to death of stopping for a herd of sheep."

Gassner seemed to forget about defending the sanctity of their mission, and he took to defending himself instead. "ROE are clear and published. It wasn't my fault. Pamphlets are everywhere. Locals know that convoys have the right of way. If they don't know by now, it's their own dumb ass fault."

"Ass fault? What's an ass fault?"

That got a chuckle out of the new kid in the back, Weber, who hadn't said a word all morning. He had recently come in to replace a guy named Ferguson who had died three months prior. He had taken a single bullet to the back of the head, just below his helmet. At first, Nick thought Ferg was faking it when his chin dropped onto his chest. It took them ten minutes of first trying to wake him before they accepted that he was dead.

"Shut up and drive," Gassner said.

Nick closed his eyes and made a show of banging his head against the steering wheel. Because of the pain in his back from the rock; because of his all-too-frequent sunburn; because of the bouncing of the Humvee and the swelling of his bladder—he refused to use the Gatorade bottle unless he truly risked urinating in his own pants—and because of the idiocy of his team leader, his platoon leader, his company commander, his brigade commander, hell, because of his legislators, president, and his entire country, Nick was now ready; ready, that is, to die.

Back in those days, when so many of them were dying, they often joked about death as they tried to convince themselves it was nothing.

Nick looked at his watch and saw they still had three hours left before they were scheduled to return to the FOB. His mood brightened slightly when he glimpsed the end of the canal road and saw the smooth hardball of Main Supply Route Tampa. Now it would be an hour and a half down the highway to Taji and then an hour and a half back up. Then it would be all over, at least for the day. If they did come across any IEDs, they'd be easier to see on the asphalt. If they missed one, it would be less lethal coming from the shoulder instead of from under the hull. Nick tapped the steering wheel, and as soon as his tires hit the road, he pressed the gas and started picking up speed. More than trying to find the IEDs on Tampa, the platoon simply tried to outrun the blasts.

The traffic thickened as they neared Ad Dujayl. For a while, Nick had enough space to either maneuver around cars or push them out of the way with the heavy cattle guard on the front of the vehicle, but it wasn't long before he was forced to stop. Rusted Japanese minivans and white-and-red taxis filled the median and shoulders. The local cars blocked both lanes of traffic.

"Hold short, Anhalt," said Gassner.

Jalaladin called from the backseat, "Hold short, Annie." He cracked up and started singing a show tune from the Broadway musical, infusing it with his thick Arabic accent: "Tomorrow, tomorrow, I love you tomorrow. You're only a day away."

"I'm going to kick you out of this truck and make you walk back to O'Ryan," Nick told him. The stop irritated him, but mostly, he grew angrier about the rock in his body armor.

Gassner keyed the radio to talk to Archer One-Six and Archer One-Six told him to stand by while they figured out a new route. The longer they stood still, the more comfortable the multitudes felt closing in on them. Kids inched in, hoping for some candy. Young men paced back and forth, scouting. Cars scooted by, ignoring the rules that prohibited them from passing convoys. Everyone hoped to find an opening in the jam.

Jalaladin pointed out the window at a donkey pulling a cart full of grass right next to their truck. "You have got to be filling me full of crap," he said. He pulled on Hooper's leg in the turret and said, "Hey, can you get this IED-making dirt farmer out of here, dude?"

Nick heard yelling and three percussive warning shots. The donkey went trotting away. A little barefoot boy wearing a McDonald's T-shirt smacked the ass with a stick, yelling in Arabic as he beat the beast.

"Thank you, gunner, sir," said Jalaladin, and he flopped back in his seat, satisfied. "These people suck." No one said anything. "These towel heads are ignorant and they are all criminals." He paused, hoping for the usual laugh that accompanied the denigration of his own people. "We should shoot them all. They need a dictator like Saddam. Someone to keep a big thumb on their heads. You see what happens when we overthrow him?"

Just as they had paid no attention to Nick earlier, the other men paid no attention to Jalaladin. They listened to the sounds of the street. The car horns. The unintelligible yelling. The braying of donkeys.

They looked for any sign that they might be seconds from an explosion. A bulky burqa. Sagging suspensions. A lone, clean-shaven, military-age male chanting to himself as he clenched a steering wheel. A man on a roof with a cell phone. A kid with his hands stuffed in his armpits, hiding grenades.

The enemy surrounded them.

The heat from the transfer case radiated next to Nick and with each passing second, he grew more restless, more scared, more hot and sweaty, and more pissed at Levi for the rock in his shirt. He nearly threw the Humvee into park to step outside to take care of the stone once and for all, screw the risk, when Archer One-Six crackled over the radio, "Turn around and Charlie Mike. I have a new route. I'll let you know when we break free. Over."

Hooper stood tall in the turret and waved. When the waving wasn't enough, he shot a pen flare at a hesitant driver.

Nick watched the gleaming red pyrotechnic bounce off the windshield before the car skidded to a surprised halt in the median.

After getting out of the traffic and back onto the open highway, Nick accelerated. "Thank God we're out of that mess," he mumbled to himself.

"You are not kidding me, my man," said Jalaladin. "But now we'll be out here twice as long, and I'm already starving."

More than a cheeseburger, Nick just wanted the irksome gravel out of his shirt. He took his eyes off the road and tried twisting his arm up under the back of his body armor to get it. If it weren't for that rock, he no doubt would have seen the three 155-millimeter artillery rounds rigged up to a Motorola Talkabout radio on the left shoulder, right there on the surface, as obvious as an ark in the desert.

Tom dropped into the center of the Humvee. He clubbed Nick's shoulder in the process.

Just when Nick was about to yell at him, he felt a painful crack in his ears. He instantly felt his body flood with adrenaline. The steering wheel pulled hard to the right, and dust obscured his view. Out of the corner of his eye, he saw Hooper lose his balance and fall onto Gassner in the TC seat.

The windshield cracked. Smoke and dust covered the road in front of them. He couldn't see a thing so he slammed on the brakes. Hooper slammed into the flat front of the Humvee dash.

"Are you stupid?" he heard.

Obscenities piled upon obscenities.

"Get out get out get out," he heard.

He hit the gas, and the Humvee lurched into action, slowly gaining speed. Nick tried looking in his side rearview, but the driver's side window was shattered worse than the windshield, and it, too, was covered in black soot.

Over the radio he heard, "Victor One, what's your status? Victor One?"

Gassner keyed the radio. "Archer One-Six, Archer One-Six, this is Victor One."

The radio crackled again. "I repeat, Victor One, Victor One, what's your status?"

"Archer One-Six, Archer One-Six, Victor One. Do you read me?"

"I repeat, Victor One, Victor One, what's your status?"

Gassner looked over at Nick, who was looking at him. "Stop looking at me, douche."

Nick turned back to the front, despite his inability to see.

Gassner repeatedly slammed the handset against the steel body of the SINCGARS radio. He threw the mic against the windshield and let it dangle by the cord in front of him.

Nick kept his foot on the gas pedal, and when he felt the tires hit the gravel shoulder on the left, he pulled hard to the right, using all the strength in his arms to keep the beast on the road. By the way it was handling, he was certain the power steering was gone or the tie rod was bent. It was drivable, but it wasn't easy. When he felt his tires hit the gravel on the right, he veered to the left until he drifted onto the left shoulder. He played ping-pong with the shoulders, praying the locals got their sedans and donkeys out of the way. "What do you want me to do?" he asked, looking over at Gassner again.

Gassner didn't reply. He stared at the dirty front window.

"Corporal Gassner. What do you want me to do?" Nick asked again, growing more frantic.

Once again, no response.

"Corporal Gassner," Nick cried out.

"Dude. Shut the hell up," Gassner yelled back. "Stop right here. Just stop. Hooper, get your ass back in the gun and stop northbound traffic. Everyone else, fives and twenty-fives." Before Nick could bring the Humvee to a complete stop, Gassner opened his door and stepped out onto the hot asphalt, gun up, looking for a target. He scanned the area, ignoring his own advice to search the immediate five meters around the vehicle for additional hazards before moving on to the next twenty-five meters.

Because of Gassner's abrupt exit, Nick slammed on the brakes so his squad leader didn't go rolling across the highway, the result being that Hooper lurched into the front of the turret. "What the hell is wrong with you today, Anhalt?" Hooper yelled down.

PFC Brian Weber, the green replacement troop, dismounted and earnestly began his fives and twenty-fives. He said nothing, but simply got down to business. Nick made a mental note to get everyone to call Weber "The Mute." He walked in concentric circles, kicking disturbed earth and discarded cigarette boxes to ensure nothing was lying in wait for them. Chances were good that a secondary IED was in the general vicinity, planted by a bomber waiting just for them or the explosive ordnance disposal troops who would set up to interrogate the blast site.

Jalaladin stayed in his seat. He clung to the handle on his door with both hands, and he squeezed so hard his brown knuckles turned ashy.

Nick put the Humvee in neutral and pulled up on the brake. He had to ram his shoulder into the door several times to force it open. Stepping out onto the asphalt was like stepping onto the surface of the sun itself—the surface of the sun with someone holding a hair dryer to his face. Before gaining his bearings or even looking for other hazards, he untucked his T-shirt and blouse and arched his back rearward, freeing the rock that had galled him all morning. It fell on the ground and he turned around to pick it up, allowing the muzzle of his M4 to clang against the road.

Upon standing, he felt dizzy, nauseous, and he nearly lost his balance. He staggered around his vehicle looking at the gravel shoulder. He tried to discern whether any of the dirt was recently disturbed. He looked south at all the vehicles stopped by Tom Hooper's menacing frame and intimidating .50 caliber fully automatic machine gun. He stumbled to the front of the Humvee, put one hand on the tire, and puked up wheat snack bread with jalapeño cheese spread and two sugar-free Rip It Energy Fuel drinks.

Nick looked back north where the remnants of the bomb's mushroom cloud hung in sky. The scorching air shimmered over the oily highway for an empty stretch a quarter-mile long. The other three vehicles in Archer platoon held the north side of the cordon, trapped on the other side of the blast site by nothing more than SOP—standard operating procedures, which said they couldn't cross the kill-zone of an IED until an EOD team had cleared the scene to ensure the absence of secondary IEDs or hazardous remnants.

Nick put his hand to his forehead to shield his eyes from the sun. Behind him, he heard Gassner get on the radio again, but nothing had changed; he still couldn't make contact with the rest of the platoon.

Nick held his rifle up and looked through his scope to get a better view. He saw a squad mount up. Their vehicle tore across the median into the northbound lane opposite the direction of travel. They hugged the western shoulder, trying to keep as much distance between themselves and the blast site as possible.

The vehicle pulled perpendicular to the road in front of the line of halted Iraqi cars. Their gunner added to Hooper's presence with his Mark 19 40-millimeter grenade launcher. The members of the squad dismounted the Humvee and dutifully performed their own fives and twenty-fives. Levi sat in the TC seat with one foot out the door on the pavement, the radio handset to his ear.

Nick placed himself between the vehicle's body and the blasted steel door. He rested his rifle over the hinges and looked out across his sector.

Levi walked up in front of him, whistling as he surveyed the damage. "Look at that. Barely a scratch. Black Cats, eh? I've seen worse on the Fourth of July back home."

Nick managed a nervous chuckle.

Levi walked in front of Nick, and Nick lowered his rifle so he wouldn't flag him. Levi looked down at his energy drink and MRE breakfast splattered all over the road. He reached his hand to Nick's face and pulled his Oakley M Frame sunglasses down his nose so he could look at his friend's eyes. "You doing okay, buddy?"

Nick looked down, "Yeah, I'm fine." His voice cracked and shook.

"Look at me," Levi said.

Nick made eye contact and held it.

"You sure?" Levi said. "How do you feel? Amped? Nauseous? Vertiginous?"

"Vertiginous?"

"Like, are you dizzy? Bell rung too hard? Do we need to get you out of here? Call a MEDEVAC?"

Nick shook his head. "Nah, man. I'm good. It was just a rush, that's all."

"You just miss it or what? Was it hidden? Hooper said it was on the surface and yelled for you to stop. How'd you miss it?"

Nick reached into his pocket, pulled out the nummular rock, and handed it over. Levi analyzed the rock and placed it in the small pouch fastened to his vest, just over his heart.

"But you're okay. And so," Levi said, trailing off. He paused. He looked Nick up and down. "All right then." He walked around the other side of the Humvee and yelled to Gassner. "LT is working on calling EOD. I told him to make sure they came up from the south so they don't hit the same traffic jam we did."

Levi let his rifle hang in front of him, and he pulled out a pack of imitation Marlboro cigarettes. He shook one out and tossed it up to his own gunner. He walked around his Humvee passing out cigarettes to his men, stopping to light each one. He walked over to Victor One and tossed a fake Marb to Tom Hooper, who lit it by shining his contraband Iranian-imported, Chinese-manufactured green dazzler laser on the end of it.

He offered one to Gassner, but he refused. "Always a gas, eh Gassner?" Levi snickered. He passed out cigarettes to Jalaladin and Weber the Mute and finished by putting one in Nick's mouth. He lit it for him. "Better just settle in boys. We'll be here a minute, I'm sure."

Nick pulled the cigarette from his lips, exhaled, and with shaking hands, put the filter back in his mouth. "Vertiginous," he thought. "Vertiginous, vertiginous, vertiginous."

2.3 WE SHOULD HAVE TAKEN UP KNITTING OURSELVES

(It Would Have Saved Us a Lot of Trouble)

hildren and men stepped out of their vehicles and walked up to the front line of cars. Rusty Toyotas and Opels crossed the median and spread across all lanes and the shoulder. Cars pressed into the barley field to the west of MSR Tampa. Had a canal not blocked the east side, surely the cars would have spread in that direction as well. Within minutes, hundreds of men and cars lined the busy highway, every one of them an enemy. Every one of them otherworldly and less than human. Every one of them apt to key a radio in his pocket to turn an unprotected, dismounted American infantryman into nothing but a torso, bleeding out where his legs used to be.

Levi had to contact Lieutenant Michaels over the net because Gassner's comms got knocked out during the blast. Lieutenant Michaels had to contact the tactical operations center; the TOC, in turn, had to contact the bomb disposal team; the bomb disposal team had to get back to the TOC; the TOC had to get back to Lieutenant Michaels; and then the LT, of course, had to get on the horn to reach Levi, who was standing less than a half a mile away.

All Levi could gather from the LT was that the EOD team from O'Ryan was tending to a large vehicle-borne IED near the south gate of Logistical Supply Area Anaconda, a massive Army post on Balad Air Base inhabited by Army Fobbits and Air Force Chairmen. The post-blast investigation for a strike against Archer platoon, which caused no significant casualties, was of little import to the execs and operations officers at the TOC. It was barely a blip on the radar. When Levi suggested to Lieutenant Michaels that they Charlie Mike—continue mission and move on—he was told that securing the scene was critical so the EOD team could collect evidence from the blast crater before clearing the scene of any additional hazards. When Levi asked the LT why they couldn't get another EOD team from Anaconda, he was told their post-blast investigation was not a priority.

Private Weber knelt between the two Humvees and quietly finished the cigarette Levi had given him. When he finished it, he put his rifle across his knee and looked out upon his sector for nearly half an hour without so much as cracking his neck or brushing away a fly. After that first half-hour, he began looking over at Levi in ever-shorter intervals. The longer Levi bantered with the LT on the radio, the more often Weber looked over at him.

"What the hell are you looking at?" Levi shouted.

Weber said nothing but turned away, looking back at his sector.

"Didn't you know that's The Mute?" Nick called over. "Hasn't said a word since he got here."

Weber looked back at Levi. Levi barked like a dog, and Weber turned back to his sector.

After a few more similar exchanges, Weber finally said what was on his mind. "Sergeant Hartwig," he called, sounding almost afraid to speak. "Do you think I'll get my CIB for this?"

Levi looked across the top of the Humvee at him and went back to talking on the radio. "Archer One-Six, personnel Weber, a.k.a. The Mute, wants to know if he'll get his combat infantry badge for being in a victor when it passed by a few fireworks." He listened to the headset pressed against his ear. "Roger, One-Six. I'll tell him."

"What'd he say?" said Weber.

"He said he'll write you a CIB in return for sexual favors."

"C'mon. Seriously. What'd he say, Sar'nt?"

"He said watch your damn sector and stop worrying about the chest candy."

After another long while, Weber called out, "How long until EOD shows up?"

"They get here when they get here," replied Levi.

"What's so important about a hole in the ground?"

"They need evidence. If they have evidence, they can tell us what bad guys to go catch. If we can kick down the right doors and kill the right bad guys, we can all stop the insurgency. Kill the bomb maker and you'll have no more bombs, but if you kill the guy who plants the bomb, all you have is another dead farmer. That's what's so important about a hole in the ground."

"Well is some scattered dirt really going to bring down the network? Aren't we just as likely to get hit just sitting here?"

"Who knows? They have to clear the blast site of additional hazards."

"Does lightning really strike twice?"

Levi looked across the Humvee at him, mouth taut. "You sure have a lot of dangerous questions for a noob."

Weber shut his mouth for a solid five minutes before shouting out, "What are we *doing* here, man?"

Levi pulled down his Oakley sunglasses and raised an eyebrow at Weber. "Since when did you find a voice?" He pushed his glasses back up. "I don't know why we're all here." Levi spread his arm out and gestured to the rest of the guys. "But I know why you're here. Would you like to hear a story that will explain why Private Weber is here?"

"Sure," Weber muttered.

"We used to have this guy in the platoon. Name was Private Ferguson. An excellent soldier. He kept his mouth shut. Didn't ask dumb questions, and he could shoot a farmer digging a hole in a road from 400 meters using just his iron sights." Levi crossed his arms and rested them on his rifle butt. He looked up into the sky, as if remembering better times. "Now Private Ferguson thrived on combat. Absolutely loved it. He would have loved today. Nothing would have made him happier than getting hit by that IED." Levi shook his head. "But he couldn't take the winter, man. Couldn't take the lull in the action. No outlet for the aggression bred in him by your United States Army. His anger manifested itself in increasingly self-destructive ways. It started with little things, like fist fights with guys who wouldn't trade him their jalapeño cheese and wheat snack bread for his peanut butter and cracker. It escalated into death threats against his TC, and to make matters worse, he started taking trips to the fence line to score needles. He literally lost his mind. Completely forgot who he was. And then one day?" Levi snapped his fingers. "Done. It was all over. No more trips to the fence, no more needles, no more nothing."

"So what'd he do?" Weber asked. "OD? Kill himself?"

"Worse," said Levi. He pulled out his box of cigarettes. He took his time taking one from the box and lighting it.

"So what'd he do then, Sergeant Hartwig?" said Weber, growing annoyed.

Levi blew out a stream of smoke. "Carpal tunnel got him."

"Carpal tunnel? What?"

Levi blew out a stream of smoke. "He took up knitting."

"Knitting?"

"You deaf? I said knitting."

Levi heard Nick snort. He looked over and nodded at him. Nick shook his head.

"At first," Levi said. "He tried cross-stitching. Old Ferg's the one who did up that really ornate looking genie lamp hanging in the TOC." Levi turned. "Hey Nick, that genie lamp still hanging in the TOC?"

Nick nodded gravely. "Sure is."

Levi continued. "But that didn't work. Too mindless is what he said. So he took up knitting. He cut his teeth by making these little—I dunno, I guess you could call them nesting dolls. You know, like, a knitted bunny rabbit with a pouch, and a bunch of tiny knitted bunny rabbits to go in the pouch so you could pull all the tiny knitted bunnies out of the pouch and make it look like the bigger bunny rabbit gave birth to all the little ones."

Weber put his rifle up to his shoulder and looked through his scope to get a clearer look at something in the distance. "That's insane," he mumbled.

"Seriously," Levi said. "But when we busted his balls for wasting his time on something so dumb, he made a pair of mittens and a nice little watch cap for every guy in the platoon. And it was winter so it was great for the rest of us. It really mellowed him out. I think it really changed his life. Heck, it changed all of our lives. Before he could finish one for the LT, however, he came down with a nasty case of carpal tunnel syndrome."

"Carpal tunnel syndrome?"

"It's a stress injury that comes from repetitive motion, numbnuts. From all the knitting. It got so bad he couldn't squeeze his trigger. They had to send him home."

"They sent a dude home because he got carpal tunnel syndrome?" Weber said. "From playing Martha Stewart?"

"You got it," said Levi. "And that's why you're here, Sunshine. Got any more stupid questions?"

"No, Sar'nt," he said, lowering his voice.

"Welcome to the party," Levi said. He walked off.

He had no real answers to give, of course. Ferguson had been shot in the head. There was no carpal tunnel. There were no bunny rabbit nesting dolls. And there were no life-changing watch caps and mittens. There was only a split-second, a chin on a chest in repose, the dull slump of a body being pulled from the turret, and then nothing. There were no real stories and there were no real answers, so they made them all up.

Now the men sweated in the middle of MSR Tampa for hours, hemmed in on all sides by geography, impassable lines of cars, and a growing mob of angry locals. Men desperate to do something—anything—smoked cigarettes and longed for nothing more than to finger their triggers.

A few minutes later, Levi heard chatter from members of Second Platoon, who were escorting the EOD team. He looked up and saw the top of a tan, boxy Air Force M116 Humvee that looked more like a bread truck than a war machine. As it grew closer and the honking of cars grew louder, he saw that the EOD team was bumping the Toyotas out of their way with the giant steel bumper mounted to the front, much to the chagrin of the locals. Levi called Second Platoon's six on the radio and let them know they had a visual on the EOD team.

When the bomb disposal team finally did break all the way through the line of cars, they dropped their black robot and got to work right away.

Levi huddled over Airman First Class Matthew Hefti's shoulder. The young Air Force EOD tech, who looked like he had barely finished high school, let a cigarette dangle from his lips as he worked. He squinted his eyes against the smoke that wafted up from his cigarette; sweat dripped from under his Kevlar, down his face, and onto his robot controller.

Tech Sergeant Pat Cazalet, the leader of the two-man EOD team, came up behind the two infantrymen. "Don't you think you two should be worried about your sectors? Let Matt here drive the robot, and he'll let you look for bad guys."

Levi sheepishly turned around. Nick, however, continued to stare at the screen. The Tech Sergeant's not-so-subtle order didn't register.

"Sergeant Hartwig," said Cazalet. "Maybe you should square away your troop."

"Nick," said Levi, looking over his shoulder. "Eyes out."

"Huh?" Nick said. He snapped out of it, and his eyes grew wide.

When Levi turned to look at what Nick saw, a white Toyota blazed down the gravel road that ran parallel to Tampa on the east side of the canal. Two military-aged males hung out the windows spraying AK fire. He looked down the sight of his weapon, but he couldn't focus on anything beyond his rear-sight aperture. When the shot was lost, he looked up over the barrel of his rifle to see Gassner already running toward his truck.

Levi barked orders as he ran. On his way back to the EOD truck, he stopped between the two Archer vehicles and looked up at the gunners. "I know you want a fight, fellas. If you have the chance, send them to their virgins, but use your brains, okay? Just look around at this mess." He gestured to the jam of cars and observers. "Some spray-and-pray potshots aren't worth the hell you'll have to pay if you hit any of these civilians." He stood there a second, waiting for acknowledgment. "Got it?"

The gunners said in unison, "Hooah, Sar'nt."

"Good. Now go get some."

Levi then ran around the truck and grabbed Nick's arm as he climbed into Victor Two with Gassner. "Nuh uh, buddy. Not this time. You're staying with me. Someone needs to guard EOD." He pulled Nick back over to the EOD truck and stopped when they reached Hefti and his robot controller.

Hefti looked up from the controller at the two Humvees tearing away. Levi put his gloved hand on the airman's shoulder. "You look this way," and he pointed with his other hand at the robot control screen. "And be quick about it so we can get the hell out of here." He removed his hand from Hefti's shoulder and put it on Nick's. "You, watch this way." He pointed behind the EOD tech and waved his arm in an arc. "One hundred and eighty degrees behind this guy. Get his back and don't pay any attention to what he's doing. Got it?" Nick nodded, but said nothing.

Levi walked around to the other side of the truck where Cazalet was on the radio with his own chain of command. He spit tobacco juice onto the asphalt and keyed the mic again. "Alamo, this is Caz. Roger, we're in contact here and gotta get movin', so we won't be using the bomb suit on this one."

The radio crackled, "Roger, team one, stand by while we seek approval for that."

Levi took a knee and faced out.

Cazalet keyed his radio again. "Negative Alamo. I ain't requesting it, I'm frickin' tellin' ya." He tossed his radio mic back into the seat of his truck and ignored their response. As he walked around the front of his vehicle, he called out, "How's it going, Matt?"

Levi glanced over his shoulder and saw a flash down the road. Cazalet flinched and hit the ground. Not a full second later, Levi heard the ear-splitting crack of the IED and he saw the main body of the robot fall from the sky onto the highway. He scooted around the backside of the Humvee and pressed himself against its protective steel as he heard the thud of rocks and the clink of metal falling around him.

When the sounds stopped, he looked around the other side of the vehicle at Hefti and Nick, who were now looking at the static on the robot screen. Cazalet picked himself up off the ground and walked toward them. Hefti dropped his cigarette on the ground and noticed that Levi was looking at him. He shrugged. "Oops," he said.

He closed the robot control unit and jumped into the driver's seat of the Humvee.

Cazalet turned to him and said, "Just a second, Matt." He walked around to the back of the vehicle to meet Levi. "Sorry, man. We gotta go down there and get that thing and clear it."

Levi nodded.

Cazalet turned around and stepped away from the Humvee to look at the dissipating mushroom cloud. "You can stay, or you can ride down there with us to be in the armor, but I think you should stay. No sense in all of us going down there. They're trying to kill us, ya know?"

Levi couldn't tell if he was kidding or not.

The EOD bread truck pulled away and rattled down the highway toward the scene of the blast. Levi nodded in the direction of the runaway and said, "Who needs to square away their troop now?"

Cazalet ran after the truck a few steps and yelled, "What the hell, Matt?" Then he gave up and watched.

"What's up with that?" Levi asked.

Cazalet shook his head in a mixture of frustration and wonder. "If he doesn't get killed down there, I'll kill him myself when we get back to the FOB."

Nick, Levi, and Cazalet watched Hefti drive right up next to the main body of the broken robot. When he jumped out of the truck, he was practically on top of it. He bent down and picked it up. Struggling with its weight, he shuffled to the back of the Humvee. He dropped it onto the ground without ceremony, opened the squared-off back hatch, picked up the robot body again, and heaved it into the truck. He scampered around the truck picking up other assorted pieces, and after making a full circle around the truck, he dumped those in the back as well. He got back into the driver's seat, stood up on the sideboard, looked around and over the top of the Humvee, sat down in the seat, slammed the door, and put it back into gear. He drove in reverse all the way back to where the other men stood. He tossed his door open. "Problem solved. Let's roll."

Cazalet shook his head, told Levi and Nick to hop in the back, and he got in the TC side.

"Caz," said Hefti when they were all in. "I had a perfectly good—"

"Not another word from you, Matt," said the EOD team leader.

Levi was secretly pleased about the EOD team's misstep. It could have taken them hours to robotically separate all the hazardous components. At least now they were on the move again. Levi's knees pressed against the steel bar that braced the back of the driver's Humvee seat. He tried adjusting himself, but despite his own diminutive stature, there was not enough room for his legs. He leaned forward to scoot his butt back on the dusty canvas seat as far as he could, which wasn't easy on account of his body armor. He put his hands on the back of the driver's seat and leaned up, pointing across Hefti's shoulder. "Cut the median and stop right before that foot bridge. I'll get out and spot you over."

"Roger," said Hefti.

"Stop here," Levi said when they had squared up in front of the wooden footbridge, which was barely as wide as the Humvee itself. He opened the door, only too happy to be out of the truck. He took a cursory glance at the ground for wires, disturbed earth, dog corpses, or any other indicator that an IED might be waiting. Nothing unusual registered so he hustled to the bridge. He jumped on it a few times to test its weight-bearing capacity, as if the weight of a man were a test of what could hold several tons of steel. He eased himself down the canal embankment to glance under the bridge. When he was satisfied the Humvee could make it over, he took his position in front of the Humvee and slowly guided the driver with hand signals. He pointed at Hefti and then pointed at his own eyes with two fingers. The airman held his gaze as Levi eased the Humvee onto the bridge and over the canal.

Each tire hung halfway off the bridge. If the bridge collapsed under the weight of the truck or if the driver turned too far to the left or the right, the truck's occupants would most likely drown in the canal, unable to open the heavy steel doors underwater and unable to extricate themselves from their own heavy body armor even if they could. Such hazards were routine.

Levi pointed left and right, and Hefti made micro-movements with the steering wheel to keep the truck on the path. When the front wheels were safely on solid ground, Levi turned around and walked forward in front of the vehicle until it was on the canal road. He looked up the road in the direction the other squads had traveled in pursuit of the white Toyota that had engaged them.

Approximately a hundred meters down the road, Levi could make out what looked like two dirt bikes laid out on the gravel in front of a hut. Two Archer Platoon Humvees stood parked in front. Several of Levi's platoon mates were standing back with their hands on the pistol guards of their slung rifles while Gassner and two other soldiers stood over two local men on the ground. The detainees were, as of yet, uncuffed. They kept trying to lift themselves to all fours to scurry away, but each time they lifted their bellies off the ground, Gassner or one of the other men placed a boot on their backs and kicked them down into the dusty gravel on the canal road. The men on the ground resigned themselves to low crawling like snakes toward their refuge near the side of the path. Mud walls, straw roof, and a rotted wooden door.

Levi cursed under his breath and took off running down the road, holding his rifle close to his body so it didn't bang against his legs. "Hey," he yelled. "Those aren't even the same guys." The heavy humid air swallowed his voice, a voice that quickly grew breathless under the extra weight he carried. He was halfway to them when they disappeared inside the hut.

He pulled up, out of breath, and called up to Tom in the turret. "What the hell's going on, Hooper?"

"Hut's the trigger point, Sar'nt. Guys had plans on them for the bomb. Like diagrams and shit. See? These are the guys that blew us up, Sar'nt." He held out a piece of lined paper, college-ruled, edges ripped from a spiral-bound notebook, grimy with the prints of hands that hadn't been washed for days.

Levi stood on his tiptoes, reached up and grabbed the paper from Hooper, and examined it. Arabic handwriting and crude drawings of wires, a battery, and a projectile covered the page. Levi stared at the page and then looked up, noticing their interpreter still cowering inside the Humvee. "Jellybean," Levi shouted. "What good is a terp who hides inside a truck? Get out here and earn your keep."

Levi pulled the door open and Jalaladin got out, looked around, and took the piece of paper that Levi thrust into his chest. "What's it say?" Levi asked.

"This looks like a kid did this writing. It's just like, some like, instructions and shit. Like, it says to just be hooking this thing up here like this in the picture, and that's it man."

Cazalet walked around so he could look over Jalaladin's shoulder. "Could you be more specific? How does it say to set it up exactly?"

"I freaking told you guys what this shit says, man. It's like some kid stuff, okay?"

Levi ripped the paper from Jalaladin's hand. He stared at it, teeth clenched, hands shaking. "Payback's a bitch," he said.

"Frickin' worthless now that all you guys put your fingerprints all over it," said Cazalet before sticking another dip in his lower lip.

The sound of someone crying out in fear and pain came from the mud hut to their left. Hefti pulled out a cigarette and leaned against his Humvee. "You gonna look into that?" he asked, looking at Levi.

Levi ran toward the hut.

After Levi kicked the door in and stepped into the dusty room with his gun up, he saw Gassner standing over the two Iraqis. Both of them lay prone on the dirt floor with sandbags over their heads. Their hands were flex-cuffed behind their backs. Privates Weber and Ott, eyes wide and brows raised, trained their M4 rifles on the two helpless prisoners.

2.4 C'MON! WHAT SHOULD THEY EXPECT AFTER WHAT THEY DID TO US?

Nick was already in there, yelling at Gassner to stop.

Gassner reared back and kicked one of the faceless prisoners in the ribs.

"Gassner," Nick yelled. "Stop right now."

Gassner looked up briefly and kicked again.

"Corporal Gassner, you gotta stop it," Nick pleaded.

Levi took several steps into the room and grabbed Gassner's shoulder. "Knock it off," Levi said.

"These are the Ali Babas," said an out-of-breath Gassner, shrugging him off and balling his fists, "who tried to kill us, Levi."

"Sergeant Hartwig."

"What?" said Gassner.

"You address me as Sergeant Hartwig," he said, his voice obdurate and commanding. "Now remove those sandbags."

Gassner didn't move.

"Now," Levi said. "Do not make this worse for yourself."

"Roger that." Gassner squared up and stood nose-to-nose with Levi. "Sergeant Hartwig." He stood there for a moment, and Levi balled his own fists, ready for a fight if it came to that, but Gassner relented and turned around. He grabbed each man in turn by the collar and pulled their necks up enough to remove the sandbags before dropping them back into the dirt.

When he had finished, he turned back to Levi. "Happy now?"

"I am the furthest thing from happy, Corporal Gassner." He took time to make eye contact with each man in the room. "Take your accomplices here and go outside. Hold a cordon and secure the EOD team."

Gassner bumped Nick in the shoulder as he walked past him, but Nick took a deep breath, told himself to turn the other cheek, and let it go. The room cleared except for Levi, Nick, and the two prisoners on the floor. Now that the sandbags were gone and his eyes had adjusted to the exiguous light, Nick could tell that these prisoners weren't men at all; they were teenagers. Practically children.

The kid on his left was scrawny, just into his teenage years with wispy hairs above his lip that couldn't properly be called a mustache. Red pimples with heads ripe for popping pocked his dark caramel skin. The other was even younger, but he shared the same unibrow and narrow chin. Probably a brother or half-brother. Back home, this kid wouldn't even have his own locker at school. He would still be playing Little League.

Even more striking than their youth was the damage done to their faces. Their split lips were swollen and bleeding, damaged too badly to blame it on the desert sun. There were other indicators that Gassner and his posse had administered more vigilante justice than the kicking he had witnessed. The nose of the older boy was cocked to the side, obviously broken. It bled into his thin mustache, down onto and even past his cracked lips. Dirt and bits of gravel stuck to the blood on his chin, which quivered in a combination of fear, anger, and indignation. The left cheek of the other boy's face was scraped raw. His eye socket and cheekbone were smashed, and his brow and forehead were deeply bruised. The dark purples and reds drew a sharp contrast to his sickly pallor, and the way he held his right eye wide open in shock drew attention to his inability to open his swollen left.

Nick approached the two detainees from the rear. He looked down at their grubby hands, disgusted. Blood oozed out of the torn skin around the white plastic flex cuffs before mixing with the henna that stained their hands.

Letting his M4 hang, he pulled his own set of zip ties from a pouch on his flack vest. He first knelt over the prone detainee on the left, one of his knees between the boy's spread legs.

"How old are you?" Nick whispered, mostly to himself. "You're just a kid."

With one hand, Nick firmly grabbed his wrists and the boy tensed, but didn't pull away. "Ssssh," Nick said. "Relax. Chill." He put his own zip ties on the kid's wrists, above the other set, just tight enough that he couldn't slip out, but not so tight as to cut off circulation or lacerate his skin. He shuffled over and did the same for the next kid.

"You guys plant that bomb?" Levi asked from over by the door. "Boom boom?"

The boys on the ground didn't look up. Levi leaned his back against the wall. He rested his forearms on his slung rifle.

When Nick had finished securing the boys with his own cuffs, he pulled a black Benchmade from his vest and told them not to move. He eased the knife under the first set of flex cuffs and sliced through the plastic, releasing some pressure from the wrists of the younger boy. When he got to the older boy, the cuffs were too tight to slide the knife underneath so he had to saw from the top, toward the boy. He slipped when he broke through the plastic, and his knife point dug into the heel of the boy's hand. The boy unleashed a choleric torrent of Arabic.

"Sorry, sorry, sorry," Nick said. He backed up onto his knees, grabbed the boy's shoulder, and pulled him up to a kneeling position. As soon as he let go of him, the boy turned his head, arched his back, and spit in Nick's face.

Nick closed his eyes when the boy spit and they remained closed for only a second, but when he opened them, he could already feel the boy's weight bearing against him. Levi, who had been casually resting against the wall, delivered a combat boot to the kid's sternum. Nick lost his balance and fell back on his elbow when the kid fell into him.

Levi reached down and pulled the kid back up by his shirt. He screamed in his face. "He's trying to help you. Are you too stupid to see that?"

Nick scrambled to his feet and put a hand on Levi's shoulder. "Chill, man," he said. "Just chill."

Levi stood fast, bent over, holding onto the kid's shirt. He stared into his face.

"Levi." Nick pulled on his shoulder. "Back off unless you want to get a face full of spit too, okay?"

Levi let go of the kid, but didn't move. He stood there content to tower over and intimidate the boy with his artificial bulk, weapon, and presence.

"Levi, I said back off. We don't both need to get TB from this kid. Just. Settle. Down. I'm okay. I got this."

Levi took a few steps back, rested his back against the wall, and slid down into a sitting position, legs spread, knees bent, boots on the floor, rifle at the ready.

Nick wiped his face on his sleeve and joined his friend in the dirt. He patted Levi's forearm. "Breathe, buddy. Just breathe."

Levi shrugged him off, shook a cigarette out of a soft pack he had wedged in the shoulder of his flak vest, and lit it. "You know what the problem is with these people? These animals never know when someone's trying to help them. Fix a road, they blow it up. Build a school, blow it up. Water plant? Boom." He took a drag and blew smoke out of his nose while waving his cigarette in the direction of their prisoners. "And these kids? They'll gank our money and our Oakleys and our Benchmades and they'll make a living selling us their stupid bootleg porno DVDs, and then two seconds later they try to blow our asses up." He took another drag and leaned forward.

"Kids have got balls though, right?" Nick said with a chuckle.

"Lucky those balls didn't get them killed."

Nick reached over and grabbed Levi's cigarette, took a drag, and gave it back.

Levi flicked it into the dirt near the kids' faces. "Animals," he said. "You should have just let the guys do what they wanted. I would've."

"Nah. You don't really believe that."

"Sure as hell do."

Nick's voice hardened in an instant. "Listen to me, Sergeant Hartwig. That is not how we operate. It's not why we put on this uniform in the first place. Right and wrong don't change because of circumstance." Nick stood up and looked down at his friend, his superior. "Furthermore, I expect you to notify Archer One-Six personally, considering you're the big, bad platoon sergeant today."

Levi looked at him, as if in shock.

"I'm not playing."

Levi rose, straightened his back, and stood as tall as he could, though he still had to look up at Nick. "Let me tell you something, *Specialist* Anhalt. I had Nick's back because Nick's been my best friend for years. But you better get something straight right now. If it comes down to a choice between helping out these al-Qaeda pricks or getting behind anyone else in the platoon?" He pointed toward the door. "Even someone like Gassner? I'm picking our guys every time, no matter what the circumstances. Do you understand me?"

Without waiting for an answer, Levi turned his back on Nick and walked out of the hut.

Nick stood in silence. Looking at the bruised and bleeding children in front of him, Nick wanted to inflict the same kind of damage on Gassner, Ott, and Weber. At the same time, he couldn't deny that they were fighting a war. Regardless of their ages, regardless of their motives, regardless of their respective faith traditions, and regardless of the politics that led them all to cross paths in the first place, there was no ignoring that each of them was trying to kill the other. The proof was in the plans; these two had been part of an attempt to blow them into a pink mist.

Nick thought of the first time his own vehicle had been struck by an IED. The front end of the Humvee flew so high he thought they were flipping over backward. The cab filled with smoke so fast he thought he had gone blind. He still didn't think he could hear right. The same rage and lust for revenge that seemed to have gripped Gassner had filled him that day as soon as he got out of the disabled truck and set foot on the ground. The difference was that when Nick got hit that first time, he felt bullets flying past his head. He fired back at the masked and faceless enemy trying to kill him. He was blessed with the opportunity to unleash the primal fighting instinct known only by those whose lives are on the line. Today Weber, Gassner, and even Nick had been hit without notice by a couple cowards, and yet, they enjoyed no such relief. In their battle, instead of stepping out to engage in a fight to the death with their enemies, they stepped onto the supply route after getting smoked by a point-blank blast of high explosives and shrapnel—concussed and confused and angry as they were—only to be told by the brass up at battalion that now their mission was to stand there in the heat for three hours to guard a hole in the road. The army had bred certain deadly instincts within them, and when the situation arose to waken those violent and reactionary forces, the army asked them to take a knee, hydrate, and wait for further direction.

2.5 I KNOW, I KNOW; IT'S NOT WHAT YOU WOULD HAVE DONE

Levi stormed out of the hut as Lieutenant Michaels and the members of first squad pulled up to the far side of the second squad victors. Gassner stood next to his Humvee whispering to Ott. The sight of them conspiring like that made Levi feel some of Nick's disgust. Levi could have given the benefit of the doubt to Private Weber, about whom he knew nothing except that he was new to the unit and greener than snot from a sinus infection. Maybe Weber didn't know any better. He could give Ott no such benefit. The kid looked like a weasel, and his favorite hobby was spreading gossip and discontent behind the backs of anyone in a position of authority while cozying up to anyone who might listen. He had already been busted in rank twice and wouldn't be in the army at all if they didn't have to cut through so much red tape to get rid of someone. And Gassner? It was a no brainer that Gassner knew better. The whole reason he had been named a corporal was because of his letter-of-the-law priggishness.

Levi unclipped his helmet to let his face breathe. He wiped the sweat pooling on his upper lip as he began the walk down the road to meet the LT.

Ott stepped in front of him. He tried to mask his body language to portray a challenge, but his voice betrayed his anxiety. "What exactly are you gonna say?"

Levi glanced up at an oblivious Hooper in the turret.

Gassner pulled Ott's arm to get him out of the way. "Leave it alone, Private. He ain't gonna say nothing. After all, he and his buddy, Annie, were in there alone. All by their lonesome for quite some time. Anything he said would be our word against theirs. Besides, who's the LT gonna listen to? The new hotshot or the old crew who've been in his outfit since he graduated from ROTC?"

Levi didn't break stride.

"You aren't gonna say a thing, are ya Levi?" called Gassner.

That was one option: saying nothing. He certainly wasn't afraid of Gassner's weak threat, but good NCOs covered for their guys. They took the fall and kept their mouths shut to cover for the failures of their men. That's what responsibility was all about: keeping your mouth shut when the other guys blew it. Not to mention, that kind of leadership instilled loyalty, and loyalty was priceless. Levi took off his glasses and used a corner of the moist shemagh wrapped around his neck to wipe them. In a way, he was grateful it had taken first squad so long to link up with them because if the lieutenant had been the one to catch the guys giving a bona fide beat down to their detainees, he would have held Levi responsible for not keeping his squad under control. You can delegate tasks; you cannot delegate responsibility. It's a tenet of leadership that colonels and generals have long since forgotten, but it's a truth that noncommissioned officers carry with them every day. At the same time, Levi did catch them, and he did put a stop to it. He still wasn't sure that was enough.

He grew lightheaded as he walked down the gravel road.

He passed the EOD truck, where the bomb techs were reconstituting their explosive charges. Levi stopped, trying to decide whether or not to bring them into it. The extent of their interaction with the EOD team had come entirely outside the wire during QRF missions to IED problems, which happened nearly every day, but still; he knew the bomb techs, not the men. A glance back at Gassner and Ott whispering together made up his mind for him. "Sergeant Cazalet," he said. "Do me a favor?"

"What's up?" he said.

"We have two detainees in that hut. It's open. It's been cleared. The detainees have been cleared. We've got two guys watching them right now. They're cuffed and ready to go." He stopped and looked around, trying to find the words to phrase his request. "Our guys," he gestured toward Gassner and Ott. "Well, let me put it this way: Do you have room in your vehicle to take them since there are only two of you?"

Cazalet hooked a finger in his lip and pulled out a wad of chew. He flung it out into the canal and spit on the ground. "We could probably handle something like that."

Levi invaded his personal space and lowered his voice. Cazalet dropped his head to hear him. "Could you clean off their faces? Give them something to drink?" Levi turned around to look at his guys. Weber was on the opposite side of the truck where Levi had no visual on him. Ott and Gassner had finally split up, but each kept stealing glances in his direction. "The guys are a bit on edge after getting hit. I think it would be best if—" he paused again to find the words. "It would be best if a neutral party took care of them and transported them back to the FOB. You know, tensions running high and all."

He looked up and met the gaze of the much larger Air Force NCO. Levi found it impossible to discern what the man was thinking, and he knew him only peripherally. Cazalet nodded slowly. "Matt and I will take care of 'em. They'll be in good hands."

"Thanks," Levi whispered before moving on.

"Everything cool?" Hefti asked as he laced detonating cord into a water bottle.

"Yeah, we're cool," Levi said. But he wasn't sure. Good NCOs didn't stand for that kind of lapse in standards. When NCOs failed to maintain the standards, everyone suffered. *You give 'em an inch, and they take a mile,* he thought to himself. Levi didn't buy into the crap about blousing pants over boots and shaving sideburns; he didn't believe that if a guy relaxed his dress and appearance, the next step was disobeying direct orders in combat as all the first sergeants liked to preach; but he had seen how once a guy gets walked on by his subordinates, it's impossible to gain respect. He needed to do things the right way. He needed to figure this out.

Levi remembered the last time he saw his parents before he left for Iraq. Everyone mingled around the verdant parade grounds at Fort McCoy for one last goodbye. His mother had hugged him and cried. She whispered to him to be safe. Levi pulled away and his father closed his arms around him.

"Any advice?" he asked his father.

His dad put his mouth next to Levi's ear. "Just do the right thing," he said. "Worry only about what you control. The rest is war." As his father let him go, he placed his hand over the flag that Levi wore on his shoulder. He shook his head and spoke sadly. "*Mundum portamus.*"

We carry the world.

They did. All those young men did. They carried the world, and it was heavy, and they didn't know what to do with it. Was this the rest? Was this the war? Things had already spun out of control and they weren't always as black and white or as right and wrong as Nick liked to think.

Levi reached the platoon leader's truck. The lieutenant sat with one leg out of the Humvee. He fought with battalion on the radio and held up a finger for Levi to wait.

Levi glanced back down the road. Cazalet and Hefti had put the detainees on their knees on the gravel road next to the EOD truck. Hefti took some pictures and then pulled out a notebook. Levi wanted to choke him, shake him, tell him to pay attention to his job and nothing else, pay attention to every detail before he got someone killed. The kid thought he was a tourist, only along to document the ride.

The detainees held their backs and necks rigid. Levi couldn't believe their stoicism. He wiggled around in discomfort after taking one knee in the grass with kneepads on. He couldn't imagine how he'd feel with the bits of gravel sticking into his kneecaps, the pull on his shoulders from having his hands cuffed behind his back, and the sharp plastic edges of the flex cuffs on the tender skin of his wrists. Yet these guys didn't move a millimeter. He admired their discipline.

Then another thought came to him. If one of these detainees lodged a complaint, and if some bleeding heart took them seriously—well, that would change everything. With the Abu Ghraib scandal still fresh in everyone's minds and with the court-martials for that mess not even finished yet, everyone knew to tread lightly. If word got out, or worse, if pictures of helpless teenagers with busted faces leaked out, the knee-jerk freak-out by the brass would be startling. Those spineless bastards would eat their own in a second just to protect their images, egos, or their next stars. And, of course, they'd be assisted by the media, and—as always—public affairs would spin everything to protect the army, i.e., whatever commander happened to own them, and they'd ensure—as always—that the official story made it clear that all the problems were isolated incidents carried out by rogue individuals. Nothing systemic to worry about here. Public Affairs: as much the enemy to ground troops as al-Qaeda. Never mind that the kids were caught red-handed trying to kill American soldiers. Never mind that the rules of engagement kept American soldiers from doing so much as sneezing in the wrong direction. Never mind that the same American lynch mobs who would be calling for their heads had trained a bunch of eighteen-year-old kids to kill people so they could sleep soundly in their cozy beds by night and troll freely on the Internet by day as if they were all masters of public policy and international relations, and never mind that those same assholes had elected leaders who had sent soldiers over there to do just what they had been trained to do, i.e., kill people.

Never mind that this was a goddamned war.

Investigations were inevitable. Levi pictured the CID guys calling the young privates into the offices, offering them coffee, only to disappear for hours at a time, leaving the young kids to think about why they were there. The kids would grow more nervous and skittish by the second. The agents would come back in and tell them someone else already squealed so they shouldn't bother lying to cover up for anyone; that would just make it worse. They'd give a little speech about the Army Values and appeal to their senses of honor and integrity, and the naïve kids would fail to understand that the omertà in an infantry platoon *defined* honor and integrity.

Barring that, someone as soft and slimy as Ott would say anything to save his own skin, and the little tiff in the mud hut would no doubt be uncovered in that way. If Levi said nothing, Lieutenant Michaels could deny all knowledge, and the worst that could happen was he'd be on the naughty list for not knowing what was going on in the platoon; which, under the circumstances and with all they had been through already that day, who could blame him for that? On the other hand, if he told the LT, even as laid back as the guy was, he wouldn't have been able to turn a blind eye to detainee mistreatment after one of his squad leaders brought it up. He would have had to report it or at the very least document some sort of discipline. Best-case scenario, he'd have to write up a letter of reprimand for Levi, and the company commander would probably write an Article 15 to bust Gassner down a stripe for the sake of posterity. That kind of punishment would tear the platoon apart. The soldiers would stop believing they could trust their platoon leadership and they'd stop believing they could trust those in their squads. When soldiers stop trusting each other, soldiers die. The more he thought about it, the more he wanted to tell Nick that right and wrong *did* change with circumstances. It was not always a simple choice between good and bad, right and wrong, or righteousness and evil.

If anything was evil, it was the war itself.

"Hello," Lieutenant Michaels said, dragging it out. "Earth to Hartwig?"

Levi snapped out of it. "Yes, sir," he replied.

"Yes what?"

Levi shook his head. "I don't know, sir. Could you repeat the question?"

"You okay, Soldier?"

"Yeah. I'm fine, sir. Just thinking about—" If Levi didn't tell the lieutenant, he would have plausible deniability. Besides, that's what good NCOs did. They stopped nonsense at the lowest possible level, leaving the brass to talk strategy and collect their medals. And that's exactly what he had already done, right? He did catch them before it could get out of hand, and he did stop it after all. No harm, no foul, right? "Nothing. What were you saying?"

"Snap out of it." Lieutenant Michaels pointed to his Blue Force Tracker, and he outlined their options. "The quickest and most direct route back to the FOB, down Tampa here, is blocked by another massive traffic jam. Initial reports were that a VBIED engaged a convoy, taking out a local oil tanker in the process. Another report, and what's more likely since EOD hasn't been called away, is that a skittish gunner opened fire when a taxi got too close to the convoy, leading the taxi to slam on the brakes, which forced an oil tanker behind him to swerve and crash over onto its side, leaving black gold all over the road. Either way, that's blocked." He hit a button, zooming out to show more of the map on the screen. "We have essentially two options then: We can get off this canal road up there and then head north until we hit Route Heather. Take that until we get to Balad. Go in the north gate there. We can chill out real quick, get some good chow, and smell the pretty girls. Then we come out the south gate and it's straight up Dover to home."

Levi wrinkled his nose. A few of the privates liked the opportunity to live the high life with the Fobbits on Anaconda. They liked getting their Pizza Hut and gorging themselves on Dairy Queen, and a few would probably beg to stay long enough to go to the theater and watch a movie. Many of the guys, however, despised going anywhere near the huge base. The place was full of staff officers and senior NCOs with nothing better to do than play uniform police and check reflective belts. The whole roundabout trip would take forever. They'd be lucky if they returned to the FOB by ten and finished reconstituting their gear by midnight. With that scenario, it would be a miracle if they got four measly hours of sleep before waking up to do it all over again.

"The other plus side to that option," Lieutenant Michaels continued, "is that we can drop off the detainees right away when we get to the Anaconda side of the base. Have them swabbed right away for explosive residue. Check them in. Done. Not our problem anymore."

This idea sent chills through Levi. That option left no time to squirrel them away at O'Ryan to allow them to heal. If they took the prisoners back to O'Ryan to sit for a few days, any bruises and lacerations would have faded into signs of a simple struggle and nothing more by the time they took them to the main base. By that time, any complaints by the detainees would be the baseless and desperate pleadings of some bomb-setting terrorists who were looking at disappearing into the deep black abyss of America's infamous detention system.

"What's the other option?" Levi asked.

"Skip that little footbridge we crossed, follow the road here to Boa. Boa to Trouser, Trouser to Dover, Dover to home. Riskier, but quicker."

Levi whistled slowly. With that route, none of the roads before Dover were paved, and the dearth of patrolling in that area would mean IEDs could be hidden anywhere. But that route, as dangerous as it was, would get them home within ninety minutes. If they pushed it, they might get home before dark. Levi knew that with the long winter and recent rains, any IEDs that did lurk behind the road would be tough to spot before they hit them. On the other hand, if they did find something before it blew them to pieces, they had the bomb squad guys right there with them so they wouldn't have to wait. He squinted down the road at the detainees made of stone, at Nick and his slumped soldiers, at Hefti and the camera hanging from his vest, at Ott and Gassner staring him down.

The lieutenant said, "I'm inclined to hit the base, get a haircut, and let the guys get chow. What do you think?"

Levi turned back. *Mundum portamus,* he thought. "I think Annie got his bell rung by the IED pretty bad. He says he's okay, but he probably has a concussion. He's been puking and acting pretty lethargic." He took off his sunglasses and wiped them again, avoiding eye contact as he focused on the menial task. "As much as I'd love to let the guys get their milkshakes at Anaconda, I think we need to get home as soon as possible. Let Annie get checked out at the aid station, see what they say."

Lieutenant Michaels shook his head. "I was looking forward to my own milkshake. But it doesn't look like we have much choice in the matter. Looks like it's Boa." He pulled his leg inside the Humvee so he could close the door. "Get everyone mounted up. If we push, we'll be scratching our balls and playing Xbox by the time the sun goes down."

2.6 IF I NEVER SEE THE SUN SET AGAIN, IT WILL STILL BE TOO SOON

Nick took a knee by the Humvee and faced out toward Tampa so as to give the illusion of attentiveness. The IED blast and the subsequent hours of waiting, the drama in the hut, and the knowledge that the day was far from over left him drained. His adrenaline had waxed and waned so much during the day that all he wanted to do was curl up on the road and take a nap, to just put his head down for a few minutes and close his eyes. He sucked his CamelBak dry, but his mouth still felt stuffed with cotton. He was so busy fighting his pounding head, sour stomach, and general anger, that he didn't hear the first call to mount up.

"I said mount up," shouted Levi.

Hefti pushed closed the rear door of his Humvee, ensuring he didn't slam it on the teenager bound in the backseat.

Nick watched Levi stalk over to them. "Hey, Hefti," he said. "Didn't you know it's against General Order Number One to take photographs of detainees? Hand over that camera."

The airman looked honestly stunned, but he handed over the camera. "I had no idea," he said.

"You're no journalist, dude. You don't get to sit back and report on all this like some bystander." Levi looked at the images and pressed some buttons. "You brought a gun over here, not a camera. You don't have the privilege of pretending you had nothing to do with it all. You own this shit too."

The airman looked embarrassed and he said nothing as Levi handed his camera back.

When the young airman whispered, "Roger, Sergeant," Levi walked away.

Nick plodded along to his own truck and took his seat as driver. He stared out the front window with his hands at ten and two on the steering wheel. The glass was still cracked, but someone had cleaned off the dirt and soot. He didn't have great visibility, but he would at least be able to finish the mission.

Hooper shouted something down to him from the turret, but he didn't bother to respond. Jalaladin slept in the backseat with his head tilted back and his mouth hanging wide open. Weber the Mute sat in the backseat staring out his window. The LT and squad leaders conferred.

When they had finished, Gassner knocked on Nick's window. Nick opened the door.

"Turn around," Gassner said. "I'll spot you."

Without a word, Nick put the truck in reverse and waited while the other trucks did the same. In turn, each truck maneuvered forward and backward, forward and backward until they were turned around. When they were turned and once again in the lead, Gassner took his spot in the TC seat.

"Take us home," he said. "Tampa's blocked or something and there's another jam by Ad Dujayl, so head to Boa, then to Trouser, then Dover to home."

"Boa?" Nick said. "Are you serious?"

"That's what I said."

"So we can just get blown up again?"

"Hello? Were you with us today? You think Tampa's any better? No difference." He stared out the window. "Less traffic on Boa. Means sooner to chow."

"This is insane," Nick said.

"It was your boy Hartwig's idea."

Too frustrated, tired, and angry to get into it, Nick shook his head and drove.

He bumped along the canal road at about twenty-five miles per hour. Any faster on the rough terrain would bruise the forearms and ribs of all the gunners in the turrets. Not to mention, the lack of steering power would mean a certain loss of control if they went any faster. Hooper leaned back into his sling, which creaked under his weight with the swaying and bouncing of the Humvee.

After nearly fifteen minutes, Nick turned west onto Route Boa. He flipped down his visor to shield his eyes from the orange setting sun looming large on the horizon, but it did little good. The orange light glared off the cracks in the windshield, and the tall grasses lining the shoulders cast dark swaying shadows across the road. Nick drove as much by feel and memory as he did by sight. He pressed on the gas pedal. The engine whined. Nick gritted his teeth, stared straight ahead, and thought about cheeseburgers. Big fat American cheeseburgers. The kind Oma made at her tavern, so slimy the grease leaked through the paper used to wrap them.

The men rode in silence into the sunset, and the falling sun grew bigger and brighter as they drove, and finally, it burst in front of them.

The next thing Nick saw was the driver's seat, that is, the seat he had been sitting in. Flames licked at the seat, and the olive drab vinyl boiled and bubbled in front of him. The electronic countermeasures crushed his leg, and his driver's side door came to rest on the highway. He looked down at his chest and saw an arm, and the arm was not his own. The blast had torn the passenger's side door from the vehicle, and the opening poured thick black smoke into the air. Nick stared at the opening, catching glimpses of the orange sky during gusts of wind in which the smoke billowed away for less than a moment. He could not move, and he could not hear.

2.7 THIS IS GOING TO HURT

They had spent many hours crawling down the dusty canal roads. The monotony of it all, the slow pace, the lack of conversation, and the crash from the day's earlier adrenaline rush nearly caused Levi to fall asleep. He stretched as well as he could in such a small space, and he complained about being bored.

His driver, Specialist Pete White, looked over at him and nodded in commiseration, but he had nothing to say.

After Levi saw his best friend's Humvee disappear into a cloud of fire, dust, and gravel, both time and sound stopped, which left Tom Hooper flying through the air, suspended against a backdrop of smoke and flames, weightless and serene. His unbloused DCU-patterned pants were rumpled by the wind; his limbs were spread against the sky, one foot bootless but still covered by a green sock. Levi stared in wonder at his friend, who was not flying, but was simply the subject of a photograph, oblivious to his surroundings, or to gravity.

When Levi lurched forward because White had slammed on the brakes, time started again and Tom hit the gravel on the side of the road. Despite the height from which he fell, his form did not bounce, roll down the shallow embankment into the tall grass, or move in any way at all. He simply stopped when his body met resistance. Tom lay supine, staring up into the sky, one arm stretched out, the other seemingly twisted under his back. Levi looked left at White, but he only saw wide eyes and a moving mouth.

Levi turned to the side and fumbled with the steel handle of the heavy door. His gloved hand lifted and pulled on the lever, and he slammed his shoulder against the door. When his foot hit the ground, his ears opened again. He heard the blast wave echoing while something else whistled past his head. He set the other foot on the ground and Lieutenant Michaels appeared in front of him. Levi looked down and saw the lieutenant's palm outstretched on his vest.

He heard the LT yell, "Contact. Get down," and he watched helplessly as his own left hand thrust the officer's arm from in front of him while his right fist struck a blow to the man's chin, a blow that released the chinstrap on the LT's Kevlar and knocked him to the ground. He did not hit the man out of anger, but because he stood as an obstacle, and Levi would not be stopped.

He ran toward the cloud and the Humvee wreckage, and because time does not exist in combat, and because his legs were heavy and slow, he had the time to gawk at the squat palm trees sitting on the side of the path like overgrown pineapples. Because there was no time, he was able to take the time to see that Tom Hooper's eyes were wide open, his mouth was wide open, and he was dead. His arm was not twisted behind his back as Levi had thought, but instead, it was not there at all. He admired the orange horizon and the way the smoke went straight up into a shimmering column, the same way it had the night that he and Nick had graduated from high school.

With bottles of champagne and six-packs of Coors, Nick, Eris, and Levi spent the night at his dad's hunting cabin toasting the end of four years of veritable prison. They celebrated the beginning of adulthood and a new adventure. They started the bonfire just before dusk. They drank and smoked and the boys played their acoustic guitars while the smoke drifted into that orange sky. Eris swooned, and later, when Nick fell asleep on one of the two couches, Levi claimed the lone single bed. Eris climbed under the covers with Levi, and between the champagne and the beer, Levi thought that even though he had been too chicken and confused since he had met her freshman year, he might finally have enough courage to make something happen before life changed for all of them. But she was asleep within seconds, and he spent the night unable to sleep, acutely aware of every accidental touch, of every innocent brush of one of her silk kneecaps against his leg as she moved in her slumber. He was afraid to embrace her and too timid to wake her, but he spent the night hoping she would rise and touch him on purpose. He was a fool for thinking such things.

And at such a time as that.

As his steps pounded the gravel, as his rifle clanged against his thigh, as he marveled at the pineapple palm trees and the sky, and as he ignored what was going on around him, he was oddly aware that he was doing it again: daydreaming, that is. He knew full well that his mind was not present with his body, as was so often the case.

As Levi neared the truck, he heard a tumultuous crash. A great crack stung his ears and he felt the peal rumble through his stomach. He wondered why it would be thundering when there were no clouds in the sky. It was only after the second crack of thunder shook his head and nearly knocked him over that he realized it was not thunder at all; but rather, it was the warheads of rocket-propelled grenades exploding near the left side of the truck. With this realization came other realizations. The smaller cracks he had been ignoring were bullets snapping past him. The more sporadic and lower-pitched pops were rounds burning and exploding like popcorn in the rear of the Humvee. As he heard his own rapid panting and the hollow drumming of his heart inside his chest, he realized he wasn't bored anymore.

When he reached the truck and climbed up onto its side and looked down in the passenger's door to view the gruesome scene within, he realized that the wailing he heard was not coming from within the wreckage at all, but from Brody Gassner lying in the road in front of the Humvee. Gassner was stranded and he was pushing himself up with an elbow trying to sit up, but his left leg was shredded near the knee. He kept falling back. Blood pooled beneath him.

Levi glanced up and saw two bearded men prone in the long grasses nearly fifty meters away. They were firing AK-47s while a third man knelt a few feet from them, aiming what appeared to be his final rocket-propelled grenade. Levi jumped down the seven feet to the road. His legs buckled beneath him and he fell back onto his butt. He leaned his back against the flat bottom of the Humvee. He tried to get up again, to go get someone, but as soon as he was up, he dropped down again as he remembered that his reason for jumping down in the first place was because he needed cover. The RPG whooshed harmlessly over the Humvee with an arch too high for contact. It traveled into a grove of palm trees and disappeared without exploding. Levi closed his eyes and took three deep breaths to steel himself.

One of the front tires still burned. It poured a black column into the sky, but every few moments the wind shifted and sent the thick smoke down the road toward Gassner. Levi crawled toward the front of the Humvee and the burning tire, and he waited for another shift in the wind. The smoke wouldn't provide much of a screen, but it was all he had.

When he felt the early evening air blow against the sweat on the back of his neck, he waited three seconds for the smoke to move out ahead of him; then he ran toward his wounded comrade. Gassner drew in his breath, choked down his screams, widened his eyes, and held out his hands like an infant waiting to be picked up. Without a word, Levi ran behind him and pushed his own rifle to his side and underneath his armpit. He tucked his hands beneath the shoulders of Gassner's body armor and spun him around, watching the bone and shredded skin and muscle scrape against the gravel as he turned his torso. Levi pulled as hard as he could. He shuffled backward in a crouch toward the cover of the Humvee.

The collar of Gassner's body armor pulled up into his throat and all he could manage were a few gulping whimpers as he was pulled violently across the gravel. A crater bigger than any foxhole Levi had ever dug in training spread across the north side of the road. Levi aimed for this hole in the earth, which had been created by the blast that had blown the Humvee on its side. When they reached the blast crater, Levi dragged Gassner down into it. He let go of his vest, and Gassner's head dropped onto the dirt.

He climbed out and hustled to the back of the Humvee. He took a knee in a position where he could look up the road for his platoon while also looking around the truck's rear corner to survey the enemy. One gunner up the road engaged the enemy in the opposite direction. The other two fired in the direction of the three men Levi had spotted in the grass.

After looking up the road, Levi peered around the truck. His breathing was shallow and rapid, his heart soared, he could not articulate a thought, and he could not name which cardinal direction was which. From his low vantage point, Levi could see dirt kicking up in the grass from the firing of the heavy fifties. He scanned the field, trying to pinpoint where he had last seen the men.

As he scanned left, a man dressed in a black salwar kameez popped up and ran through the grass toward him. Levi brought his rifle to his shoulder, closed his left eye, and peered through his ACOG with his right. At first, he could see nothing through his scope but the grass field shaking. He opened both eyes and looked over his scope again and pointed it toward the man. Through the magnification of his optics, he could see the look of terror on the man's face. Although he was bearded, giving him the appearance of age from a distance, Levi's scope revealed his soft skin and delicate neck. Levi squeezed his trigger. After he had fired his third round, he realized his eyes were closed.

When he opened them and looked over the barrel of his rifle, he saw that the man was still running toward him. He held an AK-47 in one hand at his side, both his arms flailing as he ran. He kept looking up the road at the heavy machine guns that fired into the field at him. The young man hadn't even seen Levi yet, and with everything else going on, he hadn't noticed that Levi had fired at him and missed. Levi took a deep breath, exhaled, and held it. He looked through his optic once more and aimed for center mass. He pulled the trigger with just the pad of his index finger, slowly, not allowing himself to be surprised by the shot. He remembered his fundamentals. The shot went high and Levi saw the man's head pop back as if he had just taken a jab to the nose. As the man fell and turned, Levi saw the gaping hole in the back of his head. He let his breath explode out of his mouth in a rush, astonished. A sudden wave of euphoria consumed him and he looked around, wondering if anyone had seen his shot.

He did another quick scan of the field. Then he unclipped his rifle and leaned it against the Humvee. He grabbed one of the heavy cargo rings on its bumper. He wanted to take advantage of the covering fire from the gun trucks as he once again began scaling the Humvee to enter through the passenger door in case maybe, just maybe, someone in that mess of blood and limbs was still alive. He hadn't gotten halfway up when Gassner caught his eye, and he noticed the blood still leaking from his leg.

He dropped down and ran back to him, sliding down into the crater on his bottom. He cursed himself for wasting valuable time with indecision. He looked at Gassner's right shoulder and didn't see the combat action tourniquet that was supposed to be there according to their unit SOP. "Gassner," he yelled. "Where's your CAT?"

The only response was a wide-eyed stare accompanied by Gassner's incessant bawling.

"Your CAT, Gassner. Your tourniquet. Where is it?"

He rolled Gassner onto his side so he could access the first aid kit attached to the side of his vest. He breathed a sigh of relief when he saw the tourniquet inside. It meant he would not have to use his own, which he very well may have needed sooner rather than later. He ripped open the plastic, undid the Velcro, and loosened it enough to slide it to the middle of Gassner's thigh. Levi had to lift a piece of mangled muscle to get the tourniquet up the leg. He was not as much surprised at the slickness of the mangled flesh as he was by how cold and lifeless it already felt. When he had the tourniquet a few inches up onto what remained of Gassner's leg, he stopped.

Before he started tightening, he thought back to their pre-deployment time at Great Plains Joint Training Center in Salina, Kansas. While going through Combat Lifesaver class, Levi, Nick, White, Hooper, Gassner, and even the LT played a game with their devices. They had each cranked their own tourniquets onto their legs as tightly as they could until they could no longer bear the pain, the twisting of their skin, the pulling of their body hair, and the total occlusion of their blood vessels. The first person to say Uncle lost and had to buy drinks that night. Levi did not lose, but it was a Pyrrhic victory. He had a deep cherry bruise for weeks, which made him wish that he had lost.

In the crater he told Gassner, "This is going to hurt," and as he cranked the windlass, he realized how stupid he sounded telling a man without a leg that a tourniquet would hurt. He twisted until he could twist no more and until the stream of blood turned into a trickle and then an ooze, before finally, it stopped.

Gassner screamed. It was shrill and it was loud. He only stopped to take a breath so he could continue screaming.

Levi stood and grabbed Gassner under his shoulders. "Shut up," he said. He propped Gassner's back up against the side of the crater so he nearly sat upright while still enjoying the scant cover provided by the hole and the Humvee behind it. "Quit screaming, okay?" He looked down at Gassner's nine mil holster, but was not surprised to see that the weapon was no longer there. He climbed up out of the hole and scooted over to grab his own rifle, which was still leaning against the Humvee. He thought to himself as he moved to grab it, I'm an idiot. God, why am I such an idiot? He jumped back down and unholstered his own pistol for Gassner. He looked up at the Humvee and changed his mind. He placed his rifle in Gassner's lap instead, taking his hand and forcing it around the grip for him. "Shut up and take this," he said. "I'll be right back."

Gassner shook his head with wide eyes. "I don't wanna go out like this. Not like this," he screamed.

"Shut up," Levi screamed back. "Just shut up. You're not going out. Do you understand me? Your leg is gone, but you're not dying. Okay? Now take this. You can still shoot. Now shut up and watch this sector." Levi leaned over him and placed his own face next to Gassner's to see if he could see over the edge. He had a clear line of sight for twenty meters ahead, up until the tall grasses fanned out before the grove of palm trees.

"I don't want to."

"I don't care what you want," Levi hissed into his face. "You're getting out of here today. Look out this way. Shoot anything that moves. Anything. You hear me?"

Levi ran around to the back side of the Humvee again and peered around. The gun trucks had shifted their fire farther east, but Levi didn't see anyone in the field. He waited a moment to see if anyone would pop up again, and when he saw no one, he took the opportunity to heave himself back onto the truck.

He choked on the smoke pouring up out of the door. The overwhelming smell of burnt barbecue stung his nose. He covered his mouth with his shemagh, lay prone, and peered down inside. He saw Nick directly below him. He was crumpled against the driver's door, a severed arm on his chest. His eyes were open, but they did not see. He opened and closed his mouth, like a fish, but slowly. He blinked. One leg was twisted under the radio and Duke, both of which had come detached from the mount. The other leg stuck nearly straight up, across the seat. The leg of his pants was black, charred, and still smoking.

An opening at the back hatch allowed visible flames to lick at the backseats. The popping of the extra ammunition had slowed, but each occasional burst made Levi wince and jump, hoping he would not get caught by fragments from the rounds. Chunks of deep red flesh and muscle stuck to the ceiling of the Humvee.

Two bodies huddled in the back against the rear door that now served as the vehicle's floor. Their interpreter lay on top facing down. Private Weber, who hadn't said a word until today, embraced Jellybean and stared up without blinking, his mouth agape, his flesh a sickly gray. Levi knew they were both dead, although how he knew, he could not then articulate. Nearly hyperventilating, and not sure what to do, he lay there in another moment of indecision. He straightened his helmet and pulled on a strap near the temple to tighten his chinstrap. He thought, Oh God, how do I do this? How do I do this God how do I do this God oh God how do I do this? He could not speak; he was breathing so fast and so hard.

2.8 IT WASN'T SO MUCH A CRISIS OF FAITH AS IT WAS A BAPTISM BY FIRE

The Sunday before Nick and Levi had left for their deployment, Uncle Thomas had asked them if they'd be willing to come to the front of his church to receive a blessing and a prayer before they went on their way. Levi excused himself by citing his integrity and his need to live an intellectually honest life, but Nick, of course, agreed.

Many of the faces in the church were the same faces he had left behind when he had joined, only now they were older, many of them sallow. There were very few new members, that is to say, young members. On his way in, Nick greeted the members of his old church family and politely smiled at the equivocal comments, noting just how much he had changed.

The night before the service, Uncle Thomas had given Nick the choice between several passages which invariably called down curses upon God's enemies and called for victory and vengeance for His people. No doubt the preacher's intentions were good with Nick going to war and all, but the crusading Psalms he had cited always made Nick uncomfortable; and though he had always believed such violent musings somehow fit into the larger plan of divine justice, retribution, et cetera, Nick preferred to leave the reconciliation between law and gospel to the theologians—or better yet, to the Judge himself. As an alternative, he requested something more uplifting and reassuring.

The next morning, he made his way to the front of the church and knelt under Uncle Thomas's long shaking fingers. As a result of Nick's discomfiture with the very book he professed, all 233 members in attendance at Immanuel Lutheran Church's early service heard Uncle Thomas provide a divine promise of Nick's safety with the words of Holy Scripture. He heard the old preacher intone the dismal and foreboding, yet strangely reassuring words from the ninety-first Psalm: "A thousand shall fall at thy side, and ten thousand at thy right hand; but it shall not come nigh thee."

Such memories are only recognized as significant in rewrites and retrospect. That is, if they hold any significance at all. But those words of promise did spring bitterly to the front of Nick's mind as he fought against gravity and the weight of the destroyed equipment pinning him into the burning truck.

When the smoke began entering his lungs and when the flames crept closer to his legs, increasingly desperate words flew forth from his soul. He called upon the name of his God, because this surely was his day of trouble. Yet, the longer he waited for rescue, the more frantic he became.

The flames reached his pants and they burned. They reached his sleeve and it, too, burned. Pain does not begin to describe a broken femur, compound fractures, and flames biting at every inch of exposed skin. Nick gave up on rescue and simply prayed for death. When this did not come, his previous reluctance to curse his enemies disappeared. As each second of the blinding, bleeding, blistering pain of hellfire stretched into what felt like years, other words, imprecatory words sprung to his lips. He had no compunction when he begged for the complete destruction of that place, that feigning whore Babylon. He had no regret when he cried out a prayer that their wives would be widows and all their children would be dashed against the stones.

And later, when he could no longer fight, when he could stand the flames no longer, and when he still had not been saved, blackness edged into his vision and closed in. The darkness did not overtake him until one sad, final question fell from his lips: "My God, my God, why hast thou forsaken me?"

2.9 SHOOT ANYTHING THAT MOVES

Although each detail entrenched itself indelibly in his mind, as if he had spent hours staring at a picture of the scene, the time Levi spent surveying the inside of the Humvee could not have taken more than a second. Rather than spinning around to lower himself feet first, after his quick glance inside, he shoved off and pushed himself through the door head first. He instantly regretted it as he was unprepared to brace himself. He fell onto the radio, unable to find anything to hold onto as he plunged into the flaming truck. His neck twisted, and his helmet tilted and smashed onto his nose. He cursed and squirmed back up so he still leaned in face first, but now he locked himself into position by hooking his feet onto the bottom outside of the truck. He knew he would not have enough leverage in this position to pull Nick out, but it was the only way to reach him.

The radio did not prove difficult. He picked up the box and slid it back so it came to rest immediately behind the driver's seat. He had no real room, but he set to work pulling the heavy Duke off Nick's leg. The large electronic countermeasures console was wedged under the steering wheel, and Levi grew frustrated as he dropped it onto Nick's twisted leg again. He couldn't get it out of the space.

He forced himself to breathe, to think. If it fit in, it will fit out, he thought. He repeated this in his head as he struggled. If it fit, it will fit. If it fit, it will fit. He picked up the Duke again. He turned it and squeezed to keep it from slipping through his gloved hands. Gravity worked against him, but he finally had a chance. With nowhere to put it, he had no choice but to muscle it to the backseat. He winced as he let it drop onto the dead men.

When Levi looked down and saw the white bone sticking out of Nick's thigh, he furrowed his brows and scrunched up his face. Oh Annie, he thought. Oh Annie, you're all busted, Annie.

He stretched to pick up the arm. It was slick and the blood was cooler than the air in the burning Humvee. That coldness made it seem unreal in the same way Gassner's mangled leg had felt unreal. He knew by the freckled skin and thick curly hair, by the stubby fingernails chewed to nothing, by the garish gold ring on its pinkie finger, and by the sheer size, the sheer girth of it that it was Tom Hooper's arm. He looked in the back again to see if perhaps the bodies had moved, had reanimated. The thought crossed his mind to toss the arm in the back with the Duke, but thinking that those who loved Tom would want all of him, he turned and threw the arm up and out of the Humvee. When he looked back down at Nick, he saw that his eyes had closed.

Fighting back tears, he slid his hands under Nick's vest at the armpits. He contracted every muscle in his body and pulled with all his might, nearly bending Nick in half to raise his torso to a point where he could gain more leverage. As he pulled, he repeated to himself, don't care if it hurts. Don't care if it hurts. It was both a command to himself and an apology to his friend. Nick's neck twisted as his head rubbed against the ceiling of the truck, and when Levi could, he pushed him to the left so he rested on the side of the driver's seat.

With Nick's center of gravity higher in the truck, Levi backed himself out the door. He then climbed in feet first and was able to stand with his feet on the transmission tunnel. He squatted down and grabbed Nick's body armor again. He stood, trying to lift Nick's chest to his own, but he lost his grip and the dead weight slumped back down. Nick's right leg, however, had slipped back down behind him in the process. It no longer stuck out in front of him to impede his progress.

All Levi could hear was his own breathing, shallow, fast, and painful. Everything hurt. One lift, he told himself. One lift. One lift. One lift. He grabbed hold again and pulled his friend up. He had him in a near-standing position with Nick's legs hanging dead beneath him. Levi forced one of his arms under Nick's armpit when he had him up high enough. This allowed him to crouch down again to put his shoulder into Nick's chest. He pressed him against the ceiling of the Humvee to keep him from falling. While he had him pressed against the ceiling, he wrapped his arms around his waist and lifted him another foot. Nick's head was at the opening while Levi's face was buried at his waist.

When Levi locked his hands around Nick's hamstrings, he felt the charred edges of pants, the heat of bare peeling skin, and the slickness of blood and other fluids. He gagged at the touch and then coughed against the thick black smoke. He flexed his burning thighs one more time, trying to squat him up further. The weight was too much and the quarters were too cramped to lift him in any substantive way, but still, Nick rose. Levi almost tried pulling him down to keep him from floating away, but then he heard a voice, an American voice.

Lieutenant Michaels shouted down at him, "Let him go."

Levi cried back, "No. Don't let him go."

Once again the LT shouted down. "Hartwig, let him go. I got him. Let him go."

"Oh," Levi said. "Oh oh oh," he said, realizing that it was help. "Take him. Yeah, get him," he yelled.

He crouched down even farther, trying to force himself into the foot well so there would be room to pull Nick out. He slapped Nick's feet as they passed his face, and he laughed. They were getting him out. He coughed. When Nick's body had cleared the doorway, he took one last glance at Private Weber's blank eyes and open mouth, one last look at Jalaladin's inert form, and he stood up. He gasped at the fresh air and kicked his feet until he found something to step on. He pressed himself out of the doorway. He clawed at the side of the Humvee to pull himself up faster.

White had driven Levi's truck to the south side of the Humvee, blocking it from the field of fire. Another victor had blocked the north side. The other Archer vehicle stayed down the east side of the road with the EOD truck in the direction from which they had come. The LT dragged Nick to the edge of the Humvee and lowered him down to White, who carried him in a bear hug for several feet before laying him on the ground between the vehicles next to the crater and the platoon medic, who was already tending to Gassner.

Levi knelt on all fours on top of the Humvee coughing. He hacked so violently, he felt he would puke.

Lieutenant Michaels knelt beside him. "Are you okay?"

Levi shook his head as he coughed.

"Let me rephrase, Soldier. Are you going to live?"

Levi nodded, crawled to the edge of the Humvee, and lowered himself down to the ground, dropping the last few feet. The area between the Humvees teemed with activity. The platoon medic knelt between the two wounded men. He already had an IV in Gassner's arm and was working on sticking Nick. White bent over Nick's leg. He bandaged and splinted the gruesome broken bone. The LT placed his knees on either side of Nick's head while he jammed a pharyngeal airway in his nose.

Levi walked around the far side of them and down into the crater to retrieve his rifle. When he climbed out of the hole he asked, "Did anyone call a MEDEVAC?"

No one answered.

He yelled again, "Has anyone called a MEDEVAC?"

In the midst of their own shouting at one another, they didn't hear him, or chose not to respond. Levi secured his rifle back to the wolf clip at his shoulder and ran around to his truck on the south side. He opened the TC door. "Ott," he said. "Anyone call a MEDEVAC?"

Ott looked over, but didn't say anything.

Am I invisible? Levi thought. "Private Ott," he yelled. "Did someone call a MEDEVAC?"

Ott nodded. "Yeah. One-Six Delta's on it."

Levi slammed the door and turned to walk back to the victims, but Lieutenant Michaels cut him off. "Hartwig, grab Ott. That field to the south is the only spot that will work as an LZ here. You'll have the gunners on over watch, but it's just you two dismounted, so do your best. Basically, clear the bodies on the landing zone, do a quick scan, and wave 'em in." The LT bent over and tucked an MBITR radio into his cargo pocket. "Here," he said. "Take a second radio so you can talk to both me and the bird."

Levi nodded, glad to have a task on which to focus. He ran to the other side of the Humvee and opened the door to find Ott still sitting in the driver's seat, spitting tobacco juice into a bottle. The dazed troop stared out the windshield.

"Let's go, Ott. We need to clear the LZ and bring in the MEDEVAC."

Ott nodded, wiped his pointy white nose, and twisted the cap back onto his spit bottle. He grabbed a package of M&M'S from above the visor and put them in his pocket. He put his hands on the steering wheel and took a deep breath.

"Now, Ott. Let's get a move on," Levi said.

"Who else is going?"

"Just us. Let's move."

Ott grabbed his rifle, which was sitting next to him on the transmission tunnel. "The two of us clearing some huge field of elephant grass by ourselves? What sense does that make?"

Levi wanted to hit him to wake him up. He wanted to yell at him that the time for questioning orders was over. He wanted to blast him with obscenities, remind him that he was a soldier, and remind him who was in charge. But if Levi wanted the job done right, he needed Ott onboard. He needed him to understand the situation. Levi grabbed his arm and yanked him out of the Humvee.

He pointed around the scene. "In case you haven't noticed, we just lost five guys. Three guys are manning guns. Two guys are helping Doc with the casualties. The EOD guys are taking care of the detainees you beat up, and they'll have to get to that hole to do a post-blast investigation as soon as we can get Gassner, Nick, and the bodies out of there. We have the rest trying to save some lives. Everyone is doing a job. We still need 360-degree security, which means two guys watching north, two guys watching east, and two guys watching west. Which leaves how many guys to clear the LZ to the south?"

Ott looked around and started moving his lips as if he were counting to himself.

"Two, numbnuts. It leaves two. You and me. So that's what sense it makes. So shut your trap and get on line. Fifty meter spacing. We walk out to that tree line. Walk along the line doing a quick scan into the trees and then head back down the center. We check out all bodies. I know for a fact there is at least one here. You see a body, call me over and we clear it together. If it's in the LZ or in the path to the LZ, we drag it out. One guy drags it; the other stands watch. Got it?"

Ott spit on the ground and looked up at Levi like he was crazy.

"Got it?" Levi shouted.

"Roger," he whispered.

"Good," Levi said as he looked out into the field. "And a little sense of urgency from now on." He waited until Ott had walked down the road far enough, and once he was on line, Levi waded out into the thigh-high grass. With the way the setting sun shone on the grass, Levi could see the shadows at the end of the field where a single line of trampled grass coming out of the tree line signified the path of their attackers. The path stopped near the dead center of the field where he had first spotted them from the top of the Humvee. He could see the outline of two bodies in the grass at the center of the field. He knew that he would find another body, a young bearded male with a massive head wound, about fifteen to twenty meters to the left of center. He veered off his due-south path so he could find the body he knew was his. He knew it was there; he knew it was dead and posed no threat; but he felt he had to see it, had to see what his own hands had done.

As he neared the place where the body lay, he glanced over to see if Ott was still on line. Ott had done a good job of staying west and not moving ahead or falling behind, but he was in a trance, looking only at the ground and grasses in front of his own two feet. Levi paused when he reached the spot where he remembered the body falling. He looked around and saw nothing. The undisturbed grass in front of him swayed in the cool breeze as the sun sunk ever lower in the sky.

He turned around and scanned where he had come from. It had to be there. He had shot a man and seen him die. Then the man fell. There was no way he could have crawled off, and the grass wasn't so high that he'd be invisible. Or could he have crawled off? Levi turned in a full circle. He scanned the field.

Levi panicked. He imagined the worst-case scenario. It was possible that his shot hadn't been the direct hit he thought it was. It could have grazed the man's head or simply gone through part of the man's brain without damaging him. Levi had read stories about men walking into emergency rooms with hunting knives through their eyeballs and brains without suffering any ill effects. The man could be alive out there in the grass, lying in wait with his AK-47.

Realizing that it was futile to stand there spinning in circles, he turned south again toward the trees. He picked up his pace to get back on line with Ott. Why was Ott just staring at his feet? He's not clearing much like that, Levi thought as he scanned left and right and forward, letting his eyes run over the sea of green. He looked for varying shades and shadows and shapes.

The instant he allowed himself to question Ott, his foot caught on something that tripped him up. He did not fall, but he stumbled forward, and as he turned his head to look at what had tripped him, he glimpsed—out of the corner of his eye—a man staring up at him. His beating heart stilled and he regained his balance in an instant. He pivoted and he raised his rifle as he turned. When he had squared up on the man in the grass, a million thoughts went through his mind at once: He didn't crawl away after all; he's right here in front of me; wait this isn't the same guy; he's a lot farther into this field than I remember; he's moving; he's moving; that's an AK on the ground; he's going to kill me; his eyes are wide open because he's scared; his eyes are wide open because he's dead; he's moving; if he wasn't dead before, he's dead now.

And yet, before a single one of those thoughts had time to travel through his varying levels of consciousness, adrenaline and fear had driven him to squeeze the trigger of his M4 three times in quick succession, sending three bullets toward the lifeless chest of the man on the ground. The man's chest swallowed the bullets; the body absorbed them without bouncing or jumping with the impact.

When Levi realized what he had done, he cursed under his breath. He looked around, knowing everyone would have heard the shots. He looked over his shoulder at Ott, who had dropped to a knee and raised his own rifle. The LT's voice came over the radio and he reached down to his cargo pocket. He pulled out the radio. When he had it up and out, he realized that the frantic voice was coming over the radio in the pouch on the back of his vest, not the one in his hand. He shoved the radio back into his pocket and tried reaching around to grab the radio on his vest, which he rarely used.

"Archer Three-Six report. Archer Three-Six."

Levi blindly fumbled with the snap buttons that held it in the pouch.

The voice on the other end of the radio grew more frantic. "Levi, come in. What's going on?"

Levi finally got the radio out. "Archer One-Six, this is Three-Six. All good here. One enemy dead."

Levi jumped as he heard footsteps behind him. "I'd say he's dead," said Ott.

"He moved," said Levi.

"I don't think he's moved for a while," said Ott, before spitting on the body.

"Shut your face. He moved." Levi put his radio away. "Watch him for me; I'm going to clear him." Levi tucked his slung rifle under his armpit so he could kneel.

"Watch him for what? To make sure he doesn't move again?" He snorted as he pulled out a can of dip and snapped his wrist so his index finger smacked against the can.

Levi knew he looked foolish. He knelt down anyway and made a show of patting the dead man down in a search for papers, actionable intelligence, or possible booby traps. After they had dragged him off to the side where no one going to or from the MEDEVAC could trip on him, Levi pointed out the other two bodies. His plan for a semi-orderly clearance of the landing zone had deteriorated. It had turned into Levi huffing and puffing as he dragged bodies from the center of the field to the outside edge while Ott dawdled behind him, more for show than anything else.

When they had finished with the bodies, they walked side by side to the tree line. There was still plenty of ambient light in the open, but Levi wasn't sure they'd be able to see further than a few feet into the forest of palm trees and weeds even if the sun hung high. He unclipped a SureFire flashlight from his vest and shone it into the trees to no avail. Ott said nothing. *Screw it,* Levi thought. He got on the radio and called it clear, but it wouldn't have mattered. The bird needed to land and was nearly there. Levi pushed Ott out to the southwest corner of the field. Levi took the northwest corner and waited.

White ran a few steps into the field. He threw a smoke grenade in a high arch. The spoon flew off and bright purple smoke began pouring out of the spinning grenade before it hit the ground. The purple smoke floated into the air and merged with the deep reds and oranges of the dusky sky.

The LT emerged from behind the wrecked Humvee and began pointing and shouting, offering further direction to those aiding the wounded. Levi forced himself to turn around, to focus on his sector, to do his job. The thought crossed his mind that the battle was over. Those brave enough to stay and fight were dead. Those too scared to fight were long gone. Yet, he would not allow himself to grow complacent. He thought of how quickly so many had been lost. It had all happened in one apocalyptic trumpet blast, in a flash, in the twinkling of an eye. They had not expected it.

He looked at his watch. It had only been twelve minutes since the IED detonated on Nick's truck. Something could happen again at any time.

He forced himself to pay attention, to look for threats, to keep his mind from wandering and imagining. He served as the watchman and protector. He did not allow himself the luxury of looking over his shoulder as they brought his friend to the edge of the road on a litter. Even as the helicopter roared behind him and threatened to blow him over, he kept his eyes on the tree line and on the field. Even as the helicopter carrying his friend lifted away, he vowed not to look inward. From now on, he would keep his eyes out, where they belonged.

It was only after the lieutenant called him back over the radio that he allowed himself to turn around again. By then, the helicopter was gone, the night was still, and there was nothing left of the sun.

After reaching the road, he broke into another coughing fit and collapsed to all fours. When he stopped coughing, he turned and sat down with his back against the tire of a Humvee. He leaned his head back and closed his eyes.

"Hey, Sergeant Hartwig," he heard. He didn't want to open his eyes again. He didn't want to be Sergeant Hartwig. He just wanted to rest, to be Levi for a few hours.

"Sergeant Hartwig, c'mon."

He didn't want to go anywhere, but he opened his eyes.

White held out a bottle of water. Levi shook his head back and forth. White raised his eyebrows in concern. "I don't want you to go into shock, Sar'nt."

Levi laughed. He was going to tell him it was too late. He started coughing again.

White knelt down.

"What are you doing?" Levi asked.

"Nothing, Sar'nt."

"Why are you just kneeling there?"

White said nothing, making it obvious he would not depart from Levi's side.

"Just give me a minute."

"I have time."

"You'll be waiting a while."

"I abide," said White.

Levi stared at the slow stream of smoke still coming out of the turret of the Humvee tipped over in front of him. He brought a shaking hand to his mouth and started chewing hard on the corner of a fingernail.

"Sergeant Hartwig, please don't do that," White said. "Don't chew on your fingers. Hold out your hands."

"Huh?"

"Hold out your hands. Please. Just for a second."

Levi held out his shaking hands.

White opened the bottle of water and poured some on Levi's hands. "Now rub them together."

Levi did as he was told. As he rubbed them together, White poured more water on them. Levi watched the blood rinse off into the road. He looked up at White, who was nodding at him in encouragement.

"That's right," White said.

Levi rubbed his hands together harder. He took his thumbnails and scraped at the brown that had dried on the back of his hands. White pulled another bottle of water from his cargo pocket and he continued washing the blood off Levi's hands.

When the second bottle was gone, Levi looked at his pants and saw that they, too, were covered in blood. "Guess I can't dry my hands on my pants, huh?" he said, trying to force a laugh. He shook them off and looked into White's eyes. "Thank you."

He spread his legs and lifted his knees. He rested his arms on them, folding his hands between them. He bowed his head. He breathed deeply, trying to stop his shaking. He closed his eyes, but felt dizzy and nauseous so he opened them again. *You can do this,* he thought. Just a few more hours. A few more hours, God. A few hours.

White nudged him and tempted him with a cigarette.

Levi shook his head. He closed his eyes and eased himself up. When he opened them, the world shook under his feet. He looked down at White, who still knelt while cupping and lighting his cigarette. "Screw it. I got time for one." He sat back down and took a cigarette.

He pulled deeply from it and watched the cherry glow and change shades of orange.

"What brand do you usually smoke?" asked White.

"This is fine," Levi said. He knew what White was doing. He was just trying to keep him talking. Keep him from getting too deep into himself.

"Man, I'm hungry. You hungry?"

Levi grunted.

"I can't wait to get out of this hellhole. Get back to real work."

Levi didn't say anything.

"I'm a horticulturist," said White.

Levi laughed. "Horticulture? Is that code for something? You grow bud back home?"

White smiled, as if he had heard all this before. "No, actually. May sound strange, but I think that a well-maintained lawn is an incredible work of art. There's so much that goes into it. I'd like to be a groundskeeper for a ball club someday. I think keeping the field for a pro baseball team would be my dream job."

Levi didn't respond, lost in his own thoughts. He wished someone would have tried harder to talk him out of all this.

"What about you, Sergeant Hartwig?"

"What about me?" he mumbled.

"What do you do in your civilian life?"

Levi shook his head and let out a single bitter laugh. "I don't have a civilian life. I dropped out of college and joined the active duty army in a fit of stupidity after 9/11 so I could go to Afghanistan. Wasted away in garrison for my first two years learning how bad the real army sucks. Details, CQ duty, drills, training, the whole bit, but no real work. After I realized my mistake, I enrolled in school again and took night classes. Then I heard from my mom that the National Guard unit from back home was headed over to Afghanistan. I called up a recruiter and told him I had joined to go to Afghanistan, not to do details for two years. He told me that it would be no problem. All I had to do was take the remaining time on my commitment, double it, and I could be off active duty and in the Guard in no time."

"So you did it then?"

"It was a no-brainer. I'd get to do what I came in to do so it wasn't all a waste, and with the one-weekend-a-month gig, I'd still have the money and time to finish my last year of school when I got back from Afghanistan. And here we are. In Iraq." He laughed, which made him cough again. He leaned over and spit. "So I guess I'm here because I was tricked. Or because I'm an idiot. Fool me once, shame on you. Fool me twice, shame on me. Right?"

White had no response except, "That sucks."

Levi nodded and thought, yeah it does. It does suck. And it sucks worse that I had to drag Annie along with me for all of it, and now he's dying in some field hospital in the middle of Iraq.

2.10 THEY SHALL BEAR THEE UP
IN THEIR HANDS

Nick was not in fact dying, but he did not know this. He felt no corporeal sensation because he was under the influence of heavy sedation after his first emergency surgery, although he would later determine the sedatives and painkillers were not nearly enough. He had the airy feeling that he was now a weightless ethereal being, floating through time and space while simultaneously existing independent of both. What he actually felt was his litter moving along the Balad Air Base flight line from the field ambulance to the waiting C-17 aircraft, a litter that was flanked by a physician's assistant and a cart containing various monitors, fluids, and medical apparatuses. Two air force financial officers, a navy chaplain, and a marine helicopter mechanic, who all believed volunteering to move casualties was a much better use of their down time than was flamenco night at the morale tent, carried his litter with all the pitying intensity they could muster.

Because both Nick's eardrums had blown, he could not register the roar of the propellers, the yelling of the loadmasters, and the bustling of the medical technicians and field nurses who swarmed around him as soon as his litter was lifted and locked into its position in the rear of the plane's cargo bay. This deafness kept him from grounding himself in any sort of physical reality, despite his progressive cognitive awakening. It also kept him from hearing the voices of the entire host of heaven singing praises to his Lord, which he had expected to hear now that he was dead. Of course, neither did he hear the weeping and gnashing of teeth.

The sudden realization that he was a conscious, sentient being with no physical perception sent him into a deep and shocking moment of total despair in which he believed he had been cut off and cast into the depths of a dark and limitless Sheol, where he feared he would languish indefinitely, or worse, eternally. This moment soon passed as he became aware of the burning in his throat and the tube pulling at the corner of his mouth. He struggled to open his eyes, but he found himself stuck in a painful form of sleep paralysis. This paralysis, although initially preferable to his moment of disembodiment, soon became a veritable living hell because he could feel his muscles flexing, but he could not move them; he could feel his heart pounding with his growing anxiety, but he could not breathe as he wished; he could feel a distinct pressure on the lower half of his body that did not reach a level he considered painful, but it was odd and unexpected and, therefore, no less terrifying; and he could feel his eyes scraping rapidly back and forth behind his eyelids, but they, too, burned and he could not open them.

After a thousand years of this tribulation, his eyes opened to a flood of light. He was not in a Humvee, he was not on the side of a gravel road by a grove of palm trees, and he was not in his plywood bedroom nestled deep in an old ammo bunker. He found himself in a gray cylinder with a trough of white fluorescent lights extending above his body. The lights shone into his stinging eyes, which he would not close for fear that they would remain so.

He tried turning his neck, but could not. He rolled his eyes and turned them to the left. He saw a woman rushing toward him with her own eyes wide open and frantic. She opened her mouth and yelled over her shoulder without making a sound. She put her face next to his and moved her lips and nodded her head. She took a step backward and tapped a hypodermic needle. Her mouth was tight and she had permanent wrinkles around her lip, the kind that come from smoking. She wore a tan flight suit and her dark hair was pulled into a severe bun. She wore no makeup and her cheeks were haggard. She was not aesthetically pleasing, but she was beautiful. Nick realized with a growing euphoria and rapid drowsiness that although he was not dead, he was nevertheless in the company of angels.

2.11 THE SWORD OF DAMOCLES

The men of Archer platoon did not crack jokes or whoop it up as they rolled into the gate of FOB O'Ryan. Their minds did not immediately wander to chow, video games, and showers. Crickets and charging handles made the only sounds as they cleared their weapons. Levi stood in the dark, shining his flashlight into the chambers of his men's rifles when all he wanted was sleep.

After the MEDEVAC took off, they had spent another six hours on Route Boa. Using chains and two Humvees to pull, they had been able to bring the flipped truck off its side and back onto what was left of its tires. It didn't take them long to find that the vehicle was beyond towing. The hull had been breached and the rear wheel well had been completely destroyed. After extricating Weber and Jalaladin and sealing them in body bags, they had no choice but to wait for battalion to send out a wrecker.

Now, after all they had been through, they got word to form up in front of the TOC so the commander could see and debrief them. And what did that mean anyway? Did a man who sat in a secure building watching Predator drone feeds while annoying the radio operator for updates really know something that they didn't about what had transpired? About what they had been through? What could he possibly tell them that would make it okay?

The lieutenant walked up to Levi before they mounted up again. Levi wasn't sure if his face was already bruising from the blow he had inflicted or if the dark spot on his face was nothing more than soot or dirt. Levi put his head down, not in the mood for the chewing out that was sure to come. "Lead us home, Hartwig. I told the old man he could brief us down there."

Levi looked up from the ground. It was as if the young officer had read his mind.

"He didn't much care for that idea, I don't think, but he's not in much of a position to argue. Have to take what I can get, right?"

"Roger that, sir."

They silently stopped at the fuel point. At the old bunker they called home, they went through all the motions they always did. They doffed their body armor, but the near weightlessness that came with its absence left them unfulfilled. The drivers backed the Humvees into their parking spots with the aid of spotters so they were ready to leave at the first call. They washed their windshields. They gathered their MRE wrappers, spit bottles, and bottles of sunflower seeds and threw them in the trash. They wordlessly carried their weapons, helmets, and body armor into the bunker.

Sergeant Havens held the door open. As the men passed, he muttered bromides like, "Keep your heads up, guys," and, "Tomorrow's another day."

When Levi passed and looked up to make eye contact, Sergeant Havens didn't say a word. Their interaction, or lack thereof, left Levi's imagination to run wild with all the ways the platoon sergeant was judging him, all the ways he was regretting that he didn't put up a bigger fight that morning when the LT had promoted Levi for the day, and all the ways he could have kept the same thing from happening. But Sergeant Havens was too polite to say all those terrible things aloud, so he simply nodded.

Each man retreated to his own bed, little private caves of plywood. Staff Sergeant Roper, the sick truck commander Levi had replaced that day, leaned against the frame outside his own room. Roper held a hand over his stomach and he wore a frown, but his skin held no distinct pallor and he did not look particularly ill, despite the attempt of his body language to convey otherwise. In fact, his cheeks emanated a rosy hue and his eyes glowed with the lively spark common in those rejoicing in the near miss of misfortune.

"Hartwig," he said. "I'm sorry, man. If I could have been out there, I would have been."

Levi made eye contact, but said nothing.

Roper smooshed his face and wrinkled his eyebrows into a grotesque mask. "I wish I were out there. If I could take their spots, all their spots, I would."

Levi walked on without paying heed to the empty words. He didn't doubt the heart from which the words came, but they were words spoken in ignorance. Staff Sergeant Roper did not know the difficult thing for which he wished, and he had no frame of reference from which to contextualize his expressed desires. And even if he did, Levi figured, it did no good to wish for that which could never be. And even if it were possible, no one—not one person he could think of—would willingly trade places with any of them. If they were all truly honest with themselves, they would say they were all glad to be alive. All were glad that it wasn't they who were dead, locked in an embrace with another dead man in a wrecked and burning Humvee. As guilty as it made them feel, they were all glad they weren't lying twisted and dead on the side of some unnamed dirt road in Iraq, traveling home in a steel box with a detached arm in a red bio-hazard bag. Despite the shame in it, they were all glad they were not sedated and strapped to a stretcher in a C-17 flying to Germany sans leg or covered in burns. And though they'd never say so aloud to each other or anyone else for as long as they lived, they all said a silent prayer of thanks to whatever or whomever they believed in, the words of which went something like this: Better him than me.

Levi passed the lieutenant's room on the way to his own. The officer sat on an ammo box. He had his head down, his eyes closed, and his hands folded. His closed mouth twitched furiously, praying silently to an unseen God. Levi paused and hovered at the doorway. He wanted to say something, to offer some comfort, but he didn't know how to offer comfort for something that had been all his fault. He dropped his vest and helmet on the ground.

He knocked on the frame to the LT's cubicle. Lieutenant Michaels didn't move. Levi waited. After what felt like forever, the LT took a deep breath and, without opening his eyes, he said, "What can I do for you, Sergeant Hartwig?"

Levi put his feet together, his fists at his side, and he stood at the position of attention. Standing in this manner, which he thought absurd under most conditions, was his personal act of humility, and it was the only way he could think to outwardly signify his submission. "Sir," he said, his voice quivering.

The lieutenant opened his eyes. "Why are you standing like that? Knock it off. Stand at ease."

Levi moved to a stiff parade rest. "Sir, I just wanted to," he paused and looked down. "I want to say I'm sorry. For hitting you."

Lieutenant Michaels took another deep breath and his mouth turned up in a placid smile. "You hit me?"

"Sir?"

He lifted a hand and gave a little wave. "It's fine. Whatever. That was retarded out there—what you did. Running down there, that is. But it's fine. Whatever. I get it."

The lieutenant closed his eyes and folded his hands again. He took a deep breath.

Levi hovered in the doorway.

"You're still here."

"Sir." Levi's voice broke and he took two deep breaths, in through his nose and out through his mouth, to keep himself from crying as he spoke. "You should be able to trust your NCOs. I—" He paused to breathe again. "If I wouldn't have suggested going to Boa—" He stopped short before he broke completely. "I failed you today."

Lieutenant Michaels had begun shaking his head as soon as Levi apologized and he continued shaking his head until Levi had finished speaking. "No, no, no, no," he said. "Let's get one thing straight. We were all out there and we're a team. But that was my mission. I'm the platoon leader. Ultimately, I'm in charge." He stood up. "Don't you dare try to take this yourself. Don't you dare." He turned his back to Levi and folded his arms. "Now get out."

Levi retreated into his own room and sat on the collapsible camp chair. He stared at his tan boots. Three broad and distinct droplets of blood stained his left toe. He thought there would have been more. There had been so much blood out there. His knees and arms were now crusting with the dried brown of it all. He could hear others taking apart their weapons, running bore snakes through their barrels, working the carbon off their bolts with Leathermans and steel brushes, but there was none of the usual foul talk, foul boasting, or foul insults common among men returning from a successful battle. Instead of the usual banter, he only heard the clack, clack, clack of thumbs sliding 5.56 millimeter rounds into magazines, replenishing their stores in case they had to roll out into the night, in case they once more needed to go black on ammo, in case they once more needed to unleash hell on another round of invisible enemies. Levi looked at his own weapon. It was covered in its own blanket of caliche dust, now silent and cold. He felt revulsion. He didn't want to clean it. Didn't even want to touch it.

"Archers tench-hut," he heard Sergeant Miller yell. He looked up at his green camouflaged woobie to make sure no one could see him as he remained seated. He didn't move as he heard the wooden door to the bunker slam shut.

He heard Lieutenant Colonel Bradford's deep baritone voice yell, "As you were, gentlemen."

The LT called from the common area in the center of the shelter, "Huddle up, gentlemen."

Levi heard a few assorted mumbles and a bit of shuffling, but none of the frantic hustle that would normally accompany an order in the old man's presence.

He, too, was slow to get up, but he emerged from the cave as ordered. He saw only a few privates had massed in the center near the LT while Staff Sergeant Havens quietly moved from booth to booth, telling people in a low voice that it was time to huddle up because the battalion commander was there. As if they hadn't heard.

Lieutenant Michaels stood at parade rest in front of the commander. Without his body armor or uniform top, without his helmet, patrol cap, or any insignia to display his rank, he looked like any of them. His hair was plastered to his head from wearing his helmet all day. A crust of salt made a line down his temple where his helmet strap had been. His right cheek was black and blue, and it was undeniably bruised, not simply dirty. He wore a tan T-shirt, which was soaked through with sweat. It clung to his frame, a frame that was thin, almost frail looking. It was a frame that had not yet begun to absorb the thick mass of a grown man in his prime. It was the frame of a boy. The young lieutenant's thin shoulders slumped with the weight of all sixty men in the platoon, if you counted medics, terps, and other support personnel. Now, fifty-five.

By Levi's count, forty-seven of them now chose to disobey the orders of the young man charged with their care by not huddling up. To make matters worse, they were doing it in front of his own boss while the ranking NCOs in the platoon gave them all a free pass. Levi stormed out into the common area in disgust and walked up and down the row of sleeping areas. He banged on the plywood walls and ripped the blankets from the parachute cords that held them over the entrances. "The lieutenant told you to huddle up," he shouted. "Get your asses out here now." By the time he got to the end of the row, he didn't have to yell anymore; they had all understood his point. Some of the men met Levi with dirty looks that screamed, "Who made you king?" but most trudged out with weary indifference.

Lieutenant Colonel Bradford stood with the company commander and command sergeant major in the middle of the open bay. The tired men formed a horseshoe around their three senior leaders. Bradford was tall and lean with silver hair parted at the side. He was a wealthy insurance executive in his civilian life with enough money to shame the generals he worked for in his National Guard life. Even in the desert uniform, he looked every bit the part. When everyone had stopped moving and whispering, the commander began his speech. "Men," he said. "I know you've had a rough day, but I don't even have words to express how proud I am of you all. Even after you got hit, you kept pressing. When you got hit again, you didn't give up. You fought a battle for the books. For the history books, gentlemen."

Levi tried hardening his heart to what the man said. He didn't want to be congratulated or comforted or motivated. In his head, he argued with every word that came out of the old man's mouth. *Normandy was a battle for the books*, he thought. We got hit by a glorified booby trap and then exchanged some shots with no more than half a dozen kids for all of twelve minutes. Levi put his hands behind his back and looked up at the fluorescent bulbs they had rigged overhead.

"We watched your battle as it was happening and we tried—oh, did we ever try—to get you some fixed-wing air support. I'm told that at Balad, they got so far as to get the engines fired up, but even though the bullets and RPGs were flying, they said it was too dusty. The dust storm was too bad." He paced in the small space in front of the men.

We probably killed them all by the time they dragged the pilots out of bingo night at the USO, Levi thought.

Colonel Bradford shook his head and laughed in that derisive manner that showed he was reliving the experience he had gone through, independent yet entirely connected to what they had gone through. "The dust storm was too bad?" he shouted. "That didn't stop you now. Did it?" He looked around. Dead eyes stared back at him. "Did it stop you?" he shouted.

"No, sir," the fifty-five enlisted men shouted back in unison. The lieutenant wiped at his eyes.

At first, Levi had resented the commander's presence, had despised even the idea of someone coming in to pretend he was one of them. He saw that the old man was different from them, no doubt, but he was also a part of their family in ways neither Levi nor anyone else could entirely understand. Like a father feels for his children, whom he can neither control nor shield in every situation, so a commander feels for his men.

"This man," the commander said as he put a hand on the LT's shoulder. "This man in front of you. You could not ask for a better platoon leader. You could not ask for a better warrior to lead you into battle and bring you back again."

The lieutenant sucked in his breath, frowned, and nodded his head twice in appreciation.

Bradford continued. "Some things are beyond our control and no amount of tactical skill, no amount of leadership, and no amount of training and professionalism can change the fact that we are in a dangerous business, and when people are in a dangerous business, people get hurt and die. You also have to remember that no amount of intelligence and no amount of cunning can change the fact that we're fighting cowards who don't play by the rules. These bombs," he said. He pronounced each letter distinctly as he slowly spit out, "These I-E-Ds." He shook his head. "Nothing you can do about that, gentlemen. Not a thing. But the things you could control, things like your actions after the fact, your willingness to put yourself in harm's way for your brothers, your skill in administering first aid to the wounded, your courage in laying down covering fire so your brothers could maneuver to the enemy, flank them, take the fight to them with superior firepower and guts. Superior guts, men. Yes, the things you could control," and here he shook his head again. "My God, you controlled them. And you controlled them better and with more violence than I ever could have asked for."

Levi looked around the room. The lifeless eyes of the platoon members, most of which had been fixed on the floor, were now fixed on the proud and stoic paternal leader in front of them. Some of their heads were nodding in agreement and some, almost in pride.

"Now down to business. Your company commander here is going to brief you on the nuts and bolts of the next few days."

He took a step back, and their captain continued where he had left off. "Some of you are going to be just fine. I know that. Some of you are going to have a hard time getting over this. Some of you are going to have some complex feelings you need to work through, and that's okay, and that's normal." He scanned the room and made eye contact with as many men as he could. "But we'll make every resource available to you. Both the chaplain and a representative from mental health will be here from Anaconda in the morning. I want you to know that we are here to support you in any way possible. Wolfpack will do your patrols tomorrow. I want you to take the day to yourselves. Get your gear squared away. Get your minds squared away. Talk it out if you need to. No QRF, no guard duty, no details, no nothing. You have the entire day off."

He folded his arms and looked around the room, satisfied as the men let out a collective and audible sigh of relief.

"But that's it," he said. "After that, after you get yourselves right tomorrow, I need you back out there. I need you to once again take this fight to the enemy. Hooah?"

A few men murmured back to him, crushed by the mere thought of leaving the base again.

"The best way to get over a fall is to get back on the horse, right? The best way to honor the guys we lost is to get back out there, do our duty, and crush the head of this snake. Hooah?"

The men dutifully yelled their hooah back to him.

He crescendoed, "The best thing for us to do is clean our weapons, load 'em up, and get out there and unload 'em again. Hooah?"

"Hooah," the men roared back at him.

The old man nodded in approval, spun on his heel, and walked toward the door.

"Archers tench-hut," yelled the lieutenant.

"As you were," came the call. The commander didn't bother to glance back.

As the men milled about after the door slammed shut, the command sergeant major whispered in the lieutenant's ear. The lieutenant turned pale, nodded, and followed him out the door.

Alone in his cubby, Levi placed his M4 on his lap. With one hand, he extended the butt stock. He closed the butt stock. In his other hand, he rolled a small stone between his fingers, the stone that Nick had placed in his hand after he had been hit the first time. He covered it and clenched it in his palm and clasped his hands over his rifle. He dropped his head and closed his eyes. He tried doing what he had refused to do with Nick and his contingent before missions, no matter how many times he had been asked. He remembered the prayers of his youth and he tried to bring a proper petition before his maker.

His fifth grade teacher in parochial school used the mnemonic device ACTS to teach them the structure of prayer. It stood for acknowledgment, confession, thanksgiving, supplication. Levi repeated the word in his head like a mantra, as though the words themselves were a prayer: ACTS, Acts, acts, acks, ax. If you don't know you better ax somebody. I've axed somebody. I've axed five bodies and three of them died. Plus I axed that bad guy.

You're doing it wrong.

He opened his eyes and took a deep breath. He closed his eyes to try again. It had been a very long time since he had gone to church, prayed, or done anything that was in any way spiritual. ACTS, ACTS, ACTS. Acknowledge. Dear God, I acknowledge that you're God. Can't we just move right into this with the presumption of acknowledgment? It would make sense to cut to the chase considering the following syllogism: When people pray, they pray to God; to pray to God is to acknowledge that God exists; I'm praying; ergo, I've already taken care of the acknowledgment part.

You're doing it wrong.

Okay. ACTS. Acknowledge. I acknowledge that you're God. You made me. You made all of us. You made the world. I acknowledge your attributes: almighty, omnipresent, omniscient, righteous, et cetera. You know all things. You knew this would happen. It would have been nice to get a warning. Would have been nice to get some sort of a sign, a little, Hey guys, you might not wanna take that road. Highway to the danger zone ahead. Even just a little warning. A tiny little one and we could take care of the rest. Couldn't mess up the dirt on the road a little bit? Give us a little sign that there was a surprise waiting for us down there? You know everything, so it would have been nice to have some heads up, big guy.

You're doing it wrong.

He squeezed the muscles of each hand as tightly as he could until the bones of his interlaced fingers ached with a dull pain. Forget it. Forgive me, God. Forgive me. I don't know how to pray and I don't know how to lead and I don't know how to soldier and I don't know what I'm doing here and I don't know how to not hate you for taking the one guy here who really believes in you, for hurting the only good guy among us. Forgive me forgive me forgive me. His shoulders began to heave. The tears rolling down his cheeks felt new. He did not remember the last time he had cried.

The burning and swelling in the back of Levi's throat felt foreign, almost as if he were choking. At first he tried to stop it, but as tears carved streams into the dirt and soot on his face, he felt strangely cleansed and refreshed. He realized he had nearly fallen asleep. He opened his eyes and saw that his white knuckles had relaxed their grips on each other. He did not know how long he had been talking to himself, but he felt oddly relaxed.

He tried to repeat the experience. He tried increasing the intensity of his prayer to increase the intensity of his tears, to intensify his weeping until his entire face and even his entire body were cleansed and refreshed in the same way. Forgive me. Forgive me. Forgive me.

Crying for dead people is selfish. I'm selfish. Crying is selfish. And weak. Crying is weak. There are dead people and you're being selfish and weak.

You're doing it wrong.

He had stopped crying. He once again felt calm and in control of himself, so he stopped trying to pray altogether. He gave up and opened his eyes.

He heard a knock on his doorjamb so he set his rifle on his bed and stood up. "Just a second," he said. He sniffed. He dug the heels of his palms into his eyes to wipe away the tears, and he lifted his T-shirt to wipe his running nose before he pulled aside his poncho liner.

Levi put his hands behind his back and stood at parade rest when he saw the lieutenant.

"Colonel's outside and wants a word."

Levi's adrenaline reserves were gone, but a hollow pit in his stomach grew as he imagined what the battalion commander might say to him.

"Yes, sir." He sniffed and wiped his eyes again.

Lieutenant Michaels began to walk away but paused. "Doing okay, Hartwig?"

"Yes, sir." He turned and grabbed his blouse and patrol cap. His fingers shook as he tried to button his top.

Levi's voice felt feeble as he snapped to attention when he reached the commander outside. "Sergeant Hartwig reports as ordered, sir."

"Stand at ease," Colonel Bradford said. He placed a hand on Levi's shoulder. He towered over him. "I know it's been a long day and I'm the last person you want to talk to, but there are some things I couldn't leave unsaid."

"Yes, sir," Levi said as the emptiness inside him grew.

"I heard what you did out there." He gripped Levi's shoulder more tightly.

"Sir?"

"We'll have to go through the steps, make sure everything is investigated, and we'll see what higher says." The commander looked at the command sergeant major who nodded as if to give the commander permission. "But I want you to know you'll get what you deserve."

Levi swallowed hard. Fear and guilt choked him.

"It may take time. These things do, but do you understand what I'm saying?"

Levi put on a stoic face and snapped back to attention. "Yes, sir."

The commander released Levi's shoulder. "Get some sleep, Soldier. Carry on."

"Yes, sir."

Levi waited until the commander and his entourage loaded up in their soft-top Humvee and drove off. On shaky legs he walked up the stairs to the bathroom Cadillac. He put a toilet lid down and sat on it. He stared at the curtain in front of him. He listened to the whir of the air conditioning unit. He pictured handcuffs and interviews and courtrooms. He turned around, lifted the lid to the toilet, and vomited.

When he finally did disrobe and climb into his sleeping bag at three in the morning, he had no trouble falling asleep. Until the instant he woke an hour later, his sleep had been dreamless, but then a singular image of Weber's face in death floated in front of his eyes. He woke in a violent, febrile shock. In life, he didn't know if he had ever noticed Weber's features, and he couldn't have had more than a few seconds to take them in when he had gone into the Humvee after Nick, but the image that flashed in front of his eyes before he woke could not have been more detailed or etched into his memory than if it were his own mother. The Mute now forever mute.

Weber's skin already matched the pale ash of burnt charcoal. His mouth hung open, revealing a bloated and deep purple tongue. His eyes stared through Levi, opened wide. Levi didn't expect that lifeless eyes could register emotion, but the brown glass of Weber's eyes betrayed shock, and they begged an answer for the eternal question: Why? Why are we even here? And this was an answer Levi didn't have. Wide awake and convicted by Weber's unblinking gaze, it was an answer Levi would never have for Weber's parents. Or Hooper's brothers. Or Jalaladin's wife back in Dearborn, Michigan.

And apart from the few, no one would remember. No one would care. They would get five words and a one-inch photo in the newspaper, a perennial *Faces of the Fallen* tribute in which their faces and names flashed with the thousands of other faces and names, and the people who saw these tributes and even the editors who produced them would callously skim over them and not even notice that these guys—these guys with their all-American names like Hooper and Weber and their bland unsmiling faces backdropped by the American flag in their official photos—were real people that meant something to someone.

Levi's sleeping bag was soaked with sweat. The same had drenched his boxers and the brown T-shirt he used for a pillowcase. He winced at the pain in his chest. His heart had never beaten so hard. He sat there in the cool moist fabric for a time, his bare torso exposed to the chilly air inside the bunker, and his damp sleeping bag bunched around his waist.

When he was able to calm his breathing, he got out of bed and dried his face and chest with a towel. He changed into dry boxers. He put a new T-shirt over the plush soccer ball he had been using as a pillow. He turned it over so the damp side was down. He then turned his sleeping bag inside out.

He slipped on his flip-flops and went outside, easing the door closed so as not to wake anyone. He pulled down his boxers and sat on the toilet. He rested his elbows on his thighs and his chin on his folded hands. He didn't know how long he sat there. Without ever going, he stood up and went to wash his hands, but while standing at the sink, he refused to look at himself in the mirror.

He climbed back into his sleeping bag, grateful to be warm and dry. He turned the day over in his mind, examining every detail he could remember. The thing was, it had all felt so utterly normal, even inevitable as he experienced it. He tried consoling himself with the fact that from the time the explosives detonated until help arrived and it was out of his hands, he had done everything he thought he should. He made snap decisions to leave those who couldn't be helped; he put himself in harm's way to help Gassner; he helped pull Nick from the wreckage. He had been perfect for those twelve minutes. But by that time, it was already too late. He could not find consolation in having simply done what he had been trained to do in a horrific situation, when he himself was responsible for the situation. The compounding of his tiny mistakes and missteps and failures in leadership had led to a devastating tragedy he could never undo, and he would carry that with him always.

He tried remembering the details, but it was difficult to piece together what he remembered into something coherent. He saw the moments, if he remembered them at all, in little snapshots. Yellow and hazy, it was hard to see them clearly, but every once in a while one would push its way past the others. Weber's face on Jellybean's shoulder, his arms wrapped around him in a hug. Tom Hooper's silhouette, suspended indefinitely against the cloud of smoke and flames, his one arm acting as a useless wing that would never succeed in keeping him from falling and landing and dying. A view through his scope of a man's head popping back and opening before dropping out of sight. Gassner's stump oozing blood. Three holes appearing in quick succession in a still and spongy chest.

The next day a pall hung over him, and he waited. He waited and he waited, but night fell and no one came for him. Miraculously, the sun came up the next day also, and the world continued to turn. He woke. He put on his reflective belt and went for a run. He showered. He dressed. Despite his best effort to deceive himself, he had to face the fact that as the world went on, so too did the missions. Casualties or no casualties, the three infantry platoons on FOB O'Ryan continued their three-day rotation of missions, guard duty, and QRF.

It was quieter than usual in Archer Platoon's bunker, but the men talked some. They ran. They lifted. They dressed. They ate. They started the Humvees. They checked fluids and tire pressures and lights. They oiled weapons. Then they waited for the field telephone to ring, letting them know that someone needed the QRF.

After Levi's squad did their preventative maintenance checks and services, he personally checked the lights and fluids. He opened up ammo cans to ensure the links hadn't rusted. He opened the feed tray cover on the 240B up in the turret to personally verify the cleanliness and proper lubrication of the weapon's mechanisms. He walked around to each man assigned to his truck and he made them disassemble their weapons so he could inspect their bolts and firing pins. When everyone else went to lunch, he took a Motorola handheld radio out to the line of Humvees and he personally tested each Duke in the platoon. He put fresh batteries in his GPS. He opened the combat lifesaver bag in his truck and verified that no saline bags and no packages of QuikClot powder had reached their expiration dates. He replaced the batteries in his night vision goggles, and he made sure that all his men did the same. He went to the supply NCO and got an ammo can full of extra batteries. He did all of this and then he did it again to verify that he had not missed one single thing that could mean the difference between life and death if he somehow failed to recognize the significance of some seemingly insignificant detail.

For the first two days of their QRF stint, he obsessed over everything, checking and rechecking. He was terrified that the field phone would ring. He was terrified that Lieutenant Michaels would yell, "Mount up," and they would all don their twenty-six-pound vests with the ballistic plates that would do nothing to stop the blast overpressure of a two-hundred-pound IED hidden under the road or the molten copper slugs of an Iranian EFP array.

By the third day, he had grown so anxious and fearful that he prayed the phone would ring just so it could be over and he wouldn't have to worry anymore.

It did ring. The LT did yell, "Mount up," and first and second squads did leave the comfort of their bunker. Their mission was to escort the EOD team to an IED outside Al Abayachi.

Levi's guts bubbled as they made the short drive to the staging area. His skin grew hot as they gathered around the lieutenant for the pre-convoy briefing. Levi forced himself to listen to every word. When his mind began drifting, he reached inside his pocket and he felt the rock he had dropped down Nick's body armor several days earlier. He ran his thumb over its smooth surface to remind himself that a war zone was no place for insouciance. He listened to the ROE. He made note of his place in the chain of command, fourth behind the lieutenant, Staff Sergeant Roper, and Tech Sergeant Cazalet. Though he had heard them before—had lived them before—he did not let his mind drift as the lieutenant described actions on contact.

When the briefing had been completed and each man returned to his own truck, Levi quizzed the men in his charge on what had been briefed. When they departed the gate to the FOB, they put magazines in their rifles and the fear left Levi's bowels. He turned on their Duke and he scanned the road. Rather than letting his mind drift, Levi listened to every word that crackled over the radio. Rather than singing songs in his head, composing lyrical poetry in his mind about the landscape and the sky and the trees, or daydreaming about looking up Eris when he returned home he scanned the road for disturbed earth, for black wires, for animal corpses, for the glint of copper wire against the sun. When they arrived at the bottlenecked stretch of canal road that held the IED, he secured the EOD team, and he watched his sector. He ignored the robot screen. He avoided eye contact. The only time he took his eyes off his sector was to verify that the men in his squad acted in kind.

When the EOD team conducted their controlled detonation, he did not allow himself the luxury of ooohs and aaahs. He kept his back to the blast and his eyes out, looking for threats. He did not allow his attention to waver on the way to the scene, at the scene, or during the return trip. After returning, he went through the same rituals he had gone through before the mission so they would be prepared the next time.

For months, his attention did not waver and his anxiety did not abate. He held a hard and heavy thing in his chest and the weight pressed on his stomach at all times. He slept little and ate less, but he soldiered on. Every day he waited for someone to relieve him of his duties and to punish him for his derelictions. In the meantime, he allowed himself no respite from the work of keeping his squad alive. No longer did he think of himself. No longer did he allow his ego or romanticism or grand ideas to keep him from performing in the way he knew he should. He stopped thinking about the merits of the war. If war was bad, it didn't change his mission to keep his brothers alive. If war was good, it was only because it taught you how to survive; it taught you how to endure; it taught you how to wait; it taught you how to abide.

He quit smoking. He quit going to the gym to lift, preferring to run alone. He did not watch movies or play video games. He was not there to make friends; he was there to finish his tour and take care of his troops. What good were friends if they were dead?

Each night he went to bed and in the darkness the images returned. One by one, each horrid memory swelled into focus, a moment with no context, a word with no meaning.

INTERMISSION

If You Thought I Could Write, You Should See the US Army Spin a Yarn

SILVER STAR NARRATIVE

FOR SGT LEVI HARTWIG (1-128TH INF-BN)

SGT Levi Hartwig displayed uncommon gallantry in action against the enemy on May 15th, 2005 in the vicinity of Ad Dujayl, Iraq, while acting as a dismounted team leader and vehicle commander. His heroic actions after an improvised explosive device attack and complex ambush enabled a successful counterattack that resulted in 11 confirmed enemy killed. SGT Hartwig's stalwart leadership, quick thinking, and aggressive approach directly saved the lives of two fellow infantrymen while keeping three American dead from the hands of Anti-Iraqi Forces seeking to exploit them.

On the morning of May 15th, 2005, SGT Hartwig and 19 other members of 1st Platoon, A Company conducted a movement to contact on Main Supply Route Tampa in the vicinity of Ad Dujayl and other supply routes critical to the continued operation of Forward Operating Base O'Ryan, Logistical Support Area Anaconda, and Balad Air Base. During the patrol, 1st Platoon sustained a direct IED attack and heavy small arms fire. After directing a successful counterattack in pursuit of a fleeing enemy, SGT Hartwig and his team detained two enemy fighters directly responsible for the IED attack.

While returning to Forward Operating Base O'Ryan with the detainees, the lead vehicle of the patrol suffered another catastrophic IED strike. The blast was so large, it flipped the Up-Armored HMMWV on its side, setting it on fire. The blast threw two members from the vehicle and trapped three more inside. Immediately after the strike, a band of no less than 20 enemy fighters unleashed a coordinated attack of effective small arms fire and rocket-propelled grenades.

Leaving his own position of safety, SGT Hartwig ran into the heart of the ambush to draw enemy fire away from his platoon and to aid his wounded comrades. Exposing himself to heavy enemy fire, SGT Hartwig retrieved a squad member who had been thrown from his vehicle, and dragged him to a position of minimal cover where SGT Hartwig immediately performed combat lifesaving procedures on the traumatically amputated leg of his fellow Soldier.

As the rest of 1st Platoon engaged the main group of enemy fighters to the southeast, SGT Hartwig recognized an enemy fighter advancing on the disabled vehicle and the fallen members of 1st Platoon. SGT Hartwig destroyed the advancing enemy with well-aimed fire, preventing the enemy from apprehending and exploiting fallen American Soldiers for propaganda purposes. SGT Hartwig once again exposed himself to enemy fire to enter the burning HMMWV to extricate another wounded Soldier, exposing himself to further danger in the form of flame, smoke, and exploding small arms ammunition.

Then SGT Hartwig led his team into the kill zone where the ambush had initiated to search and clear the enemy dead. While clearing the tall grasses, SGT Hartwig was surprised by an enemy fighter armed with an AK-47. He engaged the enemy at a close range of 5 meters, ensuring he, too, was eliminated.

SGT Hartwig's tactical prowess, selfless disregard for his own safety, and courage in the face of unimaginable danger directly saved two American lives and enabled three fallen Americans to return home to their families with dignity. Intelligence reports would later show that the tales of SGT Hartwig and the warrior ethos of the 1-128th IN BN would have a chilling effect on future insurgents planning attacks in the region. SGT Hartwig's bold leadership, selfless assumption of risk, and gallantry in combat were clearly decisive in the successful outcome of the ambush on May 15th, 2005 and to the entire Spring Campaign in Saladin Province, Iraq.

• • •

Before deploying, he had always wanted a medal. Nothing prestigious, just something to recognize his time and sacrifice. Something to put in a box for his kids to find in the attic. Something for them to ask about someday. But then he had seen real combat, and he had left Iraq in 2005 with no medals. All he had earned was a small rock. Just a small pebble as a souvenir. An incisive reminder to do better next time. By the time he left, he was fine with that. He had come to accept that. He was just happy to be going home at all.

[But that's not entirely true either. I expected to be happy, but let me tell you something. Anticipating happiness and being happy are two entirely different things. I told myself that all I wanted to do was go to the mall. I wanted to look at the pretty girls, ogle the Victoria's Secret billboards, and hit on girls at the Sam Goody record store. I wanted to sit in the food court and gorge on junk food. I wanted to go to Bath and Body Works, stand in the middle of the store, and breathe. I wanted to stand there with my eyes closed and just smell, man. I wanted to lose myself in the total capitalism and consumerism of it all, the pure greediness, the pure indulgence, the pure American-ness of it all. I never made it that far. I didn't even make it out of the airport in Baltimore with all its Cinnabons, Starbucks, Brooks Brothers, and Brookstones before realizing that after where we'd been, after what we'd seen, home would never be home again.]

After the beer started flowing on that first night in an Applebee's near Fort McCoy, Levi tried to believe that maybe, just maybe, he could be happy going back to real life. The second day was spent in bed. He spent day three on the computer Googling news for FOB O'Ryan and Ad Dujayl. He searched YouTube videos for video montages of photos and explosions and the green-tinted videos of night missions that could have been one of his own night missions. And that was day four, day five, and day six.

By day seven, he had set aside the war porn to barter and negotiate with the Reenlistments NCO with the hope of getting a second taste of the real thing. He waived his dwell time, signed a new contract to go regular army again, and days later he was active with the 10th Mountain. He was headed to Afghanistan, and he was fine with that.

[Truth be told, I was better than fine with that. It was the very raison d'être for our initial enlistment, back when there were still such things as the right reasons. And if I tried hard enough I could rationalize with myself; I somehow convinced myself that those reasons still existed.]

Then after a few months in country, when the Korengal Valley pass had made the canal roads in Iraq look like I-90 through farmland, when he had started smoking again, when the low ground was starting to make Ad Dujayl look like Disney, and when he had nearly forgotten that Lieutenant Colonel Bradford had made a promise—or a veiled threat—that Levi would get exactly what he deserved, his company commander materialized at their wilderness combat outpost. The man was a pale bowling ball of a captain from Mississippi by the name of Chambers. Levi had only seen him a handful of times during pre-deployment training. He flew to their little COP on a bird that wasn't part of the scheduled ring route, and he told Levi to pack his bags; he was going home on R&R

early. Some big shot general in the Wisconsin National Guard had demanded his presence.

All the old thoughts, fears, and guilt that Levi had buried to focus on the immediate task of staying alive came bubbling back to the surface, and as he packed his bags—certain he wouldn't return— he knew his reckoning had finally come.

When Levi got on the bird, which waited just for him, Captain Chambers smacked chewing gum and stared at Levi without speaking. It was all Levi could do to ignore the smug smile on the captain's face as he looked out the gunner's door at the foothills blending into vast desert below.

When they landed on Bagram and waited for transport to the PAX terminal, the captain finally broke the silence. "So what did you do?"

Levi's stomach dropped into his balls. "What did I do?"

"You deaf?"

"I don't know what you mean, sir." The thought actually crossed Levi's mind that he should contact an attorney.

"Your bit of pomp and circumstance is messing up my perfectly coordinated R&R schedule. The least you can do is stop playing the aw shucks bit and tell me whatchya did." The look on Levi's face must have betrayed his confusion because Captain Chambers blew a bubble and said, "By golly, you really didn't know?"

Levi shook his head slowly. "Didn't know what?"

Captain Chambers shook his own head, mirroring Levi. "Well let me, as your proud and somewhat envious commander, inform you of what I am amazed you did not know. You have earned the Silver Star Medal, and some Yankee general in your old Yankee guard unit told our BC that your presence is required in whatever Yankee state you come from so they can give your Yankee ass your medal in front of all your Yankee buddies."

So after four days of flying and waiting in airport terminals, more than a year since the battle in question, Levi stood in full service dress between his parents at the base theater on Fort McCoy, Wisconsin. His father wore an understated black suit with miniature Bronze Star and Purple Heart ribbon lapel pins that Levi had never seen before. His mother held a glass of juice, and she took little nibbles of a sugar cookie as if she hoped it would last forever because once it was gone, then what would she do with her hands and nervous energy?

Lieutenant Colonel Bradford—like a proud kid at show and tell—led Levi around and introduced him to three different mayors, the lieutenant governor, various county and city officials from the local area, and a boatload of flag and field officers he had never seen before. With each handshake, Levi had a new unit's challenge coin pressed into his right palm, which he had to drop into his pocket before shaking the next hand of the next officer who also felt obligated to personally honor Levi with his own personal coin to show his own personal gratitude for Levi's service and bravery. Meanwhile, Levi's vacuous thank yous rang hollow in his own ears, and his forced smile felt to him like the grimace before the tears. These people were throwing a party to celebrate the worst day of his life.

During the ceremony, Lieutenant Michaels gave an emotional and sometimes self-deprecating speech in which he relayed to the crowd an account of a ferocious and cool-under-pressure soldier willing to disobey orders to save his friends. He made no overt mention of his own physical assault at the hands of his subordinate, but he sprinkled the speech with plenty of idioms and metaphors. He referenced black eyes, busted jaws, and knockout punches. To Levi, the soldier he described sounded like a figment of someone's imagination. "Sergeant Hartwig is the kind of soldier that every platoon leader needs," he said. Before closing his speech, he paused and turned to make eye contact with Levi, who was sitting in the front row with his parents. "He's driven. He's fierce. He's aggressive. I can tell you from personal experience that anyone who tries to stand in his way doesn't stand a chance." He winked. "I couldn't be prouder to have had the honor of commanding him in battle."

The words, and particularly the heartfelt conviction with which they were delivered, created in Levi his own emotional tumult. The room erupted into applause, and Lieutenant Colonel Bradford stepped to the podium. Before Levi had the opportunity to breathe, the colonel—who had indeed promised they would not forget about him and that he would get what he deserved—spoke into the microphone. "Sergeant Hartwig, could you please come up here?"

Members of the local press sat in the front corner of the crowd with their video cameras and microphones, leaning on the edges of their chairs, moving around to catch the best angles of the stoic soldier's face. They ate up the juicy and violent narrative as a great hometown-hero feel-good piece, a success story in an otherwise disappointing and frustrating war.

Certain phrases jumped out at Levi as the colonel read, and Levi would stop listening to think about how their tone and spin ran in sharp contrast to how he had come to perceive the events in the long months since that tragic day. Since the day in question, Levi had mulled the events over in his head every night as he tried to sleep, during every conversation's lull, during every shower, every workout, and every meal. Every morning's foggy transition from sleep to wakefulness consisted of filling in the gaps where his memory failed him. He had never spoken of it, had never discussed it, and had never been pressed when he evaded the topic. He had lost his objectivity long ago, and he had accepted his own guilt-laden perspective— the one in which it was all his fault—without reasonable doubt or credible challenge.

Levi felt something inside growing softer and lighter as Lieutenant Colonel Bradford read on. The events still felt like nothing to be celebrated, but Levi had locked himself away in his own cage of guilt and regret for so long, the narrative made him feel something like grace. That day in Iraq had presented a terrible situation and he had done the best he could. The reading of the medal was something of a revelation. He listened with fascination and he thought, even if it was not true that he was a hero, perhaps it was true that he was not a criminal or a failure. The possibility existed for him for the first time that the past was mutable—that he might have a new truth, a new narrative that was truer than his own tortured memory. For the first time, he realized how subjective it all was and how the past was not as inviolable as he had come to believe. And didn't the possibility exist that his own recollection and the Silver Star citation were equally true? Perhaps that single afternoon had manifested both his greatest failures and his greatest accomplishments.

It could not last. In the middle of the bleachers on his left, he locked on to the smirking eyes of Private Ott, the kid he never disciplined. The kid who saw him pop a few rounds into a corpse because he had been scared shitless. His feeling of levity—of grace—vanished. Ott leaned over and whispered something to the man in the bleachers below him, which elicited another smirk. Levi was reminded of his own long-held understanding of the incident: He had not been a hero, and he had not exhibited tactical prowess. Instead, he had exhibited indecision and fear, and nothing more than a failure of moral integrity had resulted in their being on Route Boa in the first place. Ott's very presence, let alone his smirking and whispering, destroyed any vestigial thoughts that the Silver Star offered an alternative truth for Levi to carry—a truth that spoke of his exceptional reaction to an impossible situation. Only one truth remained: He was a coward and a fraud.

When Levi returned to Afghanistan, he put the medal away and he tried not to think about it, which proved impossible at first. There was some fanfare and some jealousy and many questions. He rebuffed questions with the answers that everyone expected: Everyone out there was just doing his best; I didn't do anything extraordinary that anyone else wouldn't have done; I just happened to be in position to get there first; it was no big deal; and finally, to his peers trying their hardest to disguise their envy, if anyone deserves a Silver Star, it's you guys.

It wasn't long before the medal was no longer news and it stopped being a conversation piece, which came as a relief because it meant that Levi no longer had to answer simple questions, the truthful answers to which no one would have wanted to hear on account of how complicated and morally ambiguous they would have been. Yet, the gradual slip of the medal into irrelevance in the collective memory of his peers also saddened him because it meant nothing was left to challenge his personal and long-held guilt about it all.

Things were so complicated, so mixed up all the time. Everything went in waves. Sometimes he would realize he was sleeping better; he was eating more; and he could not pinpoint with any precision the last time he had thought about May 15th, 2005. Other times, he would go through entire days in which he let his squad run on autopilot; he wouldn't say a word unless it was to snap at someone for doing something stupid or reckless, and he'd hear his subordinates muttering, "Sergeant Hartwig's on the rag again." On these occasions, he would open his footlocker and pull out the medal. He'd read the citation, and he'd close his eyes and try to picture what had happened in minute detail. He would punish himself by picking his scabs until they bled. In a way, he hoped that by reading this new narrative and by trying to reconcile it with his own, the new scabs would be smoother, smaller, and less painful.

But that exercise had failed, and he put the medal away for good.

• • •

Fast forward to Christmas 2008. Levi had polished off two jugs of wine and he had thrown most of his belongings in the dumpster behind his apartment. He put all his clean undergarments and a few sets of civvies in a hockey bag. He moved an olive drab M183 demolition satchel—scored on his first trip to Iraq from the EOD guys—to the bathroom, where he hung it on the doorknob so he wouldn't forget to pack his toiletries inside. He sorted through everything else that remained, putting anything bearing utility into a cardboard box to take to his neighbor Albie. He packed everything else into two footlockers. The entire ritual, the preparation, the counting of the socks and underwear into sets of sevens, the packing away and shipping off of the unessential, and the total abdication of anything excess or frivolous felt familiar; it felt like packing for war. But he wasn't packing for war; he was packing for home. That was the night he had found the medal where his mattress had been. He reflected for a short moment and then he added it to the rest of his trash in the dumpster, the small ribbon and cheap metal star meaning nothing now that he was no longer a Soldier.

BOOK THREE

OF BIRDS AND BLOOD

3.1 THE STRONGEST VOICES OFTEN GO UNHEARD

Winter, Late 2008–Early 2009

She believed history was important, and history was bred from memory. And this is how Eris remembered her whole life: in short viral video clips. Viral as infection. Her memory was high-definition media swimming in a digital pool in her brain. Every once in a while, one of these clips floated to the surface. The sounds of the present faded into the background like the oscillating surf of the sea. The colors of the other images blurred and rippled, and the buoyancy of the one that floated demanded her attention.

Here is an image, from before the war: Nick sitting cross-legged on his bedroom floor on some wild night when Levi got him high and then punched him out. And she had been stupid too, but for good reason: for him. This was the night of the drinking, the bathtub, the hospital. He was heartbreaking with his boyish cheeks, his fuzzy blond buzz cut, and the confused but trusting hopefulness of an abused child. He rocked back and forth and looked her right in the eye. He listened to every word she had to say about why she couldn't go home, about why her life had lost all meaning. He listened and he cared. That was important to her. She could hear him grinding his teeth, and yes, his eyes were so dilated she couldn't see his irises, but she could hear the sincerity in his voice when he told her, "You saved me tonight."

She leaned forward to kiss him and said, "No, you saved me."

"Because I love you." He said, "I don't want to sound vulnerable, because I'm not, but because I love you."

He didn't know irony and he didn't know lies, and she could hear that. When she began to take her clothes off, she could also hear him say, "No. Didn't you hear me?"

By then, she had only heard no. And she felt confused. He probably sensed this because he had always looked out and not in. He reached his hand out to touch her face. He ground his teeth and smiled at her. "You have to understand."

A tear rolled down her cheek. He had studied a bit of Greek at that little Christian high school of his, and it was this gibberish he used to explain himself. "There's philos," he told her. "And I love you like that. And eros. I want to love you like that. Believe me, I want to love you like that. I mean, how could I not? But I can't love you like that. Not now. But the other love, it's called agape. And that's how I need to love you. That's how I love you. So please don't take your clothes off."

She didn't understand all of that back then. Didn't care. She only heard, "I don't love you like that."

She didn't like to think of all this as before the war—as if all time should be categorized by where he went and what he had done and how he had returned—because it seemed to legitimize it all and excuse it all, and it took her out of the equation. But the problem was this: She didn't know how else to think of it. She would give anything to go back to the way it was before the war, back when he so nakedly expressed himself.

He smacked his dry tongue. "You have to understand what I mean. The words seem so inadequate, and I love you, but that doesn't begin to cover it. I wish," he said. "I wish Levi were back here because he'd have the words. He's always the one for words." He then hit his own head with an open palm trying to think of how to explain it.

"It's fine." And it was. It really was. And she was glad Levi wasn't there. He may have had the words, but they always lacked love. She sat on the floor in front of Nick and looked into his eyes for an eternity. Each one a sea of glass, like unto crystal, and as deep and endless as the night.

She smiled. Sniffed. She stood up. "Let me tuck you in," she said. "Let me put music on and tuck you in. You won't sleep, but you can dream."

She had pride back then. She held herself together with a sure hope that she'd have him.

And then when she least expected it, there was this: A letter from Brooke Army Medical Center announcing his return. And then another memory: Nick coming down the walkway at the airport.

She had been late. She wanted to look perfect. She ended up having to run from the parking lot, trying not to slip in her high heels. By the time she made it to the door, she felt a single bead of sweat run down her back. She wore a ribbed sweater and a long pearl necklace. A flower-patterned skirt that clung to her hips and thighs. Tall, high-heeled, black leather boots. She had ironed her hair straight. She wanted to look like a woman, not the teenage girl he'd left behind.

He stood at the top of the ramp looking nervous and unsure of himself. He was thin and pale, but even from across the airport she could recognize him. Could recognize the way he looked around at everyone and everything as he moved. He did his best to mask his limp, and he carried himself with his shoulders back and his chin up.

His Oma stood against the wall by the bubbler between the restrooms. She stood there wringing her hands together, as if she were washing them. She wrinkled her eyebrows and scanned the line of people coming down the ramp. When Eris spotted her, she couldn't believe how frail and tiny and wrinkled she had become. She was half the size and twice the age as the last time Eris had seen her. From a distance, Eris saw Nick light up and wave to the woman who raised him. He lost all sense of himself and he started shuffling down the ramp, running as well as he could.

Eris wanted to cry at how they had broken him, but she thought, "It's okay. I can still love this. I can still love him."

He wrapped his small grandma in his arms, and he hugged her face to his chest. She rubbed his back, and he held her. He looked like he might snap all her bones. She hugged him to the point of awkwardness, to the point where Eris thought she'd never let him go.

Eris stood still then. Stopped moving toward them. It was a silly thought, she knew, but as she looked at Nick's grandma pressed against Nick's chest she thought, "Is he capable of loving any woman besides her?"

The two turned and Oma locked her arm in Nick's as they started walking. In that moment she'll always remember, it was as if his limp disappeared and his face had healed. He may not have been at home in his skin, but he was at home in his role as protector. And she saw that.

She waited to give them their space, and her stomach fell when Nick didn't recognize her, though he had locked eyes with her for a moment. They couldn't have been more than ten feet away when Oma tapped his arm.

He tapped the hand that tapped his arm, and he gazed into the old woman's eyes. She tapped again. "Yes." He smiled at her.

Oma nudged him with an elbow in the ribs. She pointed up at Eris. "Aren't you going to say hi?"

He looked up. "Hmm?"

At that point, recognition crossed over his face. Oma let go of his arm. Eris rushed forward and thrust her arms under his and she buried her head in his chest and she hugged him. "You're home. You're actually finally really home." She pulled her arms from around him and put her hands on his chest. "Let me look at you." She took a step back. "Oh my," she whispered, wiping her watering eyes.

"I know." He looked down at the ground. "I look like I got blown up."

"You look beautiful," she said, embracing him again. "I've never seen anything look so beautiful."

She thought it would be perfect like that forever; she was still a naïve, foolish, stupid little girl.

To prove it, this is a memory from the last Thanksgiving, when things were really bad: Nick limping away behind a foggy windowpane. She stared at the condensation on the window in their living room. Her elbows leaned against the back of the couch that sat against the wall. The rough brown fabric felt like burlap on her knees. She looked down, wondering why she wasn't wearing pants. She didn't move, but she still lost her balance and had to brace herself. She fought to keep her bobbing head up. She wiped her hand against the cold glass so she could see outside.

She didn't hear his footsteps, and she didn't hear the screen door, yet she could see him running away again. She watched Nick limp to his car, his mouth set. He didn't slam the door. He didn't peel out. He just drove away. She would have preferred that they scream and throw things at each other; but no, he was always content with silence. A man of action with little use for words. For hours, for days, for weeks, he was happy running away to his bar to work eighteen hours a day, to come home only for a shower and a bed, or as he called it, a hot and a cot.

She turned and slid down the couch until she sat on the floor. She screamed out curses at him, although he was already gone. She could smell her own vomit on her breath as she wailed. Eris was sure Nick believed there was dignity in the way he fought, in the way he refused to be sucked into arguments, in the way he would never yell at her. She beat the floor with her fist and she threw herself down, her tears and drool wetting the fibers of the carpet. She was no longer capable of such dignity.

She crawled into the guest bedroom, the carpet burning her knees. She found a plastic bottle of cheap vodka tucked into one of Nick's old combat boots, and she drank it. Choked it down like medicine. Even after Uncle Thomas slapped her awake, she refused to pull herself together.

"Nick is hurt," he said. "I mean hurting. He's hurting."

"You'd never know it talking to him," she said. "He's a tree. A solid tree that doesn't listen or talk."

The real truth was this: Then, as now, she felt unheard. The words she said seemed no louder than the thoughts in her own head. Her conversations indistinct from her dreams.

She laughed without mirth. "He's not a tree; you can burn a tree down. They couldn't do that. But they tried. They sure as shit tried to burn him down, didn't they Reverend?"

Uncle Thomas nodded.

"He's a rock. You can't burn down a rock."

"No," Uncle Thomas said. "But you can burn down a marriage."

And that was true.

It was also true that if you ignored your wife hoping she'd just go away, she probably would.

But life has its own rules of inertia, so here is an image from today: Nick reading a postcard from Levi, a smile playing at his lips. Nick read it as he walked in from lunch. He tossed his keys on the table, and turned the card over twice, looking at both sides.

"Why are you smiling?" She didn't think it was an odd question. It had been a long time since he had smiled like that.

"I'm not smiling."

"Yes you were."

He handed the card to her, postmarked from Watertown, New York. "Levi still thinks he's living in some story." The postcard was covered in a small, slanted, cursive scrawl.

• • •

Dear Nick,

Let me introduce myself. My name is MISTER Levi Hartwig and I'm free of all obligations and responsibilities. Hitting NYC. I'll try to dance with some older women and maybe hire a prostitute, just to hear her talk. After that, home.

Levi

• • •

She, too, turned it over. There was a picture of a red-and-blue snare with two drumsticks. "I thought he was in Afghanistan."

Nick shrugged. "He was."

"So how is he coming home?"

"Who knows? It's army. Things change."

"So Levi's coming home? Is he coming back here for good?"

"He's probably not coming back at all. Soldiers are always dreaming of home."

He walked to her and took the postcard from her hands. He set it on the table next to his keys, and he hugged her. It had been months since he hugged her. He hugged her tight and wouldn't let go. As if he just now realized that if you don't hold onto her, she could leave.

3.2 THEY ESCORTED ME OUT LIKE A CRIMINAL

Levi looked up at First Sergeant Top Powers struggling to zip his Gore-Tex coat over his massive belly. "Time to go," the man said, knocking on the desk. "Need to grab anything else, or are you good?"

By no means did Levi believe he was good, but that which belonged to him was now packed in his shabby one-bedroom apartment off base; everything else he had accounted for, inventoried, and then returned to Uncle Sam, ensuring to get every checklist item on his basic item issue sheet signed and dated. "We can go," Levi said.

Snow flurries blew into the entryway. Levi pulled up the hood on his parka when he walked outside, and he enjoyed his first new privilege as a civilian: He shoved his hands deep in his pockets and kept them there as he stomped through the snowdrifts to the parking lot.

The first sergeant, unable to deploy because of sleep apnea and chronic back problems—what Levi thought of as simple symptoms of extreme obesity—breathed heavily as he shifted and forced his girth and puffy coat behind the steering wheel. Instead of scraping the ice, First Sergeant Powers waited for the defroster to do its work.

The man was a flurry of activity. First, he breathed into his hands. Then, he rubbed them together. He reached over and opened the console and took a Skoal pouch from a tobacco tin. He turned the heater to the vents, felt the air coming out, and then switched it back to defrost. He turned on the radio and after only a few seconds, he changed the station. He turned on the windshield wipers and when they loudly scraped against the still solid ice, he sighed audibly.

"Suppose I could have had you start the car while you were waiting," Top said, laughing nervously.

Levi didn't respond, but instead watched his own white breath flow out in front of him.

"Do you need to stop by finance or anything else? Final accounting of your pay, or is that all wrapped up?"

"Nope. I have already rendered unto Caesar what is Caesar's." And far more, Levi thought.

He stared out his window on their way off post. The sun shone off the drifts in blinding glares, and the thick snow and ice covered the flaws in the old rundown government buildings, shielding their dilapidation with a thin veneer of romanticism and nostalgia.

After a few moments of silence, Top Powers said, "You know it could be worse. Colonel Torres really did a good thing for you. I never seen an admin separation under your circumstances as anything higher than a general discharge before. Never seen a guy in your shoes get an honorable discharge before, but the Colonel saw that Silver Star in your package and said to me, 'Top, this guy's a bona fide war hero, and he's getting an honorable, and I don't care what the JAGs say.' That's what he called you for real. A bona fide war hero."

[By that point I was too exhausted to fight. Too exhausted to ask if that was supposed to be consolation. Too exhausted to tell him they didn't even give me a chance. Too exhausted to be bitter, sarcastic, or rude. Too exhausted to be anything.]

They passed the guard shack and the visitors' center as they exited the gate to the base. Levi took one last mental snapshot of the post through the rearview mirror. No longer could he enter through those gates. No longer was he set apart. No longer was he accepted. No longer was he part of that communal brotherhood doing powerful and mysterious things behind those tall fence lines. He felt like Adam being expelled from the Garden of Eden, except instead of an archangel with a flaming sword guarding the gate, it was an eighteen-year-old MP with perfectly erect posture and perfectly bloused pants over his immaculate and unscuffed boots. I have boxer shorts with more time in the desert than that kid, Levi thought.

"And hey," the first sergeant said. "You still got that GI Bill."

"Already got my degree," Levi mumbled.

"What's that?"

He turned and spoke up, defiant now. "I said I already got my degree. What do I need a GI Bill for?"

"Well even better," he said, still painfully affable. "I'm sure you'll find a job in no time. Highly decorated vet, leadership experience, college educated. I'm sure there'll be people banging on your door trying to hire you." When Levi didn't respond, he began asking questions. "So what'd you go to school for?"

Levi wanted to cry, wanted to yell at the guy, wanted to wallow in his own failures, but he could not bring himself to do any of those things. He whispered, his voice nearly cracking, "English."

"Gonna be a teacher then?"

[I didn't respond. Honestly, it had been years since I thought about what I wanted to do because I had been so busy doing what I felt I had to do. And I hadn't earned the degree with the night and online classes because of these big lofty dreams so much as I earned it because the army bred this compulsion in me to simply finish what I started. Until you called me out on it, I barely remembered a time in which I had planned on traveling the world and writing books to save it. It seemed—still seems?—like that person had been killed in action, and I couldn't even pinpoint when it happened.]

When they neared the apartment complex, Levi leaned so he could get to his wallet. He removed his white common-access card and placed it on the dashboard. "Suppose you need that," Levi said.

The first sergeant parked and turned to Levi. "Look, I know it's hard for guys like you to listen to guys like me. I'm not stupid. And I also know I ain't got a clue what you've been through and wouldn't ever dream of pretending I have. Now do I think the army's doing you right? No. But could they be doing you worse? Sure. But it is what it is, is one thing I know.

"Aw, hell." Top Powers stuck out his hand. "I like you, Levi. I really do. But things are the way they are. Just—whatever you do, don't let this define you."

Levi shook his hand weakly. "Roger that, Top."

The first sergeant pumped his hand and looked him in the eye like any good soldier would do. "I believe you can call me Jeff now, Mr. Hartwig."

Levi nodded and left. After filling a plastic gas station cup full of Absolut and diet pop, he sat on a packed-up footlocker in his living room. He chugged half the glass and picked up the black Steve Wariner Signature Edition Takamine that he had purchased with tuition aid money his freshman year of college. He played jangly open chords, and by the time he'd finished his first cup, he had started singing slow, sad versions of songs his band played in high school.

Halfway through his third cup, he heard a knocking on the wall and then the thickly accented voice of his neighbor. "Shut up, Meester Levi."

Levi ignored it, took another drink, and kept singing.

"I am serious tonight. Please, shut up, please. I have to work tomorrow."

Levi strummed harder. "Just come over and join me," he yelled at the wall. "I'm sure the 7-Eleven won't miss you, you walking talking Slurpee-slinging stereotype."

"I'll call the manager," his neighbor yelled.

Levi yelled back. "I'll call ICE on your ass."

"I'll call your command post or your first sergeant."

Levi laughed, lit a cigarette, and let it dangle from his lips. He squinted through the smoke. "I'll give you his number." Levi heard one more knock of resignation and that was it. He played and drank until his B string broke, at which point he let the guitar fall to the floor with a clang. He gave it a kick to send it skidding across the cheap laminate floor. It connected with the wall in a sickening crack and a metallic vibrato.

He walked to the kitchen and picked up a box he had packed full of pots, pans, and kitchen utensils. He grabbed the keys to his truck and headed over to his neighbor's apartment.

Not wanting to put the box down, he didn't knock on the door, but instead kicked it. "Open up," he yelled. "Police."

A dark-skinned Afghan even shorter than Levi opened the door. He rubbed the thick gray mustache that seemed to cover half his thin face. Once upon a time, the man in khakis and a plaid button-up two sizes too big had been a practicing physician in Kabul. This was before he left his homeland in the seventies. He went by the nickname Albie. "Why are you always screwing around? And why are you here on Christmas?"

"What do you think I'm here for, Albie? I come bearing gifts. Besides, it isn't Christmas for another two days, you heathen schmuck."

"I don't think you can call a Muslim a schmuck."

Levi kicked his shoes off as he entered, and he set the box down on the kitchen counter. He tossed Albie a bottle of gut-rot whiskey from the box. "I don't think you can call yourself a Muslim."

Albie broke into a large smile. "Now we are talking, my friend."

He followed Levi into the small kitchen and took two ornate glasses from the cupboard, each made from smooth green stone. He poured them each drinks, raised his glass, and said, "Merry Christmas, my friend."

Levi sipped while Albie drank three cups in quick succession. Levi tried to make small talk and asked about his family. Albie's wife had died years ago, but he still had a daughter teaching at a private high school in Brooklyn. She rarely traveled upstate to visit.

"She's getting so old," Albie said. "She's almost thirty and she does not even have a boyfriend." He shook his head sadly. "Soon, I shall give up all hope of having grandchildren." He sucked whiskey off his mustache with his lower lip. He leaned forward and whispered, as if someone else might hear. "Do you think she's a lesbian?"

"Introduce her to me and I'll find out."

"I put up with lots of kidding, Meester Levi, but you better not be pushing on that button."

"You don't want me pushing your daughter's button?"

Albie gave him a look that made it clear the conversation was over.

"So what about you? What's new with you? When will you go back to kill more Taliban?"

"You mean Afghans?"

Albie shook his head. "No. Afghans are a peace-loving and honorable people. See?" He put an open palm on his chest. "I have invited you—an infidel and baby killer—into my home and you are safe here."

Levi laughed. "Well, safer here than there, I guess."

"So?" Albie said. "Will you be returning?"

Levi took a drink and let the silence hang. "I'll go back and do some more soldiering when you can practice medicine again."

"Oh, I can't practice medicine here. You know that." Albie clicked his tongue, as if reprimanding Levi for his forgetfulness.

"I know, Albie. That's my point. They won't let me go back. They kicked me out."

Albie nodded, "Ah yes. I understand now." He frowned and looked into his glass, but he didn't ask why.

[And this is why I loved him. He accepted the news with the quiet understanding of someone who has seen tragedy, with the quiet understanding of someone who understands there is no why.]

"Don't you want to know why?"

Albie shrugged, still looking into his glass. "Probably you are too nice." He looked up and tapped Levi's chest. "Probably not enough hate in here." He tapped a cigarette from a pack on the counter. "Probably," he said, waving an unlit cigarette. "They saw you hanging out with me and think you are a terrorist now. Probably Dick Cheney listened to your phone calls and heard you talking bad about the war. Who knows why? There are so many reasons."

Levi shook his head. "No. I get too drunk and I can't shoot my rifle. I can hit the women, but I miss the babies. They're too small."

"Yes," Albie said gravely. "To be a good soldier, you must not miss the babies."

After a few more drinks, Albie's eyes began to droop. He swayed, using the counter for support.

"So you work tomorrow." Levi said.

"No. No drinking if I'm working."

"You told me you had to work."

"I lied so you would shut up."

"Good. I need a ride to the post office and then the airport tomorrow."

"Where are you going, young traveler?"

"Going to visit a buddy in Walter Reed in DC. Maybe talk to Congress and have them end the wars. After that, Brooklyn. I heard there's a lovely young teacher there looking for a husband. After that, home. To Wisconsin."

Albie shook his head and wagged a finger at him. "No Brooklyn. But I can't anyway. I don't have a car."

"You do now." Levi dropped the keys to his truck on the counter.

"You drink too much."

"I don't drink enough."

"That is too much," said Albie. "I can take some whiskey, but I cannot take your truck."

"So sell it. I don't care. The title is in that cardboard box and it's already signed over to Abdul Teyrawah, so that old truck is your problem now."

Albie dropped his burning cigarette in the last swallow of his whiskey, and he set his glass on the counter. He wrapped Levi in a hug. "You people and your Christmas," he said.

"Nothing to do with Christmas," Levi muttered.

"You come back anytime," said Albie. "And if you convert, you can marry my daughter."

"I'll think about it," Levi said as he waved his goodbye.

He stumbled into his own kitchen to pour himself another drink. He emptied the last third of his vodka bottle and threw it at the garbage can, the lid of which was closed. He opened the fridge to find an empty pizza box and a lone bottle of beer. He leaned against his fridge and lit another cigarette, smoking it as he drank the beer. He finished the beer before the cigarette, and when he had finished his smoke, he dropped the butt in the empty beer bottle. He sauntered over to the garbage can, stepped on the pedal that opened the lid, and he dropped the bottle in the can. Leaving the lid open, he unbuttoned the fly of his jeans and pissed into the garbage can before stumbling to his bedroom.

3.3 ODYSSEUS RETURNS AND THE BLUE STAR FLAG COMES DOWN

After returning home from the burn ward at Brooke Army Medical Center and before Levi returned home, it wasn't the war that kept Nick awake; it was his febrile prayers over Oma's deteriorating health. After he had returned, it was as if she had breathed a sigh of relief, a sigh in which she happily gave up her ghost now that her grandson was safe. She didn't seem to suffer, but she grew smaller and thinner. He wanted to pick up this poor old woman and rock her like a baby. And then she died.

Then there were the long months—or was it years?—in which anxiety over Eris's drinking and wandering consumed him. Even when he could fall asleep—on the rare nights she was home and sober—he'd wake in a sweaty panic, feeling around to make sure she was still there.

Other thoughts then kept him up at night. Like any entrepreneur trying to make his way in the world, thoughts of his business kept him awake. He thought about the razor-thin profit margins of the food service side of the house. He tried scheduling in his head to cut manpower expenses. After he had been taken for thousands by his manager, Kathy Stenson, he stayed up contemplating the cost versus benefit of boosting his in-house security to prevent employee theft.

Since firing Kathy, he had been working every shift every day, and it had almost gotten to the point where he was too tired to sleep. Now, on the eve of Levi's return, something else, something like trepidation kept him up. He leaned against Eris's back and put his mouth on her neck and kissed her, trying to wake her.

She reached her arm behind her and swatted at him. "Leave me alone," she said. "Lemme sleep."

He turned on the lamp. "I get home, and you're sleeping," he said. "I wake up, and you're gone."

"So."

"So you're the one who complains we don't talk." Nick turned on his back and laced his fingers behind his head. "I just don't know what to do."

"Start by turning the lamp off."

"That's not what I mean." But he did turn the lamp off.

After two hours on the cusp of sleep, he got up. Through the window, he could see the streetlights shining off a thin layer of snow. He cleared his driveway and the rest of the walks on his block before driving to the Hartwig house in Bangor to shovel their driveway and sweep the snow from their deck. The snow was light and the work was easy, so making the rounds with a shovel and a broom seemed as good a way as any to release the nervous energy that fizzed and popped inside him.

As he walked around the back of the house and onto the deck, Kevin opened the sliding door and poked his head out. He held a cup of coffee and wore the flannel pajamas and slippers that Nick imagined were common for men of his age and economic status. "You didn't have to do this," he said.

"You're old. Didn't want you to have a heart attack."

Levi's dad laughed. "Well, when you're done, come inside. Charlotte wants to show you something."

Levi's parents hunched over the island bar. "Come here," Charlotte said. "Look at this."

They were looking at a mahogany frame. Levi's Silver Star citation was framed in the top, and replica Silver Star and Purple Heart medals sat centered in the bottom half of the frame. The deep forest green of the felt background made the blue, red, and purple of the ribbons pop in contrast.

He had read the narrative many times before, yet he still found himself amazed as if reading it for the first time. He had no recollection of the blast and no recollection of the subsequent firefight. The last thing he recalled was driving down Boa, squinting against the setting sun. Different images returned to him from time to time—a bloody arm on his chest, smoke obscuring the sky—but these seemed distant and surreal. These images were no more than something he had seen in a movie once. His real battle had been his recovery.

Charlotte put her hand on Nick's elbow. "Well," she said. "What do you think? We're going to give it to him when he gets home."

Nick traced his finger around the edge of the frame. "I think it looks great." For a moment, he felt a twinge of guilt at being the cause of such mayhem, but he quickly pushed the thought away. Whether he failed to spot the bomb or not, he wasn't the one who had planted it. *What's done is done,* he thought.

He excused himself, and he drove back to La Crosse. He cleaned himself up and took Eris to church before they took Uncle Thomas out for steak and eggs as they did every Sunday.

Nick's mind wandered all morning. Levi's homecoming was no small news. Plenty of people in Oma's Pub had been peppering him with questions all week. In the afterglow of the presidential inauguration, all the common-sense Democrats in the small village of Bangor, Wisconsin, viewed Levi's return as proof-positive that they had voted correctly and the wars were ending. The Republicans viewed his return as evidence of a mass exodus of heroes from the military now that the Commander-in-Chief was so antimilitary and soft on defense. Charlotte had spread the word all over town, and she had passed out invitations to everyone at Saint Paul's Lutheran Church, but Nick wasn't even sure Levi would show up at the airport. He'd sent a postcard from Manhattan with a flight number, and Nick hadn't heard a thing since.

Nick's Uncle Thomas chewed on toast and talked with his mouth full. "So where'd you go?" he asked.

Nick looked up from his eggs, which he had been moving around on his plate. "Huh?"

"Got that thousand-yard stare again." He sipped his coffee. "So where'd you go?"

"Nowhere."

"Suit yourself."

The anxiety only grew through the afternoon. It peaked as he drove alone to the airport. He scanned the faces of the masses as they walked down the ramp from the secure area. He thought he spotted a man that might be Levi walking behind a group of people near the tail end of the herd. He had a difficult time being certain because the man was a ways off, but the slight slump of the shoulders, the way he slightly bobbed with each step in what could be mistaken for a cocky swagger, and the way he held his head down as if he had no idea what was going on around him were all unmistakably Levi. The long, flared sideburns that Nick remembered from high school already crept toward Levi's jaw, and the rest of his hair wasn't far behind.

Levi had been carrying a messenger bag loosely on one shoulder. When he saw Nick, he threw the bag toward his back and started pushing through the other travelers with their rolling suitcase-sized carry-ons and the casual lumber of cattle.

"Let me through," he yelled. "That's my brother up there."

Nick's dread melted away with Levi's smile, and he couldn't help but laugh as Levi cut around an old man in khakis, loafers, and a Packers sweatshirt. He did an actual spin move around a little girl in a red dress decorated with candy canes.

Nick tried to brace himself to keep from being crushed, but Levi wrapped him up. He pinned both of Nick's arms against his sides. He picked him up, bending his legs to bounce. Each bounce punctuated his speech: "It is. So so. Good. To see you." He dropped Nick and stepped back. He looked Nick up and down. He winced. "Oh man. Sorry, dude. I didn't hurt you, did I?"

Nick laughed. "I'm not a porcelain doll, ya douche."

Levi reached out and touched the tight wrinkled skin that spread up the left side of Nick's neck and ear. "Does it hurt?"

Nick tilted his head, pulling his face from Levi's touch. "Did the army close all the chow halls? You must have lost like thirty pounds."

Levi flexed his bicep and kissed it. "And I could still kick your ass."

"You wish."

They looked at each other in silence, the stupid smiles of old friends unsure of what to say to each other. Nick knew that it was Levi in front of him, but his eyes had grown more intense. His cheeks had hollowed out, enhancing the lines in his smile, which seemed almost manic. Despite the broad grin that spread across his thin face, there was an incongruity in the way his thick eyebrows pulled together and in the way his forehead wrinkled.

Nick bit his lip while they waited for luggage. He still had to broach the subject of the party. "So, I know you said no ticker tape parades, but your parents insisted on a party."

Levi shrugged. "Cool."

"I mean, they kind of invited everyone in town to their house for a coming home party."

Levi took a few steps and picked up a black hockey bag moving along the conveyor belt. "They kind of did or they did?"

"Well, they did. They're all waiting there now. They wanted it to be a surprise, and I'm not supposed to tell you, but I know I wouldn't want a bunch of people jumping out and yelling at me. I'll tell you that for free." Nick put his hands in his pockets and looked expectantly at Levi, who was digging in the hockey bag. "You know, or we could just like, blow it off or whatever."

After finding what he was looking for, Levi picked up the bag and slung it over his shoulder. He took a long pull from the flask he had taken from the bag. "Ah, what the hell. Let's go party." He handed the flask to Nick. "Here. Drink and be merry."

Nick took a sip of the straight liquor—vodka from the bottom shelf—and he smiled with relief. "Okay then. Your chariot awaits."

In the parking lot, Nick opened the hatch to Eris's blue Volvo. Levi whistled and dropped his bags in the back of vehicle. "Fancy," he said. "The old bar and grill must be doing pretty well. Living large, eh?"

"It's Eris's actually." Nick patted the top of the car. "She wanted something all-wheel drive for the snow. My truck was a mess, so I stole this for the afternoon."

"So how is she? Eris."

Nick didn't know how to explain things. The question felt loaded. It seemed like the kind of question whose answer required context and history. It seemed like the kind of question that needed its own chapters so he simply said, "She's good. She works at a bank now."

Levi smiled as he stared out the window of the car, looking at—or past—the virginal snow on the pastures and the barren stalks of the cornfields. The all-volunteer village council had commissioned a Kinko's to create a big banner that said, "Welcome Home Staff Sergeant Levi Hartwig, Silver Star Winner and Our Hometown Hero!" They tied it to the splintered wooden sign that boasted Bangor as the home of the Lady Cardinals, High School State Basketball Champions of 1995. After coming up from Interstate 90, they drove up Highway 162 under a canopy of naked maples. They bumped over the railroad tracks, past the Log Cabin Tavern, and around the blind turn into Bangor where Levi saw the sign that welcomed him.

"Are you kidding me? What the hell is that?" Levi looked at Nick with a perplexed smile.

After stealing a glance at Levi to gauge his reaction, Nick turned back to the road. "President Obama may as well have ended the wars already. Bangor has her hero back, and hope is in the air."

Levi turned back to the window, shaking his head. He rubbed his hand across the back of his head, through the hair that was already long enough to reach his collar.

Instead of pulling into the packed driveway, they joined the two rows of cars on the frozen front lawn. They stepped out, each with a foot in the car and a foot ankle deep in the cold snow.

"Well," Nick said. "Ready to do this?"

Levi pulled the flask from his back pocket and drank. He kept his eyes on the house as if it might reach out and grab him if he looked away. "Why the hell not?" he said, as much to himself as to Nick. He took one more swig before tossing the empty flask on the passenger seat of the car.

They stomped through the snow toward the house. When Levi reached the sidewalk, he paused and looked up at the tattered blue star flag that hung there. He untied the rope and let the flag down, catching it before it hit the ground. He rolled it up in a ball and walked it over to the trashcan, where he dropped it without ceremony.

His mother opened the screen door first. She lumbered down the stairs and shuffled along the sidewalk. Tears streamed down her face and she held out her hands. Levi stood still on the sidewalk, waiting for her to reach him. She put her hands on his cheeks and said, "My baby. Oh, my baby's home."

Levi hugged her back. He lifted his chin and set it on top of her head. He patted her back. "It's okay, Mom." His dad waited at the bottom of the stairs, hands behind his back with an air of self-confident patience. Levi brought his eyes up. His dad met them, smiled, and nodded. "Okay, Mom," Levi said. "I need to say hello to Dad too."

She let him go and put both hands on his cheeks again. He raised his eyebrows. She patted his right cheek. "Okay," she said, wiping a tear away. "Okay."

Levi kissed her forehead and walked up to his dad, who hugged him tightly. His father closed his eyes and exhaled. Nick could see the weight lift from his shoulders as they embraced. He rubbed Levi's back. "Welcome home, Son."

Levi's sister, brother, and brother-in-law all waited at the top of the stairs and one by one they came down to greet him. Levi hugged and kissed Elizabeth. "Good to see you, Sis." She couldn't speak because she was crying like her mother, mascara-filled tears drawing black lines in the thick foundation on her face.

Levi rolled his eyes and pointed at his sister as he shook hands with her husband, Chris.

"Welcome back, Bro."

Then Levi moved in to hug his brother, Paul, who stuck out his hand for a formal handshake. Levi recovered by grabbing Paul's hand to pull him in for a one-armed hug. "Long time no see," he told him.

"No kidding," said Paul.

"So, couldn't hack it in DC? Working for the old man now?"

"Something like that. You know we still have an opening at Hartwig and Sons."

Levi pulled away. "It's probably time he renamed it Hartwig and Son."

"I've been telling him that for years." Paul reached his hand up and tousled his little brother's hair. "You sure do look older."

"Go figure."

Having completed all his formal greetings, Levi stood at the bottom of the stairs and crossed his arms. His family stood around him shivering and smiling. "Geez," Levi said looking around at them. "Take a picture."

"Right," said his dad. "No sense in standing out here freezing your *tuchis* off." He spread his arms out as if to gather his family under his wings. He gestured for everyone to walk up the stairs. "In, in," he said. "We've killed the fattened calf and we've prepared a feast in your honor. Please, inside."

Nick fell in next to Paul, behind the rest of the family. Paul put his arm around Nick's shoulder. He wore a cruel smile as if he were doling out congratulations after losing a hard-fought game. "Must be nice," he muttered to Nick. "I didn't get a party like this when I got back from DC."

Nick patted him on the back in consolation. "Who needs a party when you inherit the family business and get your name on the door of a law firm?"

Paul frowned and nodded, as if thinking of that for the first time. "Touché," he said. "Touché."

3.4 IF I HAD KNOWN, I COULD HAVE BEEN A BIT MORE SENSITIVE

She recognized many, but she knew none. Eris tried her best to give polite smiles to the many guests at the party, and she graciously uttered her thanks when she accepted her drink from Mrs. Hartwig, but she was all too happy to find herself alone in the back den where she could look up and down the bookshelves without having to make small talk.

Levi had already barreled through the house giving bear hugs, patting backs, shaking hands. He disappeared out the back door only moments before entering the front.

Nick came up behind Eris and put his hand on her shoulder. She turned, holding the stem of a wineglass in her right hand near her chest. She traced the edge of the glass's circular bottom with her left index finger. Nick put his hand on her waist and kissed her cheek. He turned so he stood next to her and faced the same direction. In a low voice he asked, "Whatchya got in there?"

She ran her eyes over the crowd. "Champagne. It's a celebration." She took a sip and went back to tracing the bottom of the glass.

Nick reached to grab it. She turned her body to protect it and she sent an elbow into his stomach, but with playfulness and not malice. "Oh relax, Dad. It's ginger ale."

He grunted. "Was that really necessary?" He grabbed his stomach.

Annoyed now, she hissed at him. "Like it would make a difference. You'd still hover around like a little hawk." She then threw her voice into her nose, "Whatchya doin? Whatchya drinking? Ginger ale? Lemme taste it." She rolled her eyes. "Four hundred and twelve days, Nick. Four hundred and twelve days sober. But you probably know that better than I do, don't you, Nick, because whenever I start to forget that I had a problem, you have to remind me, right?"

He looked surprised. "I wasn't trying to—"

"Listen. As many problems as I've had, I'm in control. Remember our wedding? With my mother there? I was sober there, remember?"

"I was sober too."

"Not the point. If I could make it through that outrageous and depressing display of drunkenness bordering on debauchery, I can make it through this." She noticed but could not help that her voice rose as she spoke.

A woman Eris didn't know bent down in front of them to grab a slice of summer sausage and cheese from the plate on the coffee table. She looked over her shoulder at them as she stood up, and she gave a patronizing smile as she lingered. "Excuse me," she said. She walked to the other side of the room, tossing one more glance at the couple fighting in the corner.

Nick crossed his arms and lowered his voice, trying to get Eris to do the same. "How many times do you have to bring up the wedding? I'm sorry. I should have thought about it more. I should have thought about your mom. I'm sorry. The Hartwigs are sorry. I'm sorry. I'm sorry. I'm sorry. Okay? Need me to say it for the rest of our lives together? I'm sorry."

He leaned in. He tried to kiss her. She pushed him away.

"Not the point." She turned to him. "The point is, you can take the kid gloves off any day now and try a little thing called trust." She lifted the wineglass to her lips and sipped, pretending she was in control.

As if by instinct, Nick leaned down to her glass to smell it.

"Are you kidding me?" She spun on her heel and stormed away two steps, though she had nowhere to go. She turned around to face him. "Seriously?"

He reached out. "I didn't—"

"Unbelievable." She huffed and turned to the window.

And then he was there in her vision again, but she could not see him clearly. The husband she saw on the back deck—gregarious, laughing, and gesturing to other guests with a beer bottle—was not the husband that she knew. The Nick she saw through the window was the man she recognized from the bar, from the backyard barbecues, from the coffee hour after church, from the chance encounters in the grocery store. This was not the Nick she knew from home, from the kitchen table, from the bedroom. That Nick was quiet, pensive, suspicious. The husband of the home lived almost entirely within himself. Even their arguments were punctuated by brutal and agonizing silences. She did not know if he didn't speak because of his great anger or because of his great indifference.

She also recognized Levi, but barely. He was no longer a little boy, although he still had no substance to his frame. When she first walked to the window, he lay supine in the snow, waving his arms and legs to make an angel in the snow. A little girl she did not know jumped on top of him and kneed him between the legs. He sat up and picked her up in the process. His movements were decisive—explosive—and she flew up and out of his hands as he threw her into the snow. Another girl made a tiny snowman by herself. She watched patiently, waiting for her turn with crazy Uncle Levi.

A boy of about ten—Eris remembered it was Levi's nephew, his sister's child—jumped on his back. He wrapped his arms around Levi's neck. Levi stood up and roared. The boy lost his grip and fell in the snow. In retaliation, he packed a snowball and threw it, hitting his uncle in the face. Levi brought the two young girls to himself and spread his arms around them. He gently folded up the stocking cap of the older girl and he whispered in her ear before rolling her cap back down. He patted her head. The girls spread out, and they all pelted the young boy with snowballs. He squealed so loudly Eris could hear it through the window, and he ran across the yard in retreat. Levi and the girls chased after him. The boy ran behind a tree and Levi stooped to pack a snowball. He waited a beat, and as soon as the boy stuck his head around the tree, he was met with a frozen splash to his face.

Though Nick stood in a circle of men smoking cigarettes on the deck, he had relinquished the center of attention to someone else. He followed the backyard battle with his eyes. He laughed when the boy was hit in the face. Nick's head and eyes followed Levi as he moved through the yard.

Levi's sister Liz appeared on the deck with her hands on her hips. She was blond, beautiful, put together, painfully nice, and entirely too high-maintenance for Eris's liking. The little girls ran inside. Levi sat in the middle of the yard in the snow with his hands in his lap. The little boy stood half-behind his mother, crying into the hem of her shirt.

She waved a hand and said something to scold Levi. She knelt down and examined the boy's face, and she kissed his forehead. The kid's face was red and his eyes were swollen from crying, but it didn't look like he had any cuts or bruises. He wiped his nose on his sleeve and shook his head no, burying his face in his mom's shoulder. She patted his back. Eris wondered what it would be like to have such a helicopter for a mother. She would never know.

Levi, still sitting on the ground, messed with the snow between his outstretched legs. He was nearly laughing. Eris heard his muffled shout through the window: "He started it." He staggered as he stood up. His eyes were wild and young and they searched around, looking for kicks. Eris recognized this Levi.

His sister turned and went into the house. She slammed the sliding patio door. Eris quickly turned away from the window, not wanting to make eye contact with Liz as she stormed in, but then she felt silly. She was practically invisible at her station, surrounded by a sea of people moving and talking. Everyone else sharing of themselves.

She turned back to the window to see Levi's face darken. He threw a snowball where his sister had been. It smacked and rattled against the patio door. He walked over to Nick. He put his hand on her husband's shoulder and leaned on him. He pulled out a cigarette and lit it. He took a single drag and waved it around. He stepped back and gesticulated; he threw his barely smoked cigarette on the ground and stamped on it. "Tell your kid to stop being such a pussy," he yelled at the door. Eris did not know this Levi.

Nick and Levi walked in together. Her husband didn't look her way as the two old friends tumbled through the patio door and through the room next to her. Levi reached into a cooler and pulled out two beers. He put his canine tooth under each cap and pulled the bottles down in turn, prying the caps off. He handed one to Nick and held out his bottle as if they were the only two people in the room. "Cheers," he said. They walked to the stairwell by the door that went to the basement, bottles tilted the whole way, draining down their throats. When the bottles came down empty before they even reached the other side of the room, Levi slapped the back of the closest person, a thick old man in a suit. "Hey, thanks for coming," he said. Nick slapped someone's back. "Great to see you again." They reached the stairwell to the basement and Levi nudged Nick and whispered something. They looked around as if partners in a conspiracy.

Eris had been in this house once before, when they were juniors in high school. Levi's older brother and sister were off at college, and his parents were out at some fundraiser for La Crosse's aspirant district attorney. The night began with Nick, Levi, and Eris mixing orange juice with a bottle of Grey Goose pulled from the fully stocked basement bar. It ended with Levi puking in the sink while the DA's wife—looking fun in a little black dress overflowing with all her embonpoint—rubbed his back and informed Levi's dad that she'd have whatever the boy was drinking.

She knew all about that basement, and those boys were idiots if they thought they were fooling anyone.

Eris turned back to the bookshelves. She set her glass down and flipped through a poetry anthology. "Oh, Ezra," she thought. "How I've missed you." She had once loved to read. She had loved art, poetry, and music. Then life happened. She put the book back and traced the bottom edge of her glass again. When she could no longer take the combination of boredom and anxiety from standing alone in a room full of people, she looked for an opening in the crowd.

When she was halfway down the switchback staircase, she could see Nick, Levi, and an older man slamming shot glasses down on the bar. By the time she reached the bottom, the older man was holding up a chunky brass challenge coin in front of Nick's face. "You see that there, Nick?" the man said.

Nick nodded politely while Levi stood behind the man's shoulder making the shape of a gun with his thumb and forefinger. He placed the forefinger inside his mouth, pointing up through the roof, and he mimed cocking the hammer with his thumb. He then jerked his head back as if he had shot himself, and he dropped his chin on his chest and let his tongue hang out.

Nick put his hand on the man's shoulder. A gesture to reassure. "Yeah, I see it Robert. I see it."

The man turned around, and Levi popped his head up and raised his eyebrows. The man slammed the coin down on the bar next to Levi. "One Hundred and Eighty-Second Airborne." The man enunciated every word. "Da Nang Air Base. Sixty-nine." He nodded silently as if he were remembering something significant and serious. "I never saw much action, but let me tell you, it was the constant fear that got to you."

As Eris approached, she made eye contact with Levi for the first time. He cocked his head like a curious dog, as if he disbelieved his own eyes. Eris grabbed Nick's elbow and pulled him toward the empty media room.

Once they were alone, she turned to face him. She crossed her arms and leaned in, but she didn't bother to whisper. "So are you wasted too? You smell like a distillery."

"What do you mean?"

"Are you as hammered as Levi?"

"No. This is my first beer."

"Whatever."

"Honey. Gimme a break. I haven't seen the guy in over three years."

"I said whatever. Do what you want. But give me my keys. I'm not driving that stupid truck again, and I'm sure as hell not letting you drive my car like this."

He reached into his pocket and grabbed the keys. She reached for them. He lifted them and held them above his head. Did he expect her to jump for them? And that stupid smile.

"What have we here?" Levi leaned on the doorjamb. "A lovers' quarrel?" Levi tilted his head so it, too, rested on the doorjamb, and he flashed a big carnie grin. "Hello, Eris. Like a fine wine, you've refined with age. You look as beautiful as ever." He then righted himself and walked across the room, swaying as if the walls and floor were fun house mirrors.

"Hello, Levi." She looked down at the carpet, embarrassed for them all.

Levi reached out and took one of her hands. He kissed the top of it. "Where've you been? Why're you hiding away in here?"

She pulled her hand back. "It's nice to see you again." She was polite. Formal.

"So Eris, do you know any of these people?"

She shook her head no.

"Nick?"

"Sure. People that went to our church growing up. Friends of your parents. I see a lot of them at the bar. They're all people from town here. The town where you grew up."

Levi put an arm around Eris. She stiffened.

"So Eris," he said. "That makes the two of us then. You and I. That is, you and I don't know anyone. And so."

"So what?"

"So come join the party."

She said nothing.

"C'mon. I'll mix you a rum and coke. The three of us can play cards, and it'll be like the old days."

She could see Nick out of the corner of her eye shaking his head no, drawing a line across his throat. She tried to smile politely. "No, thank you. I'm fine."

In a way, she could sense it already. The way it would be. Now no different than it used to be. And she felt small. Silent. Pushed to the margins. Nothing more than an object between them. Forget that she was real.

Levi took a drink from his own highball glass and let go of her. "Suit yourself." He took another large gulp and wiped his mouth with the back of his hand. "Suit yourself. But really, you should have a drink."

"Yeah," her husband said. "Why don't you have a drink?"

They all stood there staring at each other.

Nick then looked down at his feet. Levi either didn't pick up on the silent tension, or he didn't care. He took another drink and looked from Eris to Nick, from Nick to Eris.

Finally, Eris patted Nick on the chest with an open palm as she walked past him to leave. "I think you've drunk enough for all of us."

Levi spun around and called after her. "Aw, now I know why Nick married you." He held up his glass in a toast. "It's not everyone that knows how to use the past perfect of drink like that."

She turned when she got to the door. She held her peace. "I'll see you at home, Nick."

"What?" Levi called. "You're leaving? You just got here. I just got here."

She lifted a hand to wave but didn't turn around. In a way, she envied him. His wild eyes and oblivion.

"I haven't seen you in years, and you're leaving? C'mon," he called after her. "Have a drink and take the stick out."

She walked away. She didn't blame him. They wouldn't enjoy her company anyway. Sometimes she didn't enjoy her own.

She melted along the line of the wall, up the stairs, and into the crowded living room. Eris looked around for Charlotte Hartwig to tell her goodbye, but she stood at the kitchen island with a gaggle of women.

Charlotte told the other women, "We never expected it and still don't even know how it all worked out, but he came home early and Jesus kept him safe, just like we prayed."

"The Lord does work in mysterious ways."

"Mmm, mmm, mmm."

Eris thought of waiting until the conversation was over, thought of returning to the window to stand alone again. Instead, she turned back toward the door to leave. The sea of people parted and moved around her as she murmured and touched elbows.

"Petals on a wet, black bough," she thought.

3.5 I'D BE REMISS IF I DIDN'T ADDRESS THE WHOLE SILVER STAR THING

L evi thought he had escaped Robert Wright, his challenge coins, and his war stories. He had not. When he tried passing him again to use the restroom, the man put a big farmer's hand on the back of his neck.

"Like I was saying before. It was just the fear, more than the combat." Robert put a fist on his chest and belched with a closed mouth, only to blow the noxious odor in Levi's face. "But I don't really have to tell you boys that, what with all those roadside bombs and booby traps. Not to mention, you're supposed to be fighting a war, but they tie your hands with all these rules of engagement. And you don't know who the enemy is, right? I mean, could be anybody. Nope. Don't have to tell you boys, do I?"

"No. You certainly don't have to tell us."

"Real quick. Let me tell you about the night I landed in country, just to put it all in perspective."

[Why do we feel the need to assail each other with our war stories? That was the last thing I wanted. I looked down into my glass, but he carried on anyway. Certain words jumped out at me— mortars, wire, listening post, jungle rot, dancing girls—but I couldn't tell you what he said. I was already plenty drunk. I really only snapped out of it when he laughed and slapped his palm on the top of the bar, and by that point all I could do was snort in commiseration and tell him something like, "Robert, you're the real hero here."]

He waved Levi off, but Robert grinned from ear to ear, clearly enjoying himself. "Nah." He unwrapped that tired old cliché that Levi knew so well, "Anyone would have done the same thing."

His mother appeared at the bottom of the stairs. "Sorry to interrupt, gentlemen, but your presence is requested upstairs."

"Pourquoi?" said Levi.

She smiled, stuck her tongue out, and curled it. She rubbed her hands together. "You'll just have to see, Smarty Pants."

Levi walked up the stairs behind Nick. "Too bad she didn't show up ten minutes earlier."

"Right," Nick said, laughing.

The guests gathered in the living room and crowded to one side. Liz's kids sat on the floor with their legs crossed. Nick stood next to Paul at the edge of the crowd. Levi's dad stood in a cleared space in front of the horseshoe of people. "Come here, Son," he said.

Levi stood and turned so he faced both his father and the crowd. "What's going on here?" he whispered to his father.

A few people in the crowd chuckled. Everyone but Levi was in on the joke, and he didn't like the feeling.

"We couldn't be happier now that you're home. We're just really proud of you Son, and we—that is, your mother and I—got you a little coming home present." He turned to his wife, who hovered in the doorway that led to the dining room. "Dear?"

She leaned through the door and pulled out a large frame. Beaming from ear to ear, she handed it to her husband. Levi's dad held it out so people could see it. He slowly turned his body with the frame out so everyone got a good look. Then he held it out so Levi could look at it. "We had your medals framed with the narrative and citation," his dad said, nearly busting with pride.

Levi sucked in his lip. "Yeah. I see that."

His dad brought the large frame closer to his body and let it rest on his hip. "It reads as follows—"

"It's okay, Dad." Levi put his hand over the words. "That's not necessary." He shook his head and laughed, trying to be a good sport. "I can't thank you all enough for this." He took a moment to respectfully admire his gift, knowing their intentions were pure. "I don't deserve this. Thanks."

His dad handed it back to his mom, and she held it out and started reading, "Sergeant Levi Hartwig displayed uncommon gallantry in action against the enemy on May 15th, 2005—"

"Mom. You don't have to read it."

She smiled at him and kept reading. "In the vicinity of Ad Dujayl, Iraq, while acting as a dismounted team leader and vehicle commander."

"Mom. It happened, like, four years ago. It's not news anymore." He looked around, as if for help. "Please, just—"

She waved a hand at him and smiled. "Oh, it's okay, honey." She looked back down. "His heroic actions after an improvised explosive device attack—"

He erupted before his brain could catch up with his mouth. "Mom," he shouted. "I said don't read the goddamned medal."

His dad stepped in front of him and put a hand on his chest. The shuffling, murmuring, whispering, laughing, and background noise had all fallen away. Everyone heard him whisper, "Check yourself, Son."

The damage was done. His mother quietly said, "Oh," and she pursed her lips and looked down at the medal in her hands.

Levi took a deep breath and unclenched his fists. "Mom. I'm sorry. Really." Trying and failing to recover, he said, "But thank you. It's very sweet. I'm sorry."

She set the frame on the ground against the wall and folded her hands in front of her. She lifted her chin and set her jaw. "No. I'm sorry. I should have—" Her voice cracked. She stopped and cleared her throat. She finished in a whisper. "I should have listened the first time."

"Mom?" Levi scanned the faces of the silent guests. "Well, shit," he said. Levi locked eyes on Nick trying to shrink away behind Paul. "Oh yeah, Nick. Hey Nick. Come over here." He held his arm out and waved him in.

Nick hesitated. Levi's dad shook his head in exasperated resignation. Nick took a few tentative steps toward the front of the silent room.

"C'mon, Nick, don't be shy." Levi put one arm around his friend and slapped his chest with his other hand. "This guy needs to be recognized. Not a day goes by that I don't thank my lucky stars that my friend, my brother from another mother, the real hero here, *my* hero, Nick Anhalt is still with us." He looked around. "Right?" A few people in the crowd nodded their heads while looking around to see if they should. Levi looked at his dad. "Right, Dad?"

His dad looked at the ground.

"Ladies and gentlemen," Levi said. "I give you Specialist (Retired) Nicholas Anhalt. Recipient of the Purple Heart Medal and Army Commendation Medal with Valor device." He clapped and whistled and lifted his palms to encourage the rest of the people. It was all very theatrical, like Levi was a caricature of himself.

When the crowd failed to rebound, his face fell. "Thanks for coming everyone." He brushed past his dad, past his mom without a word, and through the kitchen. He slammed the door to the garage as he left. He trudged through the lawn getting cold snow down his shoes where it melted into his socks under the arches of his feet. When he reached the sidewalk, he stomped the snow from his shoes and kept walking.

Levi felt terrible for how he had snapped at his mother, but everything would have been easier if they would have let him forget it, if they would have just let him move on. Instead, that medal kept popping back up, and it forced him to dig graves that were better left filled.

3.6 HOW TO DRINK WISCONSINABLY

Nick's second grade teacher was one of the last to leave. She hugged Charlotte and whispered something in her ear. She then came over to Nick and gave him a hug. "You take care of your friend."

"Sure."

"I mean it," she said. She closed the front door quietly.

Robert Wright swaggered up to Kevin Hartwig just before leaving. He pumped his hand, not letting go of it as he talked. "You know, when I got home from Vietnam, I went through the same thing. Ain't easy, just switching worlds like that." He pulled his hand away and snapped his fingers. "Just like that. Hell, I coulda told ya. Well you know as well as I do, having been over there yourself. You don't win a medal like that without having been through hell, ya know?"

Kevin chose his words carefully. "I don't blame him for not wanting to relive it all."

Charlotte had disappeared and Robert had been the last to leave. Nick walked around with a trash bag cleaning up paper plates with half-eaten pieces of cake and plastic cups that weren't quite empty.

Paul leaned against the refrigerator and drank a bottle of beer. When he had finished, he looked at his watch and said, "I suppose." He put his bottle in Nick's trash bag, left the room, and came back in a black peacoat. "I'll be seeing you."

When they had finished with the bulk of the cleaning, Kevin and Nick sat at the island across from each other. They drank in silence for a while. Kevin pinched his lips between his thumb and forefinger, wiping off the excess beer. "I should have known better," he said. "I don't know what I was thinking. Just proud I guess. And thinking more about showing off than thinking about what he would want." He looked down and peeled the label on his beer bottle.

"Don't beat yourself up," Nick said. He wished he could say something more edifying, something less cliché, but nothing came to him. "You meant well." That too sounded weak.

Kevin nodded and dropped little bits of metallic paper on the counter as he continued to pick at his label. Nick wished he could go over and hug him—after all, he had become as much a part of that family as any of Kevin's own children—but he kept his seat.

They heard a clunking in the back. Nick spread the blinds to look out the window above the sink. "It's Levi."

"Better if you talk to him," Kevin said.

Nick took a seat on the cascading step next to Levi. He set an extra beer on the landing between them. He grabbed a cigarette and held the pack out to Levi, who tried grabbing one between two fingers. He swayed and his eyes crossed and uncrossed. His face was slack. He missed twice before finally grasping one. They sat on the step, their backs against the edge of the deck, their cold breath indistinguishable from the smoke that filled their lungs.

"Think I'm like the worst person ever?"

"No," Nick said. "Not the worst ever."

"I'm the worst person ever." Levi nodded and took a drink. "Trust me on that one."

Nick looked out toward the swaying shadows of the denuded trees. "Who am I to judge?"

"So do my parents know?"

"Know what?"

"That it's all a bunch of bullshit?"

"That what is?" Nick knew what he was talking about. He could Google as well as anyone. He knew that his letters home had no truth in them, that his brigade had not been sent home early, that his service commitment should have kept him in the army for the next two years. But he wanted to hear him say it. He wanted to hear the details. He wanted him to open up to him so he could help him. So he could somehow be a friend.

"Whatever."

"So then, tell me what happened."

"Rough night tonight, huh? I sure was a dick to my mom."

Nick kept quiet, hoping he'd keep talking.

"Just drank too much is all." Levi took another drink. "I drink too much." He turned his chin toward the sky; he extended his neck. He tried and failed to blow smoke rings. "I have drunk too much." He lifted a finger and pointed it at his head. "And tomorrow?"

"You will have drank too much?"

"Nope." Levi shook his head in disappointment. "No, sir. I will have drunk too much."

Levi's dad opened the sliding glass door. "I'm headed to bed, boys. Don't throw your butts in the lawn. Your mother hates that."

Levi didn't turn around. He took another drag off his smoke, and he drank another swallow of beer.

"Levi, it's good to have you home."

Levi lifted a hand and let it drop.

His dad waited for a moment, and when it was clear that was the only response he would get, he turned and quietly closed the door.

"Anyway," Levi said. "Married. Renting? Owning?"

"We bought a house in La Crosse. North side. The drive to the bar every day sucks, but Eris likes living in town, in her old neighborhood."

"Can I stay with you for a while?" Levi made eye contact for the first time since Nick came outside. "I hate to ask—"

"No, no. That's ah. That's fine."

Levi turned away again and flicked his cigarette into the lawn. "Forget it. I should have given you notice. I'll figure something out. I'll get a hotel or something." He shook his head. "I just can't stay here. A grown man living with his parents? It's pathetic."

"No," Nick said. "It's fine. Stay with us. I'm sure Eris won't mind."

"Oh yeah. Forgot you're domesticated now. You need permission for everything, I s'pose."

Nick bristled at the suggestion he wasn't in charge of his own decisions. "Gimme a break. We've shared tents, bunk beds, the cover of a tire under enemy fire; I'm pretty sure you can share our house for a while. Besides, it isn't like Eris never stayed at our apartment when the two of us were in college."

"Ah yes." Levi closed his eyes, turned his head toward the sky, and breathed deeply through his nose.

"Yes what?"

"Nothing. Sure it's not a problem?"

"Not a problem. Anyway, I'd say I owe you."

"I'd say." Levi punched him in the shoulder. "You owe me every year of your life."

Nick looked over at him to gauge his mood, but he sensed no jocularity. "Okay then. Need to grab anything?"

"Nah. All my crap is still in your wife's car." He stood up and spread his arms. He breathed deeply, let out a tremendous yell, and threw his beer bottle over the fence into the neighbor's yard. It fell with a great crash of broken glass. "Hello, Wisconsin," he screamed into the cold night.

Before getting in the car, Levi turned. "Hold on a sec." He ran to the front door. Finding it locked, he lifted a flowerpot near the steps. He unlocked the door with the hidden key and disappeared inside. When he reappeared, he was carrying the frame. He set it in the bed of the truck on a blanket of snow before getting in.

"Pardon the mess," Nick said. "I don't usually have company."

"What is all this crap?" Levi kicked around the garbage on the floor of the passenger's side. He started lifting things and throwing them through the back window into the rusted bed with the frame and the snow. "Cigarette boxes, an old newspaper, a McDonald's bag. Classic: a half-finished breakfast sandwich."

He pulled out a flat black box, slightly larger than his hand. "What the hell is wrong with you?" he said. "You have your Purple Heart on the ground with all your garbage?" He opened the box and ran his fingers along the ribbon.

Nick pushed in the cigarette lighter. "What the hell do I care? Just a bit of string and steel."

Levi shook his head slowly and his mouth dropped open. Nick was unable to determine if Levi's exaggerated display was ironic disbelief or if he was being serious.

Levi set the box on the dashboard. "Well what about your Comm with Valor?"

"Keep digging." Nick drove. Fresh snow fell and the headlights shone on each sparkling flake. Nick weaved across the powder-covered highway lines.

3.7 NO, THIS IS NOT A FRAT HOUSE

When Eris was a girl, she spent a summer with her mother at a beachfront home on Florida's Emerald Coast. The home was owned by a family friend, and they had gone there during one of the separations before the divorce. It was the first time Eris had ever been near the ocean and she could not sleep for days. When she closed her eyes, the rolling of the waves made her sick, as if she herself were rocking. Her mother spent her days in bed before she dressed up, put on makeup, and left for the nights. Eris spent hours alone watching the caps break onto the white sands that spread out from the condo. The sands glowed in the moonlight. When she eventually returned home, she could not sleep without the waves.

The memory was remote and distant, as if it had happened in a dream rather than in her childhood. She had not thought of this period in her life in years. Yet, this is what she thought about as she tossed and turned, unable to sleep without her husband by her side.

By the time Nick did return—drunk, tiptoeing, bumping into furniture in the dark—she only had two hours before she had to rise for work. He was snoring within seconds, and within minutes he had pulled the quilt from her and wrapped himself into a chrysalis. As uncomfortable as she was with her meager sliver of top sheet, she finally drifted off to sleep until her alarm woke her.

She showered and dressed in a pinstriped skirt and a button-up top. She went to the living room to find a pair of tights from the baskets full of laundry she hadn't gotten around to folding. Just as she found one, she heard a rustling behind her. She jumped up and hit the light switch on the wall.

Levi lay on the couch, his eyes wide open and locked in on her, his brow furrowed in concentration. His hand frantically swept along the floor next to the couch as if he were trying to grab something that wasn't there.

"What the hell?" she shouted. "What are we running here, a frat house?"

Levi let out a deep breath. "You just about gave me a heart attack," he said. He lay back down on his side and turned to face the back of the couch.

Eris stared at the lump of blankets on the couch for a moment before heading back up the hallway. She then turned back and hit the wall with the towel she held, wanting to impress upon him the level of her displeasure. "What if I had been naked?"

"Nothing I've never seen before."

"What did you say?"

He rolled over and sat up, but gave her no response.

"Did you say what I think you just said?"

He wiped his eyes. She couldn't tell if he was giving her a sleepy smirk or if he was just squinting against the light.

"Are you still drunk?"

"Sorry," he said. "What?"

She stormed back to her bedroom and threw the towel at her sleeping husband. "Get up." He made no move. "Is someone else opening for you today or what?"

"No," he said. "Tired."

"Get up. No one made you stay out last night."

He sat up and put his feet on the ground. He sat with his head in his hands a moment before standing. He looked down at his watch. "It'll be fine. I'll make you some coffee. Want eggs?"

She sat on the bed and put on her tights.

"Eggs?"

"You know I don't like eggs." She zipped her boots before following him into the kitchen.

She felt intense jealousy when he walked into the kitchen wearing nothing but a pair of boxer shorts. His immodesty offended her. Maybe offended was the wrong word, but apart from the doctors and nurses, she was the only one who had seen him in anything except full pants and a collared shirt. Yet here he was walking around exposed when they had a guest.

Levi leaned against the sink looking out the window. He was barefoot in jeans and a white undershirt. He held an empty glass.

Nick slapped his butt on the way to the fridge. "Good effort last night."

Levi nodded. He turned on the tap and refilled his glass with water. He chugged it down. "Not so bad yourself."

He turned around. Eris saw the way Levi's eyes only flickered along the motley colored scars that ran the length of Nick's body. He acted like he didn't notice the appearance that was marred beyond that of any man she had ever known. She saw the way Levi averted his eyes from the scars on his legs and torso and stared only at Nick's eyes. It was the same way that men refused to break eye contact after they had been caught staring at your breasts.

"What's on your schedule today?" Levi said. He didn't even glance at Eris.

"Work. I should have been there half an hour ago."

Levi turned to look up at the clock on the soffit above the window. "This early?"

"Lots to do. I have to reconcile the books, do some inventory, meet with our food service rep. Not to mention, it's crunch time on getting W-2s out and then prepping for taxes. The place doesn't run itself, contrary to what my wife thinks."

Nick set a cup of coffee in front of Eris, who sat at the round kitchen table, ignored until then. She rolled her eyes, but no one noticed. It wasn't that she thought the place ran itself or that someone didn't need to put the hours in, she just didn't understand why Nick had to do it all himself.

As if reading her mind, Levi said, "Geez. Don't you have your people to do that?"

"Don't I have my people? My peeps?" Nick laughed and turned around to pour himself a cup of coffee. "What people?"

"I don't know. Like employees."

"Can't afford more than a short-order cook and a few bartenders. Certainly can't afford what a good manager would deserve right now." He took a sip of his coffee. "Of course, Eris disagrees." He said it as if she weren't sitting right there. As if she didn't have a voice of her own.

Eris stood up. She reached behind Levi and dumped her coffee in the sink. "Excuse me," she said. "And excuse my husband."

She saw Levi point at her and lift his hands like, What's her problem? As if she weren't there. She also saw Nick shrug and shake his head like, How should I know? As if she weren't there.

She was still angry by the time she reached her first break at work. She went outside to smoke a cigarette, and as she sat there shivering and alone behind the building, she said a quiet prayer for the strength to let it go, whatever it was. As part of her program, she was supposed to identify her triggers, and she had been trying to carry that philosophy into every aspect of her life. She was trying to be a better person. She had been angry when she had found Levi on the couch, but her anger had come more from her fear.

Everything else was more complicated. She had been angry when Nick hadn't thought of covering himself in front of Levi. She felt protective, and yes, jealous. She was the one who had nursed him, who had rubbed salves on his tight, inflamed skin. She was the one who had seen and loved him through his secret pains when no one else could. She was the one who had waited for him to finally trust her enough to accept him. She was the one. She had always been the one.

Now there was Levi. Breezy, carefree, self-absorbed, wild, and rude. Worse than all of that, dangerous.

She lit a second cigarette and closed her eyes as she inhaled.

But wasn't it unfair of her to deny that those two also had a history? To deny that they shared formative years before they met her? And before they left for the war like a couple dunces, hadn't she been the third wheel anyway? But there was also the secret history. There were those things they did together in the dark of night or in the heat of the blistering sun on strange highways and in dusty towns a world away. They shared things she knew nothing about. There were things they had done and things that had been done to them, and she knew nothing of those things except the damage they left behind.

One late night shortly after Nick had returned home—before they were married, when things were complicated, when Eris didn't know what they were together—they had gotten drunk behind the pub after it closed. It was four in the morning, and the alley smelled like cigarette smoke and rotten garbage. She couldn't remember what song it had been, but Nick played his guitar gently, with only the side of his thumb on the strings. His voice was near a whisper. When Eris started humming a harmony, he started crying. Weeping, really. She asked him what it was.

"Nothing," he told her.

"You can tell me," she said.

"You don't need to know."

"But I want to know."

He laughed and sniffed and wiped his eyes. "So do I."

She must have started crying as well because he reached up and wiped a tear from her cheek.

"It's okay," he said. "I'm okay. But I can't answer questions about what I don't know."

Since that night, he had offered nothing more, and that was the last time she had seen him cry.

But now, she had to know. For herself and for Nick, she needed to share that too, whatever it was. She decided she would go home at lunch and apologize to Levi. She would talk to him.

She wanted to be a better person. She wanted a better marriage.

When she walked in, Levi was hunched over a notebook, writing. A small stone sat on the table in front of him. He finished a line, dropped a period onto the page with finality, and he closed the notebook. It was one of the cheap black-and-white composition books that he had always carried around in high school.

"What are you writing?"

"Nothing." He put his hand over the stone on the table as if to hide it. "So do you still write poetry?"

She shook her head. "What kind of nothing?"

He slipped the stone into his pocket. "One rung below juvenilia."

"Still want to be a writer?"

"No."

"Why not?"

"I'd rather do something useful."

She sat down across from him. "So what are you doing that's useful today?"

"I need to buy a car."

"I can get you a good interest rate at our bank. I know someone who works there." She winked at him, trying to be casual. Trying to be friendly.

He didn't smile back. "I don't need a loan."

"Sorry." She picked at her fingernails.

"I set up in the basement. Nick said that was okay. Is that okay?"

"Yeah sure. Sure, that's okay."

"Okay. Because if it's not—"

"Tell me some war stories," she said.

"What?"

"Tell me some war stories."

"Why do you want me to tell you war stories?"

"Nick never has."

"Then why should I?"

"So I know what happened over there."

"We played Xbox over there."

"What else?"

"We watched movies over there."

"What else?"

"We went running before dawn when it wasn't too hot. We started running west so we could see the sun rise on our way back to our hooch."

"What else?"

"We lifted weights at night when we couldn't sleep."

"What else?"

"We took up chewing tobacco to quit smoking cigarettes and we ended up doing both."

"What else?"

"We read cheap books that people sent to us and we learned the value of pulp fiction."

"What else?"

"We filled a shower entirely with shaving cream and videotaped some new guy opening the curtain."

"What did he do?"

"He said 'aw' and went to another shower."

"That's it?"

"That's it."

"What else?"

"We played our guitars together late at night when we got back from missions. The adrenaline flowed, so we'd start loud. Other guys sat around us and smoked Cuban cigars. Each night, like a ritual, we slowed down."

"What else?" she whispered.

"We were the lullabies." Levi picked up the coffee mug that sat next to his closed notebook. He looked in it, swirled it. "This guy," he said. "A big guy named Tom Hooper liked to sing harmony."

She said nothing. She held her breath, hoping he would say more.

He set the mug on the table, picked up his notebook, and stood up. "I suppose I have things to do."

"C'mon. What else?" She did not want him to stop.

"What do you want from me?"

"I want to know what you guys did over there. I want to know why Nick never talks anymore."

"He never talks because he listens."

"He doesn't listen to me."

A pained look came across his face. He put his hand on the doorknob.

"Another time?"

"I don't know," he said looking down. He looked up and into her eyes. He looked conflicted, but as if he were searching her instead of himself. "Sure. Yeah. Sometime. I don't know. Maybe."

"Decisive. So I can take you at your word?"

"You can take me however you want."

"What is that supposed to mean?"

He sighed deeply. "Okay. Yes."

3.8 CHEKHOV'S GUN

I had a 6,000-word section here in which I described the few weeks I spent bumming around right after leaving the army. I tried to explain my lack of direction. I bemoaned how the army didn't even give me a chance to plan my exit, just kicked me out the door. My to-do list included only two things: 1) Going to Walter Reed every day for two weeks to visit a member of my unit named Toby, and 2) Getting extremely wasted for the entire month after the visit except for the hours I spent laid out in my Weston bed in the perfect midday blackness of my hotel room.

Toby was already a skinny kid, but he instantly lost seventy-three pounds when some pressure plate hooked up to a jug of homemade explosives took both legs and an arm while we were on a dismounted patrol on some unnamed goat trail in some worthless village between Sperwan and Masum Ghars. The sad thing is, Toby didn't get the worst of it. He just stared at the wall while I was there—his silence making no secret of his bitterness.

And so I tore up all those pages because you don't need to hear about that. You don't need to hear 500 words on the loneliness of the hospital bed because you've been there. You don't need me to pontificate on the fierce warrior-ethos of so many and the deep despair of more. You don't need a graph on the medicinal sting of the air, because it resides in your own memory. Mostly, I thought as I tore up all those pages, you don't need to be reminded of how when I visited you, I spent all of five minutes in your room before once again leaving you to deal with it all alone.

I tore up the pages because I didn't want to share with you that—despite the fact that Toby wanted to curse God and die, despite the fact that he wanted nothing do with me or anyone else—I stayed. I showed up and I stayed, just to be there. Sure, I was hung over every day for every visit; and yes, just like with you, I had nothing to offer, nothing at all that would make it better; but at least I was there. In a way, it was easier to stay with him because even in our silence we commiserated. Our shared gall made us a kindred pair.

I destroyed the pages because I didn't think you should know any of that. I didn't do it because you'd think less of me. I thought it would make you think less of what I think of you. And that's the last thing I want this note to do. The thing is, everyone there who knew I was there to see you raved about what an inspiration you were, how you touched so many.

I could see it even in those few minutes. You were so positive. You were so optimistic. Worse, you were so *thankful*. I had none of that in me, and I was ashamed. Worse, I was angry that something like that could happen to you. And every cheery word you said about the goodness of God made me want to slap you across the grafts on your melted face for your stupid and misplaced foolishness.

The truth is, along with everything else, I'm sorry for that too. I'm sorry I wasn't there for you.]

Now that Levi had returned home, he felt as lost as ever. He was back, but he didn't know why. There had been no job lined up, no school admittance, no plan of any kind. His return, rather than serving a purpose, felt like nothing more than natal homing.

Nick told Levi to make himself comfortable in his house, but after showering and setting up a small space in the basement, Levi felt strange wandering the home of a friend he hadn't seen in years, sitting in the kitchen of his wife, who—with her laundry baskets, bold green curtains, matching sofa set, bank job, and probing questions—seemed strange, domestic, adult, completely humorless, and utterly normal. This new Eris, although still a beauty to behold, seemed nothing like the sensuous, snarky, and rebellious girl he had wanted when he was younger. This new Eris matched his friend. In fact, she seemed made for him.

To get away from her, he had gone down to the basement with meaningless mumbles and stammers. He lay on the simple double mattress set up in the corner of the broad semi-furnished room. He knew he had things he could do—get a car, apply for jobs, pick up his stuff from his parents, find an apartment—but he was tired, hung over, and overwhelmed. He didn't know where to begin.

He'd start with a car, he thought. Then a job. He'd look for an apartment next week, or the week after. He just needed a little time to get over whatever funk he had been in, or whatever it was. Maybe he had been spending too much time alone. Maybe in his quest for the perfect ascetic life, he had given up too much. Maybe he just needed a little time around normal people, friends, a little normal conversation. Maybe he just needed someone who would drink with him. Someone to talk to. He needed time to hear the thoughts of someone other than himself. He needed some time to get it together. Just a little time. It wouldn't last forever. He'd start with a car. But he was so tired, he couldn't get going.

[Of course because of the party I had slept poorly, but I had woken worse.

That morning, even as drunk as I was, I woke in a snap to footsteps near my head. I kept my eyes closed and stayed still, but I was certain that if movement didn't give me away, the thunderous beating of my heart surely would. I moved my fingers gently under the pillow, trying to get a firm handhold on my M9 without being too obvious, but I couldn't find it. I swept my hand along the ground to put my fingers on the rifle that slept mere inches beneath my cot, but that wasn't there either. The adrenaline rush had turned into a full-blown panic. I popped my eyes open, ready to catapult into whatever Afghan National Army troop was getting ready to blast me, hoping at least to surprise him, or at the very least, keep his fire from becoming accurate or lethal. I was not ready to be the next victim in some green-on-blue shooting, which had grown all too common while I was over there in Afghanistan.

Of course, all I could see was your wife bent over a laundry basket.

I closed my eyes again to take account of my senses. My hip sank into a plush cushion. Too soft for a cot. My fingers had been dragging along the pile of thick mid-grade carpet. Too nice, too soft, too clean. Too dissimilar from wood, concrete, or dirt to be the floor in a safe house, qalat, or combat outpost. No rifle because they took that from me. Breathing through my nose had been difficult, as stuffy as it was, yet still, I smelled vanilla, not goat dung.

Eris had no idea what I had been through by the time I rolled over, looked at the ceiling, put my hands on my chest, and told her that she scared the hell out of me. Perhaps if she did, she wouldn't have given me such a hard time.]

Yes, he'd get the car. But first, a nap.

He drifted into a semi-somnolent state, which wasn't quite sleeping, but it wasn't far from dreaming. The fresh image of Nick's scarring manifested itself in front of his eyes. Although the burns weren't as gruesome as when they were fresh, their permanence almost made them worse. He replayed the particulars of the attack in his mind and he thought of how he had pulled and yanked on Nick. How much worse had that injured him? He could almost feel the skin sliding away from Nick's hamstrings and buttocks as he lifted him toward the opening where the door had been. He thought how if the IED would have gone off a second—one single second— earlier it would have rung all their bells, but they would all be alive. Everything would have been different.

He thought the same things he had thought a thousand times: One wire touches another and the stupid bomb shorts out. A tanker doesn't crash and Tampa doesn't get backed up, changing their plans. Gassner doesn't go nuts on some kids and Levi doesn't try covering it up. EOD shows up sooner to clear the first IED site. Nick drives the Humvee one foot farther left as he travels along Boa. Anything. Any little stupid thing. One single change of one single link in the chain of events and things would have been different, and Levi wouldn't have been trapped staring down an eternity of circuitous and obsessive thoughts that wouldn't stop turning, churning, burning, and repeating in his mind. If it wasn't the attack in Iraq, it was any number of battles on his first trip to Afghanistan. If it wasn't that, it was what got him kicked out of the army.

And this, he thought. All of this is what it means to regret.

He flung off the blanket, enraged that he should never be allowed to enjoy a moment's rest, even when alone with no agenda. He threw his pillow across the room, furious that he should never enjoy a single moment of silence for as long as he might live because the memories never left and the pictures and images remained and the questions were never answered and the past could never change.

He left the house and waited for half an hour in a Plexiglas booth, shivering the entire time. He stepped onto the first bus and stopped at the first car dealership he saw. He bought the cheapest car on the lot, a rusted-out maroon Blazer, circa 1992. He paid with his debit card, had the temporary plates fixed, and he drove straight to his parents' house in Bangor.

He hoped to get some of his stuff before they got home from work. He knew he'd have to sit down and apologize to his mother for how he had embarrassed her at the party, but he was not yet ready for that confrontation. He knew that the boxes he had mailed had to be there by now, and that included all the boxes of books he had mailed back from Iraq and Afghanistan and everywhere else because he didn't want to lug them around the world, yet neither could he bring himself to get rid of them.

He first went to the unfinished half of the basement with the storage shelves and the laundry machines. He found some taped-up cardboard boxes underneath the stairs, but they only contained Christmas decorations and ornaments. Checking his bedroom next, he grabbed a paring knife from the kitchen and walked down the hall, expecting to find the heavily taped boxes stacked in the middle of the room. When he opened the door, sunlight framed two white-and-blue-striped curtains, which hung mostly closed on a modern stainless steel rod. There were no boxes on the cream carpet, which had stripes from a recent vacuuming, even visible in the relative darkness. Levi didn't recognize the queen bed that took up half the room's right side, nor did he recognize the red, white, and blue striped bedding. The wall on the left held an elaborate modular shelving system, which had been set up around a dresser matching the bed's headboard.

He nearly didn't enter the room at all, thinking maybe his parents had set up a guest room, or maybe they had a strange arrangement with a boarder that he didn't know about, or maybe Paul had moved the stuff in since returning from DC. The bed, however, had a folded note on the pillow, and it was this note that piqued his curiosity enough to get him in the room. He flipped on the light and thought it strange that he should feel like an intruder.

He picked up the note, which was short and written in his mother's handwriting.

• • •

My dearest Levi, Son,

Forgive the liberties we took with the furnishings. We figured you were a little old for the single bed and basketball curtains that were in here when you left. Combo to the safe is your birthday. Books are in alphabetical order, in the same way you packed them in the boxes. OCD much?

I can't tell you how happy we are to have you back. You make us both so proud.

All our love,

Mom and Dad

• • •

He read the note again and turned around to look at the shelving system lined with all the books he had mailed back. Sherman Alexie . . . Charles Bukowski . . . Stephen Crane . . . David James Duncan . . . Denis Johnson . . . Ken Kesey . . . Jack Kerouac . . . Tim O'Brien . . . George Saunders . . . Kurt Vonnegut . . . David Foster Wallace. *Sure enough,* he thought. Everything in order, spines flush. Sitting on top of the dresser and recessed into the shelving system was a small digital safe, similar to the ones found in hotel closets.

He opened the drawers in the dresser and found the T-shirts he had mailed back, all neatly folded. He shook one out and smelled it. His mother had washed the laundry he had mailed back. She had folded it. She had placed it in drawers for him. His heart broke as he pictured his mother whistling and smiling and putting this room together with the best of intentions.

He turned around and rushed to the closet, fearing what he would find. Indeed, when he pulled the string to turn on the light, all the pants and the few button-up shirts he had mailed home hung in a neat row. Several pairs of boots and low quarters sat in a neat row on the floor. His class A uniform had the position of honor. It was encased in plastic that was clear except for the logo of the local dry cleaning shop. Each ribbon and accoutrement had been returned to its proper place on the uniform with care and precision. Levi pictured his mother asking his father a million questions as she tried putting the uniform back together before his dad got tired of answering questions and got up from his recliner to patiently do the work himself, referring his questions about new and unfamiliar ribbons and their proper placements to an Internet search engine.

He pulled the string and turned off the light. He slid down with his back on the doorjamb of the closet until he sat on the floor. He shook his head in disbelief. He wanted to hug them for their sweetness and their unconditional love and their misguided pride and their total obliviousness to everything about him. But did they really expect a twenty-six-year-old combat vet to come home and live in his childhood bedroom?

He was past all that. A grown man. Self-reliant.

He stood and grabbed one of the trunks from the back of the closet and tossed it onto the bed. He flung it open and pulled his pants and shirts from the closet. He threw the clothes into the trunk. He pulled an assortment of books from the shelf and did the same with them. Likewise, he packed a handful of clothes from each drawer. The safe once again caught his eye, and he punched his six-digit numerical birthday into the number pad on the safe. He opened it, and his Glock 19 lay inside. Two loaded magazines and two boxes of ammo lay next to it. He had mailed it home rather than get arrested with it in DC. The magazine well of the weapon was clear, but Levi racked the slide to be sure the chamber was clear. He put the weapon, magazines, and ammo in his trunk. He gave the foreign room one last lingering look before turning off the light and closing the door.

3.9 DID YOU THINK I COULDN'T HEAR EVERY WORD THROUGH THE VENTS?

When Nick got home from work, he didn't see the Blazer in the driveway, nor did he see it parked on the street. He crawled into bed with his already sleeping wife. He asked if she had seen Levi since that morning. She mumbled into her pillow. He couldn't understand her so he asked, "What did you say?"

She lifted her head slightly, but kept her eyes closed. "You need to knock this off. Hire another manager already."

He said, "This again? Should I just start ticking down the list of why that won't work right now? You want to quit your job to get your graduate degree. Great. I'm proud of you, but it's not free. We have renovations left to pay off. Your idea, by the way. We have a mortgage here. Your idea, by the way. The profit margins are nonexistent, and we lost too much with the whole Kathy ordeal. Hired on your recommendation, by the way. Should I keep going?"

"Whatever." She turned her head so her mouth wasn't smooshed into the pillow. "Then sell the place. You ever do the math? With what you bring home and with the hours you're working, you make like, three bucks an hour."

"Five years. Five years is how long most businesses in the food industry take to turn a profit. Do we really need go over this again too?"

"Ha." There was only cynicism in her laughter. "Most businesses in the food industry need to secure financing to open. They need to build from the ground up. Most haven't been around fifteen years before being inherited."

"Hello?" He propped himself up on his elbow. "You're the one who convinced me to *get* financing for the renovations that were *your* idea. Do you really want to start a fight or throw this back on me now that it's too late?"

She sat up and tugged a blanket from him and pulled it toward her side of the bed. "I agreed to spruce it up a little. I didn't think you were going to tear the place apart."

He tossed himself back down onto his side and pulled the covers violently around himself. She pulled back, but he had a handful of the comforter at his chest and he held firm. "If I'm going to do something, I'm going to do it right."

"You and your big dreams for your small town bar. Stop overshooting your demographic. Just pour the beer, put on a game, serve some cheese curds, and they'll be happy. That's it. It's not that hard."

"If you're so smart, why don't you come run the place? Or at least help out a bit? Or are you just going to deride me all the time? Be the machete that hacks my legs out from under me every night when I come home for a few hours rest?"

"Yeah right," she said.

"What's that supposed to mean?" He sat up again.

"Nothing."

"No, seriously. What's that supposed to mean?" He wanted her to say aloud what he knew she thought, that the place was a crummy hole that he never wanted in a crummy little town where he never wanted to live, and now that his grandmother was dead, he had no reason to hang onto it.

"How's a recovering alcoholic supposed to work at a bar?"

He lifted a pillow to his face. He didn't want to look at her and say what he thought, which was, *Stop using your own lack of willpower as an excuse for everything.* "Gimme a break," he shouted into the pillow. He pulled it away and spoke slowly. "You quit cold turkey, dear. Either you have exceptional willpower, or you're not an alcoholic."

"The Holy Spirit works wonders on our frail natures," she said, her voice high and innocent, like a child's. And then instantly biting, "You taught me that."

He closed his eyes and counted to five. She knew exactly how to get under his skin. "Sure. In that case, you can do it. And it's not like you have to be a bartender. Do the books. Take inventory. Order products. Research cheaper deals. Find ways to cut costs. Just help out a little."

"You don't get it, do you?"

He said nothing more. He got it. He got it all too well. He had left town as a stupid teenager, partly as a matter of conscience to escape the destructive allure of the booze, drugs, and fast crowd, and partly as an escape from a life running the family business—a life that had been planned for him before he had outgrown Little League. And then what did he get for trying to do something noble and right? Skin grafts, brain injuries, and pins in his leg. All of which sent him right back to the place he had left, just so he could inherit the life he had tried to escape.

Even the silver lining had turned ugly when his old friend and confidante had turned into a beautiful woman and swept him up in a love that he never knew they shared. And then she married him—scars and all—before revealing herself as a clone of her mother. Or more accurately, since she kept it as no real secret, when he allowed himself to recognize what he had always known.

He got it all right. How could he not when she had made it so evident last year? He had come home from physical therapy, and at four o'clock in the afternoon—before most people even got home from work—she was curled around the toilet. She was drooling into the bowl and sleeping with her face squashed against the porcelain rim. She had little chunks of vomit on the ends of her hair. He had woken her, wiped her face, prayed for her, undressed her, bathed her, and cleaned her up. He then sat behind her on the floor and brushed the hair on her lolling head, but when he rose to help her into bed, she slapped his hand away.

She had slapped his face and said, "Don't you look at me like that. Don't you dare pity me." She slurred and spittle flew from her mouth and she cried, "I pity you." She wiped her mouth. "I pity you," she whispered.

Nick did not believe she had said it reflectively, as in, I pity you that you have to put up with a drunk for a wife. No, he believed she had meant she pitied him for his scars, for how he looked, and for how he would always walk like some sort of cripple. And at that instant, in his shock and pain and misunderstanding, he told her she should pity him. He stood and left her there on the floor, and looking down on her he had said, "You *should* pity me. You should pity me that I'm stuck with you. You should pity me that I was duped into spending the rest of my life with someone who only married me because she felt sorry for me."

He left her there and didn't turn back when she crawled after him. He didn't turn back when she pressed her face against the glass of the living room window and pounded on it as he climbed into his truck. He drove to the bar and slept on a couch in the back office. He was convinced that his marriage was a sham bred from pity. At the same time, he was terrified the end of his marriage was imminent. He wasn't stupid or deaf. He had heard things—rumors about her on the loose lips of heavy drinkers at the bar. It wasn't like this was an isolated incident. Far from it. He had cleaned her up and put her to bed in the same fashion a hundred thousand million times. Gone most evenings. Stumbling in during the early morning hours. Possessive about her cell phone on which she was constantly texting. E-mailing old high school boyfriends. Changing her Facebook passwords. The signs were all there and he had been an oblivious idiot.

He had put a sign on the door of the pub, unplugged the phone, and gone on a three-day bender himself. He didn't go home the entire time, and he didn't hear a word from her. It wasn't until Uncle Thomas finally drove to Bangor, broke a window to get in, and rebuked Nick for his drunkenness, selfishness, and the abandonment of his sick wife—who was now threatening suicide—that Nick finally went home, took a shower, and brushed his teeth for the first time in over seventy-two hours.

Although Nick asked, Uncle Thomas refused to provide counseling because of the family connection. He instead recommended a colleague from across town—Reverend Bartles—to bring them through what he referred to as their dark night of the soul. When they had walked in to meet the man at his church in what looked like a broom closet attached to the sanctuary, he had them sit in two folding chairs.

He immediately launched into a lecture. "If you're sitting in my office for marriage counseling, it means you've reached the point where you need the directions spelled out for you in black and white." He leaned back in his own metal folding chair, and he put one hand in the white hair behind his head while he rested the other arm across his portly belly. He looked at the ceiling in exasperation.

"Well, I guess it's inevitable sometimes. But when a marriage reaches this point—and I don't care whose fault it was or who said what or who started it or who bears most of the blame—you only have two options left." He slammed his hands back onto the table. "And this is what they are: The first option," he said without a hint of irony, "Is that you can be absolutely miserable together." He made eye contact with each of them in turn. "Would you care to guess at the second option?"

Nick folded his arms and looked down. "I dunno. We can leave the church and get a divorce?"

Once again, Pastor Bartles looked at the ceiling in exasperation, or maybe it was in commiseration with God, as if he were saying, Look, Lord. Look what I have to deal with down here. And these are supposed to be your people?

He drew out his words like a moody teenager. "Wrooong. Wrong wrong wrong. Your other option?" He leaned forward again and smiled broadly, spreading his fingers and turning his palms up to show them it wasn't magic and that he had nothing up his sleeves. "Your other option is to be happy together.

"But, that's it. Those are the only two options. Be miserable together, or be happy together. Divorce is not an option. If we can start from that premise, we can work together. If not," he shrugged. "Your loss. The bottom line: This is marriage counseling. Not divorce counseling."

Nick looked at Eris. Eris looked at Nick. Staying together and being this miserable for the rest of their lives was not an option. Being happy seemed impossible because they were young and had not yet learned how to fight for each other. They were young and had not yet learned to forgive. But there in that little closet that the pastor liked to call a sacristy, they decided to try.

In that little room, they were more open with each other than they had ever been before. Nick finally yelled and let his frustration out. He recounted the whole messy scene for Pastor Bartles, detailing the hurtful things she had said. He explained how he understood the drinking was a sickness. He had seen her mother growing up. He had seen how Eris had tried to change so many times and he was proud of her for continuing to try. And it's not like he didn't have his own problems, Lord knows he did, so who was he to judge? He would patiently wait with her and hold her hair over the toilet for as long as they lived, in the same way he'd hold her hand in the hospital if she had cancer. In sickness and in health, right? But he made it clear in no uncertain terms that he could not live with someone who felt sorry for him.

Eris explained with tears and sobs that she didn't remember saying she pitied him. She had never pitied him. The scars were a reminder of everything that made him good and pure and righteous and bold. And she pushed the folding chair behind her; she actually got on her knees, put her head in his lap, and let her tears run onto his jeans as she pleaded with him to believe her. "If I did say that I pitied you," she had said between sobs, "It was because you got stuck with a drunken whore for a wife."

This admission, coupled with her insistence that she didn't even remember the exchange, made Nick feel like he should be the one on his knees begging for forgiveness. He had never wanted anyone else, and in fact, had never been with anyone else. Sitting there with her head in his lap, humble and completely broken of spirit, he couldn't help but push his own chair back and get down on the floor. There on his knees he confessed his own shortcomings to her with tears in his eyes so he could profess his forgiveness and receive hers. They embraced right there on the floor of the little sacristy as if no one were watching but God.

That is, until Pastor Bartles cleared his throat. "Okay, okay. Get off the floor. This isn't a Nicholas Sparks book."

Pulled from the moment, they sat back in their chairs.

The old pastor raised a hand off the desk. He gestured in front of him, his hand shaking as if he were getting ready to throw the dice at the craps table. "This is all good and beautiful and necessary," he said. "But it isn't that simple. This is only the beginning. The rest of it—well, the rest of it takes actual work. It's easy to say you forgive; it's easy to say you love; but to do it?" He slammed his hand down on the Bible, making them both jump. "To do it is a different matter. You must do it every day. Sometimes every hour." His voice raised in a crescendo. "Sometimes every single stinking second." He had reached the point of yelling. Nick imagined the fire and brimstone sermons the man must be able to deliver on Sunday mornings. "And you will both fail. Time and again you will fail and it will no doubt be just as hard in the future as it is now. Words are cheap. Tears are cheap. But sacrifice—taking action to sacrifice, to give of *yourself* to show love—to *show* it and not just say it—that kind of sacrifice—" He lowered his voice to a growling hiss. "Well, it actually costs something." His eyes blazed and once again he made eye contact with each of them.

"Thankfully," his voice ascended on an optimistic scale. "You don't have to do it alone." He looked up. "Jesus Savior," he said. "Jesus Savior pilot me. Our battle here is over, done, and won. Easy peasy apple pie. Nothing easier in the world."

Sitting in that office with the blazing eyes of a man who cared nothing for their self-esteem, it did seem as simple as that. In a way, it reminded Nick of his time in the military. He was given a mission and feelings just didn't play into it. The truth counted. The actions counted. But the intentions? The words? Cheap. His mission here was to love his wife. He intended to do that.

When they had returned home, it still seemed that simple. That's not to say it didn't take work, but it wasn't complicated. Doing the right thing usually isn't complicated, Nick figured. It's just hard. Eris quit drinking cold turkey and started going to some meetings. Now she even had the idea to go to grad school to counsel other people suffering from addiction. They continued to meet with Pastor Bartles once a month just to follow up and hear what they needed to hear. They threw themselves back into the community of their own church—Uncle Thomas's church—with a vigor and enthusiasm they didn't have before. They spent more time in Bible study and more time volunteering. Even their lovemaking had grown more frequent and passionate. Things improved and, until recently, had never been better.

Then when Nick caught Kathy cooking the books and siphoning cash orders into her own pocket, everything exploded again. Nick refused to call the police and press charges; nor would he take her to court to sue for restitution. The issue had caused Eris to fly off the handle, but he would not bend, preferring instead to fire Kathy quietly, forgive her, and turn the other cheek. His compassion moved Kathy to return $763.14, but that was not enough for Eris, and it was peanuts compared to what she took.

The result was that Nick had to pick up the slack. He couldn't afford to hire anyone full-time so he worked insane hours trying to keep the doors open. He had a handful of bartenders and a short-order cook, but they were part-timers down on their luck, and he certainly couldn't trust them to run the place. He slept at home, took Sundays off for church, but had time for little else. He rarely saw his wife, and on nights like this one—nights in which she picked at everything he did, second-guessed his decisions, criticized the way he supported their small family, and essentially derided his humble inheritance—he felt the pain return. The old questions and insecurities nagged at him all over again. He slept without sleeping, the little earwig of doubt worming its way through his thoughts and keeping him from rest. She pities you. She pities you. She pities you, it whispered.

3.10 I SWEAR THIS ISN'T FAN FICTION, BUT EVERYONE'S INSPIRED BY SOMEONE

OR

LEAD ME NOT INTO TEMPTATION

Eris returned home from work each day shortly after five in the afternoon. It seemed that Levi typically woke and got his day started slightly earlier than that. Nearly without fail, the shower floor would be wet when she returned. The chemical scent of a man's mountain fresh or cool spring body wash lingered in the air.

It had been Eris's habit to do a load of laundry every other day as soon as she returned from the bank, but with Levi living in the basement, she decided to wait for an opportunity when he wasn't there before going down to do her work. She didn't want to intrude on his privacy. During the first week, she came home and watched television. She made dinners that required little effort to prepare—cup of noodles, grilled cheese, tuna with crackers—and she went to bed without hearing a sound. Apart from the Blazer parked in front, there was no indication that she was anything but alone in the house.

By the following week, his odd hours forced her to go down there to start working through the mountain of laundry that had built up on the floor of the master bedroom. She carried a pink basket downstairs on her hip. Levi lay on his stomach in bed writing in a notebook. After starting the laundry, she stopped on her way back up.

She walked over to the bed and picked up a paperback, *A Farewell to Arms*. He looked up at her.

She wrinkled her nose. "Yuck."

"You don't like?"

She shook her head. "He believes in heroes. His men are hopeless barbarians. And his women are fools for loving them."

"You know nothing about it."

She was not offended. She threw the book back on the bed.

"Who would you rather I read?"

"Danielle Steel."

"Shut up."

"Tim O'Brien." She had read a lot of war literature since Nick had come home. Anything to learn what he was about.

He nodded and went back to writing.

"You sure write a lot for someone who doesn't want to be a writer."

He looked up. "Do you want to be a boring old banker?"

She shook her head.

"You sure spend a lot of time working at the bank for someone who doesn't want to be a banker."

He wrote. She lingered.

"War stories?" she asked.

"A love story."

"Yeah right."

"Yeah right?"

"There are no true love stories."

He closed the notebook, rolled over, and sat up. "Trouble in paradise?"

She looked down, embarrassed. "Forget it," she said. "I shouldn't have said anything. I don't know why I said that."

He gestured to a folding chair in front of the bed.

She stayed where she was. "Forget about me. Are you going to tell me about your adventures over there?"

"We braided bracelets from parachute cord."

"What else?"

"We played prison card games and gambled for cigarettes."

"What else?"

"We started our Humvees and let them run. We checked fluids and tire pressures and lights."

"What else?"

"We oiled our weapons."

"What else?"

"We waited for the field telephone to ring, for someone to tell us we had a mission."

"Did it ever ring?"

"Did it ever ring. Are you going to tell me why there are no true love stories?"

"Maybe I was wrong."

"Or maybe you were right."

"A true love story is never romantic."

"It only instructs, encourages virtue, suggests models of proper human behavior, et cetera?" he asked.

She nodded sadly. "We're incapable."

"You can tell a true love story by its absolute and uncompromising allegiance to selflessness and sacrifice?"

"And unhappiness," she said. "A true love story must be full of much unhappiness."

"What else?" he said.

"Another time," she said before walking upstairs.

The next night she invited him up for pizza. He joined her, and he did not take his eyes from her the entire meal. Even as she looked down and cut her slice with the side of a fork, she could feel his eyes on her.

Finally he said, "I never expected Nick to come back here. I never expected him to go back to the pub. He hated this place. Hated that place."

"Well." She dipped a forkful of pizza into the little puddle of ranch dressing on her plate. "He's here. We're here."

"But why?"

"Why ask why? At least that's what he'd say. He believes in the sovereignty of God."

"I had a friend named Albie who would say the same thing." Levi wiped his mouth with a napkin. "I never expected you'd be married," he said. "I never expected you'd work at a bank."

"I never expected you'd be homeless and living in my basement." He smiled.

They spoke of her plans to go back to grad school for psychology, or social work maybe. She marveled at the foolishness of how she spent her days looking at loan applications, enabling or crushing the hopes of normal people like her by plugging numbers into a formula. It was so pointless. Her life had taken her so far from where she ever expected she would go.

When she began clearing the paper plates from the table, Levi excused himself.

The next night they had spaghetti. He spoke of his lingering hangover. He commented on the improved look of the bar district. "I mean, it still looks like La Crosse," he said. "But they really gave downtown a face-lift. Especially the riverfront."

"Different bars, same culture," she said.

"I missed it here."

"You can keep it," she told him. "I'm over it." The way he stared unnerved her. She snorted like a cynic and looked down.

For a week they did not speak of love and they did not speak of war.

The following Monday, she gathered her husband's underwear, socks, and dirty jeans from the floor of her room. The hallway by the bathroom did not smell of shampoo or a man's cologne. When she carried the laundry past Levi's room, she saw that he was not there.

She microwaved a Hot Pocket for dinner. She held a paperback in one hand and her dinner in the other as she sat on the couch. She heard the door open and the stomping of feet.

Levi walked in and put his hands on the back of the recliner that gave the room shape and separated the hallway from the rest of the room. "Sorry I'm late," he said as he looked at her with furrowed eyebrows that sought forgiveness. He said it as if they had a standing date. As if he had missed the family dinner. Like his constant stares, she found it unnerving, for she had never had a standing date with anyone. She had never shared a regular family dinner. She had never had reliable company.

"You're not late for anything," she said as she kept her eyes on the page of her book.

"I got a bottle of wine," he said. "When's the last time you had a good wine buzz? Whaddya say?"

She shook her head no.

"So what about Nick? Think he'd be interested in being my drinking partner?"

She looked up at him. "Nick? Who's Nick? Name rings a bell. If you ever see him here, you can ask him."

Levi turned and walked back to the kitchen. He returned with a large jug of sangria and two plastic cups. "Well if he's not in, you'll have to do."

She tucked her legs beneath her and stuffed her book between the cushions.

"What are you reading?"

"I'm not telling."

"Why not?"

"You'll make fun of me."

"Will not."

"You're a book snob."

"Am not." He poured a cup of the red wine.

"I'm not drinking," she said.

"You're not drinking?"

"I don't drink anymore."

"Why not?" he asked as he poured himself a glass. He sat back in the recliner.

"Nick doesn't like me when I drink." She shook her head. "I don't even like me when I drink. Let's just say it's caused a few problems in our marriage."

"Suit yourself." He sat back and quickly drank one cup down. He took a sip from the second and leaned his head back. He closed his eyes and smiled.

The silence made her feel uncomfortable, as if she were required to give a better explanation. "Did Nick tell you?" she said.

"Tell me what?"

"We had to get counseling, you know."

He said nothing, but shook his head ever so slightly.

"Marriage counseling."

He took another sip but did not open his eyes. His smile had retreated.

"It was with this really old pastor from across town, not with like a real psychologist or anything. He was some friend of Uncle Thomas's. He was a real Bible thumper," she told him.

He opened his eyes and finally acknowledged she was talking to him. "Well I would imagine so, if he was a pastor."

"No. I mean he literally thumped his Bible. It sat on his desk and he'd smack it with an open palm. Or he'd pound on it with two fingers when he was trying to make a point." She puffed her cheeks out and lowered her chin into her chest. She tried speaking in a deep voice to imitate him. "The way this works," she mocked, "is the way God says it works, right here in this book right here. She beat down on the worn leather Bible that Nick kept on the side table."

Levi leaned forward, but let the silence prod her on.

Matthew J. Hefti

"I don't know how it could properly be called counseling. He lectured us. Seriously. He went on and on and on. How can it be counseling if neither of us says a single word?"

Levi sipped. "I wouldn't know."

She grabbed the bottle and poured herself a cup. Levi raised an eyebrow at her but remained silent. She drank half of it in silence as she looked out the window at the street, at all the vehicles passing her by, and then she refilled it.

"Did you know Nick called me a whore?"

"He did not."

"He did. He said I should pity him because he married a drunken whore."

"That doesn't sound like Nick."

She took another large drink. "Of course," she said, "it's all about what I did wrong. How I'm the alcoholic. How I was the one who said hurtful things. Forget his own response, which was what? To nearly drink himself to death for three straight days. Of course he failed to mention the hurtful things he said and did."

She felt disloyal for telling him all of this. She felt dishonest as well, because the truth was, they gave their marriage a second shot only because Pastor Bartles was a genius, because he thumped his Bible, because he had little patience, and because he only told them what they needed to hear and never ever what they wanted to hear. But the wine was sweet, and it made her feel warm, and Levi listened to what she said.

"That's not the whole truth either," she confessed.

"No?"

She shook her head, took another sip, and wiped her mouth with the back of her hand. "I know I'm not perfect. I did some bad things—"

"Like what?"

"Like what does it matter? But I told him as much. Explained how I knew I was to blame, and then the next thing you know I'm weeping on the floor of this pastor's office. There I am on my knees, practically begging my husband to stay, like some archetypal helpless damsel, or worse, the scarlet harlot in some bad romance novel written by a man. I mean, who does that?"

"That doesn't sound like you," he said.

"No, it doesn't, does it?"

They sat in silence again for a few moments.

"After it was all said and done?" she said. "Pastor Bartles—that was his name—he thumped his Bible again. Tapped on it, really. He assumed this light, natural tone as if we were at the bar, as if those fiery outbursts had never even happened." She lowered her chin again. She lowered her voice and said, "Here is the blueprint, the design, the example. Simple as that." She shook her head, as if it were all so stupid. "I did everything I knew how to do to make him happy. I bought a beautiful wooden plaque that had been detailed with a wood-burning pen. It had flowers and gorgeous scrollwork. It said, 'The Couple That Prays Together Stays Together.' I hung it up above the bed."

"But did you actually pray with him?" Levi asked skeptically.

She leaned forward and pushed his shoulder playfully. "Whose side are you on here?"

He looked away from her for the first time. "I didn't realize there were sides to take here." He swirled the sangria in his hand. He looked down into the glass as if he might find what he was looking for in the bottom.

"And so, that's enough about me," she said, embarrassed now. "I filled you in on my life, now you fill me in on your life since—what? Christmas 2004? Was that the last time I saw you before now?" She had tried to say it lightly, had tried to sound cavalier, but she felt the air shift as well as he had.

He shook his head. "I don't think I'm qualified to pick sides."

"Forget about that," she said. "Tell me about what you did the past few years. You played video games, you slept, you waited for phones to ring. What else?"

He picked up the jug of sangria and stood. He looked down at his own glass and frowned. He looked down at hers.

She felt naked. She set down her cup. He set down the jug, poured her cup into his own, and he picked up the jug again.

"What else?" she whispered.

"That's it. There's nothing else. I have nothing else to tell you. I'm sorry."

3.11 IF THIS IS GETTING REDUNDANT AND RELENTLESS FOR YOU, IMAGINE HOW *I* FEEL

evi's sleeping hours were dominated by the green glow of night-vision goggles; surreal images of rooms full of teenagers and young men with sandbags over their heads and flex cuffs around their wrists; and intense close-quarter combat in which he'd be face-to-face with another man, close enough to count the hairs between his enemy's eyebrows, only to wake covered in sweat because no matter how hard he tried, his finger had frozen, and he could not pull the trigger on his rifle.

On several occasions, he had spent the entire night behind the wheel of a Humvee driving down the same stretch of Tampa alone. No traffic, no bombs, no gunfire, no donkeys, no mindless chatter. Just an endless stretch of road, the grasses and squat palm trees moving past him, and the *cri de coeur* of the engine trying to move the weight of all the extra armor.

Some nights it was Afghanistan. The long hikes on cold mountain passes or the slow methodical movement through dry desert wadis. He often felt that he wasn't sleeping alone, but that he was surrounded by the dozen brothers who would die for him and the two dozen Afghan National Army soldiers who wouldn't. Sleep doesn't come easy when your bunkmates may want to kill you.

[I'm sorry, it's just, the thing I want you to realize is this: Once sleep becomes an issue, it's like everything becomes an issue. The real truth is that most nights there were no dreams at all. Most mornings

I woke with an aching head and a sore jaw from clenching my teeth while I slept. Each side of my tongue had painful sores from where I bit it during the night. That is, if I slept at all. I think I've made it pretty clear that I was drinking a lot. Far too much, really.]

Each moment awake was a moment in which he wished he could sleep. Every moment he slept was a moment in which he wished he could wake up and get on with his life.

3.12 YOU DIDN'T HAVE TO PRETEND YOU WERE DOING LAUNDRY

One late Friday afternoon, Nick left the pub in the hands of his bartender, Shirley, so he could drive back to La Crosse. He wanted to catch Levi awake and present during normal hours just to say hi, just to talk. When he got home, Eris lay on the couch watching the local news in a pair of yoga pants and a long-sleeved sleeping shirt. "A little early for pajamas, isn't it?" Nick asked her.

"You the clothing police now?"

"Seen Levi?"

"Nope." She didn't take her eyes off the television.

"The truck's here. Is he here?"

"Dunno."

"Have you heard him down there? Has he come up to use the bathroom?"

"Nope."

Seen him at all during the rest of the week?"

"A little."

Nick walked over and turned off the television. Eris showed no reaction. "I'm trying to talk to you."

"I'm answering."

"So a little like how? Like what? Like does he come up and watch TV? Eat dinner? Take a dump?"

"I dunno. A little, I guess. Like he comes up and goes to the bathroom sometimes, sure. Then he stands there at the edge of the room just lurking like you're doing now. He's like, 'Hey, Eris.' I'm like, 'Hey.' And then he goes back downstairs to do his lurking there."

"Just hey? You don't even make small talk?"

She sighed. "How long is he staying?"

"I don't know. As long as he wants. Why? Is he bothering you?"

"He'd be bothering me less if he weren't just the ghost in the basement." She looked down at her hands. "I think he's depressed."

"What, did he tell you this? Are you two sitting around having heart to hearts?"

She rolled her eyes. "No. I never even see him. He never comes up. It's weird. And it's scary."

"Maybe he just feels awkward having to stay here?"

"I think he's taking advantage of you."

"Cynical much?"

"Why does he need to stay here? Why doesn't he just get an apartment or something?"

It was Nick's turn to shrug. "I don't know. He's incapable of being alone? He's all PTSD-ed out? He's broke? He doesn't have a job? He has a drinking problem and no responsibility? He doesn't know how to interact with normal people anymore? How should I know?"

"So talk to him then," she said, pulling the throw blanket over her shoulders before reclining again.

"And say what?"

She picked up the remote from the floor. "We aren't eighteen anymore? Things change? Hey, dude, this ain't no commune? Get a job? Go to school? Go live with your parents? Go to counseling? Or like, if you can't interact with normal people and carry on a normal conversation, go back to the army?" She flipped through a few channels while Nick stood at the edge of the room. "Just go down there and give him the old fail safe." She craned her neck and looked up at him, resting her head on her left palm. She smiled. "It's not you; it's me."

Nick couldn't help but laugh at that one. It was a loud and hearty laugh that carried through the house.

He went back to work, having gained nothing from his trip home. He didn't return until late. By then Levi was gone again, out who knows where.

After coming home from the hospital in early 2006, Nick had set himself to working hard, to praying hard, and to ignoring every reminder that Iraq had ever existed. The few dreams that plagued him in the burn ward had vanished, and he couldn't even pinpoint when it had happened. He could, however, pinpoint exactly when they returned.

That night, the start of his dream was pleasant. He and Levi had been playing basketball on a concrete pad in the middle of O'Ryan. The land was flat and there was sand, but the ground sat low so there were tall grasses, vegetation, and mosquitoes. Massive concrete trapezoidal ammo bunkers dotted the horizon of the small post. They were joking and laughing when the distant concussion of an unseen mortar caused them both to freeze in their tracks. The second concussion was much louder, and they both dropped to the hot concrete, covered their heads with their hands, and opened their mouths to protect against the coming blast waves. The third concussion grew closer, and Nick felt more helpless.

Taking direct fire is one thing. Adrenaline and anger and inhumanity charge through blood vessels so quickly that fear transforms into oppositional reaction before it even registers as fear. Indirect fire, on the other hand, is a terrifying beast in which only the strong of faith come out psychologically unscathed. The adrenaline and fear have nowhere to go, no action to take, and the only option is to hit the deck in submission to the advancing explosions. The impossibility of action during accurate and prolonged indirect fire forces a position of prayer. The saying that there are no atheists in foxholes is, of course, rubbish. Atheists abound. But to the terrified soldier lying humble and prostrate on the ground in utter submission to forces greater than self-reliance, each explosion is its own sermon.

It was this kind of fear and humility that now gripped Nick. Reverting to what he had known since infancy, he whispered a petition in which he gave himself up to the mercy of his creator.

He then opened his eyes and listened. He heard another thud, but now that he had woken, he recognized it as the basement door slamming. The other thuds must have been the car door slamming, the front screen door, and the door from the foyer to the kitchen. Nick listened to Levi tromp down the stairs. He heard a stumble and a few more steps until, once again, silence filled the house.

Nick felt his house was no longer his own. Charity and love—not to mention no small bit of guilt and a sense of great indebtedness— had forced him to share his home with his old friend. The friend who had saved his life. This guitar-playing, poetry-writing, heavy-drinking, smug, and broody war hero who years earlier had a real thing for his wife. The crazy friend who by coming back into his life automatically made it more complicated, more difficult, more dangerous, and more unpredictable. And this, Nick thought, is how Levi always shows up: He consumes attention; he monopolizes frames of vision; he steals oxygen from fires; he's all anyone can ever see.

When Nick woke in mid-morning, he found Eris drinking coffee and surfing the web at the kitchen table. He poured himself a cup and opened the freezer to get some ice so he didn't have to wait for his coffee to cool before drinking it. He saw a frosted bottle of Absolut in the freezer.

He held it up. "This yours?"

She looked surprised, and then hurt. "Of course not."

"Need anything washed?" he asked her.

"You're going to do laundry?" she asked.

"I do laundry sometimes."

She closed the laptop and stood up. She had already showered and dressed. She hugged him and buried her head in his chest. Her hair smelled like Herbal Essences and he loved it. "You're such a liar. But really, it's not that big a deal."

"I know," he said. "But I don't want it to become one."

The only laundry Nick could find in need of washing were the clothes they had worn the day before, which barely filled a basket to halfway. He grabbed the bottle from the freezer, put it in the nearly empty basket, and he took it downstairs, feeling a bit silly. He made sure to stomp loudly as he walked, so he didn't inadvertently surprise Levi in a moment that required privacy.

Levi sat on the bed, leaning against the wall, a book in his lap. He glanced up at Nick as he came down the stairs. Nick lifted the basket as if explaining why he would enter his own basement. Levi looked back down at his book while Nick scurried into the laundry room.

When he returned to the stairs, Nick saw that on the wall of the landing at the bottom of the stairs, Levi had hung the medals his parents framed and presented to him. He paused to look at it more closely, surprised he hadn't seen it on his way down. He turned to look at Levi and realized that his friend had been watching him.

Levi said, "What?"

The way Levi stared at him, the immediacy with which Levi hung the medal on the wall, and the placement right at the landing where anyone coming down would be eye-to-eye with it, the complete and absolute heavy-handedness of it seemed like a threat to Nick. It seemed like Levi was a dog marking his territory or asserting his dominance, but more than that, it seemed like Levi didn't want anyone to miss that fact. The medals hanging on the wall was a statement that proclaimed: Say something; I dare you.

"Nothing," Nick said. He took a few steps into the room. "Sorry if I bothered you."

Levi raised his eyebrows, obviously expecting something more. "Don't mind me," he said. "It's your house." His eyes dropped down to the vodka bottle in Nick's hand. Say something; I dare you.

"Just doing laundry." Nick knew it was a stupid and obvious thing to say, but he felt like he was back in high school trying to make a new friend. "Sorry I haven't been around to hang out much," he said. "Been working a lot."

"No worries, dude."

"Whatchya been up to?"

"Not much. Trying to get acclimated I guess."

Nick looked around the room. Levi had a pile of books stacked next to the bed. His footlockers sat closed at its end. Two restaurant to-go boxes sat opened on the folding card table adjacent to the bed, both of them encrusted with the remains of some type of beans and rice.

"Listen," Nick said holding up the bottle. "I know I told you to make yourself at home, and I meant it, but I can't let you keep alcohol in the house."

"You own a bar," Levi said, as if that fact alone made Nick's statement ridiculous, which Nick had to admit, in a way, it did.

"No, you're right. Yeah. I just—I didn't tell you before because it's kind of a sore subject, but Eris kind of has—well, she's had some problems and she's on the wagon now. She doesn't ever come to the bar. It wouldn't be a good idea for us to keep booze in the house."

Levi closed his book and set it down next to him before pushing off the bed and standing. "I'm sorry. You never said anything about it." He walked over and grabbed the bottle.

"No. Not your fault. How could you know?"

"I couldn't," Levi said. He stared at Nick, as if he were examining him. He stared so long, Nick looked away in discomfiture like a submissive dog.

He turned to head back upstairs.

Levi called after him. "Do you want me to leave?"

Nick saw the medal again. He took a deep breath, closed his eyes for a moment, opened them, and turned back to Levi. "Been looking for work by any chance?"

"If this is a problem, I can get a different place, or I can pay rent. Like, that's not a problem. I've saved up a lot."

"No, not at all," Nick said as a matter of reflex, though some additional cash flow would help them out a lot. "No problem. I was just wondering." Worried that he had caused offense, he blurted out, "It's just that Eris has been bugging me to hire a manager. Problem is, I haven't been able to find anyone I trust. I was thinking now that you're back—" Nick let his voice trail off.

Levi put his hands in his pockets and looked down at the floor and then back up at Nick. He pursed his lips and scrunched his eyes. "I don't know," he said. "I don't know anything about that kind of business."

"Well," Nick said, selling it harder than he had intended. "You know how to lead people and I trust you. That's like 99 percent of it right there. I can teach you the simple day-to-day stuff. I mean, like, a monkey could run the place if I could trust him."

"No offense, but I don't really—"

"No it's cool."

"And I've kind of already got a job doing this online writing slash editing thing on a freelance basis."

"Yeah, no problem. Sure. No. Sorry I brought it up." Nick turned to go back upstairs. "Don't be a stranger, okay? Don't just be the ghost in the basement, okay?"

Levi's head snapped back in surprise. "Okay, yeah. Sure."

Over the course of the next week, Levi came into the bar to eat a burger and make small talk on several different occasions. The following week, he came in one time and left after having two drinks in silence. The week after that, he didn't come in at all. Entire weeks disappeared.

Eris brought it up to Uncle Thomas as they ate brunch after church one Sunday in late March.

"Why don't you say something?" Uncle Thomas said, looking at Nick accusingly.

"You guys don't talk," Eris said. "Friends are supposed to talk to each other. No one talks. If you guys would just talk about how you feel."

Nick looked over to Uncle Thomas. "If it bothers her so much, why doesn't she say something? Why doesn't she talk to him?"

"I never even see him," she said. "He's always gone by the time I get home."

"He's not hurting anyone," Nick said.

The same nights kept playing themselves out. Nick's new dreams continued. He drove in a Humvee. He craved a cheeseburger. An explosion widened his eyes. The weight of another man's arm lay heavy on his chest. He continued to awaken with the realization that the concussions were only the slamming of doors. "When are you going to do something about that?" Eris would ask. His acquiescence melted with the snow as his nightmares, the loud late-night arrivals, and the complaints from Eris continued.

He began doing more laundry. Each time he limped down the stairs he planned on telling Levi off. Giving him the business. Telling him he needed to get it together. Get a job. Get a life. Get some friends. Stop drinking so much. Stop being the weird freak in the basement. Snap out of it. Each time he walked down, he saw the frame as a reminder that he owed Levi more than a little patience. Sometimes he wanted to tear the medal off the wall. Sometimes he craved violence again. He just wanted to do *something*.

Levi grew larger and larger, and Nick kept getting smaller and smaller.

3.13 WE'RE NOT ALL PSYCHOS INCAPABLE OF CONTROLLING OURSELVES

She had only wanted to invite him to their Sunday breakfast, to get him out into the world. She sensed he needed that. The lamp by his bed was on. A hardcover copy of *One Hundred Years of Solitude* lay on the floor with the cover up, pages bent, and spine splayed as if it had fallen from the bed. Levi lay on his stomach, one arm under his pillow, one arm hanging over the edge of the bed. His laptop sat open on one of the footlockers. One of his shoulder blades stuck up in a jagged peak on his bare back. His mouth was slightly open. He looked peaceful, like a skinny, sleeping child.

She tapped on the doorjamb with her knuckles. In the sudden way that a viper grabs a mouse, he rolled up and extended his arms in front of him. The violence of action, the quickness of the movement surprised Eris, and it took her a moment to realize what had happened.

She stood still—more stunned than scared—until she realized that what he held was a gun. The muscles in his arms were like ropes. The lines of his face were hard and angular, almost to the point of being gaunt. His torso was not large, but his chest was tawny and defined. His abs were hard. His cheeks were hollow and his eyes were as cold and unflinching as granite, or as the steel of what he held in his hands. She did not recognize the boy she had known for such a large part of her life years ago. For the first time, she saw him for what he now was: a hard man, a soldier, a killer.

He looked, in a way, as if he didn't know who she was. He looked as if he didn't know who he was. In that moment, she turned and ran.

She shook Nick awake with one hand as she bawled and wiped away tears with the other. "Get up," she cried. "Get up and get him out of here."

Nick jumped up, flinging the covers off the bed. "What? Why? Calm down."

She shoved him hard. "Calm down?" Sobbing, she punched the front of his shoulder with a closed fist. She hurt her knuckle when she caught the edge of his clavicle, so she punched him again. "He pulled a gun on me. Don't tell me to calm down."

"Wait. What?" Nick squirmed into a pair of jeans and stepped into his unlaced boots. "Who pulled a gun on you?"

"Levi." She crossed the room and grabbed a tissue from the dresser and wiped her eyes and blew her running nose. "He pulled a gun on me and you brought him here."

"Slow down. Are you sure? Tell me what happened." He pulled a T-shirt over his head.

She spoke rapidly with her exhale. "I went down to ask him to breakfast with us. I thought it would be nice." She gulped because she had run out of air. "And when I tapped on his door, he was holding a gun on me, and he had a crazy look in his eye."

"And then what? Did he actually point it at you? Did he put it down when he saw you?"

"No. Not at first." She gulped. "Maybe. I don't know. What difference does it make? He has a gun down there, Nick. A gun."

Nick, who had woken in a panic of rage, seemed to have deliberately slowed his movements. He stepped to her and enveloped her in his arms. She cried against his chest. As he held her, he took slow, deep breaths in sharp contrast to her own.

"Calm down," he said. "He didn't shoot you. I'm sure he didn't mean it. You probably just startled him."

She pushed him away. "Don't tell me to calm down." Her voice rose in pitch and intensity. "I have a gun pulled on me in my own house and you tell me to calm down? I've had enough of your tiptoeing around." She stepped up to him and put her index finger in his chest. "It's time you pulled yourself together and went down there and told your friend to pull himself together." She tapped his chest for emphasis with each reflexive pronoun.

"Don't," he said. "Don't." He grabbed her hand and pressed it back down to her side. He did it firmly and with force, but there was no doubt he was in control of himself. He did it without anger. He walked past her and walked toward the basement.

She followed and stayed at the top of the stairs, watching until he was down and into the next room. She stopped halfway down. She listened.

"I'm sorry, I'm sorry, I'm sorry," she heard Levi say. "I'm packing up and then I'm gone, okay? I'm sorry."

She walked down the rest of the way and peeked into the room from around the doorjamb.

The pistol lay on the side of the bed, on top of the plush comforter. Nick walked in and picked it up off the bed. He turned it in his hands and barely looked at it. He released the magazine from the well and pulled back on the top of the pistol. A round flew up and he caught it deftly. Eris was surprised at how comfortable he looked with the weapon. He returned the round to the magazine and tossed it on the bed. He then tossed the pistol on the bed like it was nothing worth worrying about. Like it was nothing more than an inert piece of steel.

Like riding a bicycle, she thought to herself. She marveled at this part of Nick that she had never thought about, had never allowed herself to think about too deeply.

Nick sat on the edge of the bed and folded his hands. "What if you had shot her?" He said it in a voice near a whisper.

"She's overreacting. I didn't shoot her. I didn't even point it at her." Levi paced around the room grabbing books and clothes, stuffing food trays into a garbage bag. "Our story has enough guns without another one going off," he muttered.

"What?" Nick said.

Levi stopped his frantic movement and stood still. "Look. If you're expecting some big dramatic breakdown from me, some violent episode to show how psycho I am, it's not going to happen. I'm in control, okay." He moved to the footlockers and tried closing one. He fought to keep the lid down as the rumpled clothes pressed against it. "A gun can serve a purpose without ever going off."

Nick's voice remained calm. It provided a soothing counterbalance to Levi's manic pacing and packing. "I know you didn't shoot her, Levi. But you could have. You probably didn't mean to pull a gun on Eris, a friend of yours; but you did."

Levi gritted his teeth and finished closing up his belongings in the two footlockers. "I do exactly as I'm trained, exactly as the two of us did for years—assess the threat and control my fire—and you act as though now all of a sudden carrying a gun is dangerous."

Nick waited in silence. Eris wiped her nose and pressed her cheek against the doorjamb. Finally, Levi threw a hand in the air. He yelled quickly, with passion, and without taking a breath. "You think I don't know it's dangerous? You think when I woke up, when I realized that I wasn't on top of Sperwan Ghar, when I realized it was your wife, that I didn't almost vomit right there from the sickness of it all?" He moved in front of Nick and spoke lowly. "I'd rather put that thing in my own mouth and blow my own brains out." He stood there with his fists clenched, staring down at Nick on the bed.

Eris turned, crying, and sat on the step.

"It's okay," she heard Nick say. "It's okay to cry."

When she stopped her own crying, she still heard shaking sobs coming from the other room.

"It's okay. It's okay to cry. We can talk. You don't have to leave. Let's just talk."

The sobbing stopped. Levi cleared his throat. His voice was suddenly cold. "We're going to talk? And what are we going to talk about? We haven't talked for months and we've lived in the same house."

Eris listened to the silence.

"That's what I thought," Levi said. "I do my lurking in the basement, Nick. I don't live in a vacuum, and I don't live in outer space, contrary to what you and Eris might think."

"What do you mean?"

"You think I can't hear what goes on in this house? The things that are said?"

"Levi—"

"Stop. It's cool. I know I'm not Mister Congeniality lately, okay? And don't think I don't appreciate the help you've given me. But—"

"But what?"

"But you and Eris have made a life for yourself. She's right. We're not eighteen anymore. This isn't a commune. And maybe I have been taking advantage of you. Hell— Hell. Hell. Hell." Levi laughed. "Maybe I should just join the army again."

Eris scooted to the side as he carried his first footlocker up. She sat with her chin in her hands as Nick stood in front of her looking up the stairs. She tried to curl into herself as Levi came stomping down to get his second trunk.

Levi put his hand on her head before he walked up for the final time. She flinched.

"Eris," he said. "It's not you; it's me."

She felt Levi's gravity diffuse into her through the palm resting on her head, and she could not get up when Levi dragged his trunk up the stairs to leave.

3.14 A YEAR LATER AND I'M STILL THE BIGGEST CLICHÉ OF THEM ALL

April 5th, 2010

Levi's father stared ahead at a 19-inch television screen playing the soundless Opening Day Brewer's game. When Levi slid onto the stool next to him, his father popped up from his chair to give him a hug. Just like when Levi was a kid, his father hugged like he was going to crush ribs, and he held on far too long.

"Mom coming?"

"No. No, she couldn't make it; she was busy." The white lie sounded slow and strange coming from his father's ethical and well-guarded tongue.

"I meant to call her. Or to visit."

His father let the silence hang.

"And so," his dad said eventually. "How goes it?"

"Oh, don't worry about me. I'm fine." He felt disloyal to Nick, bellying up to the only other bar in town.

[You know, my dad doesn't even like baseball. And looking at him there? I felt embarrassed for him. The lines around his eyes ran even deeper than the last time I had seen him. His coarse gray hair fell further down his neck. The flecks of pepper had long since disappeared and he now wore a closely trimmed beard that held only salt. He had grown old on me. Looking back, I think I just felt embarrassed for myself. Probably ashamed is a better word. Even after he kept calling me every single week and getting rejected every single week, he wouldn't quit calling, wouldn't quit offering me a place at home, a place at work. And sitting there with him, I felt ashamed that the distinguished old man would humble himself to show up in the kind of mindless holes that I frequented because it was the only way to reach me.]

The bartender walked over and slung a towel over his shoulder. "Kevin," he said. "You didn't tell me Levi was in town."

Levi and the man shook hands.

"How long you been back now?"

"Little while, I guess."

His dad said, "It's been over a year now."

Levi spread his hands out in front of him and felt the familiarity of a two-part, clear polymer epoxy resin bar top. He did the math in his head and realized his father was right. It certainly didn't seem like it had been that long since his triumphant return. It had been nearly eighteen months since he had spent four days in PAX terminals on his way back to Fort Drum from Panjwai Province, Afghanistan, nearly a year sooner than expected. All the memories were still so vivid. The humiliation so fresh. The wounds not yet scabbed.

The bartender poured Levi a beer. "You won the Silver Star, right?"

"That was a long time ago." He pulled his wallet from his pocket. "Can I open a tab?"

"Put that away. The first one's on me. It's not every day I get to serve a war hero."

"Thanks," Levi said. *Thanks for thinking some bits of string and steel actually mean something,* he thought. He put his wallet on the bar without opening it. "But really. I can pay."

"I insist," said the man.

"I appreciate your generosity." Levi hoped to create distance with his formality. He lifted the glass a few inches off the bar in cheers before turning his attention back to the game.

The man remained, hands on the bar. "So was it in Iraq? Where you got the medal?"

[I mean, you had to have dealt with the same kind of thing, right? I had four choices as I saw it: The first was to tell the guy bluntly that I appreciated the beer but didn't enjoy talking about my time in the army; the second was to play it cool, nod when appropriate, and hope the guy just got the hint; the third was to engage, tell some stories, read the man's cues to get a feel for his political leanings, rant about the current or former administration, shake my head when talking about the media, give him the stories that he wanted instead of the truth he didn't, and collect free beers all night; the fourth would be to describe in detail what it feels like to grasp the power of having another man in the sights of your M4, describe the adrenaline rush of pulling the trigger after higher gives you the okay, make him feel the overwhelming satisfaction of removing evil from the world as you watch the enemy crumple to the dust from which he came knowing that you just kept a bullet from going into your gunner's brain or you kept an IED from being planted beneath your buddy's truck, and then as the bartender leans closer and his mouth opens a little wider—devouring every salacious word that comes from my mouth—I could tell him about the dump truck load of bricks that drops in your stomach when you stand over the dead man realizing that he wasn't in fact armed, that the Kalashnikov you saw against the pickup from a hundred meters away was really nothing more than an axe, and what you thought was a shovel was just a pitchfork, a simple farmer's tool.

I chose to sip my beer and nod.]

"Been to Afghanistan too?"

Levi nodded again. He felt like one of the Bobblehead dolls they were probably handing out to the fans at the baseball game on TV.

The Brewers had never won the division during Levi's lifetime and had only made the playoffs once. But the thing he loved about baseball was that it was so different from life. It was a metaphor for how life could be, or at least should be. At any time, things could change for the better. Every season was a fresh start. Maybe this year they could turn it around. Maybe one solid game could end the drought. Maybe one quality start at home could turn the tide and carry them through the long season. It could happen.

"So what was it like over there?"

Levi looked down into his beer, which was nearly empty. "Can you believe this? Just when you think we can contend again."

The bartender turned and looked at the screen. "Oh yeah. I'll tell you what; I can't watch anymore. Not since the strike and then all that steroids business." The man took Levi's glass and walked away.

"You know," his dad whispered. "He's just trying to make conversation."

"What'd I say?"

"All these people here in town, Son. They remember you kids from when you were little. They all know and remember you more than you remember them, that's all."

Levi pulled out his pack of cigarettes. "Mind if I smoke." It wasn't a question.

The bartender brought back a full glass of beer with an ashtray. He set the beer and the ashtray down and hovered. "Pretty bad then, huh?"

Levi looked at his dad. His eyes silently nudged him forward. "All right. You want to know what it was like over there?" He took a slug of beer and the man leaned forward. "Your wife ever take you shopping? Mall of America? Valley View, wherever?"

"Sure, yeah."

"Afghanistan was like that. You walk around all day and you don't have a single clue about what the hell you're looking for."

The man threw his head back in a hearty laugh. "That's great. I guess that's about what my dad said about the European front. Hurry up and wait, right?" Satisfied, the man walked back to his post near the taps.

"Happy?" Levi whispered. "I don't even know this guy's name."

"Hey, Brad. Think we can get a few more?" While Brad poured new beers, Levi's dad whispered back, "Happy?"

The men watched the game. Between innings, the bartender would bring Levi another beer and empty the ashtray. As he brought Levi's sixth beer, Levi's dad said, "You mind bringing me a plate of that roast beef special, Brad?"

"Sure. Levi? Hungry?"

Levi shook his head. He tried smiling to show the man some semblance of warmth, but after downing several drinks in quick succession, he felt his face was as distorted as his thoughts.

"So," his dad said.

"So."

[Ya know, by this point, I should have felt ready to loosen up, start buying shots, start riffing and having a good time. This was usually the point when life stopped being so drab, but the silence was oppressive. The ice machine rattled and the Miller Genuine Draft sign buzzed, sure, but they only made me more aware of the silence. Kind of like when you notice no one is talking at dinner and suddenly it sounds like your chewing could be heard in China. The things is, I had seen my parents like a handful of times, maybe, since I got back, so what did I have to say? And even if I could think of something to say, I wouldn't feel comfortable saying it because the longer I stayed away and the longer I didn't talk to anyone, the more guilty I felt about not talking to them, and then the more guilty I felt about it, the harder it was to open up and talk about it. It was, and is, this self-perpetuating problem.]

"Work things out with your sister?" said his dad.

"Mmm. She told you about that?" He sipped his beer. "Yeah, anyway. I acquiesced. No sense keeping up a fight over something dumb. She's fragile."

"Not as fragile as you think. She stands up to you, doesn't she?"

Every time she called Levi on the telephone, she spoke in low hospital-bed tones. The week he had moved out of Nick's and into his own apartment, she stopped over to drop off a casserole. To be specific, she had stood there smiling—she was always smiling, even when he knew she must be revolted at the smell of cigarette smoke and the shredded commercial carpeting found in the hallway of the industrial building offering studios for less than 300 bucks a month—and she had said, "I thought you might like something low maintenance to heat up in your bachelor pad and all." All white teeth and bubbles. "It's a duck cassoulet with artichokes. And then this Tupperware here doesn't even have to be reheated. This one is a chilled beet soup with crème fraîche and dill. It's so yummy. Your nieces love it." He invited her in, but she stayed in the hallway as if she were scared to go in, like if she went into his apartment she might find the bodies of dismembered hookers; or at the very least, she'd find the dried-out ears and fingers of enemy combatants.

For a year she'd been doing the same thing as his dad. She'd been calling him every week, begging him to come over for dinner, forcing him to talk, to engage with her for full minutes at a time. Finally he accepted, almost as a last-ditch effort to be left alone for a while. It turned out to be as bad as he'd anticipated. When he arrived, she escorted him into the living room to see his nieces and nephew. She stayed close as if he were a rescued dog, ready to latch onto an internal jugular at any moment. She said, "Hey guys," and she moved like an inch a minute because sudden movement might have startled him. "Do you remember your Uncle Levi?"

The kids looked up at him, excited, but his mood had already soured. Of course they remembered him. He had seen them when he came home and he had seen them once a year every year he wasn't deployed. And it's not like he had any control over the rest of the missing time. Something about two wars, three deployments, the exigent scheduling of the military industrial complex, and the vicissitudes inherent in weaving that blanket of freedom under which she loved to sleep.

Her husband Chris had offered him a drink on the patio, and then he offered a few more. The switch had been flipped. That was it.

It was hardly Levi's fault that Chris asked him to demonstrate some hand-to-hand combat. And it wasn't his fault Chris was so drunk that he wouldn't give up. He didn't remember much, but he remembered being unable to control his laughter after she began shrieking that the kids were asleep. It was too ironic. He assured her that the cries of, "You're almost thirty, for Pete's sake!" and "You need to get help!" were far louder than the wrestling they were doing in the basement. He didn't remember putting a hole in the drywall, but Chris fixed it the next day; so what was the big deal?

"You know," said Levi to his dad. "I don't think she trusts me around the kids."

"She just needs to see you more. She never sees you. We never see you. She doesn't know how to act."

"What, and I do?"

"None of us do." They watched Prince Fielder take ball four and lumber to first. "I'd like to talk about that."

Brad placed a plate of roast beef and vegetables in front of Levi's dad.

Levi's dad picked up his knife. "I know how it is. I know how easy it is to get a bit rough around the edges, and I know things haven't been easy." He set his knife down and scratched his beard. Levi turned away from the game and toward him. "I've been there myself, which is why I've tried to give you some distance. Sometimes a guy just needs to work things out for himself."

"Exactly." Thinking they had reached some sort of understanding, Levi turned back to the game.

"Are you thinking of suicide, Son?"

The suddenness of the question caught Levi off guard. "What? No."

Rather than accept his answer, his dad gazed into his eyes as if he were searching for something truer than words. Levi's mind flickered to the debacle in Afghanistan that got him put on the first plane back to Fort Drum. He tried to keep his eyes steady so as not to betray anything to this experienced interrogator. "Hell no. Why even ask that?"

"It needed to be asked."

"Nick say something?"

"I've talked to Nick, sure. But he's never spoken a single ill word of you. This isn't about him. Let me put it bluntly." He put his hand on his son's shoulder. "I think the time has come for you to talk to someone."

Levi let out an exasperated sigh.

"I have some pamphlets in the car."

Levi removed his hands from his glass and laced them behind his head. He looked up at the ceiling, contemplating the idea.

[Perhaps it would be more accurate to say I pretended to contemplate the idea. I had been on that stage before in forced visits to the mental health clinic at Fort Drum, and before that, the joke of a system in Afghanistan, where they made me video-teleconference on some crappy satellite connection with some prick on Bagram. They cleared out the single concrete room in this bombed out UNICEF school on Sperwan Ghar—the same room where we all lived together—and they did it so my discussion with the shrink would be considered "confidential." Could anything get more degrading or humiliating than having your entire platoon uprooted to go stand on some mountain in the middle of nowhere so you can have your forced visit with the shrink? And how could I ever lead any of those guys again after that?]

No. Levi was done with the government's idea of mental health care. And the thing now was that even if he quit being a slug and got out to talk to a group, some veterans' support group or something, it would only be for one meeting. Just the one. Because this is what would happen: He'd go to the meeting and everyone else would have something to share, the essence of which would seem so platitudinous or like, trite. He had seen every character already.

He could imagine that each meeting would be filled with the same bromidic long-winded narrators, and each one would be identical to the characters he already knew. He conjured images of the night he got home when he had been trapped by Robert Wright and his stories of his air base. The star of the show at the meeting would be a similarly quintessential Vietnam vet with the "Look-What-I-Did-Thirty-Six-Years-Ago" baseball cap adorned with campaign ribbons and mini-medals. A graying ponytail would hang out the back of his baseball cap. Just like Wright, he'd be the broken-record type who probably didn't say a word to his family, but every weekend he went to hang out with his brothers-in-arms at the VFW who couldn't let go of their history—a history Levi would just as soon forget—and in the presence of his fellows he felt it was okay, necessary even, to rehash his battles.

A few months earlier he had paid a visit to Nick at Oma's Pub. The same kind of guy—sans ponytail but with the campaign hat—told all his stories. Nick had abandoned Levi, feigning work to excuse himself.

Levi couldn't take it. The guy continued to tell his stories. He kept pulling poor Shirley the bartender over to the conversation. With every calculated pause and well-time choke-up, with every attempt to connect or convey some real sentiment, Levi wanted to scream and tell the man how sentimental it was, and didn't he know that sentimental stories were inherently bad? And the stories were always so didactic; and didn't he know that audiences wanted to be entertained, not instructed? Didn't he know that audiences didn't want to be dragged down with the wisdom and moral lessons he was seeking to impart? He wanted to scream, but that wouldn't have been polite, because this man—this storyteller—was an American war hero after all, at least in the sophistic sense of the word; so he never screamed out his frustration, never put a stop to the narrative, and so the war stories, of course, continued. Would always continue.

[Don't think for a second that the irony here escapes me.]

"Like what then?" Levi asked his father. "Support groups? Therapy?"

"Sure. Could be. There's no one-size-fits-all approach."

"Let me tell you how that will go down." The alcohol had loosened Levi's tongue and the confrontation got his blood going. "I'll go to some meeting and some guy who spent his whole tour at Salsa Night or in the morale tent on Balad or Bagram or somewhere like that—some guy who's never ever been outside the wire for even a second—will corner me. Then I'll be stuck between politeness and the coffee table that holds the stainless steel coffee urn; and when I don't, like, placate him with a concerned response about what he's been through—which may as well have been an all-inclusive Sandals Resort getaway, comparatively speaking—he'll try to keep the conversation going by asking where I was and what was my mission? And how long were you in? And what made you get out? And man, don't you just miss it sometimes?

"I'll have to wait there with a crazed and impatient look in my eye, not wanting to further damage this already emotionally wounded character."

"Character?" his dad interrupted. "But these are real people with real feelings."

Levi ignored him and lit a cigarette. "To make it worse, we'll have to sit through these AA-style confessionals in which all I'll want to do is escape or smoke, but I can't smoke, because the VA is a government building after all, and so all I'll be able to do is bite little chunks of Styrofoam from my coffee cup. I'll pray that it will all end. That it will all be over. It's the type of thing that will make me literally wish for death."

When Levi paused to catch his breath, his father waited to make sure he was finished. He said gently, "Are you sure you aren't thinking of suicide?"

"Geez, Dad. It's an expression."

"So then what? You don't think any of the guys there, anyone trying or needing to get help, will really be—what did you call it?

Emotionally wounded? Maybe they haven't been through as much as you've been through, but don't they still deserve our empathy?"

"I don't know, Dad. The drinking, the fighting, the stories, the failure to adjust. It's all just so cliché, don't you think?" Levi felt like anything he said would be wrong.

[I still feel like anything I say would be wrong. The truth is, he was right, but I still couldn't/can't help feeling this (misplaced?) anger. Guys like that—guys, who, by virtue of the fact they're there at a meeting at all, or writing a blog about their experiences, or publishing their memoirs before they're forty, or having an open-forum panel to share their experiences, or sitting at the bar telling their war stories—these guys obviously don't have a problem telling their stories and recounting their heroes and going through the whole terrible and painful process of facing their demons with all the necessary emotional upheaval, if you will. All in the hopes of finding some redemption. And isn't that the problem with coming home from wars like this? We're all seeking redemption as mythical as the reasons they sent us over there in the first place.

But unlike them, I do have a problem telling my story. This generation: It's not like Grandpa or my dad—hell, or even you—who didn't/don't talk about war. No, we can't stop talking about it, blogging about it, tweeting about it, and updating our Facebook statuses about it. So what is there even left for me to say? There's nothing left. It's all been said, and it's cheap, and we're frustrated, and we're all tired of it.]

"Not to mention, Dad, it's not like the Greatest Generation who fought a great evil like the Nazis. So what kind of heroes can be in my story? I mean, really, what did our friends die for? Huh? What did I get my ears blown out for? Why did you go over there and get shot? And why did Nick get his ears blown out, his leg snapped, and all his flesh burned? Why did we go over there to fight and kill people? Not the threat of WMDs; that's for sure. And we're sure as hell not fighting for freedom. If anything, they're sending us to fight these useless wars to scare people, because when people are scared they'll give up anything. If we were actually defending freedom, the people we're fighting would actually have to threaten our freedom, and no one in Iraq or Afghanistan has ever threatened that. Not al-Qaeda, not the Taliban, not any of those primitive dirt farmers, and not even those maniacs that flew those planes into our buildings. The worst those radicals can threaten is our lives. The truth is, the biggest threat to freedom is our own corrupt government, which is bigger and scarier now than it's ever been. But hey, let's deify the troops and thank them all for defending freedom, right?

"Assuming arguendo—to use your language, Dad—that I go sit in on this Kumbaya circle-jerk to appease you, Liz, Nick, and everyone else who thinks I need help; well, once again I have to be surrounded by all these deified American vets. These guys who are walking talking clichés of the movies they see about themselves. These guys who are, sadly, just like me. And is it really even our fault? It's not like we know how to act apart from how books, movies, and the Internet tell us to act. We're all products of our generational influences, that's all. And perhaps that means there's a certain lack of culpability here, but at the same time, it makes any kind of change or rehabilitation absolutely impossible. It makes me crazier than the PTSD or whatever else you think I must have. We're all trying to boil down our meaningless experiences to fit this tiny little conventional, three-act, linear narrative to, like, somehow explain or even validate what we did over there. And of course, each story is bigger and badder and more sensational than the last, and we're all trying to impress upon people how bad it was, how high the stakes were, how damaged we now are, when the truth is, our stories aren't all sensational. They're sad in their ordinariness and they're depressing in how common they are. Each one of us hitting a climax too soon and then riding out the slow boring burn for the rest of our lives."

[And you know what? It's the denial of that, it's the attempt to give meaning to it all, or to create drama where there is none, it's that kind of blatant one-upsmanship, that kind of attention-grabbing instinct—all that ugliness that I feel and recognize in my own self—that fills me full of all this existential angst and saps me of all my goodwill.]

"So you're terrified your own story will just turn you into a cliché? Is that it?"

Levi clenched his teeth and looked at the television. Tying run at the plate in the ninth with only one out. It started with such hope. A fresh season. A new start in front of an adoring and supportive crowd.

Game over. Home team lost.

His dad continued on his dinner. "Do I seem like one of these clichés you hate? Does Nick? Do you actually *know* anyone who embodies this parody of a veteran you complain about?"

Levi shook his head and downed the rest of his beer. He was starting to feel like his flight of fancy was running out of places to go. "You know what? I don't know. I don't know anything. Maybe it would be great. You know, I'd probably walk out of the meeting, stroll to my car in the parking lot, and I'd probably even whistle. I'd feel the summer winds on my face and I'd start noticing things again. I'd see that someone took a lot of care in watering, fertilizing, and edging the nugatory island of grass in the parking lot. I'd feel that things were looking up, that there were people in this world who cared about things, and for a second, I'd probably feel something like gratitude." He lit another cigarette.

"And then what would happen?"

Levi didn't know. He didn't have an answer. What would happen then? The beer made him tired. The conversation made him tired. There had been an upswing there, a short time where he had been riffing and enjoying himself, enjoying that he was drunk and talking and letting things out and someone was listening, even if it was all nonsense, but then he had run out of answers. Or he realized his answers were no answers at all. He felt like going home and snuggling up in the patchwork quilt of anhedonia that had become so comfortable.

[And the further I get into chronicling all this, the more I realize the real problem is none of this. No amount of therapy and no amount of psycho-babble can cure what's really wrong with me. No amount of writing, self-reflection, or emotional upheaval can wash my own black heart. And I know I lack empathy here, and worst of all, I lack love, but bear with me, because I can't sugarcoat it or in any way let myself off the hook. Not if I'm going to get through this.]

Levi wished he had told the truth when his father asked if he thought of suicide. He wished he would have told him everything about all the guilt, all the mistakes. He wished he could explain how certain little mistakes in judgment had led to other little mistakes as he tried to cover up the original mistakes, thereby increasing his guilt all the more. He wished he could explain how it was all his fault that people died, and people were injured because he had been stupid and selfish and self-absorbed. He wished he could explain—without sounding like a crazy man—that it had all started with a stupid little stone. He wished he could explain to his father, the lawyer, that it may not legally or even rationally be his fault, but he nevertheless bore a certain moral responsibility for what had happened. They all did, but he especially. He wished he could explain how this downward spiral was nothing new and that he had been falling for years. He wished he could explain how despite the fact that he had taken other lives after that day and made many more mistakes, he had grown obsessive and monomaniacal about that single day in Iraq where he had taken life that wasn't his to take, or at the very least, he had set the chain in motion. Somewhere along the road he had lost his way.

He wished he could apologize to the parents of the dead.

He wished he could come clean about how he had left the army in disgrace and not as some big decorated hero. He wished he could say: Dad, I lied about how I left the army. Please take a moment to listen to what actually happened, and please don't judge me, because I've judged myself enough. Just please, let me tell you the truth.

But Levi's moment had passed. It would seem too awkward to go back to the moment when his dad first asked for a simple yes or no. He had said no, and now it would take too much energy to go back and explain.

"I don't know, Dad. I don't know what would happen then. I guess nothing."

His dad looked at his plate and set down his fork. Gravity and helplessness pulled the corners of his mouth into a frown. "I want you to know you're not alone."

Levi rooted in his pocket for a second pack of cigarettes.

"You know I got a medal once too. Not a Silver Star, but it was something. I silently took the congratulations of the base commander and whoever else was there. Some other guys got medals. I came home and I didn't think we did anything worth anything either."

"Dad, you don't have to—"

"Now I listened to you, so do me the same courtesy." Tears welled in his eyes.

Levi stared at the bar, embarrassed by his father's foreign vulnerability.

"You know what? Listen to me, Son. I can't offer you what you need. All I can do is tell you what I see that you may not see yourself.

"Now I've been where you are. I've taken a bullet for my country; you know that. I'm not just flapping my gums here. And I know it's hard to talk about it. People don't really want to hear about what it was really like over there. What we really did. But when I came back, they didn't have any programs to help us, and the ones they did have were ineffective and full of red tape."

"And our programs now are so streamlined and effective, Dad?"

"I know. I know the system is broken and the politicians creating the system will never understand the human cost, but that's not where I'm going. I can't emphasize enough that this isn't about that.

"The thing is, Levi, you're smart and you're charismatic and that's why everyone likes you when you want them to. But you're also self-ish and arrogant and prideful, and you think you've got everything figured out. And you know what else? It's easy to hide, Son. For a smart guy like you, it's nothing at all to convince people who don't know better that you've got it figured out. And people are scared. They don't like confrontation, so you give them an excuse to leave you alone, and they will. If you give enough people a reason to leave you alone, you'll end up alone. It's as simple as that."

Levi's eyes grew heavy. His mouth had begun to dry out. Where was the bartender already?

"In my case, your mother wouldn't quit on me. She's tough in the same way your sister is tough. She kept pushing me and wouldn't leave me alone no matter what I did to push her away. She's pushing me to push you. She's not naïve like you think she is. I know every-one else in the world may leave you alone when you make it clear you don't want to deal with things, but I won't. Your mother won't. Your sister won't. Your brother won't. Nick won't."

Levi sat in silence. He had run out of things to say. It was time for a nap. Or another drink. Or some levity.

The way his father looked sitting there with his silverware in front of him, cold dinner, and warm beer—the way he just looked so old, and so—Levi didn't know what. He had never seen this man before. His dad picked up the silverware and sliced furiously at a hunk of cold low-grade beef.

Levi stood up and patted his dad on the back. "So, Dad. Listen to this one. A three-legged dog walks into a tavern in the Wild West about a hundred years ago, probably like this tavern right here except without the neon signs. And so, he saddles up to the bar and this three-legged dog says—well, do you know what he says?"

His dad shook his head slowly.

"He says, 'I'm looking for the man who shot my paw.'"

His father said nothing.

Levi sighed and tossed two twenties onto the bar. "Thanks for the chat."

The man used his knife to scrape some corn into his mashed potatoes. He gritted his teeth and forked a piece of meat. He shoved it into his mouth, never taking his eyes off the plate.

3.15 CHOKE ARTISTS

Nick leaned over a booth in the back of the empty pub to wipe off the sticky remnants of spilled pop. He didn't know Levi had walked in until he left the floor, wrapped in a Heimlichian bear hug.

After Levi set him down, Nick turned to face his friend. Levi wore a broad grin. His eyes were glass, but there was a spark in them, and Nick hadn't seen life there in months.

"You smell like cigarettes and beer," Nick said. "It's not even dinnertime."

"Dad and I did lunch. Made an afternoon of it watching the Brewers tank the opener."

"You saw your dad?"

"Yeah. You catch the game?"

"Most of it. Almost rallied, just not enough."

"Choke artists."

"One hundred and sixty-one games left. No biggie."

"Have a drink with me."

"Ah, you know I can't. I've got work to do."

"Place is dead, dude. Have a drink."

They sat at the bar, and Levi ordered a vodka with Diet Coke. When Shirley brought the drink, Levi said, "One more thing, gorgeous? Bring this guy a shot. Something he can throw down before the customers flood in and see him drinking on the job."

"Don't bring me a shot, Shirley."

"Shirley, surely you can bring him a shot."

"Never heard that one before," she said.

"Shirley. Surely, you have Shirley. That is, surely you've heard the Shirley-surely bit."

"He's the one who signs my paycheck."

"And the customer is the one who provides his paycheck, and the customer is always right. Right?" Levi smacked his hand on the bar. "Ain't that right, Nick? Tell her the customer is always right."

Nick gave her a little nod. She brought him back a beer.

"Good to see you again," Nick said. He turned on the stool to face Levi.

"And you, Brother. How are things?"

"Same."

"Still working as much?"

"Yup."

"Let's blow this joint and hang out like the old days."

"Why can't we just hang out here?" Nick lifted his beer and took a drink.

"Do I really have to tell you? This is your work. Your job. Duh."

"Do people still say duh?"

"Boom. Just did. Now let's go."

"Go where?"

They sat there for a moment staring at each other.

"Crazy," Levi said. "We'll go crazy. Case of beer in the Blazer. We'll go wherever you want to go."

Levi already looked crazy to Nick. His mood, his eyes, his rapid speech made him seem lost in the throes of some type of episode, the likes of which he had never witnessed before. Nick shook his head slowly. "I'm sure it will get busy here soon. It's almost dinnertime."

Levi turned back to the bar in a huff and chugged down his drink before lifting a finger to signal for another one. After a while, he turned quickly and smiled. "Okay. Make a deal. We sit here and drink together until eight. If no one comes in by then, you leave the place in the fine and capable hands of Miss Shirley here, and we take off."

Nick looked at his watch. "Deal," he said.

After the first two beers, the drinks went down more quickly for Nick. They laughed about the old days, before they had even joined the military. Nick reminded Levi of things he had nearly forgotten, like getting beat up by Caleb Meyers out by the fence at the schoolyard in the middle of winter, the cows breathing their snot on him over the fence as he lay crying in the snow. Levi reminded Nick about falling through the ice as they attempted a shortcut through the marsh. He had to go home to Oma covered in frozen green algae. They talked about starting another band.

"We can play right here in the bar since you never leave the place," Levi said.

"Or we could play downtown La Crosse since you never come to Bangor anymore."

"But you'd have to rig some wireless hookup for my guitar since I never leave my apartment."

Levi did impressions of their drill sergeant. "You booooooys." He dragged out a long, slow, southern accent. "You still don't know yer woobies from yer weenies."

Nick's stomach hurt from laughing so hard. He had forgotten how much fun Levi could be. Yet, underneath it all, there seemed to be a dark undercurrent that Nick pushed away and ignored. He wanted to enjoy his old friend.

An elderly couple came in at quarter after seven.

"I didn't see a thing," Nick said.

"Customers? What customers?"

"Let's roll."

Levi called out, "You've been great, Shirley. And Shirley?"

She looked up and raised her eyebrows.

"Surely you've been the greatest bartender I've had all night." She rolled her eyes. Levi left a hundred dollar bill under his glass.

They sat in Levi's Blazer under the streetlights of Commercial Street, the old main drag that went down Bangor's center. They each chugged a beer and threw the empties into the backseat.

They maneuvered into the village park, which sat in a geographical bowl half a klick from their SP. They dismounted on arrival. They loaded their pockets with ammunition. They patrolled the playground equipment, dropping dead soldiers as they walked, the shiny aluminum cans acting as bread crumbs to show their path.

They stopped by the steep bank of the creek and toasted their dead friends by pouring beer over the glossy rocks leading down to the stream. They climbed a muddy embankment to the bike trail and the old train bridge that crossed the winding creek. They sat down on the bridge with their legs hanging over and they listened to the sound of rushing water.

Levi pulled a joint from his cigarette box and lit it. The sweet familiar smell wafted to Nick's nose. Levi passed it to him, and he hesitated, but he was drunk enough to only feign resistance.

"This is nuts," Nick said. "I haven't smoked since before we joined the army." He took a puff and inhaled. Held it. "I wouldn't even know where to get this stuff anymore," he croaked.

"Me neither."

"Never took you for a liar."

"Scouts honor."

They smoked.

They listened to the raging water wear the hardest of stones into nothing while it polished others into something beautiful.

Levi broke the silence. "You know they can see the cherry from this joint from over a klick away?"

"Who's they?"

"No one."

The early April clouds hung thick and heavy above the dense trees that tented the trail. Nick couldn't see a single star. He stared into the blackness. The night grew cold quickly and the damp air penetrated to the bone.

"You know," Levi said. "The stuff we're doing in Afghanistan now is way sicker than what we did in Iraq. What the two of us did in Iraq doesn't even compare." He paused and took a drink of beer.

"Hiking around. Clearing caves. Firefights all the time." He threw his beer can and opened another. "People step on mines, like, every day. In Afghanistan—" He belched. "They don't run, man. They'll fight you all day and then they'll fall on grenades when they die. That way, when you kick them over, you blow up."

Nick said nothing for a while. Talk of war bored him. He pulled his last beer from his pocket and threw his empty into the water below, thinking of something to say to change the subject. "Eris is finally going back to school in the fall."

"Finally doing it?"

"Yup."

They lapsed into another silence.

"What are you going to do?" Nick said. "Ever going to do something?"

"I am doing something. I'm a professional writer."

"C'mon. Whatever."

"It's true. I write sample essays for rich college kids through some cheater website."

"What about all the books you were going to write?"

"It's not like I haven't tried, but anything I finished would suck. It would be too preachy, too maudlin, too heavy, too sentimental. Too self-conscious. Too obviously allegorical. Too cliché. Critics would tear it apart."

"Forget about the critics. They want books written by a god they don't believe in."

Levi dropped the last burning ember of their joint and said nothing.

"Quit feeling sorry for yourself and just write the stupid book already. I don't care if it's the worst thing on the planet. Even if it is, at least you'll have done the worst thing on the planet, which has to count for something."

"What if I've already done the worst thing on the planet?"

"I don't know what you mean."

Levi said nothing for a good long while. Then he said, "I'm going to go back."

"Where?"

"Active duty. Going to join the army again."

"What? Are you nuts?"

"Ah, just playing." He hit Nick in the shoulder. "Seeing how you'd react."

It had gotten to the point where Nick couldn't hold his tongue anymore. "Get over it already," he said.

"What did you say?" Levi's voice was suddenly cold.

"I said get over it already."

"What's that supposed to mean?"

"It means what I said. It means get over it. It means you've been home over a year and you need to get over it."

Levi shrugged, as if shrugging off the whole idea. He swung his legs from the bridge like a carefree kid. "Whatever. At least in the army I had a purpose. At least back then what I did meant something."

"Don't kid yourself," Nick said. "You don't even believe that yourself."

"Sure I do. Last week on the Internet, I saw a picture of some little girl in Afghanistan skateboarding to school. That couldn't have happened before we went there."

"How many people have to die before the right to skateboard is no longer worth it?"

Levi stood up. His mood shifted like tectonic plates. "What the hell does that even mean? You think that's it? You think I didn't have a purpose? How about the one sitting right here? How about you? And your life? Don't you dare talk to me like what I did doesn't matter."

He walked back and forth across the rotting, moss-covered planks of the old bridge. He screamed into the air, "I'm just so bored now!" He paced back and forth and leaned over the edge of the rail. "I'm going to jump."

"Shut up. There are rocks everywhere. It's like, three feet deep." The weed had made Nick apathetic. He didn't believe him anyway.

"There's a place right over here that's deeper. I used to fish in that hole."

"And you're going to hit it in the dark?"

"I've hit more than that in the dark. And at a farther range too." He climbed onto the black metal supports along the side of the bridge.

"Knock it off, dude. You're going to kill yourself."

"There are worse things." He jumped.

Nick heard the splash. He popped to his feet and slid down the slick embankment under the bridge. He stopped short of the heavy rocks that led down to the water.

Levi climbed up out of the water, and he shook his head. Little droplets flung off his hair. "Whooooooooo, perfect," he yelled.

"What's wrong with you?" Nick screamed.

"What's wrong with me? What's wrong with you?"

"I'm not the one trying to kill myself."

"Oh yeah?" Levi said. "Moping around, college dropout, working a job you never wanted for practically nothing in some small town you always wanted to escape. You actually like this? You appreciate these low stakes after what we've been through? You actually like this new acoustic life? All brain dead and unplugged?" He spat it out like it was poison. "We played in a rock band, traveled the world, fought wars, blew things up; we held lives in our hands and influenced the fate of nations. We did some serious living, Brother. We were baptized by fire." Levi yelled and gesticulated wildly. Spittle flew from his mouth. "And now this? Look at you, limping around. You're pathetic. Medals in a pile of trash on the floor like you were never there. Like you've forgotten everything." Levi shoved Nick, causing him to stumble back a step.

Nick nearly lost his balance. His eyes widened in surprise and then narrowed in anger. "Yeah? Baptized by fire? Are you serious right now?" He shook his head. "But what should I expect from you? The sad vet who can't get over himself or let go."

"Shut up," Levi said, tears welling in his eyes. "Sorry we can't all inherit the family business, get the girl, and go back to life as usual." He shoved Nick again.

Nick shoved him back. "Think I didn't have problems? Think I don't still have problems? You have any idea what I've been through with that business I inherited? Or that we're probably going to lose it? Or what I've been through with my wife? And that I could have lost her? You know, I was doing just fine until you got back. Almost forgot the war until you brought it back into my house. Threw your medal on the wall to remind me every day of not only the war but also how much I owe you, huh? You, you, you. It's still all about you, isn't it?" Nick shoved him again.

Levi charged forward and slammed his shoulder into Nick's stomach, taking him to the ground. They rolled around on the thin dew-covered grass, both of them getting snotty and damp as they fought for the upper hand. Nick broke free from Levi's grasp and jumped to his feet. Levi did the same. Nick swung blindly in the dark and missed, but he felt a fist connect with his nose. He bent over, stunned, and he put his finger to his nose to feel for blood.

Levi tackled him again, and they rolled down the rocky bank into the shallow, arctic water. Sharp boulders gouged into Nick's hip and back as they tumbled in the cold stream. As they splashed down into the water, the earthy mineral flavors of the northern headwaters rushed into their mouths.

They wrestled, each trying to get the upper hand. Arms reached under legs. Hands flew under armpits and gripped hair and necks and wrenched heads. They fought dirty because winning was the only thing that mattered. Abs flexed and rotated. Heads went underwater, gulped cold water, and came back up sputtering. They both turned about, leveraging their own weight and the weight of their memories against each other. They had done this countless times, and the fluid movements and constant shifts of advantage harkened back to their long days of combative sessions during their military training.

When they had settled in the gritty silt on the bottom of the creek, Levi was on top. He put his elbow across Nick's neck and worked his knees up to pin his arms down. Although Nick had always been much larger, he had never been much of a fighter. Levi had always been full of more violence.

Nick was helpless to fight him off. He felt Levi's fingers tighten around his neck. He went slack and tapped twice on Levi's thigh, signaling that he was done. It was over. He conceded.

Levi didn't let go. The moon shone on his face, and Nick saw a snarl he didn't recognize. He tapped harder in case Levi didn't feel him the first time. When Levi didn't relent, Nick realized that everything was possible. Levi was no longer himself, and he was capable of anything.

Nick's vision began to grow dim, and the moving water of the creek now sounded like rushing rapids roaring inside his head. He panicked. In one explosive movement, he stretched his arms free from under Levi's knees. He clawed at Levi's face hovering above his own, but quickly changed course and tucked his arms in to free his own neck. His thoughts raced and the rushing in his ears grew louder.

His thumbs scraped the stubble on his own neck as he struggled to create distance between Levi's grip and his own windpipe. He lifted his hips and flopped back down. He writhed and twisted and turned until Levi shifted. As soon as he had an opening, he put a knee in Levi's groin.

Nearly as soon as it had begun, it was over, but a whole history rested in the brief struggle.

Levi rolled off, and Nick slipped up the rocks on the side of the creek. He stood on the bank and looked down at Levi holding himself in the water.

Nick screamed as he bent over in pain. "What the hell is wrong with you? I'm not the enemy here." He lifted his head and watched

Levi stand up. He shouted at him, "I'm doing something. At least I'm doing something. I'm living. And you know what? I don't need their Purple Heart." He peeled off his wet shirt, fighting it as the sopping fabric stuck on his back. He flung it aside and showed Levi the wrinkled piebald scars all over his torso. "My purple heart is right here." He turned and pounded on his chest. He kicked off his waterlogged shoes and peeled his dripping socks from his frozen feet. "I don't need to tell stories to remind people I was there, because I have all of this to remind every single person who looks at me that I was there. I don't need a medal hanging on my wall to tell me I was there, because every day, every step, every morning I wake up with my skin burning to remind me that I was there. And I'm right here. Right here on this earth, still alive, right here." He stomped on the ground as he yelled. "You can't change anything, Levi. I can't change anything. The past is done. It's over." He pulled down his wet pants and threw them to the side. "Look at this," he yelled.

Levi looked at the ground, silent and shaking.

"I said look at this." Nick looked to the sky and cried out, "You can spit out all the ridiculous clichés you want, but I *was* baptized by fire." Nick stood with his fists clenched, soaking wet, naked, and trembling.

Levi climbed up the bank and sat down on the grass.

Exposed and heaving, Nick turned and walked back to his pants. He put his bad leg in first, but the wet denim of the jeans stuck together, so he couldn't slide the leg in. He lost his balance and fell. He sat on the grass, furious that he was so crippled he couldn't even put on his own pants. He slowly pulled each wet leg of his jeans over his skin. He felt the moist, abrasive waistband scrape against the backs of his thighs. He fell and arched his back to inch the wet jeans up his butt. He stood and limped around gathering his shirt and shoes in his arms.

He walked back and said, "I never wanted to be the wounded little bird, you know. I was just trying to get on with my life." He collapsed next to Levi, and they sat there next to each other in the cold. When they both stopped shaking, Levi got up. Nick got up too, and they walked.

As they left the park, they stopped at the veterans' memorial wall the VFW had recently built. "Look at this," Levi said. He ran his hand over the smooth granite. "They have all the names of all the people that have ever served from this town. Look. Your name here. And mine here. On a memorial. Can you believe that? Like we're dead or something. Nothing but a memory." He looked over his shoulder at Nick. "Then again, aren't we?"

Nick climbed in the passenger's side of the truck. Levi, looking sad and broken, made his way to the driver's seat.

Nick slammed his hands on the dashboard. "No," he yelled. He pounded on the dashboard again. "No, we're not."

Levi revved the engine, turned the heat up. "Whatever you say."

Nick opened the door and got out of the truck. He walked across the parking lot and up the hill in the direction from which they came.

Levi backed up and drove off in the opposite direction.

3.16 DON'T HOLD IT AGAINST HER; SHE WAS ONLY TRYING TO HELP

When she saw him standing there like a stray, hair wet and matted, she opened the door to let him in.

"Is Nick home yet?" he asked.

She shook her head.

"Do you think I could wait for him for a while?"

She looked at the vodka bottle he waved while he spoke. She looked at the clock on the wall. Even though he hadn't been in the house in nearly a year, Levi opened the cupboard as if he lived there. He grabbed a glass and sat at the kitchen table.

"Do you think," she asked, "I could get you some coffee? Maybe instead?"

He waved a sad hand. "I'm good. Thanks."

"Are you okay?" She sat across from him. She knew he was not okay.

"My dad doesn't think so. He thinks I need to go to meetings. You been to meetings?"

She bit her bottom lip. She nodded.

"So, then what? You just quit, like, cold turkey or whatever?"

She shrugged.

He lifted his eyebrows and frowned deeply as if he were offended by this. She stood and got her own glass from the cupboard. She held it out for him to pour.

"Should you be doing that?" he asked.

"You my dad now?"

He poured. She sipped. He relaxed.

They sat in silence for a long time. She finished a drink. He poured her another. He worked his closed mouth as if he were having an argument in his head.

Finally he spoke. "You know what kind of meeting would be perfect? It would be a meeting for people like me. People similarly laconic. I'd go to this meeting for dudes like me—dudes who all have some completely established grief, some totally bona fide affliction they're all too incredibly strong to unleash on everyone else, everyone else being the weaker men in the world. You know, I really admire those guys, i.e., the strong taciturn men without the overwhelming need to be heard. I'd walk into that meeting, sit down, and look at all the other silent, usually unnoticed men. We'd all look around at each other and gulp our coffee without waiting for it to cool down. Then after a few moments of that—a few moments of drinking coffee and appraising one another—we'd all nod at each other with tight-lipped half-smiles. We'd get up, walk out, and go about our lives refreshed."

"If you didn't talk, how would you know they were like you?" she asked.

"I'd recognize them by their jaw muscles—prominent from lots of teeth clenching."

"Maybe Nick could join you."

He snickered.

She waited.

"You know what we did over there?"

"No."

"We stole wood from the main base and built a deck on ours."

"What else?"

"I have beers in my truck. I'm going to go get some beers."

"You don't have to."

"I do."

She looked up at the clock. She picked up the phone and tried calling Nick. It would probably be hours before he was home. There was no answer.

Levi returned with a case of beer. He set it on the table. He opened one and handed it to her.

"We had this big concrete T-wall that stood in front of our door so if mortars came in at just the right spot, the frag wouldn't fly through our doorway. We stole a projector, hooked a laptop and speakers to it, and we made our own outdoor theater."

"What else?"

"It lasted a week because the bugs were so bad. And the camel spiders."

"What else?"

"We drank liquor that girlfriends shipped over in mouthwash bottles."

"What else?"

"At night?" he said. "After missions? We played our guitars and sang songs against the war. Our soldiers smoked shisha and sang harmonies."

She said nothing, but remembered a night with Nick years ago.

"Don't you want to know what else?"

She took a drink, shook her head. "You don't have to."

"We put bullets in the faces of old men who drove too close. We detained teenagers, beat them up, and put sandbags over their heads because they were in the wrong place at the wrong time and they were born in the wrong country. We did it because we were terrified. We were terrified all the time."

She said nothing for a long time, but he stared at her intensely, waiting. She was afraid to look away.

"What am I supposed to say to that?" she finally said.

"Who said you had to say anything?"

She looked away and finished her drink.

"Let's smoke," he said.

He was sad.

She was drunk and wanted to make him happy, so they smoked in the living room. They sat on the floor with their backs against the couch. They ashed in empty beer bottles. She was glad they had changed rooms.

"You're good to me," he said. "All you've done for me. Letting me stay here, letting me smoke here." He swept his hand out in front of him. "I missed you."

"Good. We missed you."

Levi looked down at his cigarette, which he held between two fingers on a hand that rested on the floor. He rested a beer bottle on his poochy stomach. He looked like he might fall asleep like that.

His head bobbed like an old man with Parkinson's. "So," he said. "Two weeks after getting to Panjwai on my second trip to Afghanistan, we got in a TIC. Have you read that phrase in any of your books? TIC? Troops in contact?"

She nodded. She didn't want to know anymore, to drink anymore, or to talk anymore, but it was now obvious that he needed to tell her.

She asked him to go on.

"We took heavy fire. People died. Whatever."

He said this as if it were nothing.

"We walked out again, and once again, of course, we took contact. The platoon sergeant was on R&R and our LT was this young hot-headed type. He started talking all sorts of nonsense like he was going to raze villages. He was going to go out on the next mission and scorch the earth. It was probably a bunch of blustering bullshit, but there were rumblings in the platoon, and not your typical and perfectly natural revenge-speak rumblings. There were some deep, dark, seriously ominous undertones here."

He drank and lifted his cigarette to his lips, struggling immensely with the weight of it. When his palm had plopped back on the carpet, he once again stared at the smoke that streamed straight up between his fingers.

He nodded and inhaled deeply through his nose. "I was tired and I didn't want to scorch anything, so I said I was sick. I lied. I was just so tired. So they went out and I was alone. Like a big coward. I was the only one in our little wooden B-hut for hours. I cleaned my weapons. I cleaned my pistol. That nine mil looked so attractive." His voice grew soft. "And I was so tired. So tired."

He put his hand over his face.

She rubbed his back. "That's all in the past," she told him. "You're here now."

"I picked it up," he said. "I was just curious is all. I even cleared it two, three, four times. I swear I cleared it. I stood up and looked in the mirror. Curious is all. I put it to my head."

He dropped the cigarette into his nearly empty beer bottle. He turned to her. "I put it up to my temple, like this. I wondered how easy it would be to pull the trigger. I tried squeezing and I closed my eyes and I began to squeeze, but I couldn't. I opened my eyes again and saw the placid look on my face and the void in my own eyes and I saw the pistol against my head. What difference does it make? I thought. You're already dead. Have been dead for quite some time. I was going to pull the trigger for real then. I don't know. Just to see if I could. To see what it would feel like."

Eris exhaled. She reached out and put a hand on top of Levi's. She squeezed his hand. "What else?"

"I didn't get the chance."

Levi lit another cigarette with one hand. He leaned back against the couch and smoked. He left his other hand under Eris's. "I didn't get the chance. An Air Force captain I had never seen before walked in and freaked out. I guess he was part of some PRT, provincial reconstruction team, and they were stopping into our COP because they had busted a tie rod or something. He came into our B-hut because obviously the COP was nearly empty. He was looking for someone in charge."

Levi laughed. "A regular deus ex machina," he said. He shook his head and turned his arm around.

He held Eris's hand.

"Anyway," he went on. "This prick signed a sworn statement saying I had a loaded magazine with me. But I swear I cleared it. Or at least, I thought I did. But he said I had a magazine and he had two bars on his collar and I had none, so that was that. And that made all the difference between the army calling it suicidal ideation and a suicide attempt. They tried to keep it low key, to keep me in country, but once it's labeled a suicide attempt, the entire army has to have a simultaneous knee-jerk freak-out."

He waved his cigarette and grew agitated. She tried pulling her hand back, but he squeezed it and held on.

"So they made me do this video chat with a psychologist whose sole purpose—or so it seemed at the time—was to get me to tell the truth to myself. 'The truth will set you free,' he said. 'That's a quote from the Bible.' And I told him I could quote it too, and I said, 'What is truth?' I said it very ruefully."

Eris tried smiling, but it was a sad smile. "Did he get it?"

"Of course not. He didn't get it. He kept on howling that only if I tell the truth to myself can I heal, but I kept telling him the truth, which was that I had cleared the gun first. It wasn't loaded. I swore it wasn't loaded. And the Internet connection kept going out and he wasn't listening to me. I got so angry at all of it, got so angry that this was their idea of helping me, so I threw the computer monitor against the wall. That triggered an Article 15 Non-Judicial Punishment for violations of the UCMJ, the Uniformed Code of Military Justice."

"Sounds serious."

He shrugged. "So they sent me back to Fort Drum. Purgatory in rear detachment. Rear D we called it. Everyone else in Rear D were these guys who had skated the deployment, did whatever they could to get a duty-limiting profile. They were all guys who had never been in combat, so they had no clue. None. So if I was ostracized before, after the reported suicide attempt and Article 15, imagine how I felt in Rear D."

"I can't imagine." She didn't know what to say. She stood up and pulled her hand away as she did. "Do you want some water? I could use some water," she said. "I think you should have some water."

He spilled beer down his chin. "I drank a lot," he said. "If you think I drink a lot now, you should have seen me then. Ha. This is nothing. After I don't even know how many days waking up late and smelling like booze, they cut me loose. Yup. That's right," he said. "They cut me loose. Oh, but quietly, of course."

Levi spoke with bravado and he stood. He swayed with his chest out against his unseen enemy. He took a step toward her. She lost her balance and fell backward until she was sitting on the couch.

"They could have charged me with who knows how many counts of dereliction of duty and who knows what else, but the PR wouldn't look good if they took a Silver Star Winner, a bona fide war hero to court just for being tired and depressed. And we all know nothing is more important to the military than their precious PR, their precious image, no matter how many of their own they end up eating in the process. So they burned me. Escorted me off the base like a common criminal and said they were doing me a favor. And here we are."

He plopped down next to her.

"And here we are."

"Because I got my friends killed and I got Nick hurt."

She shook her head. She didn't know what he was talking about.

"It's true," he said. He put a hand on her cheek.

She shook her head.

She shook her head against all the ways he said he was to blame for what had happened to Nick, all the ways he was at fault, all the ways it should have been him instead. She shook her head when he pulled a small stone from his pocket and starting raving like a madman; when he begged her to look at it; when he pleaded for her to touch it so she would feel it too, so she would really know how heavy it was. She shook her head so hard she stopped hearing him.

"Are you even listening?" he asked. "Why some and not others?" he asked. "If it's not my fault, then whose is it? Why did it happen? Why? Why? Why?"

She cried. "Why ask why?"

"You sound like Nick."

She put her head down. She wiped at her tears.

He took one of her hands. She sniffed, stopped crying.

And she had an idea. She tried her best to sound like the best of Nick. She tried to sound full of grace and kindness. She tried to sound wise and knowledgeable and full of faith.

"When the ancient Israelites were wandering in the desert," she said, "the priests offered sacrifices to the Lord. There were sacrifices for everything."

He let his head lean back against the top of the couch, and he turned to look at her, bored, eyes glazed.

His disinterest emboldened her. She would not be deterred. She was—for the first time in her life—possessed by the Holy Ghost.

"In one of these prescribed sacrifices," she said. "To purify an unclean house? The priest would take two birds. Imagine this priest in his robes and his turban with all twelve ornate stones on his breastplate and the Urim and Thummim hidden away inside. Imagine him carrying these two doves in their rickety wooden cage to the altar where he sets it next to a small block of cedar, a handful of hyssop, a length of scarlet yarn, and clay pot filled with water.

"He did this," she said. "Picture it. He opens the cage just far enough to reach inside and grab one of the birds and he takes hold of it without letting the other go. He holds this cooing dove over the clean water and he strokes its head and then he wrings its neck. He holds it there and lets the blood drip into the pot while the other bird watches. Then he tosses the dead bird to the side, discarding it like it's less than nothing. Then he turns to the other dove, the one who saw his friend, his mate, his love killed in front of him. The priest grabs the second dove and holds it in one hand, tight enough to feel its little heart flutter with fear. And this bird looks from side to side, his eyes darting around looking for an escape. He tries lifting his wings but he can't, and his heart beats faster and faster. With his other hand, the priest grabs the wood, hyssop, and yarn and he puts them in the water. Then he holds this terrified bird with both hands and he plunges it into the bowl, down under the water, painting his white feathers red with blood. Then he takes it out to the field, wet, scared, shaking, covered in the blood of his friend, and he opens his hands. For no reason but grace, the bird flies free."

Levi let out an exasperated sigh. "Did you ever consider that bird? What a miserable life he must have led after that?"

She shook her head sadly, her fire now gone. She had no power to make the blind see. "Are you sure you don't want water?"

She stood.

He followed her to the sink. "What then?" he asked. "Is that dove ever the same? Does that blood mark him? Ostracize him? Does he share that story with all the other birds? Would they care if he did? Is he grateful? Or does he live with guilt because he lives and flies and roosts? While the other bird lies limp, broken, dead? Does he ever cry for no reason?"

"Or," she asked him, "does he savor every moment? Every taste of worm, every ray of sunshine, every gust that lifts his wings and allows him to coast upon the breeze? Does he savor every touch?"

She had read accounts of soldiers in battle being in such grave danger of getting overrun by the enemy that they had no choice but to call in artillery so close to their own position that they risked injury or death from the incoming fire they had ordered. The term for this was danger close.

As Eris ran the tap water at the sink, Levi stood danger close.

3.17 BUT DIDN'T YOU KNOW THAT ERIS WAS THE GODDESS OF DISCORD AND WAR?

Levi fell on his knees at the foot of her bed as if in worship, or in prayer. He cupped the narrow curve of Eris's left foot in his hand, and he inspected her perfectly proportioned toes, each toenail glazed with pomegranate polish. The large toenail had a minuscule chip on the right side, but they were otherwise pristine. He kissed the top of her foot and held her arch against his cheek.

"Don't," she said. Eris lay on her side with her head half-buried in her bare arms, the plain pink sheet covering her thighs, hips, and torso, up to the top swell of her breasts, just hiding what lay underneath. Levi couldn't see a bra strap, but he could see her cleavage at the edge of the linen. He thought of pulling on the sheet to expose all of her, to see exactly how far he could have gone, but he didn't dare do it.

"What," he said. "I wasn't trying to do anything."

She yanked her foot away and pulled her covers up to her neck.

"Please," he said. "I'm sorry."

"And what do you have to be sorry about?" When he didn't answer right away, she said, "Why are you even still here? You shouldn't still be here."

Was he *still* there? He remembered stumbling up the driveway, letting the screen door clang behind him as he walked into the entryway to ring the doorbell, but that was hours ago. Still awake when he arrived, she had opened the door and looked down at the bottle of vodka in his hands. She had shaken her head when he asked about Nick, looking down at the bottle again. A starving child looking at food. She hadn't even asked why he was wet.

He had talked. He remembered that he had talked, but he couldn't remember what he had said. She had looked tense. He had started crying. Blubbering like a baby was more like it. She had taken the glass right from his hands and had sipped from it before grabbing one of her own.

In the bedroom he now said, "I'm not still here. I'm here again. I thought maybe Nick would be home by now."

"He's not."

"Are you okay?"

"I'm fine."

"We need to talk about this."

"We don't need to talk about anything."

He turned around and sat on the floor with his back against the foot of her bed. He put his head in his hands and moaned. As he sat there breathing—deeply in, deeply out—his head filled with static. He knew he had done something terrible. Now he couldn't make a decision, and he didn't know what to say to lead this situation in the right direction. "I'm not myself."

"That's what everyone has been telling you since you came home," she said. It came out muffled as she tried to bury herself deeper into her arms and her pillow.

He talked to himself more than to Eris. "I was going to have adventures. I was going to do things. Important things. Good things. This isn't how my life was supposed to turn out."

"There is no such thing as supposed to."

He ignored her. "This isn't the person I was supposed to be."

"Get out."

What had he done? He tried to remember. They had drunk the rest of the bottle together. She drank fast and she drank well. He had stopped crying at one point and they had begun laughing. Out of the blue—was it out of the blue?—he had asked if she remembered the night before he and Nick had left for the army, the night they kissed. She then looked at him slyly out of the corner of her eye. "What are you talking about?" she had said. Had she smiled? "You know what I'm talking about. The single greatest night of my life," he had said. "Doesn't ring a bell," she had said smiling. "Really," he had said. He had looked into her green eyes and he refused to look away. And she had refused to look away from him. She had giggled.

He shook his head, trying to clear the memory, or to bring it into focus. He stood up and towered over her bed. "This is messed up," he said. "This here." He spread his hands out. "This is wrong. It needs to be fixed."

She sat up quickly in anger, and the sheet fell to her lap. Shadows and hair fell across her face, but soft light played on her breasts showing her dark nipples, perfect and round in contrast to her white skin. She snatched up the sheet again, but Levi still stared, filled with an inexplicable desire for her that tore against his intentions to reconcile, to apologize, to be better than who he was.

"There'd be nothing to fix if you weren't showing up at my house in the middle of the night when he's out working," she said.

He lifted his eyes up to hers. She looked down at the sheets. "What?" he said. "This isn't my—"

"You're going to somehow fix this by kissing my feet and trying to come onto me again?" With a fiery boldness she looked up again and locked eyes with him. "It's creepy."

"Again?" he said. "What do you mean, again? I never—"

Or had he? There were more gaps in his memory than details. They had drunk in the living room, smoking and ashing right there in the house. They leaned against each other as they sat on the floor, their backs against the couch. They had held hands. Of that he was sure. "Oh I missed you," she had said leaning against him. Or she had said, "We missed you." Did it matter which? At some point, they had kissed. Her lips had felt as soft as he remembered. But now, it was all fragmented. He couldn't remember how it had all transpired.

Here in the bedroom she maintained her eye contact. He felt accused. One more time, Levi fought the confusion that welled within. He surveyed her neck, her shoulders, the shadows across her face, the blazing eyes that reflected the ambient light, and he walked out of the room.

He walked down the hall and stood in the middle of the living room, lost. He looked around and noticed how ordinary the room looked. How normal. How nothing at all indicated that anything unusual had gone on. The beer bottles had been cleaned up. It smelled more like Febreze than cigarette smoke. Who would ever know?

He made a decision. He collapsed on the couch. He resolved to stay.

As tired as he was, his mind was racing, and he didn't dare fall asleep. There was a time when he would have stayed in her bedroom and fought. He would have rationalized. He would have cajoled or pleaded. He would have emerged triumphant. He knew as he stared at the ceiling that his younger self would have never retreated from a battle. He would have stayed in there and told her she had it all wrong; she was misremembering what had happened.

[I know this is painful to read, but I have to tell you.]

He would have made her question herself and everything she knew about herself as long as he came out victorious. But every old soldier knows that sometimes the casualties are not worth the win, and Levi was an old soldier.

He rested with the thought that the couch wasn't an all-out assault, but at least it wasn't an all-out retreat.

He heard her clear her throat, and he looked up. She wore a turtleneck sweater, baggy jeans, and thick woolen socks. Her arms were crossed over her chest. "What do you think you're doing?"

"Someone has to have the courage to do the right thing," he said.

"And what is that supposed to mean?"

"It means I'm staying. I'm waiting for Nick and I'm going to tell him."

"You need to leave. You need to leave right now." Her voice shook, but it was also hard.

"I'm going to tell him everything. Everything up to and including tonight. I need to tell him."

"Whatever. Just go."

"And you'll tell him?" He wanted her to get down on her own knees and plead with him not to. He wanted her to beg him not to say anything. She'd make it right. She was sorry. She'd confess her own sins and take all the blame necessary and be humble and righteous and penitent. He wanted her to swear she'd seek absolution so he wouldn't have to.

"Hasn't he suffered enough? What will that gain? Seriously. And you think he'll take your side about tonight? You think he'll listen to you? Find you blameless?"

"You don't know what we have. We're brothers," he said. "We've been through war together; we can get through this." As he said it, and as he heard his words aloud with his own ears, he felt hopelessly stupid. But still, he hoped she would fall on her knees and paw at his chest. He hoped she would pull her shirt off and slide out of her pants and claw at her socks and present herself to him. He hoped she'd lean over him naked, place her hands on his cheeks and turn his face to her and kiss his mouth, his closed eyes, and his forehead as she cried and said she'd do anything at all if he didn't tell Nick that they'd kissed. Anything. She'd do anything.

[But trust me in this: She wouldn't do anything. Nothing. She wouldn't kiss me back. She wouldn't relent. And she wouldn't do anything to hurt you. I'm the one to blame here.]

"I said get out."

He swung his legs out and sat up.

"Now."

Everything about her boiled up inside him and he stood up and moved in front of her. She didn't move, though his shoulders heaved and his breath seethed and he felt seconds from exploding in anger. She stared him down and wouldn't relent.

"Okay," he said. "Okay."

He brushed past her through the house. He closed the front door lightly, not knowing if he'd ever return. He lingered in the vestibule for a moment, and then silently placed his spare key above the door. He winced at the creaking of the screen door that led outside, and he held it so it wouldn't slam.

Levi turned the corner, walked west on Wall Street, and tucked his hands into his pockets to protect them from the early morning chill. He walked from Liberty Street, from the home Eris and Nick had made for themselves, all the way west through the mud puddles in Copeland Park, along the banks of the frigid Black River. He rested on a bench before getting up and making his way to Riverside Park. He found some rocks near the water and sat like he always used to do before he left town years ago.

He thought of nothing. He didn't think of the way the plastic on a Humvee seat bubbled and boiled when licked by flames. He didn't think of the way human skin did the same. He didn't think about the way a nine-millimeter Beretta looks in the mirror when it's pressed against your own temple. Or how before he saw the bullet-hole in Brian's neck just south of Sperwan Ghar, he saw the shock in his eyes—the wide and vacant stare that accompanied the complete and immediate occlusion of his airway, which was born from shock and not pain. The shock was born from Brian's realization that things like this really did happen to you and not the other guy, and this is exactly what it feels like. He didn't think of the screaming. The multitude of screams. The myriad screams. The plethora of screams. The innumerable screams. All the various screams. He didn't think of how, when he was cranking a tourniquet on Brody Gassner's thigh, he wanted to use the tourniquet as a garrote so Brody would just shut the hell up already. He didn't think of Tom Hooper suspended against a backdrop of smoke and flames or of the way Weber's eyes bulged in death. He didn't think of Nick, and he certainly didn't think of Eris.

CODA

REWRITES
&
RETROSPECT

IN HOC SIGNO VINCES

C.1 THIS IS WHERE WE MUST BEGIN

April 6th, 2010–July 4th, 2010

Levi didn't think of how easy it would be to walk into the water. How many kids in their twenties had simply disappeared into the water there? He'd just be one more. They could hardly even call it suicide. Just another drunk kid stumbling into the river. Happens every year in this town. As comforting as the water seemed, he could not do that to his friends and family. At least not yet. Not that he couldn't walk into the water or end it all, but he couldn't leave without telling Nick everything, without at least giving him a note to tell him why he did it.

The wind bit his cheeks. His ears burned. His toes slowly deadened, and he sat there until he could no longer move them. When he felt sufficiently numb, he stood and walked on wooden legs up State Street until it connected with Third and took him to his apartment downtown.

He smoked a cigarette outside Coconut Joe's, cupping the asthenic cherry against the ever-growing wind. After finishing, Levi trudged up the stairs to the modest apartment above the bar.

The bass music from the club bludgeoned his ears, and the sound of parties and pleasure beckoned to him. He was filled with an urge to lose himself in the drinks and the girls and the music, but for once, he resisted.

He went to the card table and folding chair he had set up in the corner of the studio. He took a black-and-white composition book from the top of a stack of black-and-white composition books, and he opened it to the first blank page. He set the book on the table, and he sat down to complete his confession.

He sat down to do what Nick told him to do.

He sat down to write.

He had to explain things, had to make some sense of everything, had to get it all off his chest. He wrote about Eris. He wrote about Nick. About his dead friends, his family, himself.

He wrote until his wrist grew sore; he took a break to ponder, and then he took up his pen and continued.

He put people in convoys and threw bullets at them, and he wrote people into Humvees with bombs underneath them. It wasn't that hard, because they were only characters, right? He forced young kids to make the worst decisions of their lives and he made them walk into no-win situations with blindfolds on. He put people in trees and threw rocks at them, most of the time not even bothering to get them down—because that's how life *really* worked.

What if? he thought. *What if Cain never killed Abel?*

He wrote about his own tight fingers around the neck of his best friend, his beloved brother, mere seconds from the satisfying pop of a crushed windpipe.

Sometimes he cried. Salty tears plopped onto the white paper, and later, when they dried, left little circular ripples that stiffened the pages; but this was all part of the process, all part of the upheaval. He put into words what he couldn't think about at the river, what he couldn't explain to his dad, and what he couldn't express aloud since he'd come home. He didn't know what good it would do, but at least he was doing something.

When he could no longer think straight and when his wrist was so swollen he could barely move it—long after the club had ushered her patrons home—when the sky turned pink and then blue outside, he adjusted the painter's drop cloths that he used to curtain the windows and he took off his clothes.

He folded them and put them in neat and sorted piles instead of strewing them across the floor as he had done for the past year. He did it consciously as if this action meant he was turning things around. As if caring about a detail was evidence that he was making progress.

As he did when he was a child, he got down to petition the Lord in the old-fashioned way, on his knees, and he said some bedtime prayers. For the first time in a very long time, he asked for mercy, for daily bread, for serenity, and for wisdom.

When he woke, he typed what he had written, and he wrote again. At some point in the night before—he didn't know when—what he had been writing turned into something more than a simple suicide note. It had turned into a love letter, and he felt like he couldn't stop until he finished. Until he had written every word he had inside him to write, he could not in any way give up the ghost.

He continued his confessional. Each night he returned to the river and thought the same dark thoughts, but he was not yet ready. Each night he returned home to pray the same desperate prayers, and each morning he woke to continue that, or rather this, note. It was in this process that Levi walked, until one night in early July, something extraordinary happened.

He typed his final word. His fingers rested on the keyboard. There was a moment of complete stillness between breaths. There was no clattering of keys. There was no percussion from the club below. There was no conversation in the hallway, no buzzing of electronics, no whooshing of ventilation, and no humming of traffic. Even the wind had stopped blowing. He was done. He had written every word. There was nothing left to be said. For the first time in his life, he was content.

Then he exhaled and the world returned. The smoky stench of the apartment filled his nose when he inhaled again. The fan rattled in the window. Tires screeched and a horn honked. Someone in the hallway yelled an obscenity and slammed the door.

When Levi was immersed in his work, he had felt better. He felt like what he was doing was important. Each word that came out of him made him lighter. Now, he was done.

Levi's heart quickened. He grew nervous. He chewed on a fingernail. He saved the file and sent it to the printer. He stood up and paced as it printed, and when the printer ran out of paper, he refilled it. He smoked a cigarette as he stacked the hundreds of pages and waited for it to quit printing. When it was complete, he picked up the stack of paper and felt the thing that he held in his hands. It was hard and it was heavy and it was just as he had feared.

It was nothing but a stack of paper. Nothing but words. He had begun the process alone and now that he had finished, he remained alone. If he had confessed, if he had explained, if he had said anything of value at all, he had said it only to himself, and that meant nothing.

He paced and he smoked. He rummaged through his cupboards looking for a drink. When he found none, he rummaged through the footlockers under his bed. Finally, he found two single-drink bottles of vodka stuffed inside some toilet paper rolls in his old duffel bag. He slurped them down, welcoming the burn down his throat.

He stood over his manuscript again. He resisted the urge to throw it in the incinerator. He turned to the end and scribbled a final apology note in his own hand. Among other things, he wrote, "I know: too little, too late."

He wrapped the thing up in a large rubber band, put it in a collapsible folder, and took it out of his apartment.

The night was hot. The air felt full and thick with humidity. Levi began sweating before he had walked across the street to the parking ramp. Once inside his truck, he drove in silence to the north side of town. He wiped his hand against his dripping forehead as he sat across the street from the comfortable home on Liberty Street where his old friends lived.

The lights were off. Levi took the folder from his passenger seat and stepped outside his truck. He left his door open to minimize noise. He walked across the street. He slowly opened the front door that led to the little mudroom between the garage and the house. He set the folder on the mat where someone was sure to see it, and he left.

He felt lighter as he left, but it was not a good feeling. He felt hollow, as if he had torn his own insides out and left nothing but the shell.

When he returned home, he was too tired to follow through with anything but sleep. He lay on his side and put his hands together under his head. He pulled his knees up and imagined himself as an oil painting of an angelic, innocent, and untainted child. He ignored the stubble that pressed into the back of his hand, and he imagined the rosy cheeks of a cherub.

C.2 YOU'RE NO CHRIST, BUT YOU MAKE A PRETTY GOOD REDEMPTIVE ARCHETYPE

Pièce de Résistance

Levi woke to the sounds of the street and of guns. It was a night that sounded like Baghdad. When he peered out the window, he saw that it was early evening, and the rapid cracking of gunfire came from two teenage boys lighting Black Cat fireworks at the edge of the alley near the parking garage.

As a matter of habit, he cleaned himself up, ate a bit of food, and put his feet to the pavement as a way to wake his mind in preparation for the writing he would do at night. But as he moved among the crowds of revelers passing in and out of bars and restaurants in preparation for a wilder celebration that night, he faced the melancholic truth that his writing was done and there was nothing, nothing at all, left for him to do.

Levi made his way to Riverside. Several middle-aged and elderly couples had arrived hours too soon to begin saving their places along the river, but the park was not yet as crowded as it would surely become. He moved south through the park, nearly as far as the big blue suspension bridge on Cass Street. He stopped at a secluded patch of grass where he could be alone to think.

Levi stood on the eastern bank of the mighty Mississippi, his feet planted firmly on the grass in front of the large rocks that led out to the river. The still water sprawled out in front of him like glass. The setting sun reflected brightly in its surface. It looked solid, as if he could walk on it like Saint Peter, if only he had enough faith. An occasional series of cracks or the whistling of bottle rockets floated over from Pettibone Beach on the far side.

He was alone.

The sound of the summer slowly and faintly gave way to that ancient instrument of war, the bagpipes, playing an old familiar song. At first, the notes forcing their way into his consciousness were indistinguishable from the cicadas and their singing tymbals. As the notes came closer, however, they grew louder until the song of the pipes carried across the river, and he had no choice but to acknowledge the melody.

He had heard this same song as the centerpiece of every funeral he had ever attended. Some of the words moved through his head with an involuntary force. *Through many dangers, toils, and snares I have already come.* He took a step closer to the water.

The music grew louder so he turned, trying to find where the notes were coming from. He saw Nick walking toward him from the edge of the open expanse of grass. Levi tried dismissing the music as nothing more than part of a parade or some other part of the festivities of the day, but as Nick grew closer, holding his standard high, looking as though he were walking in perfect step with the rolling rudiments of the snare drums accompanying the pipes, Levi began to think that Nick was somehow bringing the tune to his ears. In a way, it was as if the song were coming from inside Nick himself. He had no beauty or majesty that he should attract anyone, yet there he was, magnetic and glorious, yet terrifying because of all Levi had done to betray him.

He grew closer and closer and Levi watched wide-eyed until Nick stood in front of him. The notes from the bagpipes pierced his ears at such a close range. When it reached the point that Levi couldn't take it any longer, Nick lifted a hand. The music and the drums—in fact all sound—stopped.

Nick reached out his hand and touched his friend. "I've been looking everywhere for you."

"I didn't want you to find me."

"Why are you here?" Nick asked.

"I can't carry it any further. Not alone."

"You can't carry what?"

"My guilt. My failures. This stone." Levi held up the rock from that day long ago in Iraq.

"Come down to the river," Nick said.

They stepped along the rocks until they looked down into the water. Nick pointed at the murky waters and their skewed reflection. "Why do you still see us in old clothes?"

In the dark surface, Levi saw himself as he once was. He ran his hand down his chest and touched the brass buttons on his uniform with reverence. He straightened his ribbons and the accolades of that other life he had once known. He reached over and picked lint from Nick's shoulder. He cinched and smoothed his tie. Yet, despite the old clothes with all their superficial pomp, he saw no recognition in the eyes of the soldiers in the water. Their features were less linear. Their jaws were softer. The hair was a bit too long at the ears.

He pulled at the bottom hem of his coat. "We look like we're just playing dress up." He tried out the position of attention and lifted his chin. He tried to look proud, in control of himself, in command of things. He simply looked tired. "We were just boys playing dress up back then, and we're just playing dress up now."

"It's never too late for new clothes," Nick said.

"Didn't you read what I wrote you?"

Nick nodded.

"Didn't you read the end?"

"This isn't some story. This is your life. You don't get to choose when it ends."

"It's too late," said Levi sadly.

"It's never too late to rewrite it. It's never too late to rewrite the future."

Levi shook his head. "That's just wishful thinking."

"So then," Nick said. "Why are you here?"

Levi lifted up the stone that he still held. He gave it to Nick. "It would be well within your right," he said. "To crush me with it."

Nick took the rock, felt its weight, and looked at the rock as if he didn't recognize it. As if it were something he had never seen before. He reached back and then threw it with great force. It arched high over their heads, above the glassy surface in front of them, and it landed with a small plop in the river. The water rippled and the concentric rings coming from where it landed wiped out the reflection of their old selves. The muddied images were soon invisible and forgotten.

Levi was—for a moment—stung by the fear that there had to be more to it. He looked over at Nick, his countenance unchanged except for a small satisfied smile. "That's it?" he asked him.

Nick nodded. "It's finished."

"That's it," Levi whispered in wonder.

In this way, the stone was cast into the depths forever.

"But what about you and Eris?"

"I don't know. I wish I did, but I don't. Only characters get resolutions; real people keep living."

"I'm sorry, Nick. I never meant to—"

He shook his head. "I know." He smiled sadly. "Why don't you write us a happy ending?"

Levi nodded. "And then? And now? What am I supposed to do?"

"Walk with me," Nick said.

The drums rolled. The pipes played. Levi fell in step and they walked together; they walked home.

As they walked, they called to more people, and some of them joined their throng. A float adorned with flags and fighting men fell in line behind them. Cars and fire trucks joined, and more floats too. They walked around town and grabbed people from the bars and restaurants, gas stations and farms. They gathered the children from the Little League games and called to the parents sipping beer on the top row of the rickety wooden bleachers at the diamonds. They pulled the homeless from under the bridges and the forgotten from under their shadows. Soon the trailers and floats were swallowed by the crowd. They called to everyone they saw until they had a full parade.

As night fell, they—that is, we—*we* walked into the park. The music stopped and most found places to sit. We buzzed from excitement, waiting to see the sky light up in celebration of our freedom.

I walked with my friend, my brother, into the park where we found a grassy area next to the creek. We lay on our backs and stared at the clear sky. We felt the prickling of the grass on our bare arms and we smelled the damp must of the mossy trees. The fireworks started with a flash, and we could feel the concussions from the blast deep inside our memories. We watched the red, white, and blue explode in front of our faces. We watched those colors fade to nothing before they ever hit the ground.

ACKNOWLEDGMENTS

OR

1,000 WORDS OF GRATITUDE BECAUSE YOU WON'T ALL FIT IN A PICTURE

Monica, Madeline, Lillian, and Zoe. I could never articulate how grateful I am for you and how much I love you. I only pray I can show you. You make it all happen.

Thank you to my parents, the Reverend Roy and Alice. You taught me how to tell a story, and a whole heap more. All you've done is good.

Michael, Katie, Sarah, Chris, David, Caleb, Jenny, Nathan, and Theresa; also Geronimo, Angel, Autumn, Cody, Kyle, and Kristin: my first and last brothers and sisters—the ones I didn't get to pick—I wouldn't have picked anyone else. Each one of you has informed all of the love in this book—first those by blood, then those by the ring.

Thanks to the rest of my family: Oma and all our matriarch's descendants. Uncle John and Aunt Sue, Camie, Carrie, et al. Uncle Dave. Greg and Cristy. Danny. Nana. Grandma Mitchell. Grandma Widener and all her descendants.

Reverend Jon and Deb Rockhoff and Denise Costa: parent, friend, counselor, babysitter—you filled every role we needed whenever we needed it most.

Limitless gratitude to (in chronological order) Adam Delph, Kevin Gotfredson, Beth Hernandez, Aaron Roberts, Darrin

Skousen, Jacob Ramer, Jeremy McKissack, Ryan Hendricks, Toni O'Neill, Sarah Carlson, and Jeff Starnes. Without you all, I would have written this book from a far more uncomfortable place.

Bo Bloomer, JJ Loschinskey, and Michael Freeman: You are the three bravest leaders that I have ever met. Thank you.

For holding me up on too many nights after one too many and for listening to me fret about all the same things, I owe the liver of my firstborn male to Ben Baloga and Mike Korbely. And Allyson, a sheepish thanks to you for all the rides (and for being a great early reader).

Thanks also to Josh Flaherty, Chris Broyles, Eddie Spaghetti, Beau Chastain, Mike Wheeler, George Haka, Dustin Koslowsky, and all the rest too numerous to mention. If I forgot your name, it's not because you weren't important; it's because I've been around too many explosions. Dwayne Ferguson, Stephen Mabe, and Matt Rider—you guys hold a special place in my heart.

Thanks to those who taught me to read and write: Gwen Manke, Anne Hagel, Scott Herrewig, Ron Brown, Kristine Blauert, Dan Kunz, Keith Heinze, Dr. Bob Treu, Susan Kapanke, Cristine Prucha, Amina Cain, Peter Bricklebank, Arianne Simard, Penny Freeland, et (many) al.

Thanks to my go-to MFA classmates: Jade Moss, Denise Barkhurst, Brian Bergman, and James Luna.

Thank you to Josh Boyd, Brad Gollnik, Jesse Weibel, Hank Rotering, Ben Trehey, Tristan Weibel, Britt Peterson, Steve Harm, The Brokedowns, the Luther High class of '01 and surrounding, and all my other friends from back in the day. You were there when this story started, and you're all conflated in these characters somehow.

Chad Harbach, thanks for graciously providing feedback when this novel was nothing more than a nascent and bombastic short story.

Bryan Hurt, you alone endured the pain of the early stages. You kept this book from becoming one hot mess. Another thanks for passing it to Kate. This novel never would have seen the light of day if it were not for your patient instruction, gentle persuasion, and general good nature. I am in your debt.

Brian Castner. You have devoted more time to discussing with me all things writing, art, war, and anything remotely related to the intersection of those things than anyone else on this list. Your input polished this book into something I didn't know it needed to be. Thank you.

Thanks to the incredibly supportive community at the University of Wisconsin Law School. From the sale of this manuscript through publication, I've spent the entire ride proud to be one of you. Special thanks to all my bosses, supervising attorneys, and colleagues: Farheen Ansari, Cecelia Klingele, Ion Meyn, Keith Findley, Carrie Sperling, Steve Wright, Kate Judson, Lindsey Cobbe, Cristina Bordé, Greg Wiercioch, John Pray, and all the other members of the incredible #Winnocence Team—you probably all deserve more hours than you've gotten from me since this manuscript sold, but you haven't yet said so aloud. For that, I am grateful.

To my brothers from another mother who inspired the two brothers in the short story from whence this novel came: Nathan Anhalt and Nick Torres. "Chief. Hey, Chief." . . . "Thanks, Chief."

To my other brothers and sisters in arms who have shaped this book in more ways than you'll ever comprehend: Patrick Cazalet, Danielle Ruiz, Bryan Berky, Alejandro Rodriguez, Rob Randall, Paul Brow, Greg DiVito, Garet Vannes, Jerry "Jerbo" Shelton, Chaplain Ray Hagan, Adam Jannsen, the 1-128th INF-BN guys at FOB O'Ryan in 2005, the 3d Special Forces Group guys in RC South in 2007, the C-IED and French Foreign Legion guys at M-F in 2009, my brothers in the dark valley in Iraq in 2010, and so many more.

Jeremy, Cathryn, Kyle, and LeeAnn. I hope we take anniversary trips together until long past the time when our age and wrinkles make catching sight of us in our bathing suits cruel and unusual punishment. Thanks to everyone else at Messiah. You were our family as this book was written.

Ben LeRoy—you've been a ball to work with. This couldn't have worked out better. I really like you! To Ashley Myers and the rest of the cast and crew of Tyrus and F+W: designing, copyediting, distributing, advertising, coordinating logistics, proofreading, and who knows what else you're all doing in the background while I'm not paying attention—I don't take it for granted. Thank you.

And finally, Kate Johnson. I couldn't ask for a better teammate in all of this. Here's hoping *A Hard and Heavy Thing* is just the first of many projects together.

When I see this book on the shelf, all I'll be able to think to myself is: "You didn't build that." Because all of you did. Thank you.

READERS' GROUP GUIDE

1. What's the most remarkable (or unremarkable) thing about Levi's life pre-9/11?

2. How much of Levi, Nick, and Eris's adolescence mirrors your own?

3. How politically aware was Levi before 9/11? How much of any of his newfound "awareness" was based on serious study and how much was based on the twenty-four-hour cable news cycle? In that way, how much of a stand-in is Levi for the "average" American white male or the "average" soldier?

4. His time at war obviously leaves Levi very conflicted, especially as it relates to transitioning back into civilian life. Do you believe that this is a near universal experience for those returning from battle? Is it possible for those who haven't seen conflict to truly understand the challenges facing returning veterans?

5. Do you think that the inner conflict Levi experiences has a lot to do with the political leanings of most veterans? That is, do you believe it's easier for many veterans to simply support war because it eliminates the cognitive dissonance they'd experience if they continued fighting in a war to which they were politically opposed?

6. If Levi showed up in your neighborhood, how could the civilian population best aid him in processing his experience and integrating back into peaceful society? What can any of us do to help slow down the growing tide of veteran suicides?

7. Given what he's learned through experience, if, in the future, Levi had a child of his own who bore witness to an event like 9/11 and was contemplating joining the military, how would he advise his child?

8. Where is Levi in ten years? Nick? Eris?

9. How does Levi and Nick's faith (or lack of faith) impact their decisions to enlist (if at all)? How does it impact their decisions after leaving the military? How does religion, faith, or lack of faith affect the mental health of each individual?

10. Through their own tones as disappointed dad, irritated older brother, and concerned big sister, Levi's family tells him in various ways to man up. How does Levi interpret or misinterpret that message?

11. In what ways does Levi's authorial voice change as the book proceeds before, during, and after war? In what ways is his narrative influenced by the narratives that have already been written? How does this affect his own attempts at processing his story?

12. Levi, Eris, and Nick all have specific interpretations of their relationships and behaviors through the years. Who sees most clearly? Or are any of their narratives reliable? How reliable do you believe Levi relates to the perspectives of Eris and Nick when writing from their points of view?

13. What do you think brought Levi back from the edge? Was it Nick? The writing itself? Something else?

Matthew J. Hefti was born in Canada and grew up in Wisconsin. Prompted by 9/11, he spent twelve years as an explosive ordnance disposal technician. He deployed twice to Iraq and twice to Afghanistan. While enlisted, he earned a BA in English and an MFA in creative writing. He is now working for the Wisconsin Innocence Project as he pursues his Juris Doctor at the University of Wisconsin Law School. His words have been seen in *Pennsylvania English*; *Blue Moon Literary & Art Review*; Chad Harbach's *MFA vs NYC*; and *War, Literature and the Arts*. Along with Adrian Bonenberger, Mike Carson, and David James, he writes at *www.wrath-bearingtree.com*. Matthew is married to the woman of his dreams, with whom he has three incredible daughters.